Catherine Anderson

Forever After

AVON

An Imprint of HarperCollins*Publishers*

AVON BOOKS
An Imprint of HarperCollins*Publishers*
195 Broadway
New York, NY, 10007

Copyright © 1998 by Adeline Catherine Anderson
ISBN: 978-0-380-79104-0
ISBN-10: 0-380-79104-8
www.avonromance.com

First Avon Books paperback printing: April 1998

Avon Trademark Reg. U.S. Pat. Off. and in Other Countries, Marca Registrada, Hecho en U.S.A.
HarperCollins® is a registered trademark of HarperCollins Publishers.

Printed in the U.S.A.

HB 03.05.2024

Dear Readers:

When I was asked to talk about what inspired me to write *Forever After*, I reread the dedication page, and the memories came flooding back. *Forever After* was written as a tribute to one of the best friends I've ever had.

Goliath was a rottweiler who came into my life when he was only three weeks old. His mother had no milk—a great loss to the sheriff's department—for Goliath had been handpicked to become a canine deputy. Sadly for the sheriff, he had no time to bottle-feed a tiny puppy, so I volunteered.

Goliath grew from a handful of black fur into a one-hundred-and-fifty-pound powerhouse of muscle. He was the smartest dog I've ever known, and not only adored children, but was fiercely protective of them. He would have been a phenomenal canine deputy.

After Goliath died, I mourned him deeply. I got a burning urge to rewrite his life story the way it might have happened if he had become a police dog. Naturally, the sheriff in Goliath's fictional life had to be a totally great guy, so Heath Masters, the handsomest county sheriff this side of the Continental Divide, was born. There also had to be a frightened and endangered woman and child in the story for Goliath to fall in love with and protect, so Meredith and Sammy were born. From there, the story took on a life of its own, and to this day, it's one of the best and most romantic that I've ever written.

As you read *Forever After*, please know that practically everything about Goliath is truth, not fiction. It is a tribute, after all. Yes, he really was that wonderful, loyal, incredibly brave, and funny.

Sincerely,

Catherine Anderson

In memory of Goliath, my faithful friend and fearless champion, whose premature passing left an emptiness in my heart that will never be filled. There are those who believe a dog has no soul and that heaven is reserved for only humans. Those people must never have known a dog like you. Wait for me on the other side, Big Guy.

And also to Paula Detmer Riggs, my psychic twin and adopted sister, the only person I know who's as crazy, eccentric, preoccupied, and compulsive about spending money as I am. Here's to fender benders and tall tales, pig slippers on Main Street, sour notes at high decibels, death threats on the office doorstep, semiautomatics in the book rack, tangled wires on Monday morning, panic before deadlines, countless pots of coffee, chocolate-kiss tinfoil, hitchhiking hummingbirds, grease spots on the office rug where Goliath gnawed his bones, shopping instead of working, and last but not least, laughing in the face of adversity. You've enriched my life with the best of all gifts: a friendship that will last Forever After.

Forever After

Chapter 1

A *volley of* shouts jerked Heath Masters' attention from the report he'd been filling out. Tension bunched the muscles across his shoulders as he stared down the steep embankment. When he saw that his deputies were still combing the thick brush, he relaxed slightly. *Not another body, thank God.* Evidently, his men and the ambulance attendants had merely been talking back and forth, their voices raised to carry over the roar of the rushing water that ribboned the canyon floor below them.

Three-quarters of the way down the slope, a blue Ford pickup lay upside down at the base of a massive pine tree. The vehicle's body and framework had crumpled like so much tin foil, and the rear axle had snapped like a tooth-pick.

A sudden gust of wind kicked up from the ravine. As the updraft molded his khaki uniform shirt snugly to his torso and cut through the heavy denim of his Levis, Heath caught the faint smells of burned rubber and gasoline. Try-ing to ignore the odor, he braced his booted feet wide apart and welcomed the refreshing coolness.

For almost a week, it had been unseasonably warm for early May, and this afternoon was no exception. There were few trees to cast shade over this section of the road, and with the eastern Oregon sun baking his shoulders, he was starting to sweat. When the breeze huffed softly under the brim of his brown Stetson, tousling strands of sable hair into his eyes, he only blinked, letting the air caress his hot face.

As if to remind him he had work to finish, the wind also ruffled the sheets of paper attached to his clipboard. Half blinded by the glare of sunlight, he squinted to read his writing. His aching eyes teared in protest. Damn, but he was tired. The kind of tired that went clear to his bones. He'd been working too hard, he guessed. Three weeks running with no days off, pulling twelve- to fourteen-hour shifts.

That's what happened when there were budget cutbacks. He'd been forced to lay off deputies, and now he was running himself ragged to take up the slack. Not that he minded the hard work. No. What really wore him down was the sense of defeat that dogged him. He couldn't be everywhere at once, and when he wasn't, things like this happened. A year ago, he would have had two deputies patrolling this area when the weather turned warm. Now he could only assign one. As a result, at least two kids had slipped through the cracks, and all Heath could do was pray his men and the paramedics didn't find others.

After making another unsuccessful attempt to bring his writing into focus, he decided it was time to give his eyes a short break. After securing his pen to the clipboard, he trailed his weary gaze over the slope that yawned below him, searching the bushes and tall grass for anything that looked out of place. He wanted to believe he would see nothing. But after ten years in law enforcement, he knew better than to get his hopes too high. When high school boys cut classes to go down to the river and guzzle a few beers, they usually went in groups. Unless he missed his guess, there had been at least three youths in the cab of that truck and others riding in back. Without restraints, those in the back could have been thrown quite some distance from the vehicle. It only remained to find them.

Eventually, Heath's attention came to rest on the pickup again. As he studied it, he could almost hear the scream of tires grabbing for traction, then the crunch of metal as the truck plunged over the embankment and flipped end over end. He tried to shove the images from his mind, but they seemed to have a root system equal to that of the lofty pine that clung so tenaciously to the slope below him. *Memories*. They always haunted him at the scene of an automobile accident, but never quite so cruelly as when he looked at that old Ford truck with its chipped blue paint.

A flare on the asphalt behind Heath emitted a soft hissing sound that reminded him of compressed air seeping slowly from a tire. Kaleidoscopic flashes of red and blue came from the light bars of the county vehicles parked on the shoulder of the road. Diluted by sunshine, the rhythmic rotation of colors blurred together to create an ethereal, muted mauve that lent a strange, pink brilliance to everything. It was like staring through heat waves with rose-colored glasses.

A burst of voices from one of the radios snapped Heath back to the moment. If he meant to get this accident report finished before the news hounds arrived, he needed to get cracking.

Bracing the clipboard on his left palm, he used the information on the driver's licenses he'd found inside the two victims' wallets to fill in their names, ages, and physical descriptions. In the photos, neither youth looked old enough to shave, let alone die. His hand shook slightly as he recorded the last entry, the tip of his pen squiggling below the line. *Emotional detachment*. Every lawman knew it was necessary to perform his job. Unfortunately, it wasn't always easy to turn off your feelings.

Sighing, he returned the pen to his shirt pocket and set the clipboard on the bumper of one of the cars so it would be handy later. After fishing a tape measure and piece of chalk from his trouser pocket, Heath signaled down to Tom Moore, the deputy closest to him. "I need a hand up here!"

As Moore struggled to climb the steep embankment, Heath found himself wishing he'd asked one of the other deputies to help him. Moore wasn't exactly one of his favorite people. In the six months since he'd been sworn in, the younger lawman had stirred up trouble more times than not with his over-zealous dedication to law enforcement. He was the kind of deputy who would slap cuffs on a four-year-old for stealing a two-cent Tootsie Roll. Even worse, he expected a pat on the back for a job well done.

To add insult to injury, Moore made no secret of the fact that he had his sights set on Heath's job. *That* was frightening. Moore was state certified to do police work, but that didn't mean he had what it took to be a good cop. In Moore's case, though, that probably wouldn't matter. When your daddy was the local mayor, strings got pulled and doors were opened. It also made it difficult for your boss to fire your ass, even if you damned well deserved it.

Having been raised and tutored by a successful politician didn't hurt Deputy Moore's prospects in county law enforcement, either. He'd cut his teeth on campaign tactics, and he honestly seemed to believe that political opportunism was an addendum to the golden rule. Heath had never known anyone who could so easily manipulate a situation to work in his favor or suck up to a camera with so much charm.

At first, Heath had been secretly amused by Deputy Moore's aspirations to become the sheriff. In his opinion, the citizens of Wynema County would be better served if they pinned the badge on an orangutan. Now, however, Heath was no longer laughing. Moore missed no opportunity to make a name for himself, and he had no compunction about making Heath look as bad as he possibly could in the process.

The deputy's breathing was labored by the time he gained the shoulder of the road. Panting, he leaned over and braced his hands on his slightly bent knees. "That's one steep puppy, I'll tell you."

Heath had ascended the slope only a few minutes before, and he'd been only slightly winded when he reached the top. "Maybe you should consider joining a gym," he suggested grimly.

Moore straightened, his eyes glinting as he scanned Heath from hat brim to boot top. "Is that what you do to stay in shape, old man? Go to the gym three days a week?"

Heath chose to ignore the dig about his age. In this line of work, being seasoned was a plus, not a minus. "I have a small ranch. The hard work that goes along with it is all the gym I need."

Still huffing for breath, Moore dogged Heath's heels as he walked up the road. At the rear of the ambulance, two stretchers lay side by side on the ground. Heath kept his gaze fixed straight ahead, trying not to look at the dark green body bags secured to the stretchers with straps.

When he reached the spot on the asphalt where the black tire marks began, he bent to make a chalk mark. "You ever done this before, Moore?"

"Done what?" the deputy asked with undisguised disinterest.

A muscle in Heath's cheek started to tic. "By using the tire marks here on the pavement, we're going to calculate the approximate speed the pickup was traveling when the operator lost control. It's something you should know how to do if you want to be the sheriff someday."

Moore raked his hand through his blond hair. "I attended the state academy, remember. I know how to do it. I just need to refresh my memory on the particulars."

After carefully examining the tire tracks, Heath instructed Moore to hold the end of the tape while he took the necessary measurements. As he worked, he reviewed the "particulars" that had slipped his deputy's mind.

"Once you determine the percentage of road incline or decline, and find exactly where the driver first applied his brakes, you measure the distance from there to the point where he was finally was able to stop. Then you plug your figures into the formula. You tracking so far?"

Moore flashed him a resentful look. "I think I can keep up," he said sarcastically. "I have an IQ of a hundred and forty. As for tracking, boss, you seem to be the one who's thinking a little slow. Aren't you forgetting one important point? The truck didn't stop. It went over the frigging cliff.''

Heath dug down deep for some patience. It was his job to train the little ass, and he'd damned well do it. ''That's right. The tire marks end prematurely at the edge of the embankment, which makes it impossible for us to determine an actual stopping point. So, instead, we're going to pretend he was able to stop the truck before it went over the edge, and we'll measure from the beginning of the tire marks to that imaginary stopping point at the cliff. If we plug that distance and the percentage of incline or decline into our formula, we'll be able to calculate the maximum speed he could have been going and still have managed to stop before going over.''

''Which tells us what? As far as I can see, all we'll know is the speed he *wasn't* going.''

''Exactly.'' Heath jotted down a figure as he walked back down the road between the streaks of black. ''Since he failed to stop before going over the edge, we'll know he had to be driving in excess of the speed we calculate. It's not as close as I generally like to get, but with the embankment factored in, it's as accurate as we can be.''

Balancing the clipboard on the fender of the car, Heath quickly worked the formula. The figure he came up with was mind-boggling. According to his calculations, the pickup had been traveling in excess of ninety miles an hour.

Gripping the clipboard so tightly that his knuckles ached, he reworked the equation, scarcely able to believe he'd done it correctly the first time. When he got the same answer twice, a tingle of alarm walked slowly up his spine. He fixed a measuring gaze on Deputy Moore.

''You did say you didn't come upon the scene of the accident until after the fact. Right?''

Moore rested his hands on his hips. ''That's right. Why do you ask?''

Shaking his head, Heath left the clipboard lying on the fender and strode out to the no-passing line that evenly bisected the pavement. Anyone who drove in excess of ninety miles per hour on a narrow stretch of country road like this had to be crazy. Or suicidal.

"What's wrong?" the deputy asked.

Heath was too preoccupied to reply.

Why would a kid drive that fast? The question circled darkly in Heath's mind, and he could think of no answer. Granted, teenage boys tended to drive with one foot in the carburetor, and most of them were daredevils. But as a general rule, they didn't deliberately try to kill themselves.

Something—*or someone*—must have pushed the youth into driving that fast, Heath concluded, and he had a very bad feeling he knew what it had been.

He turned to pin Deputy Moore with a relentless gaze. "Are you absolutely positive you weren't anywhere near here when that accident occurred?"

Moore huffed air past his lips. "You questioning my word?"

Snatching the clipboard off the car fender, Heath turned away without dignifying that question with a reply. The bunched muscles in his thighs protested with every step as he strode to his Bronco. Once inside the vehicle, he radioed in to the department. After making contact with Jenny Rose, the day-shift dispatcher, he suggested they move to a less commonly monitored frequency.

Once he had switched channels, Heath reestablished his contact with Jenny Rose and then asked, "Did Deputy Moore radio in a tag number to you this afternoon? Over."

"That's an affirmative," the dispatcher replied. "He wanted me to run a twelve-seven for the RO. Over."

Heath swallowed, feeling as if the walls of his throat had been coated with Elmer's Glue. His voice had an odd twang when he spoke again. "I need the license number Deputy Moore gave you, Jenny Rose. Over."

Within seconds, Jenny Rose came back with the requested information. The plate number she gave Heath was a perfect match for the one he'd entered on the accident report. A wave of nausea rolled through his belly. "Thanks for the help, Jenny Rose. Out."

As Heath swung from the Bronco and closed the door, he moved with the cautious slowness of an old man. Heartsick, that was the only word to describe how he felt.

As he drew to a stop in front of Deputy Moore, he tapped the edge of the clipboard he held against the heel of his opposite hand. "You lied to me, Tom. You out-and-out lied," he accused softly.

"I don't know what you're talking about," Moore retorted.

"Let me draw you a picture. While you were patrolling this area this afternoon, you spotted a bunch of teenage boys in an older model, blue Ford pickup. The boy at the wheel was driving a bit erratically, arousing your suspicion. You fell in behind the truck, called in the plate number to Jenny Rose, and then you attempted to pull the kid over. How am I doing so far?"

Moore stared at the ground as if he found it difficult to meet Heath's gaze. In the past, Heath had been told by friends that his blue-gray eyes turned as scalding as twice-boiled coffee when he got mad. And right now, he was very mad. He tossed the clipboard back on the fender of the car. Moore jumped at the unexpected noise.

"When you flashed your lights and hit the siren, the kid panicked and tromped on the gas," Heath continued icily. "When you followed in pursuit, the kid drove even faster, trying to get away. Bingo. The first thing you knew, he lost control of his vehicle in a sharp curve and went over the edge."

Keeping his expression carefully blank, Moore finally met Heath's gaze. "I don't know what you're talking about."

"The hell you don't," Heath shot back. "How many times have I cautioned you not to engage in a high-speed chase when you suspect a kid's been drinking? If you try to pull him over and he speeds up, it's obvious that he's not going to stop, no matter what you do. At that point, the only safe thing to do is back off so he'll slow down. What can you possibly gain by chasing him? If he's intoxicated, his driving skills are impaired, and the faster he goes, the more risk there is that he'll have an accident, injuring himself and possibly other people.''

Angry color flagged Moore's cheeks. ''I told you I wasn't anywhere near here! You calling me a liar?''

Heath wanted to call him a worse name than that. ''Jenny Rose gave me the tag number you called in a few minutes before the estimated time that the accident occurred. It's a perfect match.''

''So? Since when is it against your rules to check out a license plate? A couple of hours earlier, I saw the truck down by the river. No one was inside, and there was no one around. That seemed suspicious, so I jotted down the tag number to check it out later.''

''Why later? Why not right then?''

''I was too busy.''

''Doing what?''

''It was my lunch break.''

Heath sighed. This was going nowhere fast. Judging by the deadpan look in Moore's eyes, he doubted the deputy was going to admit that he'd tried to pull the teenagers over and then given chase. And there was no way Heath could actually prove it. Sadly enough, even if he did, Moore's ass would be covered. Going by the book, a lawman should have pursued the teenagers. They'd been breaking the law nine ways to hell, not to mention that the one boy had been driving drunk.

Major problem. On this particular issue, Heath's law enforcement tactics parted company with the ''book.'' And he wanted his deputies to follow suit.

The boys in that truck would have faced a list of charges nearly as long as Heath's arm. They also could have been expelled from school for truancy at the midnight hour before their graduations, and after all that, they still would have had to face their angry parents whose disciplinary measures, according to the statistics, were usually unreasonably harsh, especially when meted out by a frustrated father who lost his temper and didn't realize his own strength.

Who could blame anyone for running to avoid facing all of that? With so much at stake, most kids panicked. Heath had learned that the hard way. When you mixed in a little alcohol with that panic, you came up with teenagers whose thought processes were so muddled, they might do almost anything.

The long and short of it was that Heath didn't want kids to be afraid when they saw him coming. At least they didn't run from him, which gave him a chance to get them enrolled in educational programs that strongly discouraged teenage alcohol and drug abuse.

Once you zipped a kid into a body bag, there were no second chances. It was the end, period. This afternoon was a good example of that.

"Get out of here before I do something I may regret," Heath told Moore softly. "Go help them search the brush."

Moore shifted to plant his feet more widely apart. His arms hung loosely at his sides, but Heath didn't miss the fact that the younger man was clenching and unclenching his fists. Maybe it was bad of him, but he almost wished the cocky little bastard would throw a punch. Beating the snot out of him wouldn't bring those boys back, but Heath figured it might make him feel a little better.

In the distance, he heard automobiles approaching. *The news hounds.* Damn, he'd forgotten all about them. Roving reporters generally monitored the police channels and showed up en masse at the scene of a serious automobile accident. Most times, Heath briefed himself before giving an official statement. There was no time for that today.

At the sound of squealing brakes and tires skidding on gravel, Moore glanced over his shoulder. His expression was strained when he turned back to meet Heath's gaze. "If you so much as hint that I was chasing those kids when they went over, I'll make your life a living hell," he grated out. "I'm not taking the heat for this."

Heath had never wanted to hit someone so badly in all

his life. He had a sneaking hunch that Moore had engaged in that high-speed chase hoping he could run those boys off the road, arrest all of them, and come out looking like a hero. But the plan had backfired. Two star football players from Wynema High were dead. If the news media learned the truth, they might tout Moore as a hero. Considering the popularity of the kids, though, it could easily go the other way, with Moore being dubbed a hard-nosed fanatic who chased drunk teenagers over cliffs. That would destroy any hope he'd ever have of being elected to public office.

A lovely thought, that.

The thud of running feet and the muted clanking of camera equipment acted as a prod to get Moore moving. With a final glare at Heath, the deputy took off, clearly not wishing to be caught in the limelight. Heath shared the sentiment. This was a hell of a mess, and the guy who had to hang back to do clean up was going to take some hard hits.

The reporters descended upon Heath like a colony of hungry ants on a bread crumb. Cameras flashed, making black spots dance before his eyes, and when he opened his mouth to say something, a woman shoved a microphone at him so forcefully, she damned near swabbed his tonsils.

Questions pelted him like scatter spray.

"Sheriff Masters, what were the names of the boys who were killed?" the woman with the mike demanded.

A man elbowed her aside. "At what speed was the pickup traveling when it went over, Sheriff? Can you tell us what time the accident happened?"

From somewhere at the back of the crowd, a feminine voice cried, "Have all the bodies been recovered yet?"

A man cut in with, "What were your feelings when you learned this was a wreck involving intoxicated teenagers, Sheriff? Do you see this as an indication that your present policies might need revamping?"

A woman waved a piece of paper to get his attention. "I just came from interviewing a group of angry parents who have started circulating a petition to have you recalled from office, Sheriff Masters. They claim that over the weekend, you and your deputies broke up several drinking parties and detained the youngsters involved until they were sober enough to drive. You made no arrests, which would seem to indicate that you condone such behavior. You also failed to notifying the parents of their children's whereabouts. Can you explain why? Those parents were worried sick about their kids, and they're justifiably outraged that the sheriff's department had so little regard for their feelings.''

Feeling like a dart board at which all players were throwing projectiles at once, Heath held up his hands to ward off more questions. ''Please, ladies and gentleman, I can only address one query at a time. I'll try to answer all your questions, I assure you.''

As the group of reporters fell silent, Heath scanned their faces. Male or female, they all eyed him with glassy-eyed intensity, recorders running, cameras snapping. The boys lying nearby in body bags were nothing but statistics to them.

''I'll take the last question first,'' Heath said. ''Tax cuts have decreased our county budgets, forcing the sheriff's department to trim expenses. We're presently operating with fifteen fewer deputies than we were two years ago. As we approach the end the school year, high school seniors are celebrating their upcoming graduations, and it's estimated that over seventy-five percent of those who attend parties consume alcohol. In the town of Wynema Falls alone, there are over three thousand kids who'll be walking under the arches the first of June.

''Last weekend, I and my deputies crashed five drinking parties, at which there were over three hundred kids collectively. We have no room in our jail for that many teenagers, nor did we have sufficient manpower or vehicles to transport so many back to town. Our only option was to detain them until they could safely drive home. As for notifying the parents, it would have taken hours to make over three hundred phone calls, and that's not to mention the time we would have spent beforehand, trying to get frightened, closemouthed kids to give us their names.

"Quite frankly, I don't have the manpower for an undertaking like that, and as your sheriff, I have to prioritize, concentrating my department's efforts where we can best serve the public. It seems to me that keeping our teenagers safe has to be a top priority."

Another newsman, accompanied by a plump cameraman, elbowed his way through the crowd to stand at center front. Heath recognized him instantly as Bill Krusie, a popular roving reporter for KTYX, a local television station. Heath wasn't exactly thrilled to see him.

Twenty years ago, Heath and Bill had been in the same graduating class at Wynema High, both of them eighteen and eager to grab the world by its tail. All through high school, they'd played on the same football team, been members of the Ski Club, and had frequently chummed around together, going to parties and out on double dates.

Their friendship had endured until four years ago when Heath had had the misfortune of having to arrest Bill for drunk driving. The arrest had resulted in Bill's enduring immeasurable public humiliation, becoming less popular with television viewers, losing his job at another broadcasting station, and being sued for divorce by his wife of seventeen years. Although Bill had subsequently been forced by judicial decree to go through rehab, had later become a dedicated member of AA, and now had his drinking problem firmly in hand, he still resented Heath for having been instrumental in destroying his life.

Of all the reporters Heath knew, Bill Krusie had always been the most ethical. But even Bill had his weaknesses, and his bitterness toward Heath was one of them. Bill simply couldn't reconcile the fact that the sheriff who now ran a zero-tolerance county and had tossed him in the hoosegow for driving under the influence had once been his high school drinking buddy. In Bill's mind, Heath's law enforcement policies smacked of hypocrisy, and when an opportunity presented itself, he couldn't seem to resist taking shots at Heath's character.

This situation today was going to provide Bill Krusie with plenty of ammunition.

Chapter 2

Heath felt like an accident victim in vertical traction with so many plastic bags hanging from his arms. How women did it, he'd never know, corralling kids, packing babies in car carriers, yet still managing to handle their groceries.

After closing the drop-down door of his white Bronco and rolling up the window, he headed for the back door of his sprawling farmhouse. In the distance, the Cascade Mountains looked almost purple, their rounded peaks rising like mounds of meringue-capped blueberries above the rolling green foothills. Wind swept down the draws and gullies to whisper softly in the stands of towering pines that bordered his forty-acre parcel of ranch land.

He hauled in a deep breath, soothed by the sound of cattle lowing in the fields. *Home.* After the day he'd had, the mingled scents of evergreen, sage, sun-washed grass, and alfalfa worked on his senses like an intoxicant.

Laden with new leaves, the big oak in the front yard swayed gently in the breeze, casting dappled patterns of light and shadow over the green composition roof. As Heath walked past the wrap-around veranda, he tried not to notice the chipped white enamel on the porch railing or the ankle-high weeds that peppered the lawn.

As he stepped onto the back porch, he heard the chickens out by the pole barn raising enough ruckus to wake the dead in two counties. When he turned to look, he saw red hens scattering in all directions, his dog Goliath in hot pursuit. It looked as if someone had emptied a gunnysack of red feathers downwind of a turbine.

"Goliath! Damn it all, stop that!"

The Rottweiler, unable to hear over the cacophony, never broke stride, the mahogany markings on his feet and legs a blur as he darted in first one direction, then another. With a piercing whistle, Heath finally brought the commotion to a halt.

His black coat glistening in the sunlight, Goliath swung around, his nearly tailless rump wagging with excitement, his stout, muscular body tensed. The expression on the canine's face was anything but contrite as he loped toward the porch.

"You know better than that," Heath scolded as the dog drew closer. "What am I gonna do with you?"

Perpetually wet with drool, Goliath's chin sported a goatee of rust-red feathers. *Hell.* Another of his hens had a bare patch on her ass.

"Keep it up, buddy, and there'll be no more omelets. Traumatized hens don't lay for shit."

Tongue lolling, the dog flopped down on the grass next to the steps, his soulful brown eyes gleaming with smug satisfaction.

Trying to look stern, Heath found himself smothering a smile instead. The dog had never actually hurt one of the chickens, after all. He just craved the excitement of the chase, and deep down, Heath couldn't really blame him. Since his accident nine months ago, the former canine deputy had been forced to take early retirement. Causing a brouhaha by chasing the chickens was about the only thrill left to him.

Heath shook his head, his gaze resting thoughtfully on the Rottweiler. Goliath had saved his hide more times than he could count, and he wanted the dog's golden years to be happy. Instead, the poor animal was going stir crazy.

"I took you with me to the department yesterday and

the day before that. What more can I do, Goliath? You tell me.''

The dog gazed up at him with imploring brown eyes.

''With that hip implant, you can't cut it in law enforcement anymore. It's just that simple. If going back to work is what you're angling for, it ain't gonna happen, partner.''

Even as Heath spoke, Goliath cocked one ear forward, an unfocused expression entering his eyes. On the warm evening breeze, Heath caught the distant sound of a child's voice. Since there was only one house nearby, he knew it must be his new neighbor lady's kid, a tiny, tow-headed girl he'd glimpsed in passing.

Goliath whined and pushed up on his haunches. Heath sighed, knowing the Rottweiler would give both hind legs and what remained of his tail to go down there and play. If there was anything Goliath loved more than law enforcement work, it was kids.

''Will you promise to mind your manners and not wear out your welcome?''

Goliath squirmed with anticipation.

''*Grrr-rruff!*'' the dog barked in reply.

Heath juggled grocery bags to glance at his watch. ''Only for an hour. You got it? Have your mangy ass home by seven, or I'll plant a number twelve up it crosswise.''

Before Heath could say more, the dog sprang into a run, the red-brown marking on his rump little more than a flash as he disappeared around the corner of the house.

As he unlocked the door, Heath tried not to think of his vow to avoid his new neighbors. Zeke Guntrum, the old fart who owned the property next door, was a lousy landlord and had let the house fall into disrepair. Rusty pipes, faulty wiring, rotten floors. Everyone who leased the damned place regretted it, and Heath was invariably called upon to play Mr. Fix-It. Always in the middle of the night, of course. Plumbing seldom went haywire at a decent hour. The only way to get along with his neighbors, he'd finally decided, was to stay the hell away from them.

As he stepped into the kitchen, the smell of garlic, an

unpleasant reminder of the French bread he'd cremated last night, blasted him in the face. He set the bags on the butcher-block counter, then sorted through the jumble to find the six pack of Red Dog. He plucked out a long-necked bottle, twisted off the cap, and flipped it at the trash can. Visions of a long, lazy evening in front of the television flashed through his mind.

Chugging beer, he drew off his brown Stetson and tossed it, Frisbee style, at the coat tree. The hat missed the hook, spiraled downward, and plopped crown-first on the yellow linoleum. Heath stared. He hadn't missed that hook in over six months. But, then, he hadn't had this bad of a day in a spell, either.

As he retrieved his hat and reshaped the crown, he assured himself that things were bound to pick up. He'd unplug the phone and bury his pager under the sofa cushion. Once he'd had supper and tended to the livestock, absolutely nothing would pry him out of his recliner.

Minutes later, Heath was reading the directions to make macaroni and cheese, his idea of haute cuisine, when the phone rang. He swore under his breath, wanting to kick himself for forgetting to unplug the damned thing. *Ignore it.*

Whistling softly, he stepped to the refrigerator to get the milk and margarine. Persistent, the phone kept jangling. He whistled louder. He was officially off duty. His deputies could handle any emergencies. With a grunt of satisfaction, he snagged another swallow of beer before reaching into an oak cupboard for a pan.

The phone continued to ring.

What was it about a ringing telephone that drove him so crazy? He had no wife, no kids, and no siblings. Just a father he hadn't seen in nineteen years and telephoned on rare occasion. Chances were good that it was someone from the department or, worse yet, a reporter. Tonight, all he wanted was some peace and quiet. He didn't want to hear about recall petitions. He didn't want to be interviewed about his work with teenagers. Why couldn't the world just back off for a few hours and leave him alone?

With a sigh of self-disgust, he leaned across the pile of unpacked grocery bags to grab the receiver. "Yo!"

"Sheriff Masters?"

The voice was female, shrill, and laced with hysteria. In the background, Heath heard the faint sound of a child screaming. "Yes?"

"This is—oh, dear, God, you have to get over here. Quick!"

Heath frequently got weird phone calls, and they often began just this way, with an anonymous someone at the other end of the line making very little sense.

"Just calm down, ma'am." *Domestic violence. Some drunken bastard beating on his kid, no doubt.* "Before I can help you, I need your name and address."

"Please, you have to get over here, fast!" she cried. "He's gone crazy. I think he's—oh, my God!—I think he's going to kill her! Hurry, please, hurry!"

Before Heath could ask any more questions, the line went dead.

Weird phone calls went with a sheriff's territory, but this one took the prize. No name, no address? He wasn't a mind reader. He hung up the phone. *Damn.* Another goat roper with an attitude, tanked up on cheap whiskey. Why women stayed with bastards like that, Heath would never know. Especially when kids were involved. *I think he's going to kill her!*

Why hadn't she given him her name? At least then he might have been able to locate her. The thought of some little girl getting the snot beat out of her by some two-hundred-pound jerk made Heath feel sick. He had to get caller ID on his line.

Staring at the macaroni box, he tried to concentrate on the instructions. *Please, you have to get over here, fast!* It was as if she expected him to know where she was.

A prickly sensation ran up his neck. *Goliath.* Had the dog caused some kind of trouble down at the neighbors'?

Heath threw open the back door and moved out onto the

porch. Sure enough, he heard the distant sound of a dog
barking. Not even taking time to grab his hat, he broke into
a run. He could hear the uproar long before he reached the
neighboring farmhouse. It sounded as if all hell had broken
loose, a kid caterwauling, a woman screaming, and Goliath
barking. What the Sam Hill?

He vaulted over the tumbledown fence that divided his
neighbor's patchy lawn from the adjoining cow pasture,
then circled the house, skidding to a halt about fifteen feet
shy of a dilapidated woodshed. A child, dressed in pink
pants and a smudged white T-shirt, stood splayed against
the outbuilding, strands of her blond hair caught on the
rough planks. Her eyes were so wide with fright they resembled china-blue supper plates.

Fangs bared and frothing at the jowls, Goliath lunged
back and forth between the child and a young woman Heath
guessed to be her mother, a slightly built brunette in loosely
fitting blue jeans and an oversized white shirt.

"Stay back!" he ordered.

At the sound of his voice, the woman spun around, her
pinched face so pale that her dark brown eyes looked almost as large as her daughter's. "Oh, thank God! Help us!
Do something, please, before he hurts her!"

Heath jerked his gaze back to his dog. If ever there had
been an animal he would trust with a child, Goliath was it.
Yet now the Rottweiler seemed to have gone berserk, barking and snarling and snapping at the air. Even more
alarming, Heath's presence didn't seem to be calming him
down.

Heath snapped his fingers. "Goliath, heel!"

At the command, the Rottweiler whirled toward Heath,
his usually friendly brown eyes glinting a demonic red. For
an awful instant, Heath was afraid the dog might not obey
him. *Impossible.* Goliath was an extensively trained animal
who'd been drilled, even as a pup, to respond instantly to
commands.

What in the hell was wrong with him? Heath's gaze shot
to the terrified child.

"Goliath, *heel!*" He slapped his thigh for emphasis.

The Rottweiler finally acquiesced, massive head lowered, legs stiff, his movements reluctant and abject. The second the dog got within reach, Heath grabbed his collar.

"Sammy!"

With a strangled cry, the woman bolted forward to gather her child into her arms. For a second, she simply hugged her, one of those shaky, desperate, breath-robbing hugs that conveyed relief beyond measure. Then she whirled to confront Heath, her pale, delicately molded face twisting with anger, her body quaking.

"You get that *vicious*, out of control dog *off* my property!"

The blaze in her eyes told Heath she was infused by the rush of adrenaline that often followed a bad scare. He'd experienced it a few times himself, a trembling rage that quickly petered out and gave way to watery legs.

"Ma'am, I'm really sorry about—"

"I don't want to hear it! Just get that monster out of here!"

Talk about starting off on the wrong foot with someone. And wasn't that a shame? Heath would have happily fixed this gal's plumbing late at night—or anything else that went haywire in the ramshackle old house she was renting.

Fragile build. Pixyish features. Creamy skin. Large caramel brown eyes. A full, vulnerable mouth the delicate pink of barely ripened strawberries. Her hair fell in a thick, silken tangle around her shoulders, the sable tendrils curling over her white shirt like glistening ribbons of chocolate on vanilla ice cream.

She hugged her daughter more tightly, cupping a tremulous hand over the crown of the child's blond head. "It's all right, sweetkins," she whispered. "It's all right." The child began to wail more shrilly. In a louder voice, the woman cried, "Please! Don't just stand there gaping at us! Can't you see she's terrified of your dog?"

Heath could see that, yes. Children who were afraid of

dogs didn't mix well with Rottweilers. Goliath must have scared the poor little thing half to death.

"I really am sorry about this," he tried again. "But, please, understand, Goliath would never hurt your little girl. He adores kids."

The woman retreated a step. "He almost *attacked* me!"

"I assure you he wouldn't have."

"He wouldn't even let me get close to her! Every time I tried, he lunged at me!"

"Only because he sensed that the child was afraid. You heard her screaming, right? And came running outside?"

"Yes," she admitted, her voice quivering.

"I figured as much. He *is* only a dog, you know, not an Einstein. The little girl was scared, Goliath was trying to protect her from whatever was frightening her, and you came charging out of the house. In his mind, you were the only thing around that could have been posing a threat."

"There's no excuse for that kind of behavior! You're as crazy as your dog is!"

Heath guessed she might be right. She looked furious enough to chew nails and spit out screws. Her finely sculpted face was as pale as milk except for the splashes of angry pink on her cheeks, and her huge brown eyes blazed at him. Yet here he stood, trying to reason with her. Explaining his dog's behavior would be better left for later.

She backed up another step, her gaze flicking around the yard as if she were searching for a bolt hole. She was as frightened as her kid was, whether of him or his dog, he wasn't sure. What with all the recent television coverage of police brutality and corruption, lots of people didn't trust lawmen these days.

He gave her another once-over, taking in details with a well-trained eye. Mid to late twenties, extremely skittish. The way she watched him was starting to make him feel too big for his skin. At six feet five in his stocking feet and two inches taller in riding boots, he probably seemed gigantic to a little gal like her.

"What we have here is a major misunderstanding," he tried.

"A misunderstanding? You get him *out* of here. Do I make myself clear? *Now!* Or I'm going to call the—" She broke off, her gaze flicking from the badge on his shirt to the holstered semiautomatic riding his hip. "I'll call the state police. I'm sure there's a leash law here, and you're breaking it by letting that maniacal animal run loose!"

Heath couldn't let that pass without a rebuttal. "This *maniacal* animal is the same canine deputy you read about in the newspaper several months ago. The one that went into the burning apartment building to rescue the little girl?" Her lack of reaction told Heath she hadn't read the story. *Fantastic.* "Look, lady. During the course of his career, Goliath received seventeen citations, all for rescuing children. He'd *never* harm your daughter. Die for her, maybe, because that's his nature."

She whirled and headed for her back door. "If you're not gone when I get inside, I'll call the state police. And if that dog *ever* comes here again, I'll file a complaint."

For a fast July minute Heath was amused at the idea of his neighbor reporting him, of all people, to the police. But then as fast as it had come, his amusement faded. If she involved the state cops, this situation could turn really nasty. He tightened his hold on Goliath's collar and pulled the dog from her yard as quickly as he could.

Once they reached the road, Heath relaxed his hold on the animal. "Great work, partner. You really know how to make points with the ladies."

The instant the Rottweiler was free, he tried to make a U-turn. Heath's heart leaped, a sick dread gnawing at his middle. He grabbed the dog's collar again.

"Don't even *think* about it, you blockhead. That little girl is off limits. Understand? What the hell's gotten into you?"

Goliath only whined and gazed miserably at the old farmhouse, for all the world as if he'd left his heart behind. Gently but firmly, Heath seized the dog by his ears, then leaned down for a little nose-to-nose communication.

"Goliath, listen up. You listening?"

Sad brown eyes looked into Heath's.

"That lady doesn't like you. I know that's a real hard thing for a charming fellow like you to understand. But sometimes there's just no figuring females. Show your mangy hide around there again, and she'll file a complaint with animal control, sure as the world. She'll tell them you're vicious and out of control. You know what happens then, buddy? The gas chamber."

Meredith Kenyon jerked open the back screen door, only to have the blasted thing pull away from the frame at the bottom. Understandable, since the door had only one good hinge to begin with—the top one. Arms locked around her daughter, she didn't bother to lift up on the handle as the contraption slammed closed behind her. If the remaining hinge screws pulled free from the rotten wood, so be it.

Three steps into the utility room, she halted. Sammy clung to her frantically, her small body shivering so badly her teeth chattered. Swaying from side to side, Meredith rubbed the child's narrow back, aware in some distant part of her mind that the floor gave perilously with every shift of her weight. Horrible old house, anyway. She wished she'd never rented it. Not that there'd been much choice. Now they were stuck here.

If it hadn't been so awful, Meredith would have laughed hysterically. Talk about neighbors who were her worst nightmare. A county sheriff and a berserk Rottweiler? She couldn't decide which was worse. Heath Masters had seemed as tall as a tree to her, with shoulders so broad it would take a yardstick to measure them, every inch of him roped with muscle. Those penetrating slate blue eyes had been unnerving as well, their contrast to his burnished, chiseled features and sable hair almost startling. Maybe it was because she'd lived in the city for several years and been around professional men who never turned their hands to physical work, but Masters had seemed to emanate strength.

Willing her heart to stop pounding, Meredith tried to gather her wits. She didn't like the way Sammy was trembling or the fact that she hadn't said anything.

"Hey, punkin," Meredith whispered. "You okay?"

No answer. Just an awful silence. Meredith's heart caught, and for an agonizing moment, she couldn't breathe. *Not again, God. Please, not again.* Sammy had been doing so well these last few weeks. Only occasional nightmares, hardly any incidents.

"Knock, knock," Meredith said, anxiety making her voice twang. "Is there a little girl named Sammy hiding in there someplace?"

The child squirmed slightly, making Meredith wonder if she was hugging her too tightly. Digging deep for some self-control, she forced herself to relax her arms.

"Sammy, love?"

"What?" the child finally replied in a thin, quavery voice.

Relief washed over Meredith in drowning waves that made her feel slightly disoriented and giddy. "You okay, sweetie?"

Sammy pressed closer, the brittle tension in her body conveying how frightened she still was. "You promised, Mommy," she whispered fiercely. "You promised."

An ache of regret filled Meredith. It wasn't necessary for Sammy to say more. She knew exactly which promise the child referred to, namely that once they reached Oregon, Sammy would never have to feel afraid again. Blast that man for letting such a horrible dog run loose!

"Oh, sweetheart. It's going to be okay."

Sammy shuddered. "I want to go 'way from here, Mommy. Far, far 'way."

Leaving right now was impossible. She'd been required to pay the last month's rent and a sizable deposit to lease this house, and her crotchety landlord would refuse to return the money if she failed to stay for the agreed upon six months. In addition to that, her rattletrap car needed a valve job that was going to cost a small fortune. If she meant to keep food on the table for her daughter, she couldn't afford to move until she'd drawn a few more paychecks. Besides, she had no guarantee of landing another job, especially not one that would allow her to work at home and take care of her child.

Pressing her face against Sammy's hair, Meredith struggled for calm. Instead, a helpless anger rushed through her. She and Sammy had gone through so much and come so far to get here. Now everything seemed to be going wrong.

"That big mean dog's gonna come back, Mommy. I just know it!"

"Oh, Sammy. As long as I draw breath, nothing's going to hurt you, sweetie. Not that dog or anything else. You mustn't feel afraid."

Empty words. Sammy had counted on Meredith so many times and been let down.

As she stood there rocking her daughter, Meredith realized the back of her throat was burning. She stiffened and lifted her head to sniff. Smoke trailed under the freshly painted, utility room door.

"Oh, no, the hamburger!"

The smell of burning meat seared her nostrils as she burst into the kitchen. Still clutching Sammy in one arm, she raced across the badly worn linoleum. Smoke billowed up from the antiquated white stove, stinging her eyes. After turning off the gas burner, she grabbed a potholder to move the redhot cast iron skillet off the heat.

At just that moment, the smoke detector went off, its blast so shrill that Meredith nearly parted company with her shoes. Sammy gave a start as well, then pressed a grimy little hand to her mouth, her eyes bright with tears.

"Enough, you stupid thing! We hear you," Meredith shouted at the plastic fire alarm affixed to the ceiling between the kitchen and living room. At present tally, it was the one fixture in the house that still worked properly, and given the lack of kitchen ventilation, it did so with nerve-jangling regularity.

Stepping over to the sink, she struggled to open the double-hung window. Until recently, it had been stuck shut with countless layers of enamel, and it still didn't slide smoothly. She'd meant to give the runners a few squirts of nonstick cooking spray, but what with everything else that needed attention around here, she'd forgotten.

"There," she said, dredging up a stiff smile for Sammy when she finally got the sash raised. As the smoke dissipated, the detector finally stopped blaring, giving way to shrill bleeps instead. "Thank goodness for that much. That darned thing is going to make me go deaf."

With a choked hiccough and sniffle, Sammy shifted on Meredith's hip to look at the charred remains of their evening meal. "Uh-oh," she said faintly.

Gazing down at the patties, which now resembled misshapen chunks of coal, Meredith waved a hand in front of their faces. At $2.19 a pound, the meat was no small loss. But, even so, she was glad for the distraction. At least it gave both of them something to think about besides that horrible dog.

" 'Uh-oh' is right. There's nothing to do but put it down the garbage disposal."

"We don't gots one," Sammy reminded her in a shaky voice.

Glancing at the rust-stained porcelain sink, Meredith clenched her teeth to keep from adding that a garbage disposal wasn't the only luxury they no longer had, a kitchen fan at the top of the list, central air-conditioning a close second. The warm day had left the inadequately insulated house miserably stuffy.

"Well, I guess we'll have to fix something else for supper. What sounds good?"

"More hugs," Sammy murmured, burrowing close.

Meredith was happy to comply. She had been as horrified to see that dog in their yard as Sammy had been. Even now, she still couldn't make her heart stop skittering, and when she walked, her legs felt as limp as overcooked spinach.

She kept seeing her little girl, pressed against the shed

like a sinner on a cross. Meredith didn't know what she would have done if the dog had attacked her child. She'd had no weapon handy, not even a stick to use as a club.

"Mommy, your face is all funny."

"It's just the smoke, punkin," Meredith said, shifting Sammy to the other arm. As she tightened her hold, she felt residual shudders course through the child's body.

Meredith began to pace, the toes of her sneakers catching on the occasional ragged edge of the speckled green linoleum, the floorboards creaking and groaning. At every sound, Sammy jerked to look over her shoulder.

"It's all right," Meredith whispered. "It's all right. Don't be scared, sweetie."

Still trembling, Sammy hugged Meredith's neck again, her thin arms so tense they felt like brittle twigs. Meredith rubbed the child's taut shoulders, then worked at the knotted muscles along her spine.

"Mommy?"

"What, sweetie?"

"What if that big, mean dog comes back?"

Meredith was tempted to make rash promises, anything to ease the child's mind. "I'll think of something, sweetkins. You'll be safe. I'll see to it."

Only how? Just as Sammy had pointed out, the dog might come back. What was she going to do if it did? Maybe she should buy a baseball bat and keep it by the back door. Or, better yet, build a section of fence to keep that black monster out of Sammy's play area. Getting a gun might not be a bad idea, either.

Meredith reeled to a stop. Dear heaven, what was she thinking? The last time she'd handled a firearm was shortly before she left home to attend college, and since her marriage to Dan, she could barely stand to look at a weapon.

Enough of this. She could obsess later about ways to keep her daughter safe. Right now, she needed to act calm and help Sammy put the incident behind her.

"You never did answer me," Meredith said. "What sounds good for supper?"

Sammy kept her face pressed against Meredith's neck. "I don't care."

"You don't? Wow! Does that mean I can fix"—she searched her mind for the food Sammy detested most—"*beets*?"

The child shuddered. "Yuck! Not beets, Mommy. I hate 'em."

"Well, you did say you didn't care. I've got it! How about okra?"

"Nasty. It tastes like snot."

"And how would you know?" Meredith felt the child's mouth curve against her neck in a halfhearted smile. "Sammy Kenyon! For shame."

"I di'n't never!" Sammy protested, rearing back to scowl indignantly.

Moving toward the wobbly dinette set she'd picked up for a song at a thrift shop, Meredith tweaked the child's button nose. "I'm only teasing you." The chair rocked as she set Sammy on the yellow plastic cushion and hunkered beside her. "Smiles?"

The child tried, her forced grin displaying tiny, unevenly spaced front teeth.

"Bigger," Meredith ordered with mock sternness. When Sammy grinned more broadly, Meredith tousled the child's hair. "Now I've got my pretty little girl back. How about sandwiches and soup for supper?"

"The kind with letters?"

"Soup with letters, coming up." Meredith pushed herself erect. "Do you think you'll be able to spell Samantha this time with no mistakes?"

"Maybe," Sammy replied solemnly.

As Meredith rummaged through the cupboard, she heard Sammy nervously swinging her feet, the heel of one small tennis shoe thumping the chair leg. If only her life were as easy to organize as canned goods, Meredith thought wistfully. Soups in one row, vegetables sorted as to type. Aside from a few mouse droppings that had appeared since she'd scrubbed the shelves, there were no surprises here.

If only she could say the same for Heath Masters. He was everything the newspapers and television proclaimed him to be—big, hard-edged, and intimidating. No wonder a group of parents were circulating a petition to get him recalled. Even less surprising was the fact that his law enforcement tactics had drawn national attention.

Anyone who let a dog like that run loose was a *lunatic*.

Chapter 3

Waiting for someone to answer his call, Heath held the phone to one ear and shoved a heaping spoonful of gooey macaroni into his mouth. The pasta wasn't quite done and tasted like dirty rubber.

"Wynema County Sheriff's Office, Deputy Bailey speakin'. May I help you?"

Heath gulped. "Hey, Charlie." He could almost see the deputy, fiftyish and thick at the waist, his bald head gleaming. "I need to ask you a favor. You real busy tonight?"

"Hell, yes, I'm busy. Scamp Hollister beat the shit out of his old lady again."

"Fantastic. Is Cora all right?"

"Bradford took her to the ER for stitches. The son of a bitch beaned her with a beer bottle. Other than that, I think she'll live. Scamp's bellarin' like a stuck hog about bein' locked up, though. Bein' a royal pain in the arse."

Heath shoved his bowl of macaroni away and ran a hand over his hair. "Well, I'm glad to hear Cora's okay. She's a nice lady."

"Too nice for Scamp." Bailey grew quiet for a moment. "So, what's the favor?"

"I need a twelve-seven for the RO, Oregon plate, SAV–235. Can you run it for me?"

"Son, I can eat acorns and fart oak trees. Hold on."

The phone clattered, and Heath heard the click of a keyboard. From where he stood, he could see the pasture across the road through his living room window. Deceptively placid, whiteface cattle grazed on the hock-high grass. Just hauled in from winter grazing lands, the Herefords were actually as wild and unpredictable as drunk cowpokes on Saturday night.

"You still there?" his deputy finally said.

Heath turned to grab a notepad. "Yeah, I'm here."

"Got a writin' stick handy?"

"Yeah, go."

"Registered owner, Meredith Lynn Kenyon, last name spelled Kilo, Echo, November, Yankee, Oscar, November."

Heath grunted with satisfaction as he wrote down the name. Network computer access had its advantages.

"White female," Charlie continued. "Birth date, 4/23/ 70. Five feet, four inches, one hundred and six pounds, brown hair, brown eyes, and a negatory on organ donation." He paused to give Heath time to write. "Address, 1423 Hereford Lane. That's your place, ain't it?"

"No, I'm at 1420."

"Got a problem with that new neighbor?"

"Nothing I can't handle. A little misunderstanding, is all. I need her name so I can call and apologize. If information can't give me her number, I'll get back to you."

"Son, your technique with the ladies needs work. Just go over and apologize, then ask her name. Wink and smile real nice while you're at it. Works every time."

Heath chuckled, remembering how furious Meredith Kenyon had been when she stormed into the house. "Thanks for the advice, Charlie. I'll remember that."

"She a looker, or what?"

Heath recalled her fragile build. "Not bad. A little on the thin side. Pretty face."

"Nice rack?"

"Charlie, go home to Mabel and scratch your itch. She's just my neighbor lady, all right? I didn't notice her bra size."

"I can't go home to Mabel. I'm on duty, remember? And don't lie to me. When the day comes you don't notice a woman's bra size, you'll be stone blind."

Heath was shaking his head as he hung up the phone. Gazing down at the information he'd just scribbled, he shoved another spoonful of macaroni into his mouth. Tapping his pen on the counter, he pictured Meredith Kenyon.

A generous "B" cup, no question about it. He only wished she had a few other generous traits. A more forgiving nature, just for starters.

The lights of Manhattan cast a rosy glow through the unbreakable glass window of Glen Calendri's penthouse study. He blocked out the muted drone of the traffic that passed by on the street thirty-six floors below him, listening instead, with growing impatience, to the voice coming over his speaker phone.

With each passing second, he tapped his pen on the desktop a little more loudly, the sound rhythmic at first, then increasing in tempo and volume until it resembled the *rat-a-tat-tat* of an automatic weapon with a silencer. With one final tap, he shoved back in his chair, chucking the pen onto the blotter.

"Damn it, Sanders! The bitch couldn't have vanished into thin air. How'n hell do you think she got out of the city, on a magic carpet?" He snapped his fingers. "I got it. Maybe that Scotty fellow beamed her up."

Allen Sanders' sigh of frustration echoed over the speaker into the room. "Boss, I'm doin' the best I can here."

"Well, your best isn't good enough."

"We can't come up with any leads. The last trace we got on her was that bank withdrawal. Not a damned thing since then. No paper trail, and she's not usin' plastic."

"She had to use some form of transportation. Did you check the bus stations? It can't be that difficult to track a woman traveling with a kid."

"We checked everywhere, boss, and then went back and

checked again. Every airport, every bus station. The trains, too. My guess is, she bought herself a used car from a private owner. Prob'ly paid cash and used another name. The broad's smart, I'm tellin' you, and as slippery as an eel.''

Glen pinched the bridge of his nose. "Smart? She has ovaries, for chrissake."

"That don't mean she ain't got brains. She's sharp, I tell ya."

"Luck, sheer luck. You find her, Sanders. Do you understand? No excuses. It's been five weeks. With every day that passes, the trail grows colder."

Glen rose from his chair, aborted the call with a jab of his finger, and strode angrily around his desk, his gaze fixed on the painting of his son, Daniel, that hung in an ornate, gilt frame above the mantel.

His boy.

Taking care not to step on the Dobermans that slept before the hearth, Glen drew to a stop and stared at the image of Dan's face. He tried never to think of how that face had looked when he'd gone to the morgue to identify the body. *A car accident.* Just that quick, and Dan's life had been snuffed out. Glen still couldn't believe it had happened. Even now, he kept expecting his son to walk through the door, alive and well, these past months of grief nothing but a nightmare.

Now the only blood relative Glen had left was his granddaughter Tamara. He wanted the child back. She was a Calendri, by God, Glen's only living heir, and she would be raised by a Calendri, not by that stupid little bitch his son had married. Glen would see to that. And if the broad just happened to get herself eliminated in the process, so much the better.

Sammy stood on a kitchen stool, both arms thrust into the sudsy dishwater. Standing behind her, Meredith supervised as the child ran a sponge over a plate.

"You missed a spot." Meredith pointed out a stubborn

alphabet noodle that still clung to the dish. "Very good, Sammy! Now, into the rinse water."

Sammy swished the plate in the clear water, then went up on her tiptoes to stack it in the drainer, Meredith clasping her waist to make sure she didn't fall.

"I'm almost as good at washing dishes as you are. Right, Mommy?"

Meredith was pleased to see Sammy so engrossed in what she was doing. Supper had been a trial, with the child leaping at every noise.

She bent to kiss the crown of her daughter's head. "You're the very best four-year-old dishwasher I've ever seen."

Sammy pushed an arm farther into the water, pulled the stopper, and watched the suds spiral slowly down the drain. The sluggishness concerned Meredith, making her wonder if the plumbing was partially blocked. In this house, anything that could go wrong did go wrong. High-rent districts were definitely a thing of the past. Until Sammy started to school, at least. Then Meredith would be able to work outside the home in her chosen field again, computer programming.

When she'd leased this place, Meredith had been determined to make it into a home. Now, after meeting the sheriff, she was no longer sure that staying here would be such a wise idea. Not that she had a choice. At least not for the next six months.

After drying Sammy's hands and dimpled elbows, she set the child down and returned the stool to its place under the light switch next to the ancient refrigerator.

"There. We're all done," she said, glancing around the tidy kitchen.

"Yup." Sammy hugged her waist, looking forlorn.

"Want to watch television?" Meredith asked.

The child wrinkled her nose.

"How about a game of Old Maid?"

"Nah."

It was going to be a very long evening if she couldn't

think of some way to keep Sammy's mind off that dog. "You know what sounds fun to me?"

"No, what?" Sammy asked, her blue eyes luminous in the light from the ceiling.

"Making sugar cookies," Meredith replied in a stage whisper and leaned forward to place her hands on her knees. "We could cut out fun shapes and decorate them."

Sammy's dimple flashed. "San'a Claus cookies?"

Meredith saw no reason why not. "And Christmas trees? I've got green sprinkles and confectioner's confetti."

Sammy raced to the cupboard for the cookbook. "Can I mix 'em, Mommy?"

Recalling the mess from the last time Sammy had mixed cookie dough, Meredith smiled. "Oh, absolutely. You're a much better cookie mixer than I am."

Minutes later, the counters were littered with bowls and ingredients, Meredith supervising while Sammy scooped flour from the canister into a measuring cup. The child frowned in concentration.

"One more should do it," Meredith told her.

Sammy stuck the scoop into the canister again, spilled flour from there all the way to the measuring cup, and then asked, "Now do I shake it?"

Meredith leaned down to see the red lines on the clear glass cup. "Not too hard, remember. Just a jiggle to even it out so we can tell for sure how much we've got."

Sammy started to shake the cup and lost her grip on the handle. The cup hit the edge of the counter, flour exploding upward in a white cloud. Meredith made a wild grab, but she was too late. The cup glanced off the counter, dive-bombed to the floor, and broke into a half dozen pieces.

"Oops." Sammy twisted to look. "I'm sorry, Mommy. I made a real bad mess."

Meredith swatted the legs of her jeans. "Yes, well, these things happen, punkin."

She helped Sammy down from the stool, then went for the broom and dustpan. When she returned, Sammy had already gotten the trash container from under the sink.

"Uh-oh, our garbage is filled all up. I forgot to take it out."

"Here in a minute, I'll go empty it." Meredith set to work with the broom. "First I want to sweep this flour into a pile so we don't track it all over."

"I can do garbage, Mommy. It's s'posed to be my job." Sammy picked up the trash container. "I'm sorry I broke your messing cup. I di'n't mean to."

"Measuring cup," Meredith corrected, even though "messing" seemed a more appropriate word at the moment. "And it's no big deal, sweetkins. I have another one."

Circling the flour on her tiptoes, Sammy headed for the back door.

"Don't walk on the weak spot!" Meredith called after her.

"I won't."

Meredith waited to hear the back door open. *Nothing.* After a moment, she set aside the broom and stepped to the utility room doorway.

"Sammy?"

The child stood frozen before the closed back door, one hand clasping the doorknob, the trash container sitting beside her on the floor.

Meredith wanted to give herself a swift kick on the rump. *The dog.* Making cookies had been even more distracting than she hoped. For a few minutes, she had completely forgotten about the Rottweiler, and evidently Sammy had as well.

Skirting the rotten flooring, Meredith went to crouch by her daughter. "Sammy?"

No answer. Meredith leaned around and saw the anxiety reflected in her child's eyes. "Oh, sweetkins."

"He could be out there," Sammy whispered in a shaky voice. "In the dark, he could eat me, and you'd never know where I went. I'd just be swallowed up."

Meredith's stomach rolled with sudden nausea. Sammy was still staring at the door, her small face drained of color. God knew what the child was remembering, the only certainty being that the images weren't pleasant. In that moment, if Dan Calendri hadn't already been dead, Meredith would have driven nonstop back to New York and done her level best to murder him. It had been one thing for him to make her life a living hell, but how could he have done this to their daughter?

It was a question that had no answer, and Meredith had long since stopped searching for one.

Sighing, she gave the child a heartening hug. "I'll do the trash tonight, okay?"

"No, Mommy, don't go out there! I'm 'fraid you won't come back."

Meredith was sorely tempted to take Sammy's advice and stay put. But if she humored her daughter in this, it would be the same as admitting she was afraid herself. "Don't be a doofus. Of course I'll come back. That silly old Rottweiler isn't out there."

As Meredith pushed to her feet and grabbed the trash container, she tried her best to believe that. Rottweilers, Dobermans. Except for their body builds, the two breeds were unnervingly alike.

Winking at Sammy, Meredith opened the door. Darkness lay over the backyard like a thick velour blanket. A Rottweiler would blend into the blackness, invisible until it was almost upon you.

Stop it, Meredith. Just stop it. Gathering her courage, she stepped outside.

The creak of the back porch steps made Meredith's skin crawl. Swiveling her head, she peered into the shadows, her eyes burning. *Nothing.* But then, a black dog wouldn't exactly shine like a beacon. Would it? She hauled in a deep breath, trying to concentrate on the smell of the grass hay, which reminded her of home.

"Mommy?"

"I'm right here," Meredith answered as she walked to the garbage can out by the shed. Heavens, it seemed dark. "See?" she called back over her shoulder. "No dog."

Just as Meredith lifted the metal lid, a crate beside the

can brushed against her leg. She gave a startled leap and lost her hold on the lid handle. The resultant racket was deafening. To make matters worse, she dropped the kitchen trash.

"Mommy!" Sammy cried from the doorway. "Mommy!"

"I'm all right," Meredith called, her voice quavering.

This was ridiculous. She was a grown woman, not a fanciful child. She stooped to pick up the spilled trash, patting the ground to find the stuff. When she thought she'd cleaned up most of the mess, she brushed her hands clean and groped for the lid she'd dropped. After setting it back on the can, she retraced her steps to the porch.

"See? I'm back," she called, trying to sound cheerful. "And fine as a frog's hair."

Sammy wasn't standing at the screen. After stepping inside, Meredith righted the door in its frame as she closed it, then fastened the latch for good measure. "Sammy? Where are you?"

No answer.

Meredith set the trash pail in the rusted utility sink, waited for her eyes to adjust to the light, and then began searching for her daughter. She found the child between the washing machine and wall, her small shoulders wedged into the narrow space.

"Oh, Sammy."

Taking care to be gentle, she extracted Sammy from her hiding place. "Sweetheart, I'm all right. See? Nothing bad happened to me. I just dropped the garbage can lid, that's all." The blank look in the child's eyes filled Meredith with fear. "Oh, punkin. Mommy's here. Everything's fine."

Only everything wasn't fine, and Meredith was beginning to wonder if anything ever would be again. She carried the child to the bedroom, her heart breaking at how rigid the little girl's body felt. *Disassociation from reality.* That was the clinical term a psychotherapist back in New York had used. Rigidity, a blank stare, no response to stimulus. Every time it happened, Meredith felt panicky. What if

Sammy never came out of it? That was the fear that haunted Meredith. The psychotherapist had assured her that as long as Sammy remained insulated from the sorts of experiences that had caused her illness in the first place, it was unlikely that the incidents would ever last more than a few hours. But even so, Meredith worried herself sick.

The hardest part of all, Meredith knew from experience, would be when Sammy woke up. Not that she was actually asleep. She would simply blink, as if an invisible switch inside her had been turned back on. Then she would look around, as if to orient herself, smile, and behave normally. It was Meredith's lot to behave normally as well—to act calm, to pretend nothing frightening had happened—when she yearned to hug her daughter and weep with relief.

After turning on Sammy's bedside light, she sank onto the old rocker she'd bought at a secondhand shop, cradling Sammy close and stroking her silken hair. She resisted the urge to shake the child or try to talk to her. Those tactics never worked.

With a push of her feet, she set the rocker in motion. The rhythmic creak should have been soothing. Instead, it made Meredith want to scream. This was her baby who lay so rigid in her arms. *Her baby*. Sammy needed professional help, and since their move to Oregon, Meredith couldn't provide her with it. The counseling sessions cost a small fortune, and she no longer had health insurance.

Tears filled her eyes. *Please, God, help me. I can't cope with this alone anymore*. The prayer seemed to bounce off the walls of her mind, a plea that would never be voiced. Maybe it was only wishful thinking, but Meredith believed the child could still hear her when she got like this, even though she didn't respond.

At some point, the telephone started to ring. The sound pealed through the otherwise silent rooms, monotonous, seeming to go on forever. Meredith didn't move. Since she'd come to Oregon, the only evening calls she ever got were from solicitors.

The ringing finally stopped, then started again. Her

breath hitched, and she stopped rocking. *What if it was Masters calling?* Ever since she'd learned the sheriff lived up the road, she'd tormented herself with the possibilities, all of them beginning with, "What if?" What if there was an APB out on her? What if the sheriff had seen her likeness and somehow recognized her? What if he showed up on her doorstep with a warrant for her arrest? When he drove past her house in his Bronco, he always slowed down, as if he were trying to catch a glimpse of them. In her experience, cops were suspicious by nature. That was no big problem, if you had nothing to hide.

God, she was tired. So awfully, horribly tired. Too tired to worry about it any more. If he showed up at her front door, she would deal with it then.

Resting her chin on her daughter's head, she let her gaze trail slowly over the room. She hadn't pinched pennies to decorate in here, hoping to create a place where Sammy would feel cherished, a fairy tale world, where danger and fear couldn't enter.

The clown lamp on the night table radiated light through the ruffled shade, creating a cozy nimbus of gold. Along one pink wall, Winnie the Pooh plaques held court over a Strawberry Shortcake toy chest. The bookcase farther down the wall displayed children's books, mostly fairy tales or collections of whimsical nursery rhymes.

Satin and lace. Little girl fantasies and castles in the clouds. Fairy dust and magic wands. Not so long ago, Meredith had stubbornly clung to a childish belief in those things herself—or at least in an adult version of them— that good was stronger than evil, that handsome heroes truly did exist, that anything was possible, if you believed.

His gaze fixed on the well-lighted windows of Meredith Kenyon's house, Heath depressed the receiver button on his portable phone, cutting off the connection in the middle of a ring. Why the hell didn't she answer? He rejected the possibility that she might have caller ID and simply didn't wish to speak with him.

Goliath chose that moment to rear up on the windowsill again, his claws scraping loudly on the expensive oak. Heath grabbed the Rottweiler's collar and pulled him down. "Would you stop it, Goliath? I'm not letting you out. Just go lie down."

The dog whined and circled, his stout body bumping Heath's legs.

"No," Heath said more firmly. "You'd make a beeline for that little girl. Don't think I don't know it. Now go lie down."

As the dog trotted away, Heath tossed the phone on the sofa. *Screw it*. If the lady didn't want to answer her calls, he had better things to do. What did he plan to say to her, anyway? That Goliath was a great dog, once you got to know him?

Disgusted with himself, Heath crossed the living room, flopped down on his manure brown recliner, and jerked up the footrest. A cold beer, as yet untouched, sat on the end table, condensation pooling on the coaster. He reached for the satellite remote control, hit the power button, and then poised his finger over the selection browser. *Police shows*. He saw enough in real life, not to mention mysteries to solve, and unlike in the movies, solving them was never easy.

Meredith Kenyon was no exception. Something about her troubled him. He wasn't sure what. He only knew there was more going on with her than met the eye. He couldn't stop thinking about her. Had he seen her someplace before? Was that it?

A niggling suspicion formed. Maybe the lady was wanted for something. Usually when Heath felt a nagging sense of familiarity when he first met people, it was because he'd seen their pictures come in over the wire at one time or another.

Nah. He gave himself a hard mental shake. If he didn't watch his step, the first thing he knew, he'd be suspecting harmless old ladies of being ax murderers.

Fed up, he turned off the set, pushed up from the chair,

and grabbed his untouched beer. Goliath fell in behind him en route to the kitchen. After emptying the bottle and stuffing it into the recycling bin, Heath stared down at the pile of rinsed dishes in the sink. Seven plates. That meant he still had five clean ones left.

Since he had the evening off, he toyed with the idea of washing dishes—just for the hell of it. But, nah. If he ran out of pots, he could always muck one out.

Before heading for bed, he stepped outside so Goliath could take a leak. From down at the pond, frogs croaked, creating a cacophony. As accompaniment, cattle lowed in the distance, and occasionally a horse whinnied. To Heath it was like listening to a symphony. He loved ranch life. As a young man, that had been his dream, to be a rancher. On a much larger scale than this, of course.

A sad, lost feeling settled over Heath as he remembered the young man he'd once been. One bad decision had altered the entire course of his life. For the most part, he was happy. At one point in his life, working in law enforcement had been his salvation, and even now, his work with teenagers helped keep his demons at bay. He was certainly too busy to spend much time mourning over the dreams he'd left behind. But deep down, in a secret place he seldom acknowledged, the yearning to have his own ranch was still there, waiting to assail him when his defenses were down.

He took a deep breath, savoring the smell of alfalfa and grass hay, wondering what it was within him that made him love it so. Thinking of his dad, he knew damned well it had nothing to do with genetics. Granted, Ian Masters owned a large ranch, but he seldom spent much time there.

Heath shook off his nostalgia and squinted to see through the moon-silvery darkness. Goliath had wandered up the drive and looked as if he were about to bolt. "Don't even think about running off," Heath warned.

Goliath came loping back to the porch. Heath didn't miss the look of longing the Rottweiler sent toward the Kenyon house before he bumped open the screen door to go inside. Heath turned to follow, wondering if he should flip on the air-conditioning. He decided to just open a bedroom window. In this country, the ambient temperature plunged drastically in the wee hours of the morning. This being only May, it'd be colder than a witch's tit by dawn, and he'd wake up freezing with the air conditioner on.

Meredith squinted into the morning sunlight, one hand pressed to the small of her back, the other clenched on the cracked handle of a sledge hammer.

"Whew!" she said, smiling at Sammy. "Fence building is hard work."

Sammy settled a bewildered gaze on the tangled sections of hog wire and rusty metal posts that Meredith had dragged from the shed. "It isn't gonna be very pretty when you get done, neither," she observed with a child's candor.

Meredith was far more concerned with functionality. "No, but it's free. Lucky for us, someone who lived here stored this stuff instead of throwing it away." She glanced over her shoulder at the sagging fence dividing their yard from the cow pasture. "If I have any posts left over, maybe I can use them to shore up that old thing as well."

"How come do we gots to have fences?"

Already sporting blisters on her palms, Meredith gingerly shifted her grip on the sledge hammer, her mind racing for an explanation Sammy would believe. Admitting the truth, that she was terrified the Rottweiler next door might return, would only fuel Sammy's anxieties and make her afraid to play outside. Meredith figured she was worrying enough for them both, thus her decision to enclose the backyard. The dog would play heck trying to reach Sammy through a fence.

"I'm going to have a garden," she improvised. "What do you think about that?"

"What kind've garden? For flowers?"

"Vegetables. I was your age when I planted my first row in my mom's garden."

"Was it fun?"

"Well, yes, it was. My mom left the responsibility of it

completely to me. I had to water my row and weed it, and I got to pick my own veggies and wash them for supper.''

Sammy frowned. ''I still don't know how come we gots to have a fence.''

''To keep the cows from trampling our plants.''

Sammy glanced at the pasture. ''They don't never come over here, Mommy.''

''No, they haven't yet. But if they get loose, they might. Cows love gardens, you know. What plants they don't manage to eat, they cut to pieces with their hooves.''

Sammy made a face. ''We gonna grow okra?''

Meredith laughed. Her daughter didn't share her enthusiasm for Southern-style food. ''Maybe. But we can plant other things, too. Broccoli, cauliflower, green beans, turnips, and cucumbers. Squash, too, and maybe even some taters. They have potato farms here, so they must do well.''

Now that the thought of a garden had occurred to Meredith, she quickly warmed to the idea, wondering why she hadn't considered the possibility before. Too many years of city living, she guessed. As a girl growing up in Mississippi, she wouldn't have been able to imagine people not having a garden. It was a way of life for her folks.

Given the state of her finances, Meredith needed to economize, and growing her own produce would cut back on the grocery bill. If she started collecting quart-sized jars and lids, she'd have plenty to use for canning by the end of summer, and she could probably pick up a pressure cooker at the thrift shop.

Visions of her kitchen shelves lined with neatly labeled jars filled her mind. She and Sammy could make relish, catsup, pickles, and jelly. Not only would it be fun, but it would save her a load of money.

She surveyed the backyard, trying to decide where might be best to plant a garden. ''It'll be so much fun, punkin. We can plant peas and corn, too.''

Sammy brightened at the mention of her favorite vegetables. ''Yummee.''

As Meredith bent to get another post, she found herself

glancing at the rickety old house and remembering all the grand plans she'd had when she moved in. Last night, she'd felt so defeated and afraid, her one thought to pull up stakes and move as quickly as she could. Now, her optimism was returning. With a fence, it was unlikely that the Rottweiler would get in the yard again, and with that threat out of the way, she'd have no more run-ins with Masters. Maybe they could make their home here, after all.

Hope burgeoned within her as she ran her gaze over the sagging back porch and weathered red shingles. Definitely not a palace, but to a dyed-in-the-wool country girl, fancy houses held little appeal. This place needed lots of work, but if she kept after the landlord and did a lot of it herself, it would get done eventually.

"What's wrong, Mommy?"

Meredith snapped from her reverie to focus on her daughter. "Nothing, sweetie. Everything's right, absolutely right."

Chapter 4

Over the next two days, Heath's life was a whirlwind. The recall petition was causing a stir, and he'd been called before the board of county commissioners three times, only to accomplish nothing. He refused to toss teenagers into overcrowded cells, even for short stays until their folks could come get them. *A look at the dark side, up close and personal?* Not while he was sheriff. As for calling parents, no problem. He just needed fifteen more deputies and another pair of hands to do the job.

Then there'd been the accident, for which Heath would always believe Tom Moore had been responsible. At final tally, seven boys had lost their lives, all honor-roll seniors who would have gone on to universities next fall on football scholarships. They'd been well liked by their teachers, popular with classmates, and deeply loved by their families. It was a devastating loss. Heath had attended the memorial service, and he'd spent most of the first day after the wreck at the school, giving lectures on teenage alcohol abuse, counseling kids with drinking problems, and enrolling drinkers and nondrinkers alike into prevention programs, sponsored by businesses in the community.

In addition to the problems caused by recall and the accident, Heath had been dealing with what he was coming to think of as the "Moore Factor." The younger man was about to drive Heath and everyone else at the department crazy. The possibility of Heath's recall pleased the deputy, no end. For the last two days, his uniforms had been starched so stiff, they looked as if they could walk by themselves. And when he came in to work, he all but danced a jig. He actually seemed to think that he would have Heath's job in the bag if Heath were out of the picture. *Right.* Moore had a lot of growing up to do before he'd be ready. In ten years, maybe, *maybe* being the keyword. If he kept pushing Heath's buttons, he might not live that long.

Being so preoccupied, Heath might have forgotten the pretty little brunette down the road but for one small detail: nearly every time he drove past her house, she was outside tackling some chore that made him feel guilty as hell for not stopping to help. One time, she was building a fence, which he assumed was to keep Goliath out, the next time swinging a hoe as if she were killing snakes. Another afternoon, she was trying to fix a section of fence between her yard and the pasture, wrestling with a post bigger than she was. Two days later, he saw her removing a sheet of particle board from the top of her battered Ford sedan. What in the hell was she up to over there?

He'd chewed on that question ever since. *Not my business. The lady wants nothing to do with me, and if I'm smart, I'll keep it that way. What am I gonna do? Repair the place for her? Like I have time for that.*

Logical reasons notwithstanding, Heath still felt like a heel for not helping. Not that she'd accept. He wouldn't be welcome if he went back over there, dog or no dog.

This is ridiculous, Meredith thought one morning as she stared at the black dog hair on the edge of the bathroom sink. How could there be dog hair in the house after all her efforts? She'd washed Sammy's bedding and the clothes she'd been wearing the night Goliath got in the yard. Plus, she'd dust-mopped the floor in Sammy's room three times since. But the hair kept appearing. It was as if the stuff was procreating.

When Meredith went to the kitchen and sat down across

from Sammy at the table, she found another dog hair in her oatmeal. "Sammy, has Goliath been coming over to visit with you through the fence while you're playing outside?"

Holding a spoonful of cereal poised halfway to her mouth, Sammy gazed across the table at Meredith with guileless blue eyes. "No, Mommy."

While scooping the short black hair from her dish, Meredith observed her daughter, who looked as innocent as an angel. Maybe a little too innocent.

"Have you been letting Goliath in the house at night?" she asked gently.

"No, Mommy."

Meredith had never caught her daughter in a lie, and she had no reason to believe the child might be fibbing now. Even so, she looked deeply into Sammy's eyes, searching for . . . what? Some sign of duplicity? She was dealing with a little girl who wouldn't turn five for several more weeks, not an accomplished liar.

"Sweetheart . . ."

Meredith hesitated. She couldn't spout dire warnings. Did she want the child to be terrified to go outdoors? "Hmm," she mused, looking back down at her bowl. "This is too weird. I guess you're still picking up dog hair on your clothes when you play outside."

Sammy hunched her shoulders, looking as bewildered as Meredith felt.

"Well, so much for my finishing breakfast," Meredith said with a sigh. "Somehow, a dog hair in my mush doesn't do great things for my appetite."

A few minutes later Meredith settled down at her desk to put in her daily four hours working. Telephone solicitation was a dead-end, no-brainer job, and no matter how she tried, she couldn't muster much enthusiasm. But working in computer programming, the field she loved, simply wasn't possible right now, not when she had an emotionally unstable little girl who needed her mother at home. Sammy had just been taken from the only world she'd ever known and plopped smack-dab in the middle of an unfamiliar one.

She needed time—time to heal and time to forget.

Later when Sammy was stronger and able to attend school, Meredith would return to her field. There were mail order places where she could purchase a fake diploma to get her foot in the door at a company, and once there, her experience would carry her. For now, though, she was content to call strangers and book them for a free carpet shampoo, compliments of Miracle Kleen. For every shampooer her customers purchased from the sales rep who did the demonstrations, Meredith received a commission. She wasn't getting rich, but the paychecks kept the wolves from their door.

As she was making her first phone call of the morning, Meredith noticed several dog hairs on her desk blotter. Seeing them stunned her.

"Hello?"

The irritated voice at the other end of the line startled Meredith into speech. "Uh, hello, Mrs. Christiani? This is Meredith Kenyon, your local Miracle Kleen representative. My company's offering a few carefully selected dogs in Wynema Falls a free carpet cle—"

Before Meredith could say more, the woman hung up in her ear.

Two nights later, Meredith was jerked from a sound sleep by a piercing scream. Then, "Mommy! Mommy!"

Accustomed to her daughter's nightmares, Meredith was on her feet before she came fully awake. Not taking time to search for her slippers, she raced through the house, tugging on the chenille robe she'd grabbed from the foot of her bed.

"I'm here, sweetie!" she cried as she flung open Sammy's bedroom door and flipped on the light. "It's okay, punkin. Mommy's—"

Meredith's words died in her throat, and she reeled to a halt. Heath Masters' dog lay in the middle of her daughter's bed, a hulking black presence. Meredith glanced at the double-hung window, which had been pushed open, then jerked her gaze back to her daughter, who was hugging the dog's stout neck, her tear damp face pressed against his ruff. The Rottweiler lay with one foreleg curled over Sammy as if to return her hug, his massive head resting on her shoulder, his jowls dripping drool down the back of her pink pajama top. Every time Sammy sobbed, the dog whined softly, snuffling the child's hair and licking her ear.

Always before, it had been Meredith's job to comfort Sammy when she awoke from a nightmare. Now, it seemed, Heath Masters' Rottweiler had assumed that role.

Amazement coursed through Meredith. How many times had Sammy let the dog in? Judging by the way she clung to Goliath, the two had done some serious bonding.

Meredith took a cautious step toward the bed. Goliath emitted a low, rumbling growl. Meredith stopped and hugged her waist, her gaze fixed on those gleaming white fangs. *Oh, God.* She had no doubt that the dog would leap on her if she went closer.

Gathering all her courage, Meredith took another step. Goliath's snarl gained force, seeming to vibrate the walls. She pressed a hand to her throat, afraid to move. In a frenzy, the Rottweiler might turn on Sammy. The only things Meredith had in the house to use as weapons were a butcher knife and a tack hammer, and it would take her at least a full minute to go get either one.

She retreated to the kitchen and ran to the wall phone. By the light from Sammy's room, she could see well enough to find Heath Masters' phone number.

He answered on the second ring, sounding surprisingly alert. "Masters, here."

"Get over here! Your dog is in bed with my daughter! I can't get close to her!"

"Meredith?"

The fact that he'd somehow learned her name barely registered. Throwing a frightened glance over her shoulder to make sure the dog hadn't begun devouring her child, she cried, "Of course! Who else would be calling you at two in the morning?"

"I'll be right there."

The line went dead. Hanging up, Meredith pressed her back to the wall, wondering how long it might take him to get there. Five minutes?

Shaking and almost beside herself, she ran her hands into her hair. Oh, dear heaven, her *hair*! She couldn't answer the door like this.

She charged to the bathroom. In her hurry, she knocked the contact case off the counter. One side popped open. Falling to her knees, she carefully palmed the linoleum for the lost bit of fragile plastic. She had a spare set of lenses, but she couldn't recall which drawer she'd stuck them in. Oh, God, please . . .

She nearly sobbed with relief when she finally found the lens. Then she almost lost it down the drain as she rinsed it off. After popping the colored disks into her eyes, she groped for her dark wig, jerked it on her head, then reached for her generously padded bra. At just that second, a loud knock resounded through the house.

Heath Masters looked bigger than life when she saw him standing on her rickety porch, his partially buttoned uniform shirt revealing an expanse of well-muscled, deeply bronzed chest, his faded jeans encasing powerful legs that seemed to stretch forever. Dim light fell across him, casting his dark, chiseled features in shadow and glistening in the sleep-rumpled waves of sable hair that curled loosely over his forehead.

Slate blue eyes still bleary with sleep, he asked, "Where is he?"

Meredith stepped back and beckoned him inside. "Careful of the flowerpots."

She led him to the kitchen, where two rectangles of light spilled across the floor, one from the bathroom, the other from Sammy's bedroom.

"They're in there. Sammy had a nightmare. When I went in, there he was."

Heath stepped to the doorway. After taking in the situation, he bent to pat his knee. "Goliath! Come here, buddy."

When Meredith heard the dog leap off the bed, she expelled a breath she hadn't realized she'd been holding. She backed away when Heath led his dog to the kitchen.

"There's nothing to be afraid of," he said as he tugged the dog past her.

Meredith ran to her daughter. After checking to make sure Sammy was all right, she tucked her back under the covers. "I'll be back in just a minute. Okay, sweetness?"

Sammy, who seemed to have recovered with record speed from her bad dream, caught Meredith's hand. "Don't be mad at G'liath, Mommy. I'm the one who sneaked."

Meredith reached down to smooth her daughter's hair. "Oh, Sammy . . ."

"I di'n't fib. Honest, Mommy. You asked if I *let* him in, 'member? All I done was open the window. G'liath comed in all by hisself."

"I see." Meredith looked deeply into her child's eyes. Little angels, it seemed, could be as duplicitous as adults. "And why didn't you just tell me that?"

" 'Cause you was scared." Sammy wrinkled her nose. "You di'n't really build a fence to keep the cows away. You fibbed, di'n't you, Mommy? It was for G'liath."

Meredith felt heat creeping up her neck. She couldn't chastise Sammy for fibbing when she'd done it herself. "Well . . . we'll talk more about this in the morning, all right?"

"Do I gots to sit in the corner?"

Meredith sighed and drew the covers more snugly under Sammy's chin. "No. I'll probably let this slide. But we must have a discussion about your splitting hairs."

"I di'n't split 'em, Mommy. More just comed off G'liath and got all over. I think, maybe, 'cause G'liath likes to lay in the tub."

The bathtub? Little wonder she'd been finding hair in her bathroom. That horrible dog had been wandering loose in her house? The thought made Meredith shiver.

"We'll definitely have a long talk about this in the morning," she told Sammy softly. "Right now, though, I have to see Sheriff Masters to the door. Okay?"

"I'm in trouble, huh?"

Gazing down into her child's worried eyes, Meredith couldn't hold onto her anger. "No, sweetkins, you're not in trouble. Finding Goliath in here just caught me by surprise, that's all."

"The sher'ff man was right, Mommy. Goliath loves little girls, and he was lonesome for a friend. Now he's my 'tector, like for fires and stuff."

Recalling Sammy's initial terror of the dog, Meredith could scarcely credit this. "How did you figure out that he wanted a friend?" she couldn't resist asking.

"He told me." Sammy plucked at her quilt. "In dog talk. He comed to the window and scratched, and told me. Then he gived me kisses through the glass till I wasn't scared he'd bite me no more. Will you tell him g'night for me?"

"Absolutely." Good night and good riddance. Meredith bent to press a kiss to her daughter's forehead. "No more nightmares, okay? Just sweet dreams."

As she left the bedroom, Meredith drew the door closed behind her. Turning to face Heath Masters, she flipped on the light switch by the refrigerator, then hugged her waist. A sharp edge of torn linoleum jabbed the underside of her big toe, and she sucked in a surprised breath, the faint scent of musk aftershave drifting to her.

Nice, she thought, then scowled. This man was an enemy and presently stood in her kitchen like a tree that had put down roots, the chipped yellow tabletop not quite reaching his hip. Tongue lolling, Goliath sat at his feet, so well behaved he might have been a poster dog for obedience training. She couldn't decide which of them to watch.

"I'm really sorry about this," he said.

After the fright the dog had given her, Meredith wanted to give him what for, but caution won out. Her goal was to live here in obscurity, not start a feud.

He studied her as he might a puzzle piece that wouldn't

quite fit. He was undeniably handsome, his tousled dark hair lending him an untamed, hard-edged aura she might have found appealing back in her young and reckless college days. With that bronze skin and those strong, sharply cut features he could have Indian ancestry, she decided. The type of man portrayed in those ''silk and savage'' historical romances, where the towering, muscular half-breed captured a trembling white girl and made love to her in his tee-pee—and under the stars, and along streams, and in caves, and on horseback. In her pre-Dan days, Meredith had adored those stories.

These days, being overpowered and crushed in a steely embrace, kissed senseless, and then carried over a broad shoulder to a tee-pee ranked much lower on her list—three pages or so down—from getting a root canal without Novocaine.

She hauled in a deep breath, feeling oddly faint. As if the dog sensed her uneasiness, it whined. She glanced down into the saddest, most apologetic brown eyes she'd ever seen. *Lunacy*. Dogs were incapable of feeling regret.

''Mr. Masters, please don't take this wrong. But this situation can't continue. Your dog wouldn't let me near my daughter. What if she'd been hurt and needed medical attention?'' Hugging her waist more tightly, she made fists on the chenille of her robe. ''I don't want to be difficult. But if this happens again, I'll have to file a complaint.''

''I realize that.'' He bent to fondle his dog's ear. ''I don't know what's gotten into him. He's always been protective of kids, sometimes to a fault, but not without reason.''

Meredith bit the inside of her cheek. The last time this dog misbehaved, he'd tried to make excuses. ''Protective? Sammy doesn't need protection. I'm her *mother*.''

Keeping a hold on the dog's collar, he straightened. ''I'm as baffled as you are.''

''You're also trying to justify the dog's behavior. It's like excusing a lion for eating its trainer because the poor thing was having a bad hair day.''

''You're not blameless, you know. It *was* your kid who

let the dog in here. And Goliath isn't a man-eater. Your daughter's still in once piece. Not a mark on her.''

His observation sizzled in the air between them like a high-voltage wire.

"Will you at least hear me out?" he asked.

"I'm listening," she managed to say with frigid calmness.

"There's something weird going on in this dog's head."

She nearly laughed. Only it was too awful to be funny. "Perhaps you should take him to a dog psychiatrist. I'm not up on my canine psychoanalysis."

He narrowed one eye. That was it, just the narrowing of one eye. But it was all that was necessary. Six feet plus of furious male wasn't high on Meredith's list, either.

"I'm sorry. That was uncalled for. It's just—" She pried her fingers loose from the chenille to wave her hand. "This is my house. And I wake up to find *your* dog in my daughter's bed. And then he nearly attacks me? It's a bit difficult to be blasé.''

"I'm not asking that. Listening and trying to be rational would be nice, though.''

Meredith curled her toe over the rough edge of linoleum. Unclenching her teeth, she said, "Rational?"

He pinched the bridge of his nose, then rubbed his hand over his face. "Okay, my turn. That was uncalled for." His firm mouth quirked at one corner. "Can we start all over? I won't take shots if you won't.''

Meredith thought that sounded fair, which was, in and of itself, unprecedented in her dealings with men. "I'm willing. I don't want this to be an adversarial situation.''

"That makes two of us. This is no ordinary dog. He's a decorated hero. Police departments around the country pay a thousand bucks for one of his pups without batting an eye. *That's* the kind of record he's got. And now he could wind up dead over a stupid misunderstanding. Trust me, I'm as worried as you are.''

"Dead?" she echoed.

"What the hell else do you think will happen if you file

a complaint? He was a canine deputy, extensively trained. Dogs like that are dangerous if they turn mean.''

''My point, exactly,'' she said drily.

He heaved a sigh. ''This dog would never hurt a kid.''

''I realize you believe that, but—''

''I *know* that. I can't count the times Goliath has gone on a domestic violence call with me, only to take off like a shot when we entered the house. I'd find him later, standing guard over the kids. In those situations, he always acted crazy, just like he did the other night. Sometimes he wouldn't even let *me* get close—not until I called him off. He loves children, and when he acts this way, it's because he believes something or someone is going to hurt them.''

Meredith could only stand there, staring at him.

''Look,'' he said, raking a hand through his hair. ''The dog's acting crazy. I admit it. I'm only asking you to take a step back and help me figure out why. This is the second time he's come down here and stood guard over your child. There has to be a reason, even if it's not immediately apparent to either one of us.''

Meredith shifted her attention back to the dog and once again found herself impaled by those apologetic brown eyes. *Was* Goliath acting crazy? She recalled the night she'd first met Heath and how he'd tried to excuse the animal's behavior. She had pegged him as certifiably nuts. She no longer felt so sure. Dogs *did* have a sixth sense, and both times that Goliath had behaved viciously, Sammy had been terrified.

Tonight the child had had a nightmare. She'd been panicky when Meredith first opened the door. Meredith couldn't be certain what Sammy had been dreaming about, but she had a good idea. Had Goliath sensed the child's terror, possibly even the cause of it, and reacted, warning Meredith away because he perceived she might be a threat? Incredible. Yet Heath Masters was implying exactly that, whether he realized it or not. And he knew nothing of Sammy's history.

A dizzy feeling swept over her, and she clenched her

fists so tightly on the chenille that her knuckles ached. She couldn't admit that the dog might have cause to feel protective. Keeping the past a secret was vital to their future.

"At the risk of sounding unfeeling, I really don't care *why* your dog has been acting the way he has," she said softly. "I'll leave understanding him to you."

Heath nodded. "I guess I can't blame you for that."

"By the same token, I'd hate to see him put to sleep. That'd be a shame. I just don't want him here. To that end, I'm willing to cooperate with you in any way I can."

She avoided looking at Goliath, who seemed to be trying to melt her heart. *Craziness.* Five minutes ago, she'd been afraid he might go for her jugular.

A charged silence fell over the room, the ticking of her kitchen clock the only sound. Finally, Masters said, "In the morning, I'll call about getting a kennel built, and until it's done, I'll do my best to keep Goliath home. Do you feel comfortable with that?"

Meredith nearly pointed out that his best effort hadn't proved to be effective so far, but her wig felt as if it were on crooked, she wore no mascara to darken her lashes, and her padded bra was in the bath. The quicker she got him out of here, the better.

"Your best is all I can ask," she replied.

"If Goliath does get loose again, will you call me first? Instead of animal control?"

"I'll certainly try, but I can't make any guarantees. What if you're not at home?"

"Whenever I'm gone, he'll be locked up." He thrust out a hand. "Shake on it?"

Meredith glanced uneasily at Goliath.

Heath chuckled. "He won't bite you. It's kids he's protective of, not me."

Meredith gingerly extended her arm. Heath Masters' large hand engulfed hers, his palm warm and slightly rough, like fine sandpaper. With the tip of his forefinger, he traced the protrusion of her wrist bone, a twinkle creeping into his blue-gray eyes.

She was glad when he released her. Scrubbing his touch away on the nap of her robe, she led the way to the door, relieved that he still held the dog's collar. She tried not to look at Goliath. Those soulful brown eyes were getting to her.

Holding the door wide, she said, "Well . . . good night, Sheriff Masters."

"Heath. We are neighbors, Meredith. I hope we'll become good friends."

"That reminds me. I don't recall giving you my name."

He flashed her a slightly sheepish grin. "Yeah, well . . ." He shrugged. "That first night, I wanted to call you and mend fences, so I ran a check on your license plate."

Meredith felt as if the floor had vanished from beneath her feet. Just like that, he'd wanted her name and gotten it? By running a license plate check?

"I see," she finally managed to say. "Isn't that an invasion of my privacy?"

"If your first, middle, and last names are state secrets, yeah, I guess so."

Meredith didn't miss the glint of curiosity that crept into his eyes. She looked quickly away, laughing nervously. "Not state secrets. It just tends to make you feel vulnerable. I prefer the traditional introduction. An exchange of names, shaking hands."

"You're right." He turned loose of his dog to straighten and thrust out his hand. "My name's Heath Ian Masters," he said, his voice laced with teasing amusement. "I'm the guy with the crazy dog who lives up the road."

She had endured one handshake. She wasn't eager to experience another. But there he stood, waiting. She cast a wary glance at the dog then touched her fingertips to Heath's work-hardened palm, hoping to get this over with quickly. No such luck.

How was it that he could touch only her hand, yet make her feel the heat all over? A tingling, radiating warmth that shot first to her shoulder, then did a U-turn to her belly.

"And you are?"

She blinked. "Oh . . . I'm Meredith Lynn Kenyon, the woman down the road who doesn't *like* your crazy dog."

He chuckled at that, then trailed his fingertip over her wrist bone again, slowly and lightly, as if he were committing the feel of her to memory.

"Or me, either, I'm afraid," he observed huskily. He released his hold on her and turned to shoo his dog out the door ahead of him. "We'll have to work on that. Seems to me a lady living alone should be on good terms with the one neighbor she's got."

Not if she had anything to say about it, she thought a little frantically. This man threatened her peace of mind in more ways than one.

Heath was still standing on Meredith's rickety porch when she turned off the outside light, leaving him in the moonlight that slanted under the sagging overhang. She had to know he was still out here. A grin settled on his mouth.

"Well, Goliath, you've really done it this time," he said softly. "What in the hell were you thinking, huh?"

Goliath glanced at the closed door and whined.

"I don't wanna hear it, blockhead." Picking his way carefully, Heath moved down the rotten steps. When the dog didn't follow, he snapped his fingers. "Damn it, Goliath, get your keister down here."

Head hanging, the Rottweiler finally obeyed. Heath cut across the yard. At the road, he turned to look back. The floors in that house were a hazard. He couldn't believe she'd set out flower pots to divert the foot traffic. *Damn.* Why didn't she just hound Zeke Guntrum to death until the old fart repaired the place?

Somehow, Heath couldn't feature Meredith doing that. He recalled the wariness in her eyes and the nervous way she'd hugged her waist in the kitchen. She wasn't the type to stand toe-to-toe with a man. And Zeke would take advantage of it. The old man had a history of leasing this house, promising to make repairs, then pocketing the last month's rent and deposits when the snookered tenants left before the lease was up.

Heath hated to see a single woman with a kid get taken. He ran his gaze over the crumbling foundation and sagging porches, wondering if he shouldn't call Zeke himself.

The thought brought him up short. This wasn't his problem, and it sure as hell wasn't his business. Meredith wouldn't appreciate his interference. But, then, she probably wouldn't be too pleased when she or Sammy fell through the floor, either.

He remembered how fragile her wrist bone had felt. If she went through that floor, she'd break an ankle or something. The lady wasn't exactly sturdy. And if she got hurt, who'd play Good Samaritan? Yours truly, that's who. He *was* her only neighbor. That gave him a vested interest. It wasn't that he was attracted to her or anything. He was just anticipating trouble before it happened and trying to head it off at the pass.

Right. And if you believe that, next you'll be investing in the Golden Gate Bridge.

No wonder Goliath was so bent on coming here. There was something about Meredith and Sammy—he wasn't sure what—that brought out protective instincts. Those big, wary eyes, maybe? Whatever it was, all it took was one look and you were sunk.

Sighing, he fixed his gaze on her sagging front porch again. It wouldn't take much to fix the damned thing. An evening or two of work, max. Hell, give him three weeks, and he could have the whole place back up to snuff. He scanned the house from roof to foundation, a list of necessary materials taking shape in his mind. He hadn't used all of his paid vacation in over four years. If he took off early every afternoon for the next two or three weeks, no one at the department would dare to bitch.

It wasn't exactly the best timing, of course. Right now, he had career problems coming out his ears. On the other hand, though, what could he actually do about them? Worry? If the voters in this county disagreed with the way he did things, then he wasn't the man for the job because he wasn't willing to change. Doing things his way—trying to save kids—was the driving force in his life and the only reason he'd ever entered law enforcement. That was who he was, what he was all about, and if it was taken away, the job would mean nothing.

If the citizens of Wynema County hoped to back him into a corner, they were in for a big surprise. Before he'd use intimidation tactics with teenagers, he'd sign that recall petition himself.

He was whistling when he headed toward home. In the morning when he called a contractor about a kennel, he'd give Meredith's landlord a ring. Zeke was an ornery old coot and tight-fisted. But Heath had a few powerful persuaders in his arsenal, primarily a threat to testify in Meredith's behalf if she fell through the floor and injured herself.

If anything would get Zeke's attention fast, it'd be the possibility that he might get his ass sued off. When Heath finished with him, Zeke would be glad Heath was offering to do the work for free and would give him carte blanche to buy the materials. Meredith had already done wonders with fresh paint and cute little window curtains. With new floors, some linoleum, and a decent living room rug, the place wouldn't be half bad.

Remembering the way she'd doused the porch light after showing him out, Heath chuckled. She'd have to wait a spell before she managed to get him completely out of her hair. And very pretty hair it was, lying in dark, silky curls over her shoulders.

That was one thing about her he definitely liked, he decided—that wealth of dark hair.

Chapter 5

The next afternoon Sammy came running in the back door as if the devil were at her heels. Emptying potatoes from a bag into the sink, Meredith paused to glance up.

"Is something wrong, punkin?"

Sammy worked her mouth, then pointed toward the living room. "That sher'ff man is here. In his big white truck! He gots stuff all over the top of it."

The sheriff man? Her stomach twisting into knots, Meredith set the potatoes on the drain to go investigate. Glancing out into the yard through the parted living room curtains, she saw Heath Masters' white bronco in her rutted driveway, WYNEMA COUNTY SHERIFF emblazoned on the passenger door. Just as Sammy had said, there was a load of wood and other stuff on top of the vehicle.

Meredith frowned. An instant later, she heard footsteps on her porch, then the wall-shaking sound of a man's fist connecting solidly with wood.

When she opened the front door, the man himself stood on her welcome mat, his booted feet spread, his large hands resting at his hips. As her gaze met his, a jolt ran through her. There was something about him, with his broad shoulders and dark good looks, that invariably rattled her.

Today he wore a dark brown Stetson cocked at a jaunty angle, the crown adding inches to his height. The wide brim cast a shadow over his face that did little to lessen the

impact of those penetrating slate blue eyes. In the afternoon sunlight slanting under the porch overhang, the badge above his left shirt pocket flashed every time he moved.

Prying her tongue loose from the roof of her mouth, Meredith managed a tinny, ''Hello.'' She nearly added, ''May I help you?'' At the last second, she bit back the question and settled for saying, ''How are you today?'' That scored low on originality as well, but at least it didn't make her sound like a truck stop waitress.

Jabbing a thumb in the direction of his vehicle, he flashed her a crooked, purely masculine grin that was so devastatingly attractive she wondered if he practiced it in front of a mirror. ''Your landlord enlisted me to do some repairs on the house.''

She glanced at his rugged looking four-wheel drive, the tires slightly compressed from the load it carried. ''He did what?''

Evidently her stunned reaction must have shown on her face, for he quickly added, ''I'll stay out of your way. At least until I have to move inside.''

''But—'' Meredith broke off, her mind a jumble of half-formed protests.

He bounced on one foot, making her entire porch rock. ''No way around it. You or Sammy could fall through. It isn't safe. And the floors inside aren't any better.''

''I bought some particle board. I already laid some on the utility porch.''

''That's a stopgap measure, at best, not to mention that an abrupt edge like that in the center of a room is a good way to trip and fall.''

Meredith couldn't argue the point. She'd already stubbed her toe in the utility room once and undoubtedly would again if something wasn't done.

As if that settled the matter, he swept off his hat, touching his shirt sleeve to the beads of perspiration on his forehead. Looking into the sun, he said, ''I can't believe this weather. You ever seen the like? Not even June yet and it feels like midsummer.''

The warm weather was the least of her concerns. He whacked his Stetson against his leg, making her jump.

"I'm going over to my place to change before I start. I'll be back at"—he glanced at his watch—"oh, probably four-thirty. If you hear a bunch of noise, you'll know it's me."

Her mouth still slightly agape, Meredith watched him vault off the porch with surefooted agility. He cut across her yard and started up the road in a loose, long-legged jog. It occurred to her as she gazed after him that she'd just been bulldozed. Very cleverly and politely, to be sure, but bulldozed, all the same. He hadn't bothered to ask if she minded his doing the repairs on her house or tried to schedule his visits at her convenience. He was just going to barge in, and if she didn't like it, too bad.

Closing the door with more force than she intended, Meredith whirled to go back to the kitchen and nearly tripped over a flowerpot.

"Hang it!" she said, her frustration making her voice shrill. "Between that man and his infernal dog, there'll never be any peace and quiet around here!"

Pale and big-eyed, Sammy stood in the archway that led to the kitchen. Tugging on the hem of her pink T-shirt, she said, "Mommy? What's he gonna do?"

Meredith took a steadying breath and went to kneel before her daughter. Gently smoothing a golden curl from the child's cheek, she said, "He's going to fix these awful old floors, sweetness. Won't that be wonderful? And our porches, too!"

"How come don't you feel happy, then?"

Good question. It wasn't the gift Meredith had a problem with, but the packaging. "I'm just not used to having a stranger around, that's all."

Sammy rubbed her nose. "Me, neither. I don't want him here. Don't let him come in, Mommy. 'Kay?"

It wasn't quite that simple. "We do need our floors fixed. Sheriff Masters is right about that. One of us could fall through and get hurt."

Her expression glum, Sammy hugged herself. "I hope he don't gots his gun when he comes back."

Sammy got her wish. Ten minutes later, Heath Masters returned wearing faded jeans, a blue chambray work shirt, dusty cowboy boots, the same Stetson hat, and a leather tool belt slung low around his lean hips. Fanciful though it was, Meredith couldn't help thinking he looked like a gunfighter straight off the set of a Western film, the only difference being that his side arm was a claw hammer instead of a Colt .45.

He immediately started unloading the lumber from atop his Bronco and stacking it on her patchy front lawn. For such a large man, there was a curious sort of grace in everything he did, steely muscle and bone working in fluid harmony.

When he started ripping up the rotten boards from her porch with nothing but the claw hammer and forceful precision, Meredith experienced an odd, tight sensation low in her abdomen. A purely knee-jerk reaction, she assured herself. There was something potently sensual about a well-muscled man in a sweat-dampened shirt with the sleeves rolled back over his forearms. It was only natural that her eyes were drawn to his anatomy. It was on a par with admiring a sensational sunset or studying a work of art.

Meredith soon noticed she wasn't the only observant female in the house. Sammy was staring out the window as well, eyes wide with fascination. Sammy's father Dan had been the suit-and-tie type, and the child had never had an opportunity to closely observe a man doing physical labor. It was an impressive sight.

Meredith's heart kicked against her ribs when Heath paused to jerk the tails of his chambray shirt loose from his jeans. With deft flicks of his fingers, he unbuttoned the front placket. As he straightened to wipe his forehead, her attention shifted to his chest, a burnished copper only a shade lighter than his face. From there, her gaze dropped to the ladder of muscle that formed tracks across his abdomen. A narrowing swath of dark hair ran from his navel to the waistband of his jeans. He reminded her of a carving done in seasoned oak, every line masterfully defined and rubbed to a rich, dark sheen.

As if he sensed eyes on him, he turned toward the window. His gaze locked on her. Caught in the act of gaping at him, she almost dove to the floor.

His mouth kicked up at one corner, and his flinty eyes took on a mischievous, knowing glint. Cheeks burning, Meredith turned away, nearly running over Sammy who stood partially behind her. She glanced back over her shoulder to see Heath grinning and winking at the little girl.

Grabbing Sammy by the arm, Meredith headed for the kitchen. "Come on, punkin, it's not polite for us to stare. Let's go fix supper."

"But Mommy, he's got a funny-looking tummy."

Meredith wasn't about to bite on that one. Funny didn't begin to describe Heath Masters' tummy. The man was a heart-stopper, no two ways about it, which was all the more reason for her to stay away from him. She'd fallen prey to a case of raging hormones once. Look where it had gotten her.

"How about pudding for dessert tonight?" she asked Sammy in a twangy voice.

"Is *he* gonna have supper with us?"

Heaven forbid. "No, sweetness. Just you and I, like always."

Stepping back to the sink, Meredith began dumping potatoes out of the bag again. A light breeze came through the open kitchen window, cool against her cheeks. When she realized she'd dumped enough potatoes to feed a dozen grown men and one boy, she said, "*Confound it,*" under her breath and began shoving spuds back in the bag. Visions of Heath Masters still tumbling inside her head, she scrubbed the potato skins, then grabbed a knife from the wooden rack over the stove. After peeling the vegetables, she began quartering them into a pot sitting on the counter.

"Say, Meredith? About the front door."

The unexpected sound of Heath's voice coming through the window startled Meredith so badly that she jerked. Pain shot to her elbow, and almost instantly, blood seemed to be everywhere. She dropped the potato and knife into the sink and wrenched on the faucet handle to shove her hand under cold water. "Oh, my stars!"

Heath, who stood head and shoulders above the windowsill, leaned in and saw the blood streaming from her hand. "Jesus H. Christ!"

The next instant, he disappeared.

Sammy came running to Meredith's side. "Mommy? What—?" The child's eyes went wide with fright. "Oh, Mommy!"

"It's nothing, sweetheart. Just a little cut."

Using her other hand, Meredith pressed down hard over the wound, but it didn't seem to staunch the bleeding. Gingerly, she assessed the damage. The cut had deeply severed the web between her thumb and forefinger and ran halfway across her palm.

Stay calm. She shoved her hand back under the water, feeling as if she might vomit. For the life of her, she could remember very little of the first aid training she'd had. Black spots danced before her eyes.

"Sammy, love, I need a towel."

The next thing Meredith knew, Heath was standing behind her, his muscular arms bracketing her shoulders like steel parentheses.

"I'm all right," she said tremulously, craning her neck to locate her daughter.

All she could see was blue chambray. Heath had sandwiched her between his body and the counter, his hard shoulders hunched forward. When he saw how deep the cut was, he cursed again, this time under his breath.

"Really, I'm fine. I'll, um . . . just wrap it. No big deal."

"God, I'm sorry about this." His voice gravelly with regret, he shoved her hand back under the water. "I just wanted to warn you about using the front door. With most of the porch missing, it's quite a drop to the ground."

Meredith blinked, trying to clear away the black spots. The rush of the water echoed inside her head. "Sheriff Masters, it's not your fault."

"Like hell. I should've gone to the back door. I didn't mean to startle you."

The ragged edge of his breathing told her how worried he was. "I'll be fine, really."

A sudden brightness gilded the kitchen, and Meredith felt as if she were peering at everything through the illumination, her mind strangely separate from reality. *Big, tanned hands, one clamped over her wrist, the other applying pressure to the cut. The floorboards creaking under their feet. Sammy's small face, as pale as a whitewashed picket, reappearing beside them. A deep, masculine voice saying the words "stitches" and "emergency room."*

She forced her gaze away from the wound, which gaped open.

"You aren't going to faint on me, are you?" he asked.

"No, of course not. Blood doesn't bother me." Seeing her own meat and muscle was another matter entirely, though. Every time she drew a breath, her lungs hitched. "It's not really all that bad. Is it?"

"Well, it's not exactly a nick." He shifted behind her. "Sammy, can you get me a clean towel?" Meredith heard chair legs scrape the floor. "Don't fall, sweetcakes." A second later, the patter of Sammy's sneakers came up beside them. "That's a girl," Heath told the child. "This towel will work great!" As he turned back to Meredith, he said, "Are you all right, honey? You're pale. Maybe you should look at something else."

Honey.

Hearing him call her that, his voice so deep and close to her ear, made Meredith miss her dad. Right then, she would have given almost anything to have his strong arms around her. To feel safe and loved. To know that nothing could ever hurt her again.

"Meredith? You still with me?"

"What?" She glanced down to see that Heath had

cinched the towel around her palm. Crimson already seeped through the cheerfully striped linen.

He gave the towel a jerk, tightening it over the wound and applying pressure with the grip of his fingers. The faucet squeaked as he turned it off. Then he guided her to the utility porch and out the door, his broad chest like a boulder against her back. He held her with one arm clamped around her ribs, his hand splayed under her left breast.

She hoped he didn't notice the padding in her bra. The thought made her stumble, and she had to execute some fancy footwork to get back in stride with him.

When they reached the fence she'd built to enclose Sammy's play area, he jerked the wire loose from the house with one mighty tug. After assisting Meredith through the opening, he helped Sammy, cautioning her to be careful of the ragged edges.

"We don't want you to get cut, too," he told the child, giving her head a pat.

At the Bronco, he lifted Meredith onto the backseat, handling her weight as easily as he had the lumber. Once she was settled, he boosted Sammy up. Then, leaning in, he drew the seat belt strap across Meredith's body. Startled by his touch, she clutched his wrist. The corded tendons in his forearm went hard beneath her frantic fingers.

He hesitated and glanced up, his gunmetal eyes filled with questions. Her cheeks went hot. It wasn't as if he were taking liberties. She released his wrist. He fastened the buckle, then slipped his fingers under the strap to settle it between her breasts.

"Sammy, I'm gonna need you to be my medic. Can you do that for me?"

Her eyes as round as saucers, Sammy nodded. Heath smiled and positioned her tiny hands, showing her how to hold pressure on the wound.

"That's the way," he told her. "While I'm driving to the hospital, you'll have to squeeze real hard the whole time. Think you can handle it?"

The calm certainty in Heath's voice seemed to reassure

Sammy, and once again, she nodded solemnly. Meredith insinuated a thumb between her daughter's small fingers to help hold pressure. The towel was already soaked with her blood.

"How far is it?" she asked when Heath climbed in behind the steering wheel.

He glanced at her in the visor mirror. "About fifteen miles," he said with a wink. "Don't worry. I'm a certified first responder, one of my job requirements. It's a deep cut, but the bleeding's slowed down. With a few stitches, you'll be good as new."

Meredith settled back, trying not to watch her blood drip from the towel.

A perk of Heath's job was receiving VIP treatment in Wynema General's ER, whether he sought medical treatment for himself or a prisoner. In his rookie year, he'd felt guilty about that. Now he didn't hesitate. Working the hours he did, and sometimes nearly getting his head blown off in the process, had to be worth something, and he sure as hell didn't draw a big salary.

Because he'd radioed ahead, a nurse waited inside the glass doors when Heath parked by the ambulance ramp. After quickly buttoning and tucking in his shirt, he helped his passengers from the rig and up the short flight of steps. When the automatic doors opened, the nurse slipped an arm around Meredith's shoulders.

"Hi, Peg," Heath said. "Meet Meredith Kenyon, my new neighbor. She's had a little accident. Meredith, this is Nurse Staley, head honcho of the ER."

The nurse smiled. "It looks like you tangled with something mean and lost."

"A paring knife," Heath explained. "You better get someone from orthopedics on the horn. It's a pretty deep cut."

A plump redhead, Peg was a veteran at Wynema General, and she and Heath had forged a casual friendship that went back a long way. "When you gonna learn not to tell me my business, Masters?"

"Probably never. It's my mission in life to aggravate you."

Peg winked at Sammy. "And who is this young lady with the pretty blue eyes?"

"My daughter, Sammy. I'd like to take her in with me. She's shy with strangers."

Peg shook her head. "It'll be better if she waits out here."

Meredith glanced at her daughter. "I'm not sure—"

"She'll be fine," Heath cut in. "I'll watch her."

"But she's—"

"It won't take long," Peg assured her. "You'll be back before Sammy knows it."

Meredith looked at Heath. "You don't mind?"

"If he does," Peg inserted, "I'll knock him up alongside the head." The nurse grinned at Heath. "You want me to get someone down here to park that blasted Bronco of yours? As usual, you're blocking our loading zone. That space is reserved for—"

"Ambulances, I know," Heath said with a chuckle. "And, yeah, get someone down here, would you, Peg?"

As the nurse led Meredith away, Sammy tried to follow. Still holding the child's hand, Heath hauled her up short. "Sorry, honey. It's real busy back there, and little girls can't go in unless they're sick or hurt and need to see a doctor."

Sammy's response was to rub her eye with a grubby little fist, her mouth quivering. Realizing she was about to cry, Heath started to feel panicky.

"It's all right, honey. Your mama will be right back. You'll see."

She peered up at him around her knuckles, her expression both disconsolate and hopeful. Heath could only pray the latter emotion won the war.

Only a few seconds later, a blue-suited custodian came trotting up the wide hallway, the rubber soles of his work boots squeaking on the gleaming green tiles. "Howdy, Sheriff. I hear you need somebody to park the tank again."

Keeping a firm hold on Sammy's hand, Heath fished in his jeans pocket for his keys. "Anywhere in ER parking will do, Jim."

Jim glanced at the child. "As perps go, this one's a shade on the small side. What'd she do, rob a bank?"

"This is Sammy, my new neighbor. Her mother cut her hand."

Jim grinned, his dark hair tousled, his boyishly plump face flushed from running. "No unruly drunk with his head laid open today?"

"Nope."

"No criminals in handcuffs?"

"Nope, sorry."

"Well, heck. Nothing exciting has happened around here in almost a week." Jim took Heath's car keys and gave them a jaunty toss. "If there's no prisoner, why'd they call me? You don't need a parking attendant, man. You need some action to keep your life interesting."

Heath gestured at Sammy, who was staring at Jim with wide-eyed wariness. "My sidekick here is a little worried about her mama. I'd just as soon not make her leave the hospital. Besides"—he patted Jim's protruding waistline—"you can use the exercise."

Jim wiggled his eyebrows at Sammy. "Worried about your mama, are you?" He gave the child a thumbs-up. "She's in good hands. Best doctors in the state."

"Sheriff?" the receptionist called softly. "Are you ready to fill out the forms?"

"Yo." Heath slapped Jim on the shoulder then stepped toward the desk, forgetting until he nearly jerked Sammy off her feet that he had a short-legged person attached to him. "Sorry, sweetcakes. You okay?"

The pained look on Sammy's face spoke volumes. Heath had an awful feeling he'd nearly jerked her shoulder out of socket.

He shortened his stride, which still forced the child to

run to keep up. He noticed that an older woman sitting in the front waiting area was watching him with one eyebrow raised. Putting another half hitch in his get-along, he covered the remaining distance to the desk, acutely aware that Sammy's sneakers still slapped the tile in a rapid tattoo.

"All I know is the lady's name and address," he told Trish, the slender receptionist, as he drew up in front of her station. "Meredith Kenyon, 1423 Hereford. You'll have to get any further information from her."

"I don't suppose you know if she has insurance."

"Somehow, it slipped my mind to ask her that." Heath thumped his forehead. "What the hell was I thinking?"

Trish rolled her eyes. "I just asked. Don't make a major production."

He grinned. "Do you ask if your neighbors have insurance?" Then, "Never mind. Knowing you, probably."

Jim came jogging back into the hospital just then. Tossing the car keys to Heath, he said, "First row, third spot down."

"Thanks, Jim."

Putting the keys back in his pocket, Heath turned from the desk and nearly ran over his small charge. He bent down. "You want a soda, sweetcakes?"

Big, bewildered blue eyes lifted to his. Thinking that maybe she'd never heard a soft drink referred to as a soda, Heath rephrased the question. "You wanna pop?"

Her eyes went even wider, and she hunched her shoulders, trying to tug her hand free. Heath had a feeling he'd said something that frightened her, but he couldn't think what. He got a firmer hold on her hand to make sure she didn't haul ass.

"A Pepsi?" he tried.

Bingo. She looked at the soft drink dispenser against the wall, shook her head, and started rubbing her eye again. If she kept it up, she wouldn't have any lashes left.

"Well, I need to wet my whistle." Heath led her to the machine. Angling his free arm across his body, he dug into his left pant pocket for change. The dispenser clanked as it gulped the quarters. He pressed his selection. Nothing happened. *Damned thing.* Familiar with the contraption's quirks, he thumped it with the side of his boot. Sammy jumped when the pop can came tumbling out into the trough.

"Whoa, there, honey," Heath said in low, soothing tone as he bent to retrieve the soft drink. "I'm just getting this cussed machine to cooperate, that's all. Sure you don't want a Pepsi? I'm buying."

Standing well back, her captured arm extended as far as it would stretch, Sammy hid her face against her shoulder. Heath guessed that meant no.

Taking itty-bitty, pain-in-the-ass baby steps, he led her to some seating in a cheerful yellow alcove that resounded with the blare of an overhead television.

Heath sat down, propping one booted foot on his knee. Sammy backed up to the lime-green cushion beside him, went up on her tiptoes, and finally, after a great deal of wiggling, managed to get one cheek of her fanny parked. Heath let go of her hand just long enough to grab the back of her pink britches to haul her up the rest of the way.

Flipping up the tab of his soft drink can, he took a long swallow, then whistled appreciatively. "Good stuff." He shoved the can toward her. "You sure you're not thirsty, honey? I don't mind a little backwash if you don't."

She looked at him as if he were jabbering in Spanish. *Hell.* Usually when he dealt with youngsters, he was taking a minor to the juvie or providing transport for a child who'd become a ward of the court. In situations that involved a child Sammy's age, he always recruited Helen Bowyers, a female deputy, to accompany him.

Uncomfortable with the silence and the way she was staring at him, he met her gaze warily. Her hand felt so small. Little fingers, all squished together within the circle of his. Accustomed to large, man-sized things—his dog, his cattle, his horses, his Bronco—Heath felt increasingly uneasy. She was shaking, and he wondered if he was hurting her. He lightened his grip, but she continued to tremble.

"Your mama's gonna be fine. All she has is a little cut. The doctor will fix it and give her something to make it stop hurting. Then we'll take her home."

He waited for her to smile. Those big, frightened eyes remained fixed on him.

He decided to try ignoring her. Staring at the television, but not really seeing it, Heath remembered how wary of him Meredith had seemed last night. It stood to reason Sammy would share her sentiments about most things— their neighbor, included.

What had happened to make the two of them so distrustful of men? He'd been friendly and polite, even going so far as to volunteer his time to repair their house. Yet the sound of his voice had startled Meredith so badly that she'd cut herself. Something about this whole situation didn't feel right to him.

Not my problem. He'd volunteered to fix their house, yes, but not their lives. *Stay out of it. Look the other way. Don't get any more involved than you already are.*

Hell, he'd already broken nearly all the rules, self-imposed and otherwise. When Meredith had cut herself, the first thing he should have done was get the first aid kit out of his Bronco. Instead, he'd taken one look and rushed indoors. No rubber gloves. All that blood. Never once had he thought to protect himself. If he had caught one of his deputies taking a risk like that, he would have been furious.

No two ways about it, he needed to back off. Keep his distance.

That was a fine and dandy plan, but easier said than done. For starters, it was his fault Meredith had cut herself. He felt bad about that. He'd realized from the first that she was skittish. He should have had the good sense to walk around back and knock on her door. That *was* the normal way of doing things.

Now he was in charge of a little girl who looked as if she'd just eaten Mexican jumping beans.

"You ever been in an emergency room before, Sammy?"

She hunched her shoulders and hid her face again.

Uncertain if that meant yes or no, he decided to wing it. "I bet it seems scary."

A voice blasted out over the loud speaker above them, and she jerked.

"That's just a lady talking into a microphone," he explained. "Little speaker wires carry her voice through the building, and the sound comes out of those little square things in the walls." He pointed at the speaker, silently congratulating himself on handling this situation fairly well. Little kids weren't beings from another planet, just pint-sized adults. "That way, when somebody needs treatment, the lady can call the doctor, and her voice goes everywhere in the hospital."

The child peered up at the speaker, her small face solemn, her lower lip caught between her teeth.

"Inside the emergency room where your mama went, there are beds lined up along the wall, with pretty striped curtains to pull closed around each of them. Peg, the nurse you met, will stay with your mama until the doctor comes to take care of her. Pretty soon, when she's all fixed up, she'll come out those doors right there."

As she looked at the double doors, he felt a tug on his heartstrings. Though his sister Laney had been ten when their mother died, Sammy reminded him of her. The same sorrowful, lost expression. He wanted to hug her close and make her feel better.

He drained the pop can, set it on the table near his elbow, and tried to concentrate on the television program. Some broad with frizzy red hair was interviewing a bunch of married couples. Heath listened for a minute or two, realized the topic was about men who had an underwear fetish, and wished he had a channel changer. The stuff they aired in the afternoon when little kids might be watching was mind-boggling. There oughta be a law, he thought, glancing uneasily at Sammy.

A string of snot trailed from her nose. As if she sensed

him staring at it, she stuck out her tongue to lick her upper lip.

"Don't do *that*!" His stomach came up into his throat. Straightening one leg and lifting his hip, he dived a hand into the back pocket of his jeans. After determining that his handkerchief was clean, he clamped it over her nose. "Blow."

She sputtered her lips.

"No, honey. Through your nose."

She blew through her lips again, this time with more force.

Heath sat forward, twisting his mouth, wrinkling his nose, and honking to demonstrate. When he realized what a spectacle he was making of himself, he glanced around to be sure no one was watching. Then he snorted again. She finally blew for him, after which he damned near pinched her nose off trying to wipe it.

After returning the handkerchief to his pocket, he noticed her shoe was untied. When he lifted her foot onto his knee, she toppled backward, barely managing to catch herself from falling off the cushion.

Taking care of a kid was damned hard work.

"I'm sorry." He lowered her foot onto the cushion so her leg wouldn't be hiked at such an angle, then helped her sit back up. "You're not very big, are you, half pint?"

"Almost five."

He had insulted her. "I meant size-wise. You're gonna be little like your mama."

"My mommy's not little. You're just great big."

Heath chewed on that as he struggled to tie her laces. Who, he wondered, had come up with the brilliant idea of making children's shoelaces so short?

"I guess I probably do seem big to you. It's all relative, right?"

She clearly didn't know what "relative" meant. In addition to mastering nose blowing and tying impossibly short laces, a man had to learn a whole new language.

"There," he said when he finally got her shoe tied.

She started picking at the bow. "Owee! It pinches."

"It does?" Heath checked, and sure enough, he had the strings too tight. His patience frayed as he picked at the knot he'd tied. "There. Is that better?"

"Uh-huh." She squeezed her knees together and started to squirm on the cushion. Then she clamped a hand between her legs. "Sher'f man? I gots to go."

Any fool knew what *go* meant. "No problem."

Except for one. He didn't know where the women's john was, and taking her to the men's didn't strike him as a good idea. Tugging her along, he went to the receptionist's desk. "Trish, can you steer me to the ladies' room?"

Trish held up a finger, signaling him to wait until she had finished on the telephone. Heath tried not to feel alarmed when Sammy started to prance. Surely she hadn't waited until the very *last* second. He had some leeway, here. Little kids, he assured himself, probably just pranced when the urge hit, that was all.

Finally concluding her conversation, Trish pointed down the hall. "On your left, just this side of the CCU."

Stepping it out as fast as Sammy's short legs would allow, which wasn't very fast, Heath led the way. *Prance, prance.* He started to get a bad feeling about halfway there and wondered what frigging lunatic had put the women's john a mile from the waiting room. He quickened his pace. About that time, Sammy made a small sound of distress. He glanced down and saw that she was holding herself and pulling an awful face.

She wasn't going to make it. Heath swung her up into his arms and lengthened his stride, walking so fast he could have damned near competed in the Olympics.

Once outside the restroom, he set Sammy down, shoved open the door, and nudged her inside, saying, "I'll wait right here for you. All right?"

The instant the door swung closed, she let out an ear-splitting shriek.

Heath stared at the blue-and-white sign on the door, which sported a stick figure wearing a skirt.

Son of a bitch.

Chapter 6

Heath glanced up and down the hall. In the line of duty, he'd entered a lot of places where he wasn't welcome, sometimes under fire, and over the years, he'd developed nerves of steel. So why the hell was he sweating at the thought of invading a women's restroom?

Behind the closed door, Sammy's shrill cries grew louder, a damn siren knifing against his eardrums. He had to do something.

Casual does it, he told himself. *Just act normal.* He was the sheriff, after all. If some lady was in there, he had a perfectly good explanation. Right?

He nudged the door open. *Damn.* It was dark as a cave in there. He'd shoved the poor little thing into the restroom without turning on the light for her.

Screw stick figures in skirts, he decided, hitching up his courage.

With the flat of his hand, he shoved the door open all the way, then hit the light switch. Startled by the sudden brightness, Sammy shrieked and backed away from him, her hands splayed over the wet crotch of her pink stretch pants. He might as well have been advancing on her with a club. Biting off a curse, he let the door swing closed.

"Hey, sweetcakes, what's the matter?" As if he didn't know. He glanced at the wet spot on her pants. "Uh-oh. You had an accident, huh?" He hunkered down, hoping he might seem a little less intimidating. "Oh, well. It's more my fault than yours."

She gave no sign that she'd even heard him, just kept screeching and backing up. When she ran into the wall, the color drained from her face and her eyes went wide with panic. Heath's heart caught. This child wasn't just upset; she was terrified.

He extended a hand to her. "Sweetheart, it's okay. I'm not going to hurt you."

Her gaze shifted to something behind him. Before Heath could react, a huge black purse came from out of nowhere and hit him on the temple. Spots exploded before his eyes and he reeled sideways, barely managing to catch his balance with a hand against the wall. Sammy's shrieks went up in volume.

"You pervert!" an outraged female voice cried.

Heath didn't have time to stand up before the purse hit him again, this time on the shoulder. Between that blow and the next, he blinked to clear his vision and glimpsed a gigantic woman looming over him, her jowly face flushed with anger. "Ma'am, I—"

"Don't you 'ma'am' me, you no-good, lowdown *skunk*!"

As she raised her arms to swing the purse again, the hem of her blue dress rode up, revealing the tops of her thigh-high nylons, which had slipped to her knees. Above the bands of brown elastic, rolls of doughy flesh jiggled every time she moved.

"*Lady!*" Heath threw up an arm to guard his face. If this was what fatherhood was like, he couldn't say it came highly recommended. "Would you stop?"

"Pervert! Help! Someone come help! I've caught a child molester!"

A what? Heath couldn't believe his ears. "Lady, I'm not a child"—*kerwhack*—"molester! I'm the county sheriff!"

"I don't care if you're the king of England!" *Kerwhack.* "You're not going to accost a child"—*kerwhack*—"when I'm here to stop you! I've read about animals like you!

Preying on little girls.'' *Kerwhack.* ''I declare, people aren't safe anywhere nowadays!''

As the woman drew back to take another swing, he grabbed her purse. Shoving to his feet, he said, ''You've got this all wrong.''

As if to give lie to his protest, Sammy shrank farther back into the corner, her shrieks so loud his ears were starting to ring.

Heath turned back to the woman, whose short, tightly-permed brown hair frizzed out around a black pillbox hat. ''Honestly, lady, this isn't how it looks.''

Trish shoved open the door just then and poked her blond head through the opening. ''What on *earth* is going on in here?''

''This—this—'' Chin trembling, cheeks flushed, the rotund woman was so beside herself she could scarcely speak. ''This *monster* was trying to molest this little girl.''

''*What?*'' Trish fixed a startled gaze on Heath. ''There must be a misunderstanding.''

''No misunderstanding! I saw him!'' The woman turned an outraged gaze on Sammy. ''Tell her, child!'' She jerked her purse from Heath's hand. ''I won't let this awful man hurt you, mark my words. Just tell the lady what happened.''

Sammy gulped and went suddenly silent, her small face turning an alarming shade of red.

''This man,'' Trish intervened firmly, ''is the county sheriff. This child is in his care while her mother receives emergency medical treatment.''

The woman blinked and raked Heath with a critical glare that lingered on his faded jeans and dusty boots. ''The sheriff? Hmph. You don't look like a law officer!''

Heath glanced down. ''I'm off duty.''

''That doesn't mean you're not a pervert!'' the woman said with a huff. ''I read the papers, you know.''

Heath drew a fast breath. ''Yes, ma'am, and you're right to be concerned, but I was just trying to explain to the youngster here—''

"Explain, ha! Scaring her half to death, more like! And saying you wouldn't *hurt* her in that"—she shuddered, making her cheeks jiggle—"*oily* voice. I know your kind!"

"He really is the sheriff, honest," Trish said, her mouth twitching. "And as far as I know, he has no perverted tendencies. The voice *is* a little oily, though, isn't it?"

"He'd better be the sheriff, or it'll be on your head, young woman!" Shouldering Trish out of her way, she exited the bathroom.

Heath ran a hand over his hair then cast a sheepish glance at Trish, who leaned against the door frame, her arms folded at her waist. "Oily?" he said. "I'm definitely writing you up the next time I catch you speeding."

"You've never stopped me yet, and you know it." She smiled and glanced at Sammy who was alternately holding her breath and taking quick gasps of air. "Do you need some help? It looks like you've got your hands full."

"Would you mind?" Heath was relieved beyond words that she had offered. Even the soap in here smelled different, a slightly nauseating mix that reminded him of hand lotion, strawberry sherbet, and cheap perfume. No urinals lining the wall, no condom dispenser. All he saw was a coin-drop dispenser for tampons, two of which he was tempted to buy to use as earplugs. "I'm not exactly an old hand with little girls."

A twinkle warmed Trish's blue eyes. "Most men aren't." She leaned forward, hands on her knees, smiling as she regarded the child. "Hi. Remember me? I'm Trish, the lady who was sitting at the front desk with the funny looking wires on her head."

"Trish can help you get cleaned up, Sammy. Would you like that?"

"Sure she would." Trish winked conspiratorially. "Us gals have to stick together. Right?"

The instant Trish moved, Sammy started to shriek again, sharp, shrill bursts of sound that made Heath cringe. The receptionist reeled to a stop. "Maybe it'd be better if I just

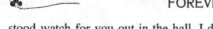

stood watch for you out in the hall. I don't think she likes me.''

Heath didn't feel very popular himself. But, then, this was his problem, not Trish's, and he really couldn't blame her for not wanting to take it on.

The receptionist wasted no time in getting out of there. Heath gazed after her for a moment, wishing he could run, too. No such luck. He turned to face the child, who was looking at him as if he were a swamp creature straight out of a sci-fi flick.

Hunkering down again, he met her gaze. When she stopped screaming for a second to take a breath, he said, ''Sammy, don't you want to see your mama?''

That got her attention. She stared at him, her narrow chest expanded, a pent-up breath puffing out her flushed cheeks. Then, with a gush of released air, she shakily replied, ''Yup.''

''Well, before we can go back to the waiting room, you have to stop crying.'' He lowered his voice to a stage whisper. ''We have to be extra quiet because of all the sick people who are trying to sleep.''

Her tearful gaze shifted to the closed door. It didn't take a genius to realize she would have made fast tracks if she could have gotten past him.

Very cautiously, Heath pushed to his feet and extended a hand to her. ''Come on, honey. Your mama should be almost finished by now. Let's go back and wait for her.''

Sammy stared at his outstretched palm. Heath took a step toward her. At his approach, she hunched her shoulders, ducked her head, and threw up her thin arms.

Heath reeled to a stop as if he'd just walked face first into a cement wall. The poor little thing was afraid he meant to strike her? He heard an odd sound, glanced down to see water pooling around her sneakers, and realized she was so scared that she'd lost control of her bladder again.

''Oh, Sammy . . .'' He dropped to his knees in front of her, his shins cracking hard against the tiles.

What in God's name had happened to this child?

Granted, it was an unsettling situation for a little kid, having her mother snatched away from her and being left with a stranger. The interference of that purse-swinging Amazon from hell hadn't helped much, either. But for her to react like this? Something was very, very wrong.

"I want my mommy!" she wailed. "I want my mommy!"

That made two of them. "Sammy, sweetheart . . . "

If anything, she only screamed louder. He doubted she was even hearing him, let alone understanding anything he said.

Acting on instinct, Heath gathered her into his arms. "Hey, hey . . . it's all right, Sammy. Nobody's going to hurt you, honey. I promise. Nobody."

She arched her back, trying to put distance between their bodies. Heath tightened his hold on her. She was such a little thing. Beneath his fingertips, he could feel the fragile ladder of her ribs, under his palm the delicate ridge of her spine. How could anyone have struck her? Yet, as sure as he breathed, he knew someone had.

Rage roiled within him, coming so suddenly and with such intensity, he started to shake. He struggled for calm. Later, he could ponder the how and why of all this, and fantasize about kicking someone's ass. But right now, Sammy was all that mattered.

He shoved to his feet and began to pace the restroom floor, jostling her and rubbing her back. With a high-pitched wail, she shuddered and shrank from his touch.

"Shhh," he whispered. "It's all right. Shhh. No one's going to hurt you."

Heath knew he was repeating himself, but there were some things that couldn't be said too many times. He paced to the wall, turned, retraced his steps. Over and over, the same movements, the same words, the same tone of voice. He'd never held a small child like this, never been called upon to comfort one, but on some level, he sensed that the very sameness of it all might soothe her.

When her cries began to lose their shrillness and became

a monotonous mewling, he knew her fear of him was finally receding.

The wetness of her pants had started to seep through his shirt, turning his skin icy. He glanced down and saw that she'd been standing near an air-conditioning vent. No wonder she was shuddering. He drew her closer, hoping to share some of his heat.

"Don't be afraid," he whispered again. "No one's going to hurt you. I've got you, honey. Never again, do you hear? No one's going to hurt you ever again."

Even as he spoke, he heard warning bells at the back of his mind. What was he saying? This child wasn't his. He was making promises he might not be able to keep.

Yet the words were there at the back of his throat, waiting to burst forth every time he expelled a breath. And, God help him, he meant them. He wanted to kill with his bare hands the son of a bitch who'd done this to her.

Oh, yes, it had been a man. He would have bet his last buck on that. Meredith, so wary and distrustful. Goliath, sneaking off to be with Sammy, then behaving erratically when she was frightened. Sammy, peering out at him through the window that afternoon, eyes wide and wary. Suddenly, all the pieces started to fall into place.

A mean-hearted bastard had to factor into the equation somewhere. Sammy's father, possibly? That made sense and would certainly explain why Meredith had chosen to live so far from town and never had visitors. She could be on the run, trying to hide from an abusive husband. There was also a strong possibility, given her reclusive lifestyle, that she was a divorced, noncustodial parent who had abducted her child to protect her. As a sheriff, Heath knew that the courts weren't infallible. Sometimes the parent least fit to raise a child was granted custody, and in a case of abuse, the noncustodial parent could be pushed into doing some pretty desperate things.

Heath had no idea how much time passed. Pacing, turning, whispering, patting. He only knew that Sammy finally went limp and that her cries gave way to occasional whimpers. He cupped a hand over the back of her head. Her hair felt like corn silk.

"You feeling better?" he asked huskily.

She snuggled closer and hooked one arm around his neck, her dainty little fingers resting lightly on his nape. As hugs went, it wasn't much. But to Heath, it meant the world. Trust. It was always a gift to be treasured, but coming from this child, it was absolutely priceless. He stopped pacing and pressed his face against her sweet-smelling curls, as close to tears as he'd ever been in his adult life.

Three women were waiting outside in the hall with Trish by the time Heath exited the restroom. He knew he ought to be embarrassed, but right then, restroom protocol seemed unimportant. Once back in the alcove, he resumed his seat, cradling Sammy against his chest. She clung to him like a baby opossum, her spindly arms around his neck, her face pressed to the hollow of his throat, her short legs clamped over his ribs.

Heath continued to rub her back. He didn't speak, and neither did she. Some things couldn't be said with words. She made no attempt to move, conveying a wealth of things, namely that she felt safe. The realization brought another lump to his throat.

Eventually her breathing changed to soft, even little huffs against his neck. Realizing she'd fallen asleep, he smiled and rested his jaw against her silken hair.

Maybe, he decided, fatherhood wouldn't be such a bad deal, after all.

Thirty minutes later, Meredith emerged from the ER, her bandaged hand held to her waist. Spots of blood stood out in stark relief on her wrinkled white shirt. Pale and wobbly, she circled a man and woman at the receptionist's desk, her gaze trailing slowly over the front seating area. Heath waved to catch her attention, then slid forward on the cushion, gently shifting the child in his arms to stand up.

As he watched Meredith approach, he was struck by an illuminating thought. Sometimes it took only a single incident to change one's perception of another person.

Less than two hours ago, he'd seen Meredith Kenyon as a shy, unassertive female who needed the big, burly sheriff up the road to intervene with her landlord and fight her battles. Now he saw a slightly built woman with a load of problems resting on her shoulders, someone who had probably survived experiences he couldn't imagine.

All his life Heath had been told that the mark of true bravery wasn't lack of fear, but having the courage to deal with it. By that measuring stick, Meredith Kenyon might be one of the bravest individuals he'd ever met. It took guts for a woman to leave an abusive husband and strike out on her own. All too often, he saw it go the other way.

The wariness reflected in Meredith's eyes as she approached him was impossible to ignore. Yet she kept coming, her gaze riveted on her sleeping daughter. That didn't say a whole lot for her opinion of him, but it went a long way toward changing his of her. He remembered how she'd stood her ground with Goliath that first night. Timid? Yes. She was that, he supposed. But she had a lot of grit as well.

Her footsteps were unsteady. When she drew to a stop near the sofa, her eyes locked with his. She was clearly wondering how he had gotten so chummy with her child in so short a time. Heath clenched his teeth. The way he saw it, if anyone had some explaining to do, it was Meredith.

"How's the hand?" he asked.

She frowned slightly, then said, "Fine. The cut is deep, but all the nerves are intact. I can't use it and have to keep it dry for a week until the doctor takes the stitches out, then baby it for a while after that. But he says there'll be no permanent damage."

"That's good." He felt at a loss. Making small talk was beyond him right then.

She shifted her gaze back to Sammy, her expression conveying that she yearned to snatch her away from him. The thought made him feel oddly empty.

He fixed his gaze on a tiny white scar on Meredith's chin

that he'd never noticed—the kind of mark that could have been left by a man's fist. He tightened his hold on Sammy to keep from touching it, his lips pressed tightly shut against questions he knew he had no right to ask.

Her eyes had a slightly unfocused look. He suspected the doctor had given her an injection for pain. "Are you all checked out?"

She blinked. "Oh . . . yes. I filled out the forms in the ER." Even with the drug-induced slur in her speech, the lilting cadence of her voice flowed warmly over him. "They'll have to send me the bill. I didn't bring my purse."

"I can take care of the bill for you, Meredith. You can pay me back later."

Her chin came up a notch. "That isn't necessary."

Supporting Sammy in the circle of one arm, Heath grasped Meredith's elbow. As he steered her through the waiting area, he couldn't help but notice how the bones of her elbow thrust against his palm. When he tightened his grip to guide her past a toddler, he made a conscious effort not to squeeze too hard for fear of bruising her.

"Watch your feet," he cautioned as he helped her down the steps outside. "You're a little wobbly."

"The doctor gave me a shot." She glanced up, her gaze once again settling on her sleeping daughter. "I really didn't want one. With a four-year-old to watch, I can't af-ford"—she stifled a yawn—"to feel drowsy."

Doped to the gills, Heath thought. Yet he could still feel tension thrumming through her. "I'll hang around at your place until Sammy's settled in for the night."

She flashed him a startled look, all trace of sleepiness vanishing from her face. "That won't be necessary. Really. I'll manage fine."

Like hell. Heath wasn't about to leave her alone until the effects of that pain shot wore off. "Hey, it's my fault you cut yourself. Necessary or not, I want to help."

He released her arm as they drew up beside the Bronco. With an ease born of long practice from having had a pris-oner in tow, he dug in his pocket for his keys and unlocked the door with one hand. Instead of putting Meredith in the back as he had before, he helped her into the passenger seat and put her daughter in her arms. Before shutting the door, he couldn't resist passing his hand over Sammy's hair one last time.

Meredith gave him another startled look that quickly turned to dismay. She obviously didn't want him to develop a fondness for her child—or vice versa.

Grimly, Heath circled the vehicle. When he climbed in under the steering wheel, he was acutely aware of the way she hugged her door. Another clear message. Clenching his teeth, he started the Bronco and drove from the crowded ER parking lot.

After merging onto Modoc Way, which accommodated a constant flow of traffic to and from the Modoc Institute of Technology, he gave his passengers a measuring look. Falling back on his law enforcement training, he decided not to beat around the bush.

"Sammy wet her pants while you were in the ER."

Cupping her uninjured hand over the seat of her child's pink britches, Meredith smiled slightly. "I noticed she felt wet."

"She waited so long to tell me, I didn't get her to the restroom in time."

Meredith bent to press her cheek to the top of Sammy's head. After a long moment, she asked, "Did she give you any trouble?"

"Depends on how you define trouble, I guess. She panicked. Thought I was going to hit her and started screaming." Pulling into the turning lane, Heath stared at the traffic light, waiting for her to comment. *Nothing*. He sneaked a glance. She still had a cheek pressed to Sammy's hair, only now her eyes were tightly closed.

"Someone has mistreated that child," he finally said. "Don't bother denying it."

She still said nothing.

At the question, Meredith turned even paler, her lashes fluttering up to reveal eyes so big and wary they reminded him of Sammy's, except for their dark color.

"It's not unusual for a little girl to get upset when she wets herself," she informed him in a tremulous voice. "You misread the situation, that's all."

Heath huffed under his breath. "I don't think so. She wasn't just upset. We're talking scared spitless."

"You're a stranger, and she tends to be shy and timid. Wetting one's pants is no small thing to a four-year-old."

Frustration welled within Heath. He sensed—no, dammit, he *knew*—that this woman and child were in desperate need of help. He would have bet his last dollar that Meredith was on the run. No matter how he circled it, that was the only explanation that made sense. If her husband was trying to find her, didn't she realize he could protect her? He was the county sheriff, for Christ's sake. Even if the courts had ruled in her husband's favor and he was the custodial parent, Heath's being a law enforcement officer gave him a certain amount of clout. He wouldn't hesitate to use his connections to help her. What did she plan to do if the bastard showed up on her doorstep?

The thought made Heath's palms go damp on the steering wheel.

"Meredith . . ."

He glanced over, took quick stock of her body language, and fell silent. Every rigid line of her body told him to back off. Talking hadn't worked with Sammy, and it wasn't going to work with her mother.

In a way, Heath guessed he could understand that. Talk was cheap. If he wanted Meredith Kenyon's trust, he was going to have to earn it.

By the time Sheriff Masters pulled his Bronco into her driveway, Meredith was having difficulty keeping her eyes open. That lasted about two seconds. The minute Heath cut the engine and spoke, she came wide awake.

"What did you say?" she asked, her senses on full alert.

He threw open his door and glanced over at her as he vaulted from the vehicle. "I said, with your hand messed up, you'll need help around the house this next week.''

"Oh, no. I—"

He cut her short by slamming his door, then skirted the vehicle to open her side. "What did you plan to fix to go with those potatoes you were peeling? It's already half past six. If Sammy wakes up, she'll want dinner."

"Hamburger patties. But I can manage."

Taking Sammy from her, he said, "You can't cook or wash dishes, for starters."

"I can wear rubber gloves."

"The doc said you aren't to use the hand, correct?"

"With gloves, I can use it as little as possible and just be very careful."

"Rubber gloves need to be snug. And water *always* slops inside the cuffs. That's not to mention they'll hurt so bad, you'll rip them off in five minutes."

"I'm sure it's all right for me to do *some* things."

He grinned. "I'll call and check with the doctor."

Meredith was tempted to kick him. She knew what the doctor would say. He'd even wanted her to wear a sling. She'd refused when she found out it would cost forty-five dollars. If the hand began to swell, she'd pin dishtowels together to make her own. "It's not necessary to bother the doctor."

Chuckling, he cradled Sammy in one arm then grasped Meredith's elbow. "Take it easy getting out. It's quite a step down. Whatever the doctor gave you, it must have been strong stuff. I get lightheaded just looking at you."

She did feel odd. As her feet touched the ground, she grabbed the door for balance. He slipped his free arm around her shoulders. "You okay?"

She dragged in a deep breath. "Yes, fine. I just need to get my legs under me."

He muttered something unintelligible as he drew her along beside him. She caught herself leaning against him for support. A warning jangled in her mind.

"I'm sorry. I'm feeling a bit spacey."

"Don't worry. I've got you."

And wasn't that the whole problem? He had her, all right. She felt as if her shoulders were wedged in a vise.

He steered left. "We'll have to use the back door. The front porch, remember."

As he led her around the house, the patchy lawn seemed to undulate like a blanket caught in an updraft. She lurched once and stumbled, which might have ended with her falling if not for his arm around her. When they reached the cross fence, he released her just long enough to pull back the panel of loosened wire.

"Easy, honey," he said as they climbed the steps. "I'll do the driving, all right?"

Honey. Just like her dad, he made free with endearments, this man. And somehow he managed to sound sincere. Broad shoulders, a solid body, an arm around her that felt like padded steel. The mix was almost irresistible. Might have been if she hadn't learned the hard way that a man's strength could be turned against her.

As he guided her into the house, Meredith's shoe caught on the abrupt edge of particle board. Once again, he caught her from falling. He bent his dark head to look closely at her, and she returned his regard. His face fascinated her. She traced the clean, sharp cut of his features and the burnished cast of his skin, the tone contrasting sharply with Sammy's golden head lolling on his shoulder. There were crinkly laugh lines at the corners of his eyes, which seemed to change color even as she gazed into them. Right now, they were the sooty gray-blue of storm clouds.

"You're mighty pale," he finally said.

"I'll live."

"God, I hope so," he said with a low laugh. "I *will* feel guilty if you don't."

He led her to the kitchen, lowered her onto a chair, and then disappeared with Sammy into the bedroom. Meredith propped her elbow on the table and rested her head on her hand. She didn't feel all that bad, just sort of disconnected from her brain.

From Sammy's bedroom, she heard drawers opening.

Then Sammy murmured sleepily, and the deep tenor of Heath's voice drifted from the room. Seconds later, the sound of his boots on the linoleum warned her of his return to the kitchen. She straightened to regard him with what she hoped was a clear-headed expression.

"I put some dry britches on her." He drew to a stop to roll his sleeves higher. "I think maybe I got them on backward. No fly."

Meredith struggled to make sense of that. "Fly?"

"You know, a fly." He gestured at his jeans. "Her trousers don't have one. I couldn't tell front from rear. There wasn't a tag inside them."

"Oh." Meredith realized she was staring at the front of his pants and jerked her gaze away. "I, um . . . sew."

"You what?"

"Sew. I made her pants. That's why there isn't a tag."

"You did a great job."

"It's one of those things you learn when you're a farmer's daughter. My mom taught me. Thank you for getting her dry. With her asleep, I can manage the rest."

His firm mouth tipped in a slow grin. "Why do I get this feeling you don't like me very well and would like to get rid of me? The faster, the better."

"Don't be silly. It isn't that."

He rested his hands on the back of a chair across from her. His stance was blatantly masculine, broad shoulders slightly hunched, one hip cocked forward. His gaze was as sharp as a razor, missing nothing. "Then there shouldn't be a problem if I hang around to help you out."

"I don't want to impose."

"Helping two pretty ladies is never an imposition."

Meredith sighed and gestured toward the sink. "Fine. Help. It really isn't necessary, though. I've got canned stuff I can fix. Soup, ravioli, spaghetti."

"And a bunch of potatoes that are already turning brown and will ruin if they aren't boiled. That's not to mention that operating a can opener might be impossible."

He had a point. She didn't own an electric opener, and

her manually operated one required two hands. Sammy probably didn't have the strength to make it work.

He strode to the sink. The rushing sound of water streaming from the faucet soon filled the kitchen. "You were gonna mash these, right?"

He turned to look at her, one large fist curled around the handle of a dented pot she'd picked up for a half dollar at the thrift store. He looked blurry around the edges, like a watercolor smeared by raindrops. "Um ... yes. Mashed will be fine."

"You use a mixer or a hand masher?"

She gazed blankly at him. After a moment, he offered her another slow, off-center grin. "Never mind, I'll just follow the end of my nose."

Meredith had difficulty even finding the end of hers. She let her eyelids fall closed, wishing the doctor hadn't insisted on giving her an injection. A loud, rattling sound jerked her back to awareness.

Hands on his hips, Heath stood gazing at the ceiling fan above the stove. "Sorry," he said. "I was hoping to get the air moving. This kitchen is stuffy as hell." He shook his head. "Jesus H. Christ! What a racket. Sounds like rocks in a tin can." He circled to get a better look. "Your squirrel cage is shot."

"Squirrel cage?"

"Layman's nomenclature. You need a whole new fan assembly."

What she needed was a way to get rid of him.

"When you get a chance, make me out a list."

"Of what?"

He arched a dark eyebrow, his eyes twinkling. "Things that don't work." He leaned over the stove to turn off the fan. "I'll get everything fixed for you."

Everything? "That could take weeks."

"No problem."

"As much as I appreciate the offer, that really isn't necessary, Sheriff Masters."

"Heath, remember? You'll be seeing a lot of me. Might as well relax."

Meredith doubted she could accomplish that feat even if she tried, which she had no intention of doing. If she let down her guard, eventually she would slip and reveal something to him that she shouldn't.

How had things gone so impossibly awry? When she'd learned the man next door was the sheriff, she'd been determined to avoid him. Now here he was, inside her house? A handsome man like him should have a wife, or at least a steady girlfriend. She had enough problems without tossing one very large male into the mix.

He seemed to know his way around a kitchen, she'd give him that. Suzy Homemaker, personified. He looked incongruous standing at her sink, the muscles across his back rippling under the blue shirt as he wielded her paring knife.

"I take it you're a longtime bachelor?"

"Mmm." He glanced over his shoulder at her, a slice of raw potato caught between his teeth. Pocketing the vegetable in his cheek, he shrugged as he chewed, his jaw tendon bunching. "Never met the right lady. How about you? Divorced?"

Meredith hadn't intended to open up a dialogue about her marital status. "I have cans of green beans in that bottom cupboard."

He quartered the potato with two deft strokes. "One can of green beans, coming right up." A moment's silence, then, "You didn't answer my question."

"What question?"

"About your husband. Are you divorced?"

Meredith's heart kicked against her ribs. "I, um . . . I'd rather not talk about that, if you wouldn't mind."

Silence descended again, broken only by the sound of the knife blade grating through pulp and the ticking of the clock. She was relieved he'd dropped the subject.

After getting both the meat and the potatoes on the stove, he came to sit across from her. Meredith fidgeted, unnerved by his intent regard. He leaned back in the chair, propping one booted foot on his knee. For reasons beyond her, he seemed bigger and broader through the shoulders than he ever had before.

"I don't bite, you know."

She threw him a startled look.

"At least not hard enough to hurt," he amended.

"It never occurred to me that you might."

"You're as nervous as a long-tailed cat in a roomful of rockers. Admit it."

She pushed to her feet, regretting it almost as soon as she parted company with the chair. Her head began to spin, forcing her to grab the tabletop to catch her balance.

"Meredith, for God's sake, sit back down."

She had little choice. The cheap plastic cushion squeaked under her weight, air rushing out through a rent in one seam. *Silence*. She searched for something to say.

"You're, um . . . right about this weather. It's been really warm, hasn't it?"

He gave a low chuckle. "Yeah, it sure has."

She knew he was laughing at her lame attempt to make conversation. Disgusted with herself for letting him rattle her, she forced herself to meet his gaze. "Your turn."

"Let's talk about you."

"Me?" That was the last topic she wanted to discuss.

His eyes searched hers. "Where are you from?"

"I've lived in lots of places."

"That cute drawl says you're from somewhere south of the Mason-Dixon Line."

After living in the North for so many years, Meredith had hoped her drawl was barely noticeable. "Arkansas," she blurted.

"Ah, Arkansas." He seemed to consider that. "Little Rock?"

The hair on her nape prickled. He had at his disposal the means to check on anything she told him. "No. I, um . . ." She flipped through the pages of her memory for the name of another town in that state. "Actually, we moved a lot, like I said."

"We?"

"My folks and I. Tallahassee, Monroe, Porterville."
Hopefully, if she named enough towns, he wouldn't be able
to remember any specific one. She glanced at his hatless
dark head. "Stetson." She nearly threw in "Levis" for
good measure, but decided that would be pushing her luck.
The hamburger patties in the skillet had begun to sizzle,
the faint aroma drifting across the kitchen. She named a
few more towns. "We lived all over the state."

"I thought Tallahassee was in Florida."

Panic. Why did he have to start riddling her with questions when she couldn't think very clearly? "There's a
town of that name in Arkansas, too."

He got up to check on the meat and potatoes. After fitting
the lids back on the pots, he laid the spatula on the counter.
"Was your dad into chickens?"

"Chickens?"

His mouth drew up at one corner. "That *is* what Arkansas's famous for."

"Oh." She gave a weak laugh. "Chickens. Of course.
Actually, no. He, um, sells cars. Used cars. That's why we
moved so much, because he went from job to job." A picture of her big, lumbering father in faded overalls flashed
through her head.

"I thought you said he was a farmer?"

Meredith couldn't remember saying that. "You must
have misunderstood. No, used cars are my dad's specialty."

He nodded. "A slick talker, polyester slacks, a fancy
gold watch?"

"My dad wouldn't be caught dead in polyester." That
much wasn't a lie, at least. Meredith drummed the fingertips of her uninjured hand on her knee. She avoided Heath's
gaze, unable to shake the feeling he was peeling away her
layers, one by one. "But he's definitely got the gold
watch." An heirloom pocket watch, passed down to him
from his father. "He's very good at what he does." There,
again, she'd told the truth.

''And you're driving a tin can held together by hope and a prayer?''

''Yes, well . . . it's been a while since I went home.''

He resumed his seat across from her, once again propping a booted foot on his knee. ''What brought you clear out here? You're a long way from Arkansas.''

''I needed a change.''

''From what?''

She dug her nails into the denim of her jeans. ''Sheriff, I feel as if you're grilling me.''

''I'm just trying to make conversation.'' The lazy smile he flashed belied the interested gleam in his eyes. ''I'd just like to know a little more about you, that's all.''

Meredith decided it was high time she turned the tables. She'd never met a man yet who didn't like to talk about himself, and as muddled as she felt, the less she said, the better. ''I lead a pretty boring existence. Let's talk about you.''

''Me?''

''I've read about your work with teenagers in the newspaper.'' She tried to remember what she'd read. ''You've reduced the alcohol-related highway fatalities by a very large percentage. Haven't you?''

''Only thirty-seven.''

''Thirty-seven percent, and you call that 'only'?''

''When you're the guy who has to tell a mother that your deputies are still picking up pieces of her child at milepost 348, that doesn't seem like much.''

''I still think it's impressive. I read you were asked to do an interview on national television and turned it down.''

He shrugged.

''So it's true. I'd think you'd want other counties to hear about your programs.''

''Spreading the word isn't what the media is after.''

''What *are* they after?''

''My ass.''

She circled that. ''Your what?''

He chuckled. ''I don't play by the rules, and a lot of

people don't like it. As for the drum rolls, making a name for myself was never my goal.''

He glanced at his watch and pushed to his feet to check on the food again. Stymied, Meredith stared at his broad back. Just like that, he'd ended the subject. Wasn't it her luck? The one time she needed to keep a man talking, and he had to be the first she'd ever met who didn't have, *Me, myself, and I,* branded on his forehead. Not only that, but now he had her curiosity piqued. What made this man tick? His job was on the line, yet he still refused to go by the book and didn't seem to care about all the controversy surrounding him. He was either the most stubborn individual she'd ever met or the most passionate for a cause. She had a feeling he was a combination of both, the latter his driving force.

After turning the patties, he said, ''Meredith, I have a favor to ask.''

She marshaled her straying thoughts. ''What's that?''

''If I kept Goliath tied, would you mind if I brought him over here while I work? Until the kennel is built, keeping him confined in the house all day and into the evening will be awfully hard on him.''

Remembering how the dog had snarled at her last night, her first impulse was to say no. But in good conscience, how could she? Heath was going to be working on her house. The least she could do was let him bring his dog.

''If you promise never to let him get loose,'' she conceded. ''But you'll have to tie him out front. I don't want him in Sammy's play area.''

''No problem. He's really a great dog, you know. Once you get to know him better, you won't be afraid of him.''

Meredith doubted that, and she had no intention of getting better acquainted.

With his back still toward her, he said, ''Another thing. If I'm going to be cooking for you this week, it will be easier for me to just eat over here. Otherwise, I'll still have to fix dinner when I go home. Is that all right with you?''

She felt as if she had stepped off into deep water. She

couldn't very well let him fix their meals, then refuse to welcome him at their table. The southern hospitality that had been ingrained in her since birth wouldn't allow her to be that rude.

She settled for saying, "You're more than welcome to share supper with us, Sheriff Masters. But before we make any definite plans, let's wait to see how things work out. I really do think I'll be able to manage on my own."

He flashed her a grin over his shoulder. "I want to help. I shouldn't have poked my head in your window like that."

"It really wasn't your fault. Hollering through the window was a perfectly natural thing to do. You just caught me off guard and startled me."

He didn't argue the point. "On the way to work in the morning, I'll drop off some food from my place. I have a big appetite, and I don't want to clean you out."

"I have plenty of food, and if—"

"I can see that you have plenty," he cut in. "But that doesn't mean you took me on to raise. I won't feel right about eating here unless I pitch in."

Meredith had a feeling that he was going to be a permanent fixture around here for at least the next week, no matter what she said. She could continue to protest, ad nauseam, or give in gracefully.

Wasn't that a fine kettle of fish? He was a law officer, and from the things he had just told her, she could only conclude he was more dedicated than most. If she forgot that, even for a second, she'd be sorry.

And her little girl would be the one who suffered for it.

Chapter 7

Heath swung the hammer with enough force to drive the nail clear through the board. The entire porch frame vibrated at the impact. Wiping sweat from his brow with a shirt sleeve, he straightened to take stock of his progress and rest his back for a moment. Half of the new planks on Meredith's front porch were finally in place, and he'd soon have them nailed to the joists. Given the fact that he'd been working on the damned thing for nearly four hours, he hadn't accomplished very much, but at least now no one would step out the front door and do a four-foot free fall.

Grimly, he stepped back to survey the overall picture. It wasn't good. To get the porch in tiptop shape, he'd had to scrap practically the whole thing and start over from scratch. What was worse, now that he had the framework finished, the carefully plumbed angles looked oddly out of line with the house, which was as crooked as a bookie at a cockfight. That meant every repair project was going to take him twice to three times longer than planned.

When he shared that news with Meredith, she wouldn't be pleased. He had a feeling that the sooner she got him out of her hair, the happier she would be.

He cut a glance at the drawn curtains over her living room windows. Since his arrival at three, she'd been hiding out in there. At least, that was how it seemed. How the hell was he supposed to make any headway with her if she dove for a foxhole every time she saw him coming?

God, he was thirsty. Maybe he expected too much, but it seemed to him the least she could do was offer him a drink of water. Fat chance. Unless of course, she decided to lace it with strychnine.

With a grunt of disgust, he tossed the hammer on the porch, tugged off his leather gloves, then circled the house to get a drink from the outside faucet. Goliath, tethered in the shade of a billowy oak, whined pathetically for attention.

Poor dog. Heath had kept him confined all day, and now he'd be tied up all evening.

"Sorry, buddy," Heath said softly as he detoured to give the dog a scratch behind the ears. "Keeping you tied is part of the deal. Otherwise, you'd have to stay home."

Goliath whined again, his soulful brown eyes pleading for a reprieve. As Heath straightened, he glimpsed a flash of red in the overgrown tangle of shrubbery along the pasture fence. His gaze became riveted to the spot. *Sammy*.

Seeing her outdoors came as no big surprise. Several times this afternoon, he'd caught her spying on him from the living room windows. It had made him feel like a freak in a sideshow.

Judging by her scramble for cover, he'd nearly caught her in the act of visiting with Goliath, a turn of events that would undoubtedly send Meredith into cardiac arrest if she knew. He glanced at the panel of hog wire he'd jerked loose from the house yesterday, a slight smile tugging at his mouth. So, Sammy had sneaked out of her backyard prison, had she?

"Hi, there!" Heath called. "How are you today?"

The patch of red in the bushes went absolutely still. Heath saw one blue eye peering out at him from behind a fan of leaves. An electrical tension filled the air, the taste of it almost metallic at the back of his tongue.

After their ordeal at the hospital, Heath hadn't expected Sammy to still be afraid of him. Some really bad shit must have happened to the kid, that was all he could say. Meredith could deny it until hell froze over, but a little girl didn't act this way without some kind of reason.

The thought grabbed him by the throat, an awful, strangling sensation. If he scared her so much, why had she come out here? To be near Goliath, he guessed. Yeah, that was probably it. Even so, he couldn't help but wish her reasons ran deeper than that. Fragile and fleeting though it had been, a friendship had been forged between them yesterday. Wasn't it possible that Sammy remembered and felt drawn to him? That in her little-girl fashion, she was trying to reestablish the bond, but simply wasn't brave enough to approach him?

It took all Heath's self-control not to wade into the shrubbery after her. What did he plan to do, drag her out by the scruff of her neck? No. He had to bide his time, let her call the shots. She'd make a move when she felt ready.

He sauntered over to the side of the house where the faucet protruded. Trying not to think about the rusty residue he would undoubtedly be drinking, he opened the spigot and bent to catch water in his cupped hands. After drinking his fill, he crouched lower to stick his head under the stream. The iciness made his skull ache. Pushing erect, he gave himself a hard shake, shuddering as frigid rivulets ran down his spine and soaked his shirt.

From her hiding place in the dense foliage, Sammy was gaping at him as if she'd never clapped eyes on a man before. He reached up to feel his hair. It was standing on end, the wet spikes going in all directions. He raked his fingers through it. No help. Giving up, he swiped the water from his eyes.

"I'll bet you've never seen such friendly hair," he called.

Her blank expression told him she'd never heard the joke. *Damn*. Learning how to communicate with a four-year-old was a whole new ball game for him. He rubbed his hand back and forth over his head to make his hair stand back up.

"See? It waves at people."

No smile. Okay. So he'd better keep his day job.

"You want a drink, honey? It's nice and cold."

Through the web of branches, he watched her do a belly crawl deeper into the bushes. As answers went, he guessed that was clear enough.

Finger-combing his hair, he cut back around the house to resume his work. After jerking his gloves back on, he grabbed a handful of nails and stuck them in his mouth, clenching the heads between his teeth. As he picked up his hammer, he glanced back at the spot of red in the bushes. She was watching him again.

He wondered what she was thinking, then decided he probably didn't want to know because it obviously wasn't good.

If only he could coax her out of the bushes, she might discover he wasn't so bad. *Right, Masters. Like mother, like daughter.* Besides, even if, by some stroke of genius, he did coax Sammy closer, what then? He knew next to nothing about little girls. As best he could recall, all he'd cared about at her age was toy trucks and catching frogs.

Sammy was undoubtedly interested in more dignified pursuits, like playing with dolls and reciting nursery rhymes, or learning to count and say her ABCs.

Heath was about to start hammering again when sudden inspiration struck. Four years old or eighty, he'd never met a female who could resist correcting a man.

He spat out the nails, laid them on the porch, and belted out the first few lines of the alphabet song, deliberately saying the letters in the wrong order. *No response.*

Abandoning his erroneous version of the alphabet, he began singing, "Old McIntyre had a farm, eeyie, eeyie, oh-hh-h. And the cows went 'quack.' And the horses went 'ba-aaa-ah.' "

Sammy's head emerged from the evergreen boughs.

"Old McIntyre had a farm, eeyie, eeyie, oh-hh-h. And the cat went, 'woof, woof, woof!' And the lamb went"— he broke off to throw back his head and give his best impersonation of a collicky horse—"and the dog went, 'meow, meow, meow.' "

Pretending to be absorbed with his work, Heath drifted from song into nursery rhyme, from nursery rhyme back into song, his selection limited because he couldn't remember all that many childhood ditties or poems, at least not the kind Sammy was probably familiar with. There again, as a little boy, he'd been more interested in learning dirty words than sissy stuff like Mother Goose.

He purposely made mistake after mistake, all the while watching her from the corner of his eye. If anyone drove by and heard him, they'd think he was a frigging lunatic. The cat that jumped over the moon? God, he was losing it, really losing it. Any minute now, the guys in white coats would pull up in their paddy wagon and advance on him with a straightjacket.

Lunacy or not, the ploy was working. Sammy's head and shoulders had emerged from the bushes, and there was no mistaking the scandalized expression on her small face, particularly when he made the dog sound like a cat. She was definitely a stickler for details, just like every other woman he'd ever known.

He started all over again with the alphabet song. With each incorrect rendition, the child crept closer, at first venturing only a few feet from her hiding place, then clear out into the yard, then nearer and nearer to the porch. Each step she took was so hesitant, her body language conveying such trepidation that it nearly broke his heart. For the dozenth time, he wished he had the bastard who'd done this to her by the throat.

Come on, sweetheart, take a chance, Heath thought. At one point, he became so focused on the child that he forgot and said the letters of the alphabet in the correct order. Sammy didn't seem to catch the slip.

Finally, she came to sit a safe distance away from him on a porch joist, one of her red canvas sneakers swinging rapidly back and forth, short white laces dangling.

"C-D-F-A," he bellowed before hauling in more air. "B-G—"

"It's A-B-C-D!" she called to him, her expression indignant.

Heath pretended not to hear her. "E-M-O—"

"You're sayin' 'em wrong!" she cried.

Struggling not to smile, Heath feigned an exaggerated start. "Sammy! Where'd you come from? You scared me out of a year's growth."

"You're sayin' your letters wrong. Di'n't your mommy teach you the ABCs?"

"My mom died when I was pretty young." That much wasn't a lie. His mother had passed away when he was only eleven. "I guess I've forgotten some of the things she taught me." That was the truth as well, as far as it went. "Maybe you could refresh my memory."

A wary expression crept into her eyes. Heath guessed he was rushing her fences. Pretending to concentrate on hammering nails, he began making animal sounds again.

She wrinkled her nose. "Cats don't go 'woof'!"

"They don't?"

She shook her head. "Dogs 'woof.' Cats go 'meow.' "

"Really?" He assumed what he hoped was a bewildered looking frown. "Are you positive about that?"

She looked at him as if he'd just crawled out from under a rock. "You ever heard G'liath go 'meow'?"

Heath pretended to consider. "No, now that I think about it, I can't say I have."

She nodded sagely. "You're making lots of 'stakes, Mr. Sher'f Man."

After circling that for a moment, Heath determined that she meant mistakes. He heaved a loud sigh and resumed hammering. "Old McIntyre had a—"

"It isn't McIntyre who gots a farm," she broke in. "It's MacDonald!"

"You sure?" He shrugged. "Oh, well. I'm just singing for me, not anyone else. If it bothers you, run along and play somewhere else."

"But you're making 'stakes! My mommy says if you're gonna do somethin', you should do it right."

That sounded like something Meredith might say.

Once again pretending to be oblivious of her, he made more animal sounds, doing cows that brayed like donkeys, cats that clucked like chickens. When he began tossing in a few jungle animals for good measure, Sammy finally rewarded him with a strangled giggle. Muffled by her hand though it was, the slight sound flowed over him like sunshine.

Heath glanced up. As their gazes locked, she went utterly still, as if she'd only just now realized how close she'd gotten to him. For a second, he was almost afraid to breathe, and he wanted nothing more than to reassure her. But, no. Pretending he didn't care if she stayed or not was the ticket. The instant he let on otherwise, she'd run like a scalded dog.

He started to sing again. Hesitantly, softly, so as not to startle her. *Old McIntyre has a farm.* Horses that squealed like pigs, pigs that crowed like roosters. He wasn't sure what sounds he made or what words he said, only that pretty soon Sammy started to laugh again, this time without reservation.

Warming to the game, he tossed down his hammer to act like an ape, scratching his armpits and loping around the yard, all the while bleating like a sheep. Sammy giggled so hard, she nearly fell off the joist. He switched from his ape act to mimic a duck crossed with a goat.

God, but she was precious, and her laughter, so hard won, was about the sweetest sound he'd ever heard.

"Ducks don't do that!" she said, fastening bright eyes on him.

"They don't?" Heath traced her small features with his gaze. Except for her coloring, she was the spitting image of her mama, her face a delicate sculpture of ivory with a slightly upturned nose and a perfectly bowed mouth. She even fidgeted like her mother did. "What do ducks do then, Miss Smarty Pants?"

She hopped off the joist and joined him in the yard. Heath didn't miss the fact that she kept a safe distance between them as she tucked her hands under her arms and began flapping her elbows. ''They go, 'quack, quack, quack'!'' she cried, and proceeded to walk across the patchy grass bent at the waist with her fanny poked out. Between quacks, she wiggled her imaginary tail feathers. ''Now you try.''

Crouched and bent forward, Heath followed in her wake, doing his best version of a duck waddle, which he totally ruined by mooing like a cow. Sammy fell to the grass, convulsed with giggles.

He executed another turn around the yard, waddling, swinging his ass and mooing. It occurred to him as he made his third pass that if Meredith was watching, he would blow any chance he'd ever had, however slim, to worm his way into her good graces.

Meredith tightened her hand over the window frame, her eyes going bleary with tears as she watched her daughter through an opening in the curtains. Sammy was laughing as Meredith had never heard her laugh, and as only a little girl could, her giggles making her breathless and so weak her little legs would barely hold her up. It was obvious to anyone who cared to look that the child craved a man's affection, that having a father like Dan had left a gigantic emptiness in her life.

Oh, Sammy, Meredith thought sadly. *I'm so sorry.*

She closed her eyes, the sound of her daughter's laughter sweeping her back through the years to when she'd been a child herself, being swung high in her father's strong arms. Because of Meredith's stupidity in choosing a husband, Sammy had never experienced that, not even once. *Until now.*

Meredith lifted her lashes to watch Heath Masters through a shimmering blur as he took Sammy's little hands in his large ones and swung her in wide circles around the yard. The child shrieked with delight, crying, "Higher! Higher!" until Heath obliged her.

On an upswing, he suddenly let go and caught her in his arms as she came back down. From out in the side yard, Meredith could hear Goliath barking excitedly, as if warning his master to be careful. Sammy giggled and threw both arms around Heath's neck, her blond head pressed close to his dark one.

The two of them might have been father and daughter at play, with the family dog barking on the sidelines. There was a part of Meredith that wished with all her heart that it was so. *This* was what Sammy needed. To be jostled and tossed about by someone who seemed as big as a mountain to her. To be hugged and made to feel special, and loved, and absolutely secure. The child was blossoming under Heath's attention like a little flower in the sun.

"Do it again!" she pleaded. "Please, Mr. Sher'f Man? Do it again."

Heath laughed, the sound husky and resonant. "You're wearing me out, sweetcakes," he said, his voice reminding Meredith of whiskey and smoke. "You've got to let this old man rest."

He hoisted Sammy onto his shoulder, grimacing slightly when she grabbed handfuls of his hair to steady herself.

"Easy up there. You'll snatch me baldheaded."

He strode with her to the half-finished porch. As he sat down, he swept her from his shoulder to perch her on his knee.

Her emotions in an impossible tangle, Meredith turned away from the window. A part of her yearned to pretend she hadn't witnessed that scene in the yard, to simply turn a blind eye and let Sammy enjoy the budding friendship. God knew, the child deserved whatever happiness came her way. But another part of Meredith knew she couldn't possibly let this continue.

Just for starters, Sammy was only four, which was far too young to be constantly on guard and remember there were certain things she could never tell their neighbor. If allowed to spend too much time with Heath unsupervised, she would slip up, sooner or later, and reveal something to him that could destroy their lives. Secondly, as inexperienced as Meredith was with men outside her marriage, she wasn't completely clueless. Heath had a hidden agenda in trying so hard to befriend her daughter, and it wasn't because he had an insatiable yearning to fraternize with a four-year-old.

Normally, Meredith didn't consider herself to be particularly desirable to members of the opposite sex, but there was little doubt in her mind that she'd somehow managed to capture her neighbor's interest. All the signs were there. His arranging to do the repairs on her house. His insistence that he help her with the household tasks until her hand healed. His arrival that morning with all those groceries. The man had attached himself to them like a tick to a dog's back, and he was doing everything possible to worm his way into their affections.

She remembered the interested gleam in his eye that first night and the way he'd watched her this morning in the kitchen as he'd unpacked grocery bags. He was attracted to her, no question about it, and if she were brutally honest, she had to admit she was equally attracted to him. He was devastatingly handsome and extremely likable, which was a dangerous combination. Every time she looked into those slate blue eyes of his, her heart skittered and her mouth went dry.

If she'd never been with Dan—and if her present circumstances had been different—she might have taken one look at Heath Masters and fallen head over heels in love with him.

Unfortunately, she had been with Dan and her circumstances weren't different.

Chapter 8

"Merry? Hey, Merry!" Heath called, his voice booming through the house so loudly that it startled Meredith clear out on the utility porch. "Where are you?"

Mary? For an awful moment, her legs went watery, one thought slicing through her mind. *He knows. Somehow, he found out.* Then, as quickly as the terror rushed through her, sanity returned. *Merry,* not *Mary.* He'd shortened Meredith into a nickname, that was all.

Before fleeing from New York, she'd run her finger down the columns of a Manhattan phone book to choose an alias. Now, when it was too late, she realized she'd made a bad mistake; in her attempt to pick a name similar to her real one, she'd chosen one a little too similar, especially when shortened. Her fault, not his.

"I—I'm out here," she called. Abandoning the pile of clean laundry she'd just brought in off the line, she reached to open the utility room door. "It's wash day. I've been folding clothes."

Heath was striding across the kitchen, the thick muscles in his thighs bunching with every step to stretch the denim of his jeans taut, his dusty boots thumping solidly on the worn linoleum. Even in a red work shirt instead of a uniform shirt, he exuded authority, his presence dominating the room and everything in it. Sammy trailed behind him like an adoring puppy.

He glanced at his watch. "It's about that time. What culinary delight should I whip up tonight?"

As Meredith stepped into the room, she couldn't help glancing down at her daughter, whose small face was flushed from giggling, her eyes sparkling. Regret welled up within her, forming an ache in her chest that made it difficult to breathe. He had no right to toy with Sammy's affections. The child had been hurt enough already. Couldn't he see that?

"I planned to have hamburger stroganoff," she replied with a calmness that belied her inner turmoil.

Rolling back the sleeves of his shirt, he said, "Would you mind having steak?"

Meredith nearly laughed. Would she mind? It had been so long since she'd sunk her teeth into succulent beef that her stomach growled when she thought about it. These days, she could scarcely afford chicken. Fish, except for cheap cans of tuna, had become nothing but a fond memory.

"You're the chef," she said. "I'm flexible."

He stepped to the refrigerator, somehow managing with effortless efficiency to brace the broken door as he opened it. When Meredith got in the refrigerator, she usually groused the entire time and was huffing with exertion.

He fetched the package of sirloin that he'd put in the meat drawer that morning. As he closed the refrigerator, he asked, "What is it with all the hinges in this place? I swear, half of them are broken."

"Rough treatment, I think." Meredith turned on the kitchen faucet to rinse her one good hand. "Rental houses take a lot of abuse, and I think this one has received more than most. I patched more holes in the walls than Carter has pills. I think someone went around putting his fist through the plaster."

He came to stand beside her at the counter to unwrap the meat. "Speaking from experience?"

She glanced up to find him regarding her with a solemn, questioning look in his eyes. For a moment, she couldn't think what he meant. Then she felt heat flooding to her cheeks.

"Not experience. Just an educated guess. The holes were about so high." She held up her bandaged hand to demonstrate. "I just naturally assumed they were put there by a fist. What else could have left holes everywhere at that height?"

"A number of things come to my mind. In my teens, I knocked holes in the walls a few times practicing karate moves," he said with a grin. "My aim wasn't all that good." Not offering further examples, he returned his attention to the meat, leaving Meredith with the feeling that he'd once again gleaned more from something she'd said or done than she might have wished. "Do you have a meat tenderizer?"

Since she couldn't afford steak, a tenderizer wasn't a necessity. "No, I, um . . ."

"No problem. An unopened can of soup or vegetables works great." He bent to open her canned goods cupboard. "Hey, Sammy. This would be a good job for you."

The child's eyes lit up at being included in the supper preparations. Heath grabbed a chair, pushed it over to the counter, and lifted Sammy to stand on the cushion. After rinsing off the container of soup, he patiently showed her how to pound the sirloin with one edge of the can. Once Sammy was happily occupied, he bent to get three large potatoes from under the sink where Meredith kept them.

"Baked potatoes," he said, grinning at Meredith. "With sour cream and fresh chives. Sound good?"

It sounded heavenly. "What can I do to help?"

He cast her a chiding glance. "Sit and supervise. What do you think?"

Feeling as if she were in the way and hating it, Meredith went to sit at the table as he'd requested. She expected to be bored, but the kitchen soon became such a hive of activity that she settled back and simply enjoyed being a spectator. After turning on the oven, Heath washed the potatoes, pricked them with a fork, and then proceeded to rub them with oil.

Looking on, Meredith found her attention riveted to his large hands as they slid smoothly over the potato skins, her traitorous mind focusing on things that no woman who wanted to remain aloof had any business noticing: the firmness of his grip, the visible strength in his long, thick fingers, the way the tendons in his brown forearms worked when he turned his wrists. She found herself wondering how it might feel if he were to touch her that way, his hands slick with oil, his slightly rough palms moving firmly over her skin, his fingers molding to her contours.

Madness. She didn't even *like* sex. Even to say she'd found the activity highly overrated would have been an understatement. Being touched by Dan had been a teeth-grinding ordeal. She had detested every second of it. And after her divorce, she'd vowed never to let another man lay hands on her again. That being the case, how could she watch Heath rubbing potatoes with oil and find herself contemplating just that, having his hands on her? Was she losing her mind?

Heath didn't give her time to ponder that question for long. Next on his list was whipping up a batch of biscuits from scratch, and he made the mistake of allowing Sammy to help. Before Meredith knew it, her kitchen looked as if it had been dusted with talcum powder, and Heath and Sammy weren't in much better shape. The front of his red shirt was streaked with flour. Sammy had dough smeared up to her elbows and white streaks all over her face.

"I'm really good at this, huh?" she asked him as she squeezed handfuls of dough, pushing the goo out between her knuckles. "My mommy says I'm the best cookie mixer she ever seen."

Heath sent Meredith a conspiratorial grin. "You're not bad at mixing biscuits, either," he said as he sprinkled a plastic cutting board with flour. "Those biscuits are definitely mixed really good. Now it's time to roll them and cut them out."

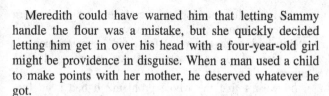

Meredith could have warned him that letting Sammy handle the flour was a mistake, but she quickly decided letting him get in over his head with a four-year-old girl might be providence in disguise. When a man used a child to make points with her mother, he deserved whatever he got.

To Meredith's surprise, this particular man wore flour quite well—down the front of his jeans, all over his dark boots, possibly *in* his boots. And to his credit, he never became cross. To the contrary, he got into the spirit of things rather quickly, giving back to Sammy as good as he got, smearing dough on the tip of her nose and even wiping his hand on her T-shirt. Sammy found the last highly amusing and giggled so hard she nearly toppled off the chair. Heath caught her under the arms to keep her from falling, and in the process soiled the only clean spots left on her shirt, the armpits.

"I think we're both going to need baths when this is all over," he told the child.

"To say nothing of my kitchen," Meredith couldn't resist observing.

He grinned in her direction. "We'll clean up after ourselves. Won't we, Sammy?"

"Yup. I'm a really good dishwasher."

"I can hardly wait," Heath replied solemnly.

Meredith was still smothering a grin when she returned to the kitchen after tucking Sammy into bed for the night. Heath was just drying his hands after doing kitchen cleanup. The aroma of sirloin steak, cooked to a turn, still lingered in the room, underscored by the smell of baked potatoes.

As Meredith drew the bedroom door closed behind her, she gave the kitchen a quick once-over, then ran her gaze over Heath. Everything looked tidy except him. He'd tried to dust himself off before attacking the floor with her broom, but his jeans still bore stubborn streaks of flour on the legs, and the stitching grooves in his brown Western boots were white as well.

"You look some the worse for wear," she commented.

He glanced down, swiped at his pants, and then shrugged. "It was fun."

And wasn't that the whole problem? It had been fun. The sound of Sammy's laughter still echoed in Meredith's mind, and because it did, knowing what she had to do filled her with sadness. "For a bachelor, you have a wonderful way with kids. You must be from a large family. Lots of brothers and sisters."

"Nope." He shrugged again. "Sammy's the first little person I've ever dealt with. I'm more experienced with teenagers."

Meredith pressed her bandaged hand to her waist, willing away the nervous flutter low in her abdomen. "Heath, we have to talk."

"Heath?" He raised one eyebrow, a mischievous twinkle creeping into his eyes. "Well, I'll be damned. The lady condescends to call me by my first name."

She dragged in a bracing breath, exhaling with a sigh. "It won't work, you know."

"What won't?"

She met his gaze. "Befriending Sammy to make points with me."

He placed his hands on his hips. The fact that his eyes didn't lose that mischievous twinkle did little to settle her nerves. "It won't, huh? I guess we'll just have to see about that."

Meredith had expected him to feign bewilderment. Instead he was throwing down the gauntlet? If she had drawn a line in the dirt and he'd stepped over it, she couldn't have felt more rattled.

"You don't seem to understand," she said, wanting to kick herself when her voice sounded shaky. "I'm not interested."

"I see." His mouth twitched at one corner. "So I'm wasting my time, am I?"

"Yes."

He rubbed his nose, whether to scratch an itch or hide his grin, she wasn't sure. "Well, I guess it's my time to waste."

Meredith stared up at him. This wasn't going the way she had hoped. "Listen, Heath. You're a very nice man, and you're very attractive."

"And?"

"*But* I'm not in the market," she finished with what she hoped was a note of finality.

"No problem." He moved toward her, his stride loose and unhurried. When he drew up in front of her, he reached out to capture a tendril of hair that lay on her shoulder. "I understand perfectly."

As he toyed with her hair, his knuckles grazed her shirt, the heat of him radiating through the cloth.

"You do?"

He wound the strand of dark hair around his fingertip, using it like a rope to haul her closer. She resisted the urge to clamp a hand to the top of her head to secure her wig. Now she wished she'd opted to dye her hair. At the time, though, wearing a wig had seemed to be simplest. Given her circumstances, she'd had no idea how long she might remain in one place, and changing her hair color frequently would have posed a problem, especially once she'd dyed it dark brown. There also would have been the worry of her blond roots showing, a dead giveaway.

When the toes of her sneakers bumped the tips of his boots, he caught her under the chin with the crook of his finger. "If you're not in the market, why aren't you running?" he asked huskily.

Because if she bolted, he would be left holding her wig, she thought a little frantically. "Why would I run? We're . . . um . . . having a conversation. And I have a point I'd like to make."

"Me, too."

She gulped. "Heath, please. I want to talk to you about Sammy."

"So talk."

"She's very—" He was bending toward her, his dark face seeming to eclipse everything else around her. "She's very sensitive. And I'm afraid she may grow too fond of you if you persist."

His breath wafted against her cheek, warm and rich with the aroma of coffee. His lips grazed her temple like the caress of a butterfly wing, light and tantalizing. "Persist in what, Merry?"

"My name is Meredith. And I don't want her hurt." She planted a hand against his chest. "Stop this. I don't want to be kissed. Not now, not ever. Am I making myself clear?"

"Then move away. I'm not holding you."

Oh, God . . . Meredith closed her eyes, battling waves of panic and memories of Dan, both of which swamped her as he trailed his lips lightly over her cheek toward her mouth. With his finger caught in her wig, she couldn't move away, and he was interpreting her staying as encouragement. "You have hold of my hair."

"Which I'll turn loose the second you move," he assured her.

Meredith clamped a fist over his finger to free her hair just as his mouth lightly touched hers. *Moist silk.* Her breath rushed from her, and he took it into himself, his lips settling more firmly on hers. He turned his hand to more fully grasp her chin and tip her head back. She curled her fingers over his shirt, forgetting about her wig, about Sammy, even about her aversion to being kissed.

Fire and ice. His firm mouth took control, his tongue lightly teasing her closed lips with tantalizing strokes. Shivers ran over Meredith's skin and shuddered down her spine even as heat pooled in her belly, radiating out from there like tendrils of fire.

Oh, God, he was good at this.

Remembering how bruising the force of Dan's mouth had become immediately after their wedding, Meredith couldn't believe this man's kiss could be so different, persuasive instead of demanding, intoxicating instead of nauseating. She couldn't feel her feet, and her legs were beginning to melt like wax placed too close to a flame.

Regaining her senses, she jerked her mouth from his and looked up at him with nothing short of stunned amazement. Unwrapping her hair from around his finger, she lurched away from him, half expecting him to stop her. *A safe distance.* That was what she needed. But at the same time, she didn't want him to think she was running.

Once at the table, she rested her good hand on the back of a chair, gripping it hard for support, still not able to believe she'd responded to him so easily. During their courtship, Dan had been sweet and gentle, too. Granted, he'd never made her feel like this—as if all her bones had melted. But she had enjoyed being kissed by him, all the same—until their wedding night. Had that experience taught her nothing? Evidently not, if all it took was some charm and a few slick moves to have her heart pounding.

Angling a glare at him over her shoulder, she said, "I don't want Sammy hurt. Do you understand that? Leave her out of this. Don't use her to get to me. I won't have it."

"I wouldn't dream of it," he replied, his smile infuriatingly unruffled. "My relationship with Sammy is totally apart from mine with you, Merry."

"Meredith!" she said with a little more force than she intended. "And you don't *have* a relationship with me."

Completely ignoring her denial that there was anything between them, he replied, "You seem more like a Merry to me than a Meredith. I'm not sure why."

It was almost as if he instinctively knew that Mary was the name she'd gone by all of her life. "I want to be called Meredith."

He inclined his head. "I'll try to remember that."

"And I *don't* want a relationship. Am I making myself absolutely clear?"

"Absolutely." He traced her features with his gaze, his smile deepening the creases in his lean cheeks. "It was only a kiss, Meredith, a pleasant pastime between consenting adults, not a lifetime commitment. People kiss each other all the time. It doesn't mean anything.''

It meant trouble; that was what it meant. He'd made her feel things she had believed she was incapable of feeling anymore. Feelings that would only tempt her to lower her guard. To take a chance she had no right to take. To risk a repeat of the misery and pain that had changed her and her little girl forever.

Like a shaky old woman gathering a shawl around her to ward off the cold, Meredith groped for her composure. ''Sammy is wearing her heart on her sleeve,'' she told him tremulously. ''If you're not careful, you'll break it. I won't stand by and watch that happen.''

He looked deeply into her eyes. ''Your daughter's heart is safe with me, Meredith.''

''Is it?''

''Yes. And so is yours.''

Chapter 9

The following evening while Heath was fixing supper, Meredith excused herself from the kitchen to use the restroom. She'd just gotten her jeans unsnapped when a deep rumble echoed all around her. The sound was coming from the bathtub. She inched over to draw back the curtain. A black and rust-colored leg was thrust up over the edge of porcelain. She poked her head around the curtain. Goliath lay sprawled on his back, all four legs limply spread, his slack jowls vibrating with every breath. *Crazy dog.* How on earth had he gotten in the house, and what was he doing in her tub?

As Meredith tried to ease away, the Rottweiler cracked open one eye to peer at her. After regarding her for a moment, he slurped his tongue over his nose, heaved a deep sigh and growled. A second later, his tongue went limp, falling back out the side of his mouth. The rumbling snore resumed.

As recently as a week ago, Meredith would have fled in terror. But it hadn't been a threatening growl, and the dog obviously had no intention of attacking her. At least not until he finished his nap. Remembering the way Goliath had curled his leg over Sammy the other night and how lovingly he'd snuffled her hair, Meredith gingerly touched his belly. Goliath arched his back, snorting and smacking his chops, encouraging her to give him a little scratch. Cautiously, she obliged, trailing her nails lightly over his ribs. The dog growled again and twisted, clearly enjoying the attention. Meredith smiled, convinced that the growl was conversational, not threatening. Heath was rubbing off on her. Next, she'd be making excuses for everything else the dog did.

"You're just a big old love, aren't you?" she whispered incredulously. "Heath should have named you Growler."

The dog rumbled at her again, turning his massive head to lick her arm. For a heartbeat of time, Meredith froze, her gaze fixed on his huge fangs. But when he continued to bathe her arm in friendly dog kisses, she finally relaxed. Lightly running her fingertips over his muzzle, she lifted his lip to look at his teeth. The fangs were the longest she'd ever seen, and his back incisors were well over an inch wide. Yet, oddly, she felt no fear.

It was a good feeling. The best. Tears stung her eyes. Somehow this dog had overcome Sammy's fear. Now he was overcoming hers, and in the process, he was helping her close yet another chapter in her life with Dan.

The Rottweiler ran his tongue over his nose, then sighed, drifting back to sleep while Meredith gently stroked his silken ears. In that precise instant, she lost her heart to the big old galoot.

After finishing her business in the bathroom, which was no easy task with only one hand, she returned to the kitchen. Heath stood at the stove.

"Your dog is asleep in my *bathtub*."

He turned a smoky gaze on her. "He is? How'd he get loose?" He laid down the spoon. "I'm sorry, Meredith. He must have slipped his collar."

She touched her hand to his sleeve. "Just let him enjoy his nap."

He lifted a brow. "In your tub? My dog, the man-eater, loose in your house? Are you running a fever?"

She laughed in spite of herself. "I've never felt better." Warmth crept up her neck. "I can't explain it. He just—" She shrugged. "I know it seems silly, but he looked so harmless. And sort of loveable. So I touched him. He didn't take my arm off, and so I—we—well, I think we've made friends."

His eyes twinkled. "You don't have to explain. He's my dog, remember? I told you all along that you'd love him once you got to know him."

"My tub will never be the same."

"Welcome to the world, according to Goliath. That's what he thinks tubs were made for. He likes the cool porcelain and sleeps in there most of the summer."

Meredith smiled, remembering how silly Goliath had looked. "On his back?"

Heath smiled. "His mother's milk didn't come down, and the county had already paid for a pup. I got him when he was no bigger than a minute and fed him from a doll bottle. The simplest way was to hold him in the bend of my arm, like a baby. He took to sleeping on his back and seldom sleeps any other way now."

Meredith tried to picture Heath with a tiny puppy cuddled in the crook of his arm, his hand curled around a bottle. "You must love him an awful lot."

His eyes darkened, and he glanced away. After a moment, he said, "Let's just say that having him around keeps my life interesting. I really missed him when they sent him away for training. It was like losing a kid."

"Was he gone a long time?"

"Only four weeks. He didn't take well to the separation, so they let me finish his training here. The school sent me an instructional video, so I'd know how to go about it. That's not usually the way it's done, but for Goliath, it worked well. He was the best dog on the force, barring none. It's a shame he was injured."

"Injured?"

Heath tapped the spoon on the edge of the pan. "When he rescued the little girl from the fire, it was the end of his career. I'm just glad I didn't lose him."

Sammy, who sat at the table making a horrific mess peeling carrots, glanced up, her huge blue eyes dark with anxiety. "You almost lost G'liath?"

Meredith saw Heath hesitate. Then he said, "Yes, honey. Goliath almost died."

"How?"

"Remember, I told you about the apartment building that caught fire and Goliath's rescuing a little girl? That was when he got hurt. The firemen missed a little girl when they evacuated the building. Goliath was my deputy back then, so he was in the Bronco with me, and he kept telling me someone was still in there." Eyes crinkling, he gave Meredith a teasing glance. "He *does* talk, you know. Dog language, of course." He turned down the flame under the pot. Then he went to take a seat near Sammy at the table. "He kept throwing himself against the door, trying to get out."

Sammy had become so intent on the story that she held the vegetable peeler poised over a forgotten carrot, her eyes fixed on Heath. "Then what?" she asked, much as she did when Meredith paused while reading to her from a book.

"Well, this lady in a beat-up old car drove up. She jumped out and started running through the crowd, screaming for her child. Then she tried to run into the building. It took two cops and a fireman to hold her back." He directed another glance at Meredith, a serious one this time. "It turned out she was a waitress who worked nights, and her babysitter hadn't shown up that evening. She'd asked an old lady across the hall to keep an eye on her little girl. When the fire broke out, the old lady got so scared, she forgot about the child and left the building without her."

"Oh, no." Meredith hugged her waist, thinking how she would have felt if it had been Sammy trapped in an inferno. "The poor woman."

Shadows darkened Heath's eyes. "By that time, the fire was out of control—so bad that only a suicidal fool would have gone back in. Two firemen were suiting up to do just that when I turned Goliath loose."

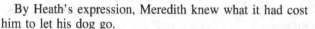

By Heath's expression, Meredith knew what it had cost him to let his dog go.

Heath glanced at Sammy. "Goliath has always had a kind of sixth sense when it comes to little kids. It's as if he can hear their thoughts or something. Sounds weird, I know. But it's true. And that night, he was in fine form. He seemed to know exactly where that little girl was. He dragged her out from under the bed where she was hiding on the third floor and pulled her to a window. Fortunately, when the little girl saw the firemen down below, holding a net, she had the good sense to jump."

"Then what?" Sammy asked.

"Well, the firemen lowered the net so the paramedics could reach her. With all the noise, they couldn't hear me yelling at them to get the net back up. Goliath was used to working with me or other deputies, and he trusted the firemen to catch him."

Sammy's small face went white. She glanced at Meredith. "That's a long way up, huh, Mommy."

"Yes, sweetkins. A very long way up."

"You ever heard the story about Humpty-Dumpty?" Heath asked Sammy. When she nodded, he said, "Well, that's how it was with Goliath. When he fell, he got busted up so badly the veterinarian here said he couldn't be put back together."

Sammy glanced bewilderedly toward the bathroom. "But he *is* back together."

"That's because there's this really wonderful vet in Eugene," Heath explained. "He does special operations on dogs, like they do on people. That vet heard about Goliath on the news and called me, offering to do all the surgery at cost. Even at that, the tab ended up being six thousand dollars by the time he was done. Goliath had a crushed right hip, three broken ribs, a punctured lung, and both his front legs were broken. Now he has an artificial hip and pins in both front legs. The firemen helped raise money to pay for the operations. Lots of people in this county donated money as well. Goliath was a hero, and everyone wanted to save him. In the end, I only had to pay three thousand."

"*Only* three thousand?" Meredith couldn't imagine anyone's spending that much money on a dog. Then again, she decided perhaps she could. Some dogs were special, and the Rottweiler snuffling and snoring in her tub was obviously one of them. She recalled Heath's telling her that Goliath had received seventeen citations for saving children during the course of his career. At the time, those had been mere words that hadn't penetrated her fear. Now she realized that for each of those citations, Goliath had saved a precious little soul. "It's a lot of money, but you can't place a price on a child's life."

Her gaze trailing to Sammy, Meredith silently added that you couldn't put a price on a child's happiness, either. Heath and Goliath. Somehow, between the two of them, they were working magic with her daughter. Magic that Meredith, despite all her efforts, had failed to work.

"He's a wonderful dog," she said with a slight tremor in her voice. "Since he can't be your partner anymore, I'm surprised you aren't training another pup."

He conceded the point with a nod. "I want to. But it can't be just any pup. It'll have to be a chip off the old block. Because of Goliath's hip, the vet said—" He glanced at Sammy. "Well, we have to let Goliath heal a little longer before he can have another family. As soon as he's up to being a daddy again, I'll take pick of the litter. Probably a female this time. Two males, even father and son, might fight."

Meredith suppressed a smile over the delicate way Heath had explained that his dog couldn't be used for stud yet. "I've, um . . . been thinking, Heath. Instead of leaving Goliath locked up over at your place tomorrow when you go to work, why don't you drop him off here? He would probably enjoy spending the day with Sammy."

"Me, too!" Sammy shouted, beaming a smile.

Heath chuckled and pushed up from his chair. "Meredith . . . are you sure? Goliath is a handful. He eats like a horse, for one thing. And he sheds. Also, it isn't just the bathtub he commandeers. If he's over here, he's liable to help himself to your bed or the sofa. And he—''

"Heath," Meredith interrupted, holding up a hand. "If your dog gets on my bed, I'll fluff his pillow."

He laughed and shook his head. "All right, I'll drop him by, but don't say I didn't warn you."

Two hours later, Meredith leaned a shoulder against the window frame, watching as her neighbor and his dog walked along the shoulder of the road toward home. Blowing in across the basin, the wind whipped Heath's dark hair. Beside him, Goliath loped along, a big black splotch in the shadows.

In the distance, tall fir and oak trees formed a perfect backdrop for Heath's rangy silhouette. She smiled, watching as his long, denim-sheathed legs scissored off the distance, his broad shoulders shifting easily with his stride.

Right after he'd finished the dishes, he'd gotten a signal on his pager and asked if he might use her telephone to call the department. From what she'd been able to gather from his end of the conversation, there was a teenage drinking party taking place later this evening that he had nearly forgotten to attend.

Meredith could almost picture him swinging out of his Bronco, looking bigger than life to a bunch of teenage boys with prominent Adam's apples and gangly builds. A towering tough guy who knew all the moves, all the lies and tricks. Heath could be intimidating with all those hard edges and that threatening glint in his eyes. On the other hand, he had a wonderful way with kids that probably served him well.

She smiled again, remembering the sound of Sammy's laughter at the supper table when Heath had made silly mistakes while reciting the alphabet, and then again later when he'd told her another story about Goliath before she went to bed. How long had it been since Meredith had heard her daughter laugh with such abandon?

Years, she realized sadly. Sammy had been a happy baby, always chortling and waving her arms, her eyes bright with curiosity. But then Dan had started exercising his visiting privileges, and slowly her child's natural exuberance and inclination to laugh had been stolen away until those inherent traits became nothing but a memory. Now, more times than not, Sammy looked out at the world with shadows of fear in her eyes. Heath Masters was the first man to work his way past the child's distrust in almost three years.

A tangle of confusing emotions swept through Meredith as she recalled his large hands and the play of muscle under his shirt every time he moved. The man was capable of bruising strength, yet he held it constantly in check. Fascinated, she'd watched him interact with Sammy tonight, remembering all the while how it had felt when he'd kissed her yesterday, his hand, touching her hair so lightly, his lips, trailing like gossamer over her cheek. She wondered how it might feel to be cradled in his arms. She could almost imagine the heat of him and the solidness of his shoulder against her cheek, the musk of his aftershave intoxicating her senses.

Oh, God . . . She was in trouble here. Meredith had never been so attracted to a man. Not even to Dan, who had swept her off her feet and into a marriage that had turned out to be a disaster. She couldn't let herself have these feelings. They went against every vow she'd made to herself after her divorce.

Shoving away from the window, Meredith moved through the house, searching almost frantically for something to distract her. When she noticed the evening paper, still neatly folded and unread, lying on the television, she grabbed it up, then nearly groaned when she saw the front page story.

Parents Protest, the headline read. Below was a grainy colored photograph of Heath on the courthouse steps, a group of angry citizens clustered around him. She returned the newspaper to its place on the television, not wanting to read more. The slant of the story was undoubtedly biased, just as all the others had been, using the terms ''rabble-rouser'' and ''unorthodox'' to describe him. He was those things, she supposed, for he was like no other lawman she'd ever encountered, from the unconventional way he dressed to the execution of his duties. But he was also much more, and now that she'd gotten to know him better, she thought this county was darned lucky to have him.

Telling herself she couldn't afford to get any more involved than she already was, she strode through the house, turning off the lights. When she reached Sammy's room, she stepped inside to stand at the child's bedside. In the shifting shadows cast by the breeze-tossed limbs of an oak outside, Sammy looked like a little angel, curled on her side, hair trailing over the pillow in strands of moon-kissed gold. Meredith bent to touch her cheek, remembering how Heath had done the same, his knuckles tracing the delicate contour of Sammy's jawline and chin.

He handled Sammy as if she were made of the most fragile crystal, always so incredibly gentle. And so very, *very* dangerous. She had come to Oregon to build her daughter a future, and this ramshackle old farmhouse in the middle of a weedy field had become Sammy's castle in the clouds.

Unfortunately, it was a castle made of glass, and Heath Masters was the stone that might shatter it.

Heath didn't bother to turn on the lights when he got home. After dumping some food in Goliath's dish, he went to the bathroom to get some towels, then to the freezer for several bags of ice to fill the coolers and ten-gallon water container he kept in the back of his Bronco. On the way out of town, he would stop at Safeway and buy several cases of cola, at least a dozen bags of corn chips, a load of candy bars, a half dozen bottles of over-the-counter headache remedy, and enough marshmallows to feed an army. If there was one thing he'd learned in his years at the department, it was to be prepared for everything at these parties, from nursing sick kids to feeding them, usually in that order.

Breaking up beer busts had managed to put a serious dent in Heath's bank account, but so far, he hadn't convinced the board of county commissioners to allocate a portion of the annual budget to snack food, ibuprofen, and pop.

As he backed his Bronco from the driveway, Heath stopped for a moment at the edge of the road to gaze at Meredith's house. One at a time, her windows were going dark. He imagined her walking through the house, turning off the lights, then stepping into her bedroom. Right about now, she'd be struggling to unbutton her shirt with one hand.

He sighed, picturing how she must look, bathed in moonlight as she undressed. White cotton sliding down slender arms, denim puddling around delicately turned ankles. A slip of a woman, the biggest thing about her a pair of brown eyes. Why that image fascinated him so, he couldn't say.

Jesus. Whether he wanted to admit it or not, he was half in love with her already. It was nuts. She hadn't given him any encouragement. But he was falling for her, anyway.

He clenched his hands on the steering wheel. Did a man start his midlife crisis at thirty-eight? Maybe that was his problem. Lately, the thought of home and hearth had an appeal that should have scared the hell out of him. Marriage, fatherhood. In the past, he'd never given those things more than a passing thought. Now they were popping into his mind frequently, making him feel as if his life lacked something vital.

He'd always gone for tall, well-rounded, sloe-eyed brunettes, and never any particular one. Big racks, slinky hips, legs that went forever. Never blondes or redheads, never anyone short. Given his size and build, he had always felt like an awkward giant with a female of slight stature.

Now, suddenly, only *one* woman appealed to him, which made absolutely no sense given the fact that she was so completely different from the females he'd always preferred. The only things about Meredith Kenyon that fitted the bill were that wealth of sable hair and those gorgeous brown eyes.

Chapter 10

Man and dog, dog and man. Over the next week, Meredith began to feel as if her previously quiet and manageable world had been invaded. After finishing the repairs on both porches, Heath moved inside to work and the dog came with him. Suddenly the drab old farmhouse had taken on a warmth it lacked before, always filled with either her little girl's giggles, Heath's rumbling laughter, or Goliath's deep barking.

Laughter. It was a priceless gift, and Heath had filled their lives with it.

During the day while Heath was at work, Goliath managed to keep Meredith and Sammy chuckling. Every time Meredith turned around, it seemed she discovered some new quirk in the Rottweiler's nature. His eating habits, for instance. The very first morning when she filled the gigantic dog dish Heath had brought over, Goliath promptly thumped it with his foot, dumping the kibble all over the floor. Afterward, he lay down in the mess to eat, oblivious to Sammy's and Meredith's laughter.

Later that afternoon, Meredith heard an awful racket in the kitchen. She found Goliath pushing the metal dish across the kitchen with his nose, occasionally whacking it with his paw to send it somersaulting. It was the dog's way of asking for lunch.

Before long, it became both Meredith and Sammy's habit

to leave the bathroom door open and the commode seat up. Goliath preferred toilet water to that in his bowl. After drinking, he invariably emerged from the bathroom with his jowls streaming water, whereupon he made a beeline for a human to blot his jowls on dry clothing.

Meredith kept her word. When Goliath got on her bed to take a Rottweiler snooze, she fluffed his pillow.

Ever watchful for dog hair, she grew accustomed to straining her coffee through her teeth. Finding stray black hairs in her food, or on her toothbrush, or even in the refrigerator no longer turned her stomach. Extra protein, Heath called it. Meredith comforted herself with the thought that at least it was black and showed up rather well. On everything. She didn't care. That big old, sloppy Rottweiler was the most wonderful dog in the world.

When the contractor finished Goliath's kennel, Meredith worried that Heath might stop bringing the dog by each morning. He didn't. Goliath, it seemed, had become a daytime member of the Kenyon family and would remain so until they moved.

Meredith dreaded the very thought of leaving. If something happened and she had to relocate, she wasn't sure how Sammy would handle it. The child adored Goliath and fairly worshiped Heath, a state of affairs that Heath encouraged on a nightly basis. No matter how tedious his work, he always had time to play. Sammy got piggyback rides around the house. Other times, Heath would suddenly jump up, grab the child under the arms and swing her in high arcs around the kitchen, Goliath circling and barking. On the sidelines, Meredith watched the three and found herself thinking that *this* was what a family should be like. By an accident of birth, Sammy had been robbed.

The child was blossoming under Heath's attention. With each day that passed, Meredith saw transformations taking place in her daughter, a process of healing that the counseling sessions and her love hadn't brought about.

It wasn't only that Sammy laughed frequently, which in and of itself seemed miraculous. She was also becoming more mischievous and actually dared to disobey Meredith sometimes, doing things she never would have done a month earlier. Unlike most mothers, Meredith silently rejoiced when she caught her daughter committing an infraction, no matter how slight. Not so very long ago, Sammy had been more a shadow than a child, never breaking rules and constantly fretting that she might have committed some imagined wrong.

The evening after Meredith got the stitches removed from her hand, she had cause to wonder if Sammy wasn't becoming a little too mischievous. Meredith was out in her garden patch, trying to get the soil ready for seeding before she completely missed planting time. Her hand, which the doctor had warned her to pamper, was aching from the unaccustomed use. Taking a break, she gazed at the turned earth, imagining how it would look in another month or so with all her vegetables flourishing in evenly spaced rows.

She sighed with satisfaction. It was a perfect evening to work outside, the air sweet with the scents of spring, warm enough for shirt sleeves, yet cool enough that she hadn't broken a sweat. On the gentle breeze, she could smell the pot of red beans she'd left to simmer on the stove. She'd had an unusually busy schedule today, doing phone solicitations, and beans didn't need much tending. Pretty soon, though, she needed to go in and stir them.

First she wanted to take a turn around the yard. Heath had finished replacing the boards in the kitchen floor late that afternoon and had gone home, saying he'd be back tomorrow to start working on the utility porch. She wanted to see if he'd discarded any board remnants she might be able to use to repair the shed.

As Meredith approached the discard pile, she heard Sammy calling her. She cupped a hand to shield her eyes against the evening sun. "I'm out here, sweetie!"

Sammy came running around the house. As she drew up near Meredith, she cried, "Momby, I can'th bweeve!"

Meredith bent to study her daughter's face, which looked oddly asymmetrical. Sammy's nose was swollen, she decided, slightly more so on one side than the other. "You can't breathe?" Meredith asked worriedly. She knelt to give the child a closer look.

"Sweetie, your nose is puffy." Meredith's first thought was of a spider bite. Her heart leaped. "You haven't been playing under the porch or out in the shed, have you?"

"No."

"Did you bump yourself?"

Her eyes filling with tears, Sammy shook her head. "Ith's the beenthz," she cried.

"The what?"

"The beenthz," the child repeated. "I sthuck 'em ind my node, and dey won'th come outh." When Meredith gazed blankly at her, Sammy leaned closer. "Yooo know. The beenthz? For thupper?"

Realization dawned. Meredith gave a horrified gasp. "You stuck beans up your nose? Oh, Sammy, no!" She'd caught the child trying to insert a bean in her ear that morning and cautioned her against it. "Why'd you do that?"

Sammy blinked, crocodile tears coursing down her cheeks. "I don'th know." She rubbed at her upper lip. "It hurths, Momby, and I can'th bweeve!"

Sensing that panic wouldn't be long in coming, Meredith gave Sammy a comforting hug. "Well, now, let's not get in a dither. We'll get those old beans out of there, straightaway. You'll be fine."

Twenty minutes later, Meredith was beginning to feel a little panicky herself. Try as she might, she couldn't pluck the beans out with her tweezers. The things had put down roots. Even worse, Sammy was crying, which seemed to make the beans swell.

Admitting defeat, Meredith gathered her daughter up from her perch on the kitchen table. "I think we'd better go see the doctor," she announced.

Sammy's wailing grew higher pitched. "I'm th-cared, Momby."

"Oh, sweetie," Meredith crooned as she grabbed her purse and headed for the car with the child cradled in her arms. "Don't be scared. The doctor will get them out. He has special tools."

What kind of tools, Meredith wasn't sure. Aside from tweezers, what could be used to make forays up a little girl's nostrils?

She bundled Sammy into the cream-colored Ford and fastened her seat belt. "Sit tight, okay, sweetkins? Be Mommy's big girl, and try not to cry."

"Thwy?"

Meredith kissed her daughter's damp forehead. "Just don't, okay?"

Running around to the driver's side, Meredith threw open the door, slipped under the wheel, and turned the key in the ignition. Nothing happened. Just an ominous click. *The battery.* She hit the steering wheel in frustration. "Confound it!"

"Whath?"

"The car won't start."

Sammy pinched the bridge of her swollen nose. "Buth I goth beenthz up my node, Momby! I goths to go to the hothpiddle!"

From a long distance away, a phone was ringing. Heath surfaced from his evening snooze, scratched his armpit, and snorted awake. *Damn.* Another call. Maintaining law and order could be a real son of a bitch sometimes.

"I'm coming, I'm coming!" he yelled, releasing the footrest of his recliner.

As he raced to the kitchen, he nearly tripped over Goliath, who was napping in the doorway. Scrambling to get his balance, he grabbed the telephone receiver.

"Hello!" he barked, wondering as he spoke who would be at the other end of the line this time. If it was that frigging reporter again, he was going to hunt the bastard down and rip his throat out. More likely, it was one of his deputies. "Masters, here."

"Heath?"

He blinked. "Merry?" She didn't sound like herself, her

voice thin and quavery. "Honey, what's wrong?"

"It's Sammy. I need to take her into emergency, and my car won't start."

"I'll be right there."

"Wait! It's nothing bad so don't break a leg getting here."

Nothing bad, but she was taking the kid to the hospital? In the background, he could hear Sammy crying. "Did she hurt herself?"

"No, she stuck beans up her nose."

Heath blinked again. "Say what?"

"She stuck beans up her nose. I let her help me sort them this morning before I put them in the pot to soak. She must have done it then. Now they're all swollen up in there, and I can't get them out, not even with tweezers. She's having trouble breathing."

"Beans up her nose? What possessed her to do that?" Heath no sooner asked than he remembered how he used to snort a cooked spaghetti noodle down his nostril, cough up the end, and drive his sister Laney crazy by pulling it back and forth through his sinus cavity. "Never mind. Listen, honey, calm down, okay? She'll be fine."

"It's just that she's panicky because she can't breathe through her nose."

"I'll be there in two minutes, all right?"

Heath hung up and went to the medicine cabinet in his bathroom to get the mineral oil and a bottle of iodine, which came with an eye dropper. Ten seconds later, he and Goliath were loping up the road. When they hit the end of Meredith's driveway, Heath could hear Sammy screeching, a good sign she was still getting plenty of oxygen.

Meredith met him at the front door. "Just let me grab my purse."

Moving aside to let Goliath enter with him, Heath stepped into her living room and closed the door. "Forget your purse, honey. I can get the beans out, no problem."

"You can?" She paused midway to the kitchen, looking

back at him over her shoulder. "I've tried and tried. They're stuck in there, tighter than a miser's fist."

Heath held up the mineral oil. "I'm a certified first responder, remember? I deal with stuff like this all the time."

In actuality, Heath had never plucked beans from a kid's nose, but the department dispatcher, Jenny Rose, had a four-year-old boy with a penchant for inserting foreign objects in his orifices.

He followed Meredith to the kitchen. Sammy sat on the kitchen table, face squinched, tears streaming, her tremulous lower lip protruding. Heath went directly to her, hunkered down, and made a big show of looking up her nose with his penlight.

"Hmm," he said.

"I can'th bweeve. My momby sethz I goths to go to the hothpiddle."

Heath directed the light up her nose again. "Nah, you're going to be fine, sweet cakes. Those beans haven't even started to sprout yet."

Sammy crossed her eyes to look down the swollen bridge of her nose. "*Spwout?*" She looked horrified at the thought.

Heath winked at her. "No beanstalks yet. Lucky for you, huh? We'll just pluck those nasty old beans out of there, and you'll be fine."

"Dey won'th come outh."

Heath gave the bottle of mineral oil a shake. "Sure they will." He handed Meredith the iodine. "Wash out the eye dropper for me, would you please?"

Meredith rushed to the sink. She returned seconds later, drying the dropper with a dish towel. Extending it, she said, "You're sure you know what you're doing?"

He grinned. "A smidgen of oil up each nostril makes it easier to pull stuff out."

"I should have thought of that."

Sammy grew rigid when Heath laid her back on the table. To complicate matters, Goliath decided to join her. Heath wrestled the dog down and asked Meredith to hold his collar. "She's all right," he assured the Rottweiler. "I'm not hurting her. Right, Sammy?"

Sammy didn't look too certain. He handed her his penlight, directing the beam at the ceiling. "Bet you can't write your name on the ceiling without forgetting a letter," he challenged. "You watch her, Mommy. If she makes a mistake, she has to start all over."

Sammy took the penlight in both hands and gazed intently at the ceiling, a frown pleating her forehead as she began reciting the letters of her name with a nasalized slur. "Tuhee . . . ahay . . . emmb—"

"S," Heath corrected as he bent to peer up her nose. "Back to square one for you, sweetcakes. Your name doesn't start with a 'T.' "

"Nuh—uh, ith—" Sammy broke off, pursed her mouth, and flashed her mother a startled look. Then she started over. "Eth . . . ahay . . . emb . . . emb . . . hawhy."

"Good!" He chucked her under the chin. "Now see if you can spell Samantha."

With Sammy's attention thus diverted, Heath went to work. After putting a drop of oil up each of her nostrils, he went fishing with Meredith's tweezers. Shortly thereafter, he plucked one of the beans from Sammy's nose. The child blinked in surprise.

"You did ith," she said, sniffing air through the one cleared passage.

"Don't sniffle," Heath cautioned. "You'll suck the other bean farther in. Swallow it, and you'll be sprouting beans from your belly button sometime next week."

Sammy giggled. He chuckled with her, then went back to work. As he drew the second bean from her nose, he turned with it held aloft in the tweezers to show it to Meredith. "Am I good, or what?"

Meredith looked so relieved, Heath thought she might kiss him. He was disappointed that she didn't. "Oh, Heath, thank you!"

"No problem." He helped Sammy sit up, motioned to Meredith that she could turn Goliath loose, and then watched with a smile as the Rottweiler reared up to plant his paws on the table. "Now, young lady," Heath said chidingly. "It's time for me to give you my official bean-up-the-nose prevention lecture."

Arms hugging her waist, Meredith stood off to the side, only half listening as Heath began to lecture her daughter on the dangers of inserting foreign objects in her nose. After Sammy's slip while spelling her name, Meredith's nerves were jangling, her heart fluttering like the wings of a frantic bird. Tammy, Sammy. The two names were very similar, a deliberate choice on Meredith's part to make it less traumatic for her daughter to grow accustomed to the change. Unfortunately, the similarity also made it harder for Sammy to keep the two names straight when she was upset.

Heath hadn't picked up on the slip, thank heaven. Because he knew Sammy had been practicing her letters, he'd assumed she had made a simple mistake. But what about next time? Sammy was so young. Since the move to Oregon, Meredith had drilled her constantly, but there was so much to remember. Sooner or later, Sammy would reveal something else to Heath, and the cat would be out of the bag.

Stupid, so stupid. Was she out of her mind? She couldn't afford to take chances like this. The man was a law officer.

Hunkered beside the table, Heath held Sammy's small chin cupped in a large, sun-bronzed hand. "So, sweetcakes, do I have your promise you won't poke any more beans in your nose?"

"I promise," Sammy assured him.

"You didn't stick beans anywhere else, did you?" he asked. "Not in your ears or your belly button or—"

Heath broke off, a dark flush creeping up his neck. It had obviously just occurred to him how creative a little girl could get with beans.

Sammy's eyes widened. "I di'n't put beans no place else."

"Well . . ." Heath *harrumphed*, then released Sammy's chin to rub his nose, his gaze flitting around the kitchen. "That's good." He shot Meredith a look that said he'd waded in over his head and was going under fast. "I, um . . . yeah." He sniffed and rubbed his nose again. "That's that, I guess."

Heath pushed to his feet, six feet plus of discomfited male. It wasn't necessary for her to usher him out. After giving Sammy's hair a gentle tousle, he collected his dog and made tracks for the front door, muttering something she couldn't quite catch about having work to do at home.

Falling in behind him, Meredith said, "Thank you for coming over. Mineral oil. I'll remember that."

He stood with his hand on the door knob, his chiseled features still slightly flushed. "Hopefully, this will teach her not to put any more beans up her nose."

Meredith flashed a brittle smile. "Yes, well, we can hope. Kids have short memories sometimes."

"I'll stop by in the morning on the way in to town and jump-start your car."

"Oh, no, really." Meredith bent to give Goliath a fare-well pat. "You've done more than enough for us. I'll manage."

He narrowed an eye. "You know how much it costs to call a tow truck? It'll take me five minutes. After I get it started, you should let it idle to recharge the battery."

"I should probably just replace it. This isn't the first time it's gone dead on me."

"Yeah, well, it's a little hard to budget for a car battery when your wages barely stretch to cover the necessities." He reached to push a stray tendril of hair from her cheek. "What you need is a second income."

"There aren't that many jobs I can do at home, and I don't want to leave Sammy with a stranger."

He rasped his thumb over her mouth. "I'm not talking about you getting another job, Merry. I mean a husband's income."

Their gazes locked, hers wary, his filled with tenderness.

A tingling tension built between them. Meredith couldn't think clearly, let alone move, not even when she realized he was leaning closer. For a moment, she thought he meant to kiss her. The blue of his shirt filled her vision, the cloth stretched taut over his chest. Her lungs hitched, her breath snagging at the base of her throat.

"A leaf."

His fingertips touched her hair. A second later, he held a leaf in front of her nose. She had a feeling he knew exactly what she'd been anticipating, and that he found her reaction amusing. A kiss, after all, wasn't that big a deal.

"Good night, Meredith," he whispered huskily.

As he let himself out, she replied in kind. "Good night." What she really meant was good-bye.

Chapter 11

Arms propped on his desk, chin resting on one fist, Heath stared down at the date on his oversized desktop calendar, which served double duty as a blotter. *Monday, May 19th.* Next Saturday would be the kickoff for Memorial Day weekend, one of the busiest and craziest holidays of the year, with drunks swarming onto the highways like armies of crazed ants, die-hard outdoor enthusiasts descending on every available water recreation site in the county, and teenagers celebrating their high school graduations. Heath knew from past experience that he would get no sleep during that seventy-two hour stretch, let alone anything remotely resembling a second of tranquility.

That wasn't what bothered him, though. *May 19th.* Nineteen years ago, the nineteenth had fallen on Friday a week before Memorial Day weekend, and Heath, a rebellious college freshman, had come home from the University of Oregon to informally celebrate his sister Laney's high school graduation at a beer bust the senior class was throwing to commemorate the coming event.

Heath squeezed his eyes closed, trying to shove away the memories. It didn't work. It never worked. The memories were part of his punishment. Punishment that would never end and that he accepted because he deserved it. Hell, he deserved worse. A lot worse.

"Sheriff?"

Heath glanced up to see Jenny Rose leaning around the partially opened office door, the sounds of ringing telephones, clicking keyboards, and bleeping computers filtering past her to defile his inner sanctum.

"Deputy Moore just came in," she said, smiling impishly. Her brown hair, skinned back into a tidy French twist, glistened in the slats of sunlight that poured through the Venetian blinds. "He's booking Alma Cresswell for shoplifting again."

"Christ." Heath raked a hand through his hair, the dull ache behind his eyes exploding into a knifing pain. "Can you call her daughter, Jen? Ask her to come down and pick her mother up."

Jenny Rose gave him a thumbs-up. "I think I should warn you, though. It's grand theft this time. The old doll walked out of Holt's Jewelry with twelve thousand dollars worth of ice dripping from her fingers."

Heath's headache mushroomed. *"What?"*

"You heard me. She went in to look, supposedly for a birthday gift for her daughter. The clerk left the case open, got busy with another customer, and forgot to watch her. Alma left wearing the whole display."

Heath stood, giving his chair such a forceful shove that it rolled back on its castors and hit the wall.

Jenny Rose jumped. "Temper, temper."

"Yeah, well," Heath grumbled as he shouldered his way past her. "Deputy Moore is a frigging blight on humanity."

Jenny Rose snickered as she drew the door closed behind them.

Heath scanned the outer office. It was a typical Monday morning, half his force off duty after working through the weekend, the other half trying frantically to deal with the weekend spillover—Saturday night drunks posting bail, neighbors filing complaints against neighbors over weekend disputes, parents searching for runaways, and the usual handful of kids who'd been hauled in off the streets for truancy.

"No, no, no!" an elderly man yelled at one of Heath's

deputies. "It wasn't just *grass* he dumped over the fence. There was dog shit mixed in, I tell you!"

Heath blocked out the babble as he circled desks and made his way down a paper-strewn aisle. He drew up beside Moore's station, his gaze coming to rest on the diminutive woman who sat across from the young deputy in a metal-frame chair. The embodiment of everyone's great-grandmother in a floral-print dress with a lace collar, Alma Cresswell smiled up at him.

She looked like an elderly angel with a halo of wispy white curls. Heath couldn't help staring in startled amazement. Perched at a jaunty angle on Alma's halo was what appeared to be the inverted bottom half of a gallon-sized, white plastic bleach jug, which she'd fashioned into a gaily decorated hat. Two tattered silk roses sprouted from the crown, waving like colorful insect antennae every time she bobbed her head. The edge of the bleach bottle had been crocheted with a two-inch wide, celery-green ruffle that reminded him of wilted lettuce.

"Hello, Mrs. Cresswell," Heath said respectfully. "How are you today?"

"Oh, you dear boy," she said, her palsied voice cracking. "I haven't seen you in a month of—" She broke off, her rheumy eyes filling with confusion. She chewed on her bottom lip, which was smeared with the same bright crimson lipstick that decorated her dentures. "When *was* the last time. Do you recall?"

"Uh, yes, ma'am. It was last Wednesday." When Tom Moore had hauled her in for stealing greeting cards from Hallmark.

"She's really done it this time," Moore informed Heath in an official, deputy voice nearly as starched as his uniform. "Twelve thousand in jewelry. That constitutes grand larceny." He gestured toward a pile of sparkling diamonds, which he had laid out on his desk for effect before bagging them as evidence. "I got her nailed to the wall."

Heath cut the deputy a glare, then returned his gaze to the old woman, a victim of advanced senility that Heath suspected was undiagnosed Alzheimer's. A former school-marm, Alma believed she was still teaching. She carried a lesson-planning book around in her large vinyl tote, along with merchandise she filched from store shelves on a daily basis as she wandered Main Street. Every Friday evening, her middle-aged daughter, an office secretary at one of the high schools, returned all the loot, paid for anything damaged, and apologized to the proprietors for her mother's behavior.

In Heath's estimation, Alma Cresswell was a completely harmless old lady whom Deputy Moore should have been helping across the street. Instead, the bastard kept arresting her.

Heath settled his seething gaze on the handcuffs that banded the old lady's wrists. Her frail hands were so gnarled with arthritis her fingers were crooked, the knuckles at least three times their normal size. Definitely not the stuff dangerous criminals were made of.

Heath balled his hands into tight fists, barely resisting the urge to pummel Moore's face. The only bright spot in the situation was that Alma remained happily oblivious. In better times, she'd probably never received so much as a parking ticket, and now, hopelessly befuddled most of the time, she couldn't comprehend that anyone might arrest her. In her mind, all she'd done was go shopping, her buying spree culminating with this nice young deputy taking her for a ride.

"Get the bracelets off her," Heath ordered softly.

"But, Sheriff, she—"

Heath leaned down to put his face a scant, threatening inch from his deputy's. Forcing a smile for Alma's benefit, he grated out through clenched teeth, "*Now*, Moore."

Tom leaped from his chair and scuttled around his desk to unlock the cuffs. He shot Heath a glare as he returned the restraints to the pouch on his belt. "I can't understand you. She *steals* things, dammit. I've finally got her for grand theft."

Heath signaled to Helen Bowyer, doing paperwork two

rows over. "Can you take it from here, Helen?" he asked. "Bag the evidence and put it in the safe. Then Alma would probably like some tea while she waits for her daughter. I always seem to make it too strong for her."

"Hi, Mrs. Cresswell," Deputy Bowyer called as she made her way toward Moore's desk. "Wow, don't you look fashionable today. I *love* that hat. Did you make it?"

"Why, yes," Alma confessed, patting the ruffle on the bleach bottle. "Would you like me to make one for you?"

Helen flashed Moore a warning glance, then smiled brightly. "Oh, I'd love one! How sweet of you to offer."

"Little Helen Evans, isn't it?" Alma asked, leaning forward to peer up at Helen's face. "My goodness, how you've grown up."

Helen, who had just celebrated her fortieth birthday, winked at Heath. Smoothing a hand over her khaki trousers, which had grown snug across her hips in the last few months, she said, "I've grown out as well as up, I'm afraid."

"I think you look lovely," Alma assured her. "How are you coming with your fractions, dear? No more problems, I hope?"

Heath had heard the latter part of this conversation last week when Alma had been brought in. The old lady's short-term memory was almost nonexistent, but events from long ago were still clear in her mind.

He planted a hand on Deputy Moore's shoulder, squeezing hard and experiencing an unholy glee when the younger man winced. "Tell Mrs. Cresswell good-bye, Tom. I need to speak with you in my office."

Face red with indignation, Tom tried to shift from under Heath's hand, the attempt aborted by Heath's tightening grip. "I'll see you later, Mrs. Cresswell."

"Thank you so much for the lovely ride," Alma called. To Helen, she added, "I do so enjoy that little radio he has. You hear all kinds of interesting things while you're driving. There was a collision at the corner of Pine and Madison just minutes ago. No injuries, thank heaven."

Heath guided Moore across the busy room. When the two of them were inside his office with the door firmly closed, he finally released the younger man to turn and advance on him, nose to nose. "Moore, do you know the one and only reason I'm not going to fire your ass?" Heath rammed a finger against the deputy's chest. "Because your daddy is the mayor, and right now, I've got enough problems without squaring off with him. But understand me, buster. I'm serving you official notice. Arrest that little old lady one more time, and your ass will be out the door. Have I made myself clear?"

Tom blinked. "I took an oath to uphold law and order. If necessary, I would arrest my own mother."

"Why don't you go do that?" Heath demanded. "Maybe then, your father will understand why you're such a pimple on my ass."

The intercom on Heath's desk buzzed. He stepped over to take the call. "Yes, Jenny?"

The dispatcher's voice crackled over the speaker. "I've got a hysterical old lady on the line. She says there's some woman parading around across the street from her house, stripped stark naked except for a red garter belt, black stockings, and three-inch heels. She's afraid her husband's going to have a heart attack."

A smile tugging at the corners of his mouth, Heath glanced over at his recalcitrant subordinate. "Deputy Moore has been angling for some excitement this morning. He'll be more than happy to get right on it."

Meredith turned, hung up the phone and bent to jot a note in her appointment book. She'd set up sixty-three shampooing demonstrations today. On an average, thirty percent of those people would buy shampooers, which meant a nice little chunk of commission for her. She leafed through the pages, looking for the following day's date. Then she set to work calling to confirm demonstration appointments with customers.

Halfway through the list of numbers, Meredith paused in

her work and glanced out the window above her desk to check on Sammy, who was playing in the yard. The child was happily occupied with Goliath, who sat patiently at the little girl's side, a frilly doll bonnet cocked at a silly angle over one ear and a pair of hot pink sunglasses riding on his broad nose.

Meredith smiled and shook her head. She was about to dial another phone number when she heard Heath's Bronco pull into the drive. This morning when he dropped off Goliath, he'd told her he planned to stop by the building supply store for more lumber on his way home. She really should go help him unload it, she thought. But after his comment last night about her needing a husband, she was more determined than ever to keep her distance from him. *And* to make plenty of money so he could never use her poor earning power as a reason to talk about marriage again.

Goliath began barking. Meredith glanced up. It sounded as if another car had pulled into her driveway. She rose from her chair to peer through the parted curtains at the front window. Heath had just removed an armload of lumber from atop his Bronco. Squinting against the sunlight, he turned to gaze at the white van that had pulled to a stop behind his vehicle. The front doors of the van both opened, and two men spilled out, both of them wearing white shirts and dark slacks. The passenger rushed around to the van's rear doors while the driver walked toward Heath.

"Bill," she heard Heath say. "What brings you out this way?"

Though Heath seemed to know the man, his greeting was cool. Since Meredith had never seen either of the men before and she still had calls to make, she nearly turned away. But then she noticed the blue lettering, KTYX, on the side of the van, which was the logo of the local television station. Her stomach clenched, and her heart felt as if it leaped clear into her throat. She raced back through the house to go get Sammy. Unfortunately, by the time she got outside, the man who had stepped to the back of the van already had his camera rolling.

Oh, God. Trying her best to appear calm, Meredith walked across the yard, picked up Sammy, and returned to the house, Goliath trotting beside her. *Why were they here?* As she let the screen slam behind her, she felt as if her legs might fold.

Calm down. Heath is always being hounded by newsmen. They've come to interview him. That's all. It has nothing to do with you.

That thought made Meredith feel slightly better. No one in Wynema Falls was interested in doing a story on her. She was just another shadowy blur in the background.

Meredith took Sammy to her bedroom, dragged out a puzzle, and got the child interested in putting it together. Only then did she go back to the living room to peer through the crack of the curtains. To combat the late after-noon stuffiness, she'd opened the windows earlier, which allowed her to hear as well as see what was going on with-out being noticed.

"Bill, please," she heard Heath say. "I'd really appre-ciate it if you'd leave. For old times sake, if for no other reason."

"I can't do that, Heath. I've been assigned this story, and it's my job to report on it. Please don't take it person-ally."

"How can I not take it personally when you bring up something like that?" Heath glanced toward the television camera. "Are you filming?"

The man named Bill nodded. Heath's shoulders stiffened. "Then I have only two words to say: no comment."

Bill shoved the microphone he held toward Heath. "Sheriff Masters, this is the anniversary of your sister's death," he said, his tone becoming formal. "According to the accident report, you were driving the vehicle when she was killed. Is that true?"

"No comment," Heath said icily as he turned his back on the camera.

Bill and the cameraman dogged Heath's heels. "Sheriff Masters," Bill called, throwing his voice as if to span a distance, "we've recently learned from a very reliable source that you were driving under the influence the night your sister died. Would you care to comment on *that*?"

Heath spun around, his dark features drawn with anger. Meredith realized she'd gasped aloud and pressed her fingers to her lips.

"There were no charges filed against you for drunk driving or vehicular manslaughter," Bill pressed. "Can you explain why? Driving under the influence *was* against the law at that time. Was it not? Just as it is now?"

Heath began to unload the lumber again while the reporter followed him around, shoving the microphone in his face.

"Do you deny that you broke the law?"

Heath dropped an armload of two-by-fours on the ground next to the porch, then stalked back to the Bronco. From her vantage point, Meredith could see the tendons standing out in his neck as his jaw grew tighter.

"You were only nineteen at the time. We realize it must be very difficult for you to recall the terrible events of that night, let alone to talk about them. But the citizens of this county have a right to know the truth. *Were* you driving under the influence that night? Were you, therefore, responsible for the accident that occurred?"

"No comment."

"Your father is a very wealthy man, Sheriff. Did he, by chance, bribe the authorities to cover this up so no charges would be brought against you?"

No answer.

"Is it true?"

"No comment! Don't you understand plain English? Leave me the hell *alone*!"

"Sheriff Masters, your refusal to comment leaves us with no choice but to draw our own conclusions," Bill said loudly. "Is it not true that you were responsible for your sister's death, that you did, in fact, *murder* her? And, due to your father's intervention, walked away, scot-free?''

Meredith's hands ached from gripping the edge of the counter. The only sounds in the kitchen were the labored rasp of her breathing, the obscenely loud tick of the clock, and the hum of the refrigerator. A few seconds ago, she had seen Heath stride past the kitchen window toward the backyard. Now a layer of red dust, kicked up by the television station's van as it peeled from her driveway, hung over the lawn like a pall.

Oh, God. She closed her eyes, her gorge rising as she recalled the cruelly flung taunts of the reporters and Heath's heated responses. *No comment.* Those two words should have revealed nothing. Yet they had. *Pain, so very much pain.*

Suddenly so many things seemed clear to her. Heath's dedication to law enforcement. His passion for working with teenagers. The rehab programs he'd started. His determination to reduce teenage highway fatalities, even if it meant sacrificing his career.

At the back of her mind, Meredith knew she had plenty of her own problems to deal with, that she should be more concerned about Sammy being seen on television than about Heath. But, somehow, knowing that and convincing herself of it were two different things. *Is it not true that you were responsible for your sister's death, that you did, in fact, murder her?*

Her palms had gone sticky with sweat. She drew her hands from the counter, working her cramped fingers as she walked to the utility porch. The back door didn't creak as she opened it. The screen, also repaired, swung easily on its new hinges. When she stepped outside, the porch didn't groan in protest. *Heath.* Everywhere she looked, everything she touched reminded her of all that he had done for them. *Is it not true that you did, in fact, murder her?* She couldn't let him deal with that alone, the devil take the cameras. There would be plenty of opportunity to worry about that later.

She found Heath out behind the woodshed. Unaware of her approach, he was leaning against the trunk of a gnarly oak, his gaze fixed on some distant spot on the horizon. The mountains, possibly? She wondered if he were imagining himself far away from here, insulated from his troubles. She did that sometimes, taking a hiatus from reality.

"Heath?"

He didn't seem surprised by the sound of her voice, merely angled her a look over his muscular shoulder. He still wore his uniform shirt. She guessed he had stopped here to unload the lumber before going home to change. She seldom saw him in lawman garb. Until now, she'd never wondered why. Had he sensed that seeing his badge and gun made her uneasy? That was so like him, always sensitive to her and Sammy's feelings.

A tight, choking sensation filled her throat. "Oh, Heath, I'm so sorry. I, um . . . heard what that reporter said. And I'm—" She broke off and gulped. "I thought you might need to talk."

"What about?" he asked in a voice gone gruff with emotion. "Arkansas, maybe?"

There was no mistaking his meaning. As long as she kept secrets from him, he would feel uncomfortable sharing his with her. She guessed she could understand that, and there was nothing she could do to change it.

She hugged herself, rubbed her arms. It was a warm evening, yet she felt a chill, probably from the frigid blast of his eyes. *Stupid*. She shouldn't have come out here. There were walls between them, impenetrable walls.

"I'm sorry. I just thought—maybe—you'd want to—you know . . . unload."

His gaze remained fixed on hers, relentless and denuding. Seconds passed. Long, seemingly endless seconds. The wind picked up, ruffling his dark hair and plastering his shirt to the hard contours of his torso. He looked as solid as the tree against which he leaned, able to withstand almost anything. But even giant oaks could fall.

Still hugging herself, she turned to go.

"Don't," he said hoarsely.

She looked back, not entirely sure if he was asking her to stay. What she saw made her feel like Lot's wife, turned into a pillar of salt for glancing back.

There were tears in his eyes.

"It's true," he bit out. "I killed her. As surely as if I'd held a gun to her head and pulled the trigger, I killed her. You still want to stay?"

Meredith had already guessed that much, and her heart broke for him. He'd been only nineteen years old, the reporter had said. That a long time ago. But Meredith knew from experience that one monumental mistake could haunt a person for the rest of his life. There was no going back to change things. You just had to live with it. Her mistake had been in saying two little words: "I do." His had been to climb behind the wheel of a vehicle while he was under the influence.

Brief seconds in time. A momentary lapse in good judgment. Life was like a blackboard, your actions the chalk marks, and God supplied you with no eraser.

"I'm so sorry, Heath."

It was all she could think of to say.

His mouth twisted, the slashes in his lean cheeks cutting deep and making him look suddenly haggard. He dragged in a breath, sounding as if he were inhaling ground glass.

"It's always hard for me on this date," he rasped out. "Stupid, right? It's been almost twenty years. It shouldn't even bother me anymore."

If that had been the case, he wouldn't have been the man he was. A caring man who felt things deeply. Judging by the look in his eyes, he would take the memories with him to the grave. That alone was punishment enough. Those reporters dredging it up had been cruel. Anything to get a story and jack their ratings up.

"Some things never stop hurting," she said softly. "The

fact that it still bothers you tells me you're a good person, not a stupid one.''

"Good?"

He moved to brace his elbow against the tree and cupped a hand over his eyes. His broad shoulders jerked. The sob that followed was so awful—so deep and wrenching—that she took an involuntary step toward him.

"Jesus!" he cried brokenly, the word both a prayer and a curse.

She could tell that he was humiliated beyond bearing that he was losing control in front of her. She didn't know whether she should stand fast and watch, which would undoubtedly humiliate him even more, or if she should go back in the house.

"Oh, Jeee—sus!"

Meredith couldn't stand it. She moved closer and touched his arm. He flinched as if she'd burned him.

"Go!" he ordered harshly. "I don't—want you—to see me—like this.''

"I can't," she whispered, tightening her hand on his arm. "I can't.''

He grabbed her then. Violently, roughly, his arms coming around her so forcefully that they slammed the breath out of her. Then, like steel vises, they clamped shut, flattening the soft roundness of her body against the inflexible flatness of his. One of his hands curled over her shoulder, his fingers compressing with such strength that she feared her bones might break.

"Bill's right. I murdered her!" he cried, the words shuddering up from his chest. "Even my own father said as much. I murdered her!''

"Oh, Heath, no . . . it was an accident." She knew this man too well to doubt that, even for an instant. "Don't do this to yourself. Don't.''

He wept then as only a strong man can, every tear wrung from him like beads of moisture from a barely damp cloth. Meredith clung to him. It was all she knew to do, simply to hold on until the storm passed. Every time he sobbed, she felt it—a deep, tearing pain low in her center. The rigidity of his body was frightening, his embrace almost painful.

When at last his arms loosened around her, she felt bruised, as though she'd been sandwiched between two cement slabs. He gentled his hand on her shoulder, lightly caressing the throbbing pressure points where his fingers had dug in. She could almost feel him returning to awareness, inch by torturous inch.

"Christ. Did I hurt you?"

It was so like him to think first of someone else. She kept her face buried against his shirt. "I'm fine."

He ran a hand lightly over her back. "I'm sorry, honey. I—" He broke off, a residual shudder wracking his body. "I lost it there for a minute. I'm sorry."

Meredith eased back to look up at him. His burnished face was tracked with tears, his dark lashes spiked. She ached to trail her fingertips over his cheeks and smooth his hair, to comfort him as she might have Sammy. But being embraced made her feel claustrophobic, and she sensed that he wouldn't appreciate her trying to mother him.

"We all lose it sometimes," she said, stepping back as she spoke to escape the loop of his arms.

He let his hands fall to his sides. "Yeah, I guess." His larynx bobbed, the constriction of his throat making a hollow *plunk*. "Some of us lose it worse than others." He tried to laugh, a bitter sound that conveyed embarrassment rather than humor, then jabbed his fingers through his hair. "Sorry about that. It's, ah, been a bitch of a day."

"There's no need to apologize. That was a pretty ugly scene that took place out there. Reporters!" She hugged herself again and rubbed her arms. "They're like sharks, aren't they? Give them the scent of blood, and they're merciless."

"Yeah, especially when they have an ax to grind." He gave a hoarse, humorless laugh. "I have to hand it to him. He waited to take his shot when he knew it would do the worst damage."

"Bill, you mean?"

He pressed his back to the tree, resting his head against the bark and closing his eyes. After a moment, he said, "He said the station got wind of the story from a very reliable source. That's an understatement and not exactly true. It was an *inside* source, namely Bill himself. I knew he'd spring it on me, sooner or later. We used to be friends, way back when. He was there the night she was killed."

"And he waited all these years to come public?" Meredith asked incredulously.

"He probably would have carried the knowledge to his grave," Heath told her. "But four years ago, I arrested him for drunk driving. Afterward, his whole life fell apart. He'd been a closet alcoholic for years, I guess. When I pulled him over, he'd been on a downhill skid, drinking more heavily, having problems at home. When it all came out, his popularity with the viewers plummeted, and he lost his job as evening news anchorman at another television station. After seventeen years of marriage, not even his wife stood by him. Like most alcoholics, instead of blaming his drinking problem, he blamed me. Still does. I'm surprised it took him this long to get his revenge."

Meredith dug her toe into the layer of decomposing leaves that had fallen from the oak last fall. The pungent smell of earth and decay drifted up to her. Great garden compost, she thought inanely. God help her, she didn't know what to say to him.

"Her name was Laney," he said huskily.

His words drifted between them, leaden with sadness and so sharp at the edges they seemed to lacerate.

"She was only seventeen." He dropped his chin and opened his eyes, which had gone dark with suffering. Meredith had a feeling that he was no longer even with her, that the essence of him had departed and traveled back through the years to another time and another place. "She died nine days before her eighteenth birthday. She never had a chance to fall in love, get married, have kids. Just like that, her life was snuffed out."

"And you've been blaming yourself for it ever since."
Guilt was something Meredith understood. It had become
her constant companion these last few years, so familiar it
was almost like an old friend.

"Damn straight I blame myself. You heard Bill. I killed
her."

"That's why you work with teenagers, isn't it? Why
you've taken so much heat for breaking up their drinking
parties and not arresting them?"

"It happened at a drinking party."

The instant the reporter had hurled those accusations,
Meredith had deduced that. Knowing Heath as she did, that
was the only explanation that made sense to her.

"I had come home from college," he went on, "to attend her high school graduation party, an all-night kegger
at the gravel pits. There were bonfires, booze. Everyone
there got drunk, me included. Me, most of all, maybe. I
was a cocky little shit back then." He swiped his shirt
sleeve under his nose. "Hated the courses I was taking in
school, hated my dad for making me take them. It was the
weekend before my finals week, and I'd been doing a slow
burn for months. The resentment had come to a head. I
don't know what I was trying to prove by drinking myself
stupid, but that's what I did."

He shrugged and gave a low, bitter laugh.

"I knew my father would be royally pissed. I guess at
that point in my life, pissing him off was enough of a reason to do almost anything."

Meredith thought of her own father, of how much she
had loved him and still did to this day. "It doesn't sound
as if the two of you had a very good relationship."

"A relationship with Ian Masters? He said, 'Jump!' and
his kids were supposed to ask, 'How high?' "

"And you were finished with that?"

He sighed and pinched the bridge of his nose. "He
wanted me to be a hotshot attorney, to follow in his footsteps. But I was raised here." He waved a hand at the
surrounding fields. "From the age of eleven, this was all I

knew, and I wanted to be a rancher. If I went to college, and I wasn't any too sure I needed to, I wanted to attend OSU, major in agriculture, take some backup courses in animal husbandry. He wouldn't hear of it. No son of his was going to wade around in cow shit for a living.'' He lifted his hands. ''We argued. He compromised. He made me enroll at the U of O, hoping that I'd change my mind once I got a year of preliminary law under my belt. I didn't.''

''So you got drunk.''

''I got drunk,'' he said with a nod, gazing across the field behind her house. ''It wasn't the first time. I spent most of my freshman year at university either drinking or hung over. When I got into trouble with the law, my father greased palms, bailed my ass out, managed to sweep it under the rug. He didn't want any marks on my record to prevent me from practicing law.'' He fell silent for a moment. ''God, he was a self-centered bastard. The heartbreak of it was that Laney yearned to become an attorney, to follow in the Masters' tradition. Go to Harvard, graduate with honors, become as famous as our dad. She would have done it, too, if only he would have let her. But, oh, no. She was a girl. She had to become a teacher, like our mother. Every single time she broached the subject of law school with him, he shot her down.''

Meredith was getting a very bad picture of Heath's father—self-centered, overbearing, chauvinistic. ''Your dad doesn't sound like a very nice man.''

''He's a selfish man. Nice? Maybe. But you'd have to dig deep to find it. I don't think he meant to be cruel. He just saw it his way, nothing could change that, and I was determined to try. Unfortunately, I chose all the wrong ways, and my little sister ended up dead.''

''How did it happen, Heath? Can you talk about it?''

''Well, now, Arkansas,'' he said softly. ''That's a good question. I've never tried.''

Again, his meaning was clear. He was telling her things he'd never told anyone. Meredith averted her gaze.

"Maybe it's time," he went on. "They say talking about stuff like this can help. Personally, I always thought that was bullshit. But doing it my way hasn't worked, and I'm—tired."

Tired. She knew what he meant. Sick to death weary. Unable to handle it all on your own any longer. "Tired" was as good a word to describe it as any, she guessed.

"Some of it's hazy. The stuff that happened beforehand. You know? It's like that one moment erased everything else."

Meredith drew a deep breath. Inside she was shaking, but she forced herself to appear calm. "Just start with what you can remember."

He frowned slightly. "Someone challenged me to some four-wheel-drive competition. I don't even remember who. Isn't that nuts? The decision that led to my baby sister's death, and I can't remember how I made it."

"Is it important?"

He made a sound low in his throat. "Yeah. I circle it, you know. Kind of like it's a rattlesnake. Why did I do it? Why? And there's no answer. Afterward, at the morgue, I stood there, looking down at her and—" His voice cracked and he swallowed. "And I couldn't remember *why* I took the truck up there."

"You couldn't have gone back and changed it, Heath. And you'd been drinking. Maybe it's a blessing you don't remember all of that part clearly."

"Maybe." He shrugged. "Anyway, I decided to go four-wheeling. There are lots of roads up at the gravel pits that are used for that, steep spots with bad traction. I and my buddy made some stupid bet. I can't remember how Laney ended up in my pickup with us. She sat in the middle, and I remember she was playing the tape deck. We were on the way up to the steeper slopes. She leaned forward, maybe to change the tape. I don't know. She'd been drinking, too. She had her feet on the console with the floor shift between her knees. Somehow, her foot slipped and hit the accelerator."

The leaves of the oak rustled above them, reminding Meredith of a thousand lost souls whispering.

"My pickup dove off an embankment and rolled. None of us had on seat belts. I didn't get thrown out of the truck, maybe because I had the steering wheel to hold onto."

"Were your friend and Laney both killed?"

"No. My buddy came through it with only a few scratches." He swallowed, hard. "The pickup rolled on top of Laney. Her skull was crushed."

Meredith balled her hands into tight fists. Little wonder this man was determined to curb teenage alcohol use. He had suffered its consequences in the most horrible way possible.

"I tried to lift it off of her," he said, his voice vibrating. "I didn't have the strength, of course. But I was drunk, and in shock, and I just kept trying, screaming all the while for someone to come help me. It was only her head. The rest of her body was clear. I thought if I could just—get her out from under there—you know? That I could fix things, that maybe she'd be all right, if I could just get it off of her."

Meredith gaped at him, her brain freezing as the images crowded in. "Oh, Heath," she whispered shakily. "Oh, dear, God . . . "

His back still pressed to the tree, he slid slowly down the trunk to sit at its base, his arms draped over his upraised knees. "A girl down at the bonfire started yelling that there'd been a wreck and somebody needed to call the cops. That was all it took, the word 'cops.' Kids piled into cars and trucks, onto motorcycles. Two high school boys on a three-wheeler collided head-on with a juniper. It's a wonder they weren't killed, too."

"You mean they all just *left* you?"

"Panic took hold. They had no way of knowing how bad Laney was hurt, and kids react that way. They're drunk, not thinking clearly. Running is instinctive. They don't want to get caught drinking. The legal repercussions are stiff, and they're scared to death of what their folks may do when they find out. Yeah, they left me.''

He rubbed a hand over his face. Meredith stared at the furring of dark hair that fanned over his wide wrist to his fingers, the strands shimmering in the fading light like threads of silk. She'd always seen him as being bigger than life, a towering powerhouse of invincible masculinity. Now she realized that in his way, he was just as vulnerable to pain as she was.

''A deputy sheriff came. Peeled me away from the truck. I think I had gone into shock. When they pulled Laney clear and tried to take her to the ambulance, I went crazy.'' His face tightened, the grooves at each side of his mouth deepening to slashes. ''Our mom died when she was ten, I was eleven. From then on, I was always the one she came to for comforting. Scraped knees. Later, over boy trouble. I'd always fixed everything. You know? And I went crazy. They wouldn't let me try, wouldn't let me touch her. And I was convinced she'd get okay if I could just reach her. There were a few obstacles in my path, cops, paramedics. I went through them like they were a half-ass defensive line. The ones who tried to stop me—hell, I don't know. They didn't stay in my way for long. I was a pretty stout boy, and my adrenaline was high.''

Meredith closed her eyes, feeling sick.

''I tried everything—calling her name, giving her mouth-to-mouth. They couldn't pull me off her. A bunch of them jumped me, pinned me down. Then somebody jabbed me with a needle. After that, I must have been a walking zombie. I can't remember but bits and snatches, like the worst parts of a terrible nightmare.''

''And they didn't charge you with any crime?'' Meredith could almost picture Heath going berserk, knocking men out of his path. ''Not assault or—anything?''

''My dad was an important man.'' He grimaced and shook his head. ''God, my dad. He's in town right now. He's going to shit when he sees the news tonight. I just pray it doesn't go to a major network. He was a son of a bitch as a father, but he doesn't deserve this. It could destroy his career.''

Just the thought of that camera footage being aired by a major network made Meredith's blood run cold. She shoved away the panicky feeling, telling herself it was highly unlikely.

''You mean it's true, then? Your father actually bribed the cops?''

Heath rubbed his thumb back and forth over his fingertips. ''Money talks. The great Ian Masters has never lacked for the green stuff.''

''You speak of him as if he's famous or something.''

Heath flashed a bitter smile. ''That's my dad, famous. You've never heard of Ian Masters, the legendary defense attorney?''

''Legendary?'' Meredith's heart stuttered. ''No, I guess not.''

''Let me think.'' He snapped his fingers. ''That senator who killed his wife. You remember him? I can't remember what state. He kept her in the freezer for over a week, then fed her to guests at a barbecue.''

''Oh, my stars!'' Meredith clamped a hand to her waist. ''That's horrible.''

''Yeah, well . . . it happened, and my dad took his case. And that woman who moved all over the country, marrying old men and then murdering them for their money? He got her off on an insanity plea. Just about any famous case you've read about, and you can bet my father was asked to take it. Now that he's older, he picks his battles, but he's still one of the biggest names in the nation. He's licensed to practice in twenty-three states. It would be big news if somebody could get the goods on him.''

What on *earth* had she stumbled into, here? Just moving in next door to a Podunk county sheriff had been bad enough. Now she discovered that this particular county sheriff was not only smack dab in the middle of a recall scandal, but the son of someone famous? Oh, God. Money talked, all right, loudly and autocratically. She needed to pull up stakes—get the hell out of here—but without money, she couldn't.

Chapter 12

The minute Meredith reentered the house, she went to get her purse off the top of the refrigerator. Pulling out her checkbook, she sat at the table and stared at the last bank balance she had entered. It was barely enough. To make another move right now, she really needed to save more. Ideally, she should get the car fixed before she left, and there wasn't money for that. She could, however, afford to make the trip if she had to, covering the cost of traveling fuel, food for Sammy along the way, utility deposits in the next town, and renting another house.

It would be tight. She didn't kid herself. No eating in restaurants, and they'd have to sleep in the car. But she could swing it. If she purchased a new battery, the Ford would probably make it if she babied it along, driving slow and watching the oil level. She'd be taking a chance that it might break down, of course, but in life-and-death situations, you sometimes had to gamble.

Relieved that she could at least see her way clear to get out of here, she tossed the checkbook aside and buried her face in her hands. Now all she could do was wait to see the news. If the picture of Sammy was clear enough for someone to positively identify her, she'd pack during the night and come morning, they would leave.

The sound of Heath unloading lumber drifted in to her from outside. She wondered if he still intended to start working on the utility room floor tonight. Probably not. She hoped not, at least. The thought of having to keep up appearances while he was here, pretending her nerves weren't raw, would be torture.

She breathed in and slowly exhaled, struggling for calm. She would deal with this, she told herself. If it looked as if they might be in danger staying here, at least it was possible for them to leave. If not, and she decided to stay, she needed to keep her head down from now on, and Sammy's as well. When Heath was here, neither of them could be out in the yard with him, just in case another television crew showed up to interview him. *Ian Masters, the legendary defense attorney.* Talk about a mess. When a high-profile individual became involved in a scandal, news crews moved in like vultures. Hopefully, Ian would be the one they hounded the most, not Heath.

Everything hinged on that news footage of Sammy now. And all she could do was wait.

Slowly Meredith fought off her initial panic and began to feel better. It was easy to overreact when so much was at stake. And that was what she was doing, overreacting. There was a strong possibility that television viewers would be able to see Sammy in the background if that camera footage was aired. But how likely was it that the picture of Sammy would be clear? And, even if her features were distinguishable, how great were the odds that Glen Calendri would see the broadcast?

Shortly after seven that evening, the phone rang. Her hands covered with cookie dough, Meredith grabbed the receiver with only her thumb and index finger.

"Hello?" She tucked the phone under her chin and leaned sideways to grab a towel to clean her hands. "Kenyon residence."

"Hi, there, Arkansas."

Meredith smiled in bewilderment. "Heath? I figured you would have settled down to watch television by now and be sound asleep."

"I kept one eye open to catch the six o'clock news."

She tightened her grip on the phone. "And?"

"I was on there, in living color."

"How bad was it?"

"Not as bad as I expected. A lot of speculation, no real proof to back it up. Their reliable *source* refused to make further comment." He grew quiet for a moment. "I guess maybe the friendship between Bill and me isn't totally gone, after all. His conscience must have eaten at him."

"As well it should. When you arrested him, you were doing your job. What he did today was sheer meanness."

"Yeah, well. He blew smoke but no fire. There were a lot of kids at that graduation party, all of them adults now. He could have claimed it was any one of them and driven the knife in deeper. Knowing what he knows, I can understand how my arresting him must stick in his craw."

Meredith could as well. Heath ran a zero-tolerance county, and Bill, who had suffered so much because of it, undoubtedly remembered Laney's death and saw Heath's policies as being hypocritical.

"The insinuations won't do my reputation a world of good," he went on, "but I don't think they'll do me much harm, either."

"That's good." Meredith was dying to ask about the background details and whether Sammy had shown up clearly on the footage.

"Remember when I told them to leave me the hell alone? They blipped the 'hell' out, making it seem like I said something a lot worse. Can you believe it? As if I'd be that stupid when they had a camera on me. I never realized how much sheer trickery and illusion goes into the news."

"That is pretty underhanded."

He grew quiet for a moment. "Oh, well. That's what I get I guess, running for public office and then bucking the establishment. I honestly didn't call to complain. I just thought Sammy might enjoy seeing herself on television. They'll probably run the footage again at eleven. Can she keep her eyes open until that late?"

Meredith's stomach tightened. "Probably not. She generally nods off about nine, at the latest."

"I'll record it for her then."

"Did they, um, get a closeup of her?"

"Nah, just a background shot. Pretty fuzzy. But she won't care. She'll know it's her and get a kick out of it."

Meredith sagged with relief and smiled. "Yeah, she probably will. It'd be neat if you could record it for her." She leaned against the counter, wanting to hoot with joy. No trip in that rattletrap car, after all. "How did the wind blow for your dad? Any indication that they may pursue the bribery accusation?"

"I wouldn't put it past them. As long as their source won't talk, though, they can't make anything stick." He gave a humorless chuckle. "Dad already called me. The last time we talked was Christmas, and as always, I called him, if that gives you any idea how pissed off he is. Called me a screwup, among other things. Said all the big boys would pick up the story and that it would irreparably damage his sterling reputation. Christ! I'd almost forgotten what a jerk he is. Not one word about what it must have been like for me, having it all dredged up again. Bottom line is, he doesn't care. You'd think, at thirty-eight, I would have figured that out by now."

Meredith leaned a shoulder against the refrigerator, feeling weak at the knees. *The big boys.* Oh, God, she prayed Heath was right, and that shot of Sammy wasn't very clear. A long silence fell over the line.

Then, as if he sensed her agitation, he said, "I'm sorry, honey. I've upset you, haven't I?"

Honey. There it was again, that offhanded endearment that always made her think of her dad. In many ways, the two men were a lot alike, she guessed, both of them big and rugged, yet wonderfully gentle.

"Why on earth would I be upset?"

"I've been blowing off a lot of steam."

She rubbed her temple. "Don't worry about it. I know this is a bad time for you."

"Is it being on television that's bothering you, then?"

This man was far too intuitive. "Heath, I'm not upset!" She tried to laugh. "Except on your behalf, of course. It'll be kind of fun for Sammy and me, seeing ourselves on television. I'll try to keep her awake. If not, maybe she can watch the video at your place soon."

"Don't you have a VCR?"

"No. I'm not much for watching movies."

She could almost hear him smiling. "Right. And the cost of a VCR has nothing to do with it."

"That, too, I suppose." Meredith stared at a cupboard handle, the beginnings of a headache throbbing behind her eyes. "A VCR is something of a luxury item."

"A good many people in this country would argue the point."

Her hand tightened on the receiver. "Well . . . you caught me in the middle of making cookies, Heath. I should probably get back to it."

"Is that anything like biscuit making?"

She smiled in spite of herself. "There are certain similarities, yes. Would you like to join us?"

"You've got to be kidding," he said with mock horror. "Catch you later, honey. Happy KP duty."

After dropping the receiver back in its cradle, Meredith leaned over the counter, resting her throbbing head on her folded arms.

After Heath hung up the phone, he frowned and directed his gaze at the living room window. Through the glass, he could see Meredith's house outlined against the darkening sky.

He'd gotten the distinct impression from talking with her that she was upset, and the only reason he could think of was that news broadcast. Her reaction disturbed him.

He shook his head, laughing at himself for the direction his thoughts were taking. He'd been wearing a badge for too long, he guessed. Getting paranoid. Meredith Kenyon was no criminal, he'd stake his life on that, which brought him full circle back to his suspicion that she was hiding from her husband. She was probably terrified her ex would see the television spot, learn her whereabouts, and come looking for her.

He wished she could be up front with him about that. In time, maybe she would be. Until then, all he could do was be patient.

Meredith sat in the shadowy living room on the sofa, her hands covering her face. The remote control, which she'd just used to flick off the television, lay beside her on the cushion. Just as Heath had predicted, she and Sammy had been on the eleven o'clock news. Given Ian Masters' celebrity status, she feared that even CNN might run the story.

The pictures she'd just seen flashed through her mind. There had been a shot of her carrying Sammy across the yard to the house, but the details hadn't been very clear. Even if the spot went national, the chances that Glen or anyone else might recognize Sammy's profile were almost zilch. As for Meredith, she looked nothing like she once had. She would venture to bet that she could walk right up to Glen in her disguise and not be noticed.

She rose from the sofa and began to pace, rubbing her aching temples with rigid fingers. *Thank you, God.* Meredith was so relieved she wanted to sit back down and dissolve into tears. They'd been lucky. This time.

Now, she just had to make sure nothing like this ever happened again.

Punching in Allen Sanders' phone number on the portable, Glen Calendri remained perched on the edge of his recliner, his gaze fixed on the image that was freeze-framed on his television screen. The phone rang several times before Sanders finally answered, his voice groggy with sleep.

"Calendri, here," Glen said abruptly.

"Boss?" There was a rustling sound at Sanders' end. "It's damned near three in the morning. What's up?"

Glen continued to stare at the television. "I recorded the

news tonight so I could see how I came off when I did that live interview with Paulson. Did you watch it?''

"Yeah, boss, yeah. You came off real good.''

"How about the rest of the news? Did you catch that story about the sheriff out in Oregon? The son of that attorney, Ian Masters.''

"That the same guy who defended Rossi and got him off?''

"One and the same,'' Glen replied.

Sanders yawned, then there was more rustling. "No, I must've missed that part. Why?''

"Because there's a kid in the guy's backyard who looks sort of like Tamara.''

"You shittin' me?'' Sanders' voice lost its grogginess. "Hot damn, boss. You think it's her?''

Glen stared hard at the child's profile. "I can't be sure. It's not a very clear picture. Probably just wishful thinking. Her hair's shorter and—'' He broke off and sighed. "Hell, I can't tell. It's just the feeling I got when I saw it. A sense of recognition. Something about the kid caught my eye. If it hadn't been on tape so I could look at it again, I would've shrugged and forgotten about it.''

"I know it must be tough, boss. You wantin' her back so bad, and all. Kind of natural to think you see her sometimes.''

Hardly hearing Sanders, Glen stared hard at the screen. "It *could* be Tamara, though. The woman carrying her doesn't resemble Mary. Dark hair, heavier build, bigger through the bust.'' He reversed the film, then ran it forward again. "The walk is similar. Could be the loose clothing, falsies, a dye job on the hair.''

"You want us to check it out?''

Glen stopped the film at the same place he'd stopped it earlier. He stared long and hard at the child's profile. "It'd be a longshot. Probably a total waste of time and energy.'' He backed the film up, then reran it. "But, hell, why not? Yeah, yeah. I want you to check it out. They're in a town called Wynema Falls. There's a car parked in the driveway

next to the sheriff's rig—a cream-colored Ford sedan, an
'85 or '86. Oregon tag, SAV–235.''

"Just a sec. I need a pen." A second later, Sanders came
back on the line. "Okay, give it to me again."

Glen did so. After Sanders had written down the information, he said, "You got a strong feelin' about this, don't
ya, boss? You believe it could be your little Tamara."

"Yeah, though God knows why. Like I said, I can't be
sure. If it is, her mother must have some kind of connection
with that sheriff. Living with him, maybe."

"Pretty fast work, if it's Mary. How long has she been
gone? Two months?"

Glen's lips thinned in a humorless smile. "Mary is attractive. She's the type some redneck sheriff might go for."

"That could make it sticky."

"Exactly. If it's Mary, you can bet that's why she tied
up with him. Probably makes her feel safe, having him
around. Tell your men to keep their heads low. For now,
all I want is a positive ID, one way or another, on the kid.
If it's not my granddaughter, wrap it up and come home,
nobody the wiser. If you find out that it is Tamara, the
snatch will have to be carefully orchestrated. I don't want
anyone to make a move without my approval."

"Gotcha, boss. You can count on me."

"No screwing up, Sanders. If that *is* my granddaughter,
I want her back, safe and sound, no trouble attached. You
tell your men I'll have their heads if they do anything to
call attention to themselves. I don't want the broad to smell
a rat and run."

Before retiring for the night, Meredith made her nightly
rounds of the house, checking to be sure all the doors were
locked and that all the appliances were turned off. That
done, she stepped into Sammy's room. As she bent over
the bed to tuck in the covers around the child, she noticed
that Sammy was smiling, even in her sleep.

Tears of gratitude sprang to Meredith's eyes, and she
sank onto the edge of the mattress to gaze at her daughter

and send up a silent prayer of thanks. They didn't have to leave. Things could go on as they had been, at least for a while longer. Her sense of relief was so great, it almost filled her with trepidation. She cared more for Heath Masters than she wanted to admit.

Knowing him had brought a lot of problems into her life, but with the problems had also come blessings. As a young girl, Meredith had fantasized about falling in love one day with a stereotypical Mr. Right. Someone tall, dark, and handsome who did wonderfully romantic things, namely bringing her roses and singing her romantic love songs. After meeting and marrying Dan, she'd quickly come to realize those had been childish imaginings, as far from reality as life could get. End of story.

But was it?

Meeting Heath had made her start to believe in the impossible again. He was definitely tall, dark, and handsome. He hadn't presented her with roses, of course. But he had sung a beautiful love song outside her window. *Old Mc-Intyre had a farm.*

She nearly giggled, remembering how ridiculous he'd looked, doing a duck waddle around her front yard and mooing like a cow. What mother could witness that and remain untouched? All her life she'd heard the old saw that the way to a woman's heart was through her child. It had definitely proved to be true in her case.

There were so many things she wanted for her little girl. A home filled with the sound of laughter. A sense of family, of security, of connection and roots.

Heath cared deeply for Sammy. That was evident every time he so much as looked at her. And sometimes, when he looked at Meredith, she sensed that he was developing a deep fondness for her as well. Wasn't it possible that there was a reason he had come into their lives? Maybe it hadn't been a disastrous twist of fate that had led her to rent this house, after all, but divine intervention.

Meredith was almost afraid to hope, but by the same token, she was so horribly tired of having no hope at all.

Heath was no fairy-tale hero, that was true. He couldn't perform magic and fix all that was wrong in her life. He certainly couldn't make her past disappear in a puff of smoke. But was it so wrong of her to wish that maybe, by some miracle, she'd met him for a reason?

Hugging herself, she fought the feelings that were sweeping through her. Against ordinary odds, Heath Masters could probably wade in swinging and come out an uncontested winner. But not even he could do battle with her dragons.

A sudden thump against the window glass jerked Meredith from her thoughts. She eased up from the bed to sweep aside the curtain and peer out into the darkness. *What on earth?* As she pressed her nose to the glass, she could barely make out a blur of black just outside the window. She smiled and tugged up the sash.

"Goliath, what on earth are you doing here?" she whispered. "Sammy's asleep."

Not waiting for her to step back, the Rottweiler hooked his front paws over the window sill and leaped into the bedroom, nearly knocking Meredith down in the process. After licking her hand as if to apologize for the jostle, he trotted over to jump on the bed. Sammy murmured in her sleep and snuggled close as the dog curled up beside her.

Meredith folded her arms. "You can't stay here," she scolded softly. "Heath will wonder where you are and worry himself sick."

The dog whined and rested his head on Sammy's shoulder, giving Meredith what she'd come to think of as his "boo-boo-eyed" look, his expression mournful and pleading. She smothered a smile and shook her head. "It won't work," she whispered. "I have a heart of stone."

Goliath whined pathetically, prompting Meredith to sigh. It would be a simple enough thing to call Heath and tell him where the dog was, she supposed. Heath had been dropping Goliath off at her house every morning before work, anyway. What difference would it make if the dog spent the night? Sammy would be tickled pink when she woke up to find her canine friend in bed with her.

"All right," Meredith conceded. "But understand, it's only this once. You can't make a habit of it. You're Heath's dog, not ours, and he won't take kindly to our stealing you away from him."

Still wide awake and staring at the bedroom ceiling, Heath answered the telephone on its second ring. He glanced at the luminous red display of his digital alarm clock. *Twenty of twelve?* It had better be damned important.

"Masters, here," he said, putting as much growl into his voice as he could muster. "What's up?"

"Heath? It's Meredith. I hope I didn't wake you."

"No, I'm still up." Pleasantly surprised to learn it was Meredith calling, he nearly smiled. Then he remembered what time it was and frowned instead. "Is something wrong, honey?"

"No, no. I just called to tell you Goliath is here."

Heath shot a look at his open bedroom window. *Damned dog.* The smile he'd squelched a moment before spread slowly over his mouth. Maybe he shouldn't complain too loudly about the Rottweiler's obsession with Sammy, not when it resulted in late-night telephone calls from his favorite lady.

"Uh-oh," he said, trying his best to sound remorseful. "I opened my bedroom window again. The house is warm tonight. I guess Goliath bailed out when I wasn't looking." He pushed up on an elbow and raked a hand through his hair, which felt as if a high-speed mixer had given it a stir. "If he keeps this up, he's going to find himself doing time in that new kennel, after all."

"Oh, no. I didn't mean to—"

"I'll be right there to get him," Heath broke in. "Just give me a couple of minutes to get dressed, all right?"

"That really isn't necessary."

"It's not?"

"No. He's already settled in with Sammy for the night,

and he won't be a bother. I just wanted you to know where he was so you wouldn't fret.''

Fret? Just when he thought he was growing accustomed to the way she talked, she threw him another quaint-sounding word. How long had it been since he'd heard anyone say ''fret''? Or was it just her honeyed drawl that made it seem so distinctive?

He settled back against the pillows, wishing he could lie there for hours and simply listen to her voice. Of course, it would have been nicer yet if she were there in bed with him, her head nestled on his shoulder, the soft huff of her breath moving warmly over his skin.

''This way you won't have to drop him off in the morning on your way to work,'' she pointed out. ''He'll already be here.''

Heath enjoyed stopping by her place every morning to drop off the dog. He'd miss not having an excuse to see her on his way into town.

''You sure you don't mind having him?''

''Not at all. Sammy loves him so.''

''He'll shed all over her bed.''

He could almost hear her smile. ''What's a little more dog hair? I'm getting used to it.''

He chuckled. ''Sorry about that. But you can't say I didn't warn you.''

''It's worth it. He's made all the difference for Sammy. Too bad you can't see the two of them right now. They're cuddled up like contented bugs in a rug.''

Heath wound the telephone cord around his index finger, wishing he could not only see Sammy and Goliath, but Meredith as well. Trying to form a picture of her, he decided she was probably wearing that pink bathrobe, her hair lying in soft curls over her shoulders. Suddenly, he found the thought of pink chenille extremely seductive.

''I think it must be true love,'' he said, his voice turning oddly husky. ''I've never seen a kid and dog so taken with each other.''

She took a moment to reply. "It definitely seems to be a match made in heaven, doesn't it?"

"Yeah, it sure does." *And what about us?* Heath nearly asked. *Are you feeling what I'm feeling? Or is it only me who's losing his mind?* Instead, he said, "Thanks for calling me, Merry. You were right. If I'd woken up and found him gone, I would have been worried."

A brief silence followed. Then, "Heath?"

"Hmm?"

Silence again. Then he heard her drag in a breath. "I, um, just wanted to thank you."

"For what?"

There was a long silence. Then she said, "You and Goliath have been so good for Sammy. It's been ages since I've seen her laugh so much. You can't know how grateful I am."

Why hasn't she laughed? Heath wanted to ask. Then on the heels of that question, another came into his mind. *And what about you, Merry? How long has it been since you laughed?* He had a hunch it had been a very long while, that moments of carefree lightheartedness came all too seldom for her. What she needed was a new husband. Someone to love her. Someone to share her burdens and protect her. Someone whose mission in life would be to make her smile at least once a day.

"What can I say? If she's laughing more than usual, we must be funny guys."

Another long silence ensued. "It'll be midnight soon. May nineteenth is almost over."

"Don't remind me. I still feel embarrassed when I think about this afternoon. My feminine side coming out, I guess."

She gave a startled laugh. "Your feminine side? There's nothing feminine about you."

"Nothing?" He ran a hand over his chest. "These are the nineties, you know. Women don't find macho very attractive."

"You're in trouble, then." She laughed again. "I guess I must not be very modern minded."

Heath grinned. "Can I take that to mean you do find me attractive?"

She laughed again. "If I were in the market for a man, yes."

"Sometimes you don't have to be shopping, you know. Things just happen."

"What does that mean? That you just sort of happened to me?"

"Yeah." He tightened his grip on the phone. Lacing his voice with levity, he added, "Sort of like when you walk across the street and get hit by a truck."

"That's not a very flattering analogy. And I happen to be a very cautious pedestrian. I always look both ways."

"Maybe I came up on you from behind."

She chuckled at that. Then she sighed. "If anyone could, it would be you," she said softly. "Good night, Heath."

The line clicked and went dead. Feeling as if someone had just buried a fist in his solar plexus, Heath hung up the phone. *If anyone could, it would be you.* What the hell had she meant by that? And what was he supposed to do now? Forget she'd ever said it? Probably. The lady was going to drive him bonkers.

I'm a very cautious pedestrian. I always look both ways.

There was something special between them. He felt it every time their gazes met. Yet she seemed determined to run from it. Was she still married? Was that it? If so, why the hell didn't she just say so? There was such a thing as divorce, after all, and he was more than willing to wait.

Heath wished he could sit down with her and discuss it, but so far, she'd shied away from revealing anything personal about herself to him. *Arkansas.* Christ. It was almost as if she'd drawn an invisible line between them, and every time he stepped over it, she panicked.

A part of him was tempted to say to hell with it. But Meredith wasn't just any woman. If she needed more time to get to know him, it was up to him to see that she got it.

How, that was the question. Once he finished the repairs on her house, he'd play heck just trying to see her.

His gaze drifted to his open bedroom window. *Goliath.* All joking aside, the dog's attachment to Sammy might soon become Heath's only remaining link with his neighbors.

Chapter 13

Wind gusted across the supermarket parking lot, whipping Meredith's hair as she leaned over the open trunk of her car to arrange several bags of groceries so nothing would spill. Ever fearful that her wig might blow off, she clamped a hand to the top of her head as she shoved a gallon of milk and a container of bleach into a space next to the spare tire.

"My goodness," she said to a man who was putting groceries into the back of a pickup in the next parking space. "This wind really has a bite this afternoon."

Closing the tailgate of his vehicle, the man tossed her a grin. "That's Wynema Falls for you, warm one day and colder than the dickens the next."

Sammy had just opened the back passenger door to climb inside the Ford.

"Sammy, you hurry and get in the car before you get chilled," Meredith called.

Before Sammy could do as she'd been told, Goliath jumped out. Meredith smiled when the Rottweiler joined her at the back bumper. Ignoring the man next to them, the dog leaped up to sniff the grocery bags in the trunk.

"He wants a dog biscuit, Mommy!" Sammy cried. "Please, can't he have just one?"

Meredith chuckled and rummaged through the bags until she located the large box of Milkbone dog biscuits.

"That's a nice-looking dog," the man observed as he got into his pickup.

"Thank you." Meredith glanced down at Goliath, thinking to herself that "nice-looking" didn't say it by half. The Rottweiler was beautiful. "We think so."

She opened the Milkbone carton and handed one of the dog treats to Sammy. "Don't feed it to him until you're in the car," Meredith told the child. "You're not dressed for this drop in temperature, and I don't want you catching a cold."

Sammy took the biscuit and bounded into the car. "Come on, G'liath. I gots a goody for you!"

Goliath was staring at something behind Meredith and didn't respond.

"Ma'am? Excuse me, ma'am?"

Meredith glanced around. A tall and slender blond-haired man in a charcoal gray business suit was walking toward her. Still holding the box of dog biscuits, she peered at him through the strands of dark hair that had whipped across her face. "Yes?"

Goliath growled, issuing an unmistakable warning. The man halted several feet away, his blue eyes shifting from Meredith to the Rottweiler. "Can you tell me where Maple Street is?"

A prickle of unease danced up Meredith's spine. Goliath had completely ignored the guy in the next parking spot, yet he was snarling at this fellow? She had to wonder why. This man looked harmless enough, a well-dressed individual in his mid to late thirties. What was it about him that made Goliath uneasy?

Meredith honestly couldn't say. She knew from experience how intuitive Goliath could be, though, and if the Rottweiler felt there was something wrong, she would be a fool to ignore him. Now that she came to think of it, she didn't like the way the man was looking at her, or the furtive glances he kept shooting at her car.

"I'm not very familiar with the side streets here, I'm

afraid,'' she told him. ''You'll have to get directions from someone else.''

As she started to turn away, he held up a piece of paper. ''According to my notes, Maple intersects with—'' He broke off at another growl from the dog. ''He's not vicious, is he?''

Meredith looped tense fingers over Goliath's collar. ''He just doesn't care much for strangers. I'm sorry that I can't help you. I don't venture off the main thoroughfares that often, and I've never heard of Maple Street. Maybe someone inside the store can help you.''

Slamming the trunk closed, Meredith hurried around the car to the driver's door, tugging Goliath along with her. The Rottweiler continued to growl until Meredith ushered him into the Ford. She climbed in behind him, not slipping her purse strap from her shoulder until she had pushed down all the door locks. The stranger still stood in the same spot, his gaze fixed on her car windows. Was he trying to see inside?

Meredith dug frantically in her purse for her ignition keys. *Oh, God, oh, God.* A few of her ex-father-in-law's employees looked like thugs, with stocky builds and pugilistic features. But most of them were very ordinary in appearance, their only commonality the suits they wore, spendy, well-tailored and usually gray, just like that man's. They were nondescript fellows, the sort who didn't stand out in a crowd, which allowed them to do Glen's dirty work without getting fingered.

Her hands were shaking as she started the car engine. Not taking the time to fasten Sammy's seat belt, she backed quickly out of the parking place, then jerked the automatic transmission into drive. As she left the parking lot, she watched the stranger in her rearview mirror. He didn't seem to be in any hurry as he returned to his car, an unremarkable gray sedan.

Even the automobile fit the stereotype. They always drove ordinary-looking cars, the better to blend in with traffic.

Her first instinct was to drive away like a bat out of hell. But then a fatalistic calm settled over her. After being seen on the news broadcast the other night, she could be jumping at shadows. For her daughter's sake, she had to know for sure.

At the first stop light on Chandler Way, she shoved the gearshift into park and leaned over the back of her seat to help Sammy with her safety belt. As she fastened the buckle, she searched the line of cars behind hers. No gray sedan.

When the light turned green, she flipped on her signal to turn left and eased into the intersection, trying not to be obvious when she looked in her rearview mirror. She'd leave an easy trail to follow, just in case he was trying to tail her. If she glimpsed a gray sedan behind her, she would know for sure that she and Sammy were in big trouble.

She circled the block, taking it slow, her gaze on her rearview mirror more often than not. After several minutes passed, the tension flowed from her body like water from a spout. No gray car had popped up in the line of traffic behind her.

Three hours later, Heath glanced up from his work to watch Meredith peer out her kitchen window at another car passing by on the road. Talk about edgy. He had a feeling she'd part company with her skin if he yelled, "Boo."

"You expecting company?" he asked.

She turned from the window with a guilty start, her eyes wide. "No. Why?"

He regarded her thoughtfully. "You keep looking out the window like you're expecting someone, that's all. I thought maybe you had guests coming."

"Guests?" She gave a nervous little laugh as she stepped back to the stove to check the roast in the oven. "I'm new here, remember. I haven't made enough friends yet to be expecting company."

That was exactly why he found her behavior so odd.

Resuming his work, he scraped angrily at the utility room

linoleum. The stuff clung to the flooring almost as stubbornly as Meredith did to her secrets. She was upset about something, damn it. But would she admit it? Hell, no. Once again, she wasn't talking, and her reticence was starting to irritate the shit out of him.

He had a bad feeling about this. Was she afraid her old man might show up? It was the only explanation Heath could come up with to explain her behavior, and the thought worried him. She'd never be able to make it to the phone in time to call him if something happened. Didn't she realize that? Stretched out in his recliner with his television blaring or sound asleep in bed, he wouldn't even know she was in trouble. The guy could kick in the door, beat the holy hell out of her, possibly even kill her, and no one would be the wiser.

Thirty minutes later, when Heath knocked off work for the evening, Meredith was still glancing out the window every time she heard a car. Fed up with such nonsense, Heath caught her by the shoulders, forcing her to look at him. As he searched her startled gaze, he realized this was one of the few times he had ever touched her, which didn't say a hell of a lot for how well their relationship was progressing. As he tightened his grip, he couldn't help but notice how fragile she felt, the bones of her shoulders prominent, her arms slender almost to the point of thinness. She wasn't eating enough, he realized. And she had dark circles under her eyes.

"Merry, if you ever need help, you do know you can count on me, don't you?" he asked softly.

She splayed a slender hand on his chest, whether to touch him or hold him off, he wasn't sure. Probably the latter, he decided, which made him bite down hard on his back teeth. She raised her chin a notch, the prideful gesture making her seem even more vulnerable.

"Thank you, Heath. I appreciate that."

Determined to hold her fast, he ignored the light shove of her hand. "Don't brush me off. I really mean it," he said, his voice turning gruff. ''If you need a friend, I'll be there, no matter what.''

She stopped trying to push him away and averted her gaze instead. ''I'll remember that.''

For an awful moment, he experienced an unholy urge to shake her. As if that would solve anything. He had a feeling she'd been on the receiving end of a man's brute strength too many times already.

He finally loosened his hold on her. What other choice did he have? He couldn't force her to accept his help.

Leaving her there alone with Sammy was one of the hardest things Heath had ever done. Once he got home, he found himself doing the same thing she had been, rushing to the window every time he heard a car. None of the vehicles so much as slowed down in front of her house. Somehow, that didn't ease his mind very much.

After about an hour, his patience frayed. He couldn't stand guard over at her place. That much was true. But there was nothing to stop him from sending his dog. If he was right, and she expected her old man to come calling tonight, the bastard would have a big surprise about the time he kicked her door in.

At the back screen, Heath knelt to give Goliath a farewell scratch behind the ears. The intelligence that gleamed in the Rottweiler's brown eyes made him smile.

''Take care of them for me. Okay, partner? If the son of a bitch shows up, rip his balls off.''

Over four thousand miles away, Glen Calendri pressed the STOP button on his VCR remote control, his ice blue gaze fixed on the dark-haired woman and towheaded child freeze-framed on the television screen. Staring at them had become his favorite pastime. A muscle along his jaw ticked as he leaned forward in his chair, narrowing his eyes to better study the blurry images he had recorded. The child definitely resembled his granddaughter Tamara.

The telephone rang just then, making Glen jerk. He swore under his breath and reached for the portable.

"Yes," he barked into the mouthpiece, drawing out the word with serpentine sibilance.

"Hey, boss. It's Delgado."

Frustration mounting, Glen leaned back in his chair. "Well, now, I never woulda guessed that if you hadn't told me. Who the hell else would be callin' me at this time of night?"

"It's only eight-thirty, boss."

"Eleven-thirty here. The time difference, remember?"

"Oh, yeah . . . I forgot."

Son of a bitch. The man was a fucking idiot. "What d'ya got for me?"

"Well, boss, it ain't been easy. We haven't been able to get in close enough yet to get a good look at the kid."

"You want easy, go teach kindergarten. That's why I pay you the wages I do, Delgado. What do you mean, you can't get in close enough?"

"Well, like this afternoon. Nelson walked right up to the broad in a supermarket parkin' lot, but the wind was blowin' like a sonofabitch, and her hair was all in her face. He couldn't see her good enough to tell for sure, you know?"

"Why didn't you just follow her into the store?"

"Well, we sure would've, boss, but we ran into some road construction on the way to town. They let her go through, but held us back. When we finally got to town, we had to drive around lookin' for her car. By the time we finally found it, she had finished shoppin' and was puttin' the groceries in her trunk."

"You find a way to get close. You got that? If that's my grandchild out there, I want her back. Not next week, *now*."

"I read you, boss. Believe me, I read you, loud and clear. Only we got us this little problem. Except for when we tailed her to town, we been watchin' her place ever since we got here this mornin', but the house is half hidden by fences and shrubbery. We can't see into the backyard from any distance with binoculars like we hoped, and there are cow pastures all around her. No kind of cover. We belly-crawled up to her fence late this evening, hopin' to get a better look at the kid while she was outside playin', but a goddamned Rottweiler jumped us.''

"A what?'' Glen asked, not quite able to believe his ears. He looked at the television, his gaze narrowing on the indistinct black dog in the background.

"A Rottweiler. You know, one of them devil dogs. Sonofabitch ripped the seat out of my good suit pants. Now we can't get anywhere close without the damned dog spottin' us. It's like the fucker's watchin' for us.''

Glen straightened in his chair. "Are you tellin' me you can't get close enough to make an ID because of a goddamned dog? *Shoot* the sonofabitch!''

"We can't do that, boss. You said to ID them without raisin' suspicion. We shoot the dog, and somebody's bound to notice.''

Glen pinched the bridge of his nose. *Incompetent idiots.* "All right, all right,'' he said, holding up a hand. "The solution to that is simple. Poison it.''

"We already tried. Went by a farmer's co-op, picked up some really bad shit that they use out here for what they call ground diggers.''

"What the hell is a ground digger?''

"They're sorta like a squirrel. Little brown suckers that burrow in the fields. Anyhow, Nelson put enough poison in a pound of hamburger to kill a horse. The dog damned near nailed him when he snuck up to throw it over the fence. And then the bastard wouldn't eat it! Me and Nelson think maybe it's one of them cop dogs. It belongs to the sheriff, and it's a smart son of a bitch.''

Glen swore under his breath. The dog had an IQ higher than Delgado's, no doubt. "Just walk up and knock on her front door.''

"Knock?''

"It's the simplest way. The dog can't be so vicious it attacks every person who goes to the house, Delgado. They couldn't let it run loose. Chances are, if you just walk up onto the porch like a normal person, instead of trying to sneak, the dog will leave you alone.''

''What if it don't?''

Glen ground his teeth. ''Your family will be well taken care of.''

''What?''

The man truly was an idiot. ''Just try it, Delgado. All right? When the broad answers her door, you'll be able to get a good look at her, and maybe at the kid as well.''

Delgado was silent for a second. ''What'll we say to her?''

''About what?''

''Well, we gotta have us a reason, don't we? For knockin', I mean.''

''Jesus Christ. What am I payin' you two idiots for, to play with yourselves? Make something up, Delgado. Say you're taking a census.''

''A what?''

Glen rolled his eyes. ''Forget that. Tell her you're selling encyclopedias. That'll work. You do know what an encyclopedia is, don't you?''

''Sure. What'd'ya think I am, stupid or somethin'?''

After hanging up the phone, Glen placed a call to Sanders. ''I want two more men on the job in Oregon, Allen. Nelson and Delgado can't handle it, at least not alone. They've encountered a few difficulties, and neither of them is bright enough to screw in a lightbulb, let alone iron out wrinkles.''

''You got anybody special in mind?''

''Get Parker and Matlock. I'd like them out there by morning. They're both sharp. They can get the job done.''

''I don't know if I can book them flights out of here that fast.''

''Use the Lear. It's probably best to go that route, anyway. Not as much red tape when they bring the kid back.''

''If they bring her back. We don't know for sure it's even her yet.''

Glen sighed. ''Yeah, 'if.' '' He glanced back at the television. "I've got a hunch it is, though, and my hunches are seldom wrong."

"Hey, boss? I think maybe I should go out with Parker and Matlock."

"You can't. If that's Mary out there, she'll recognize you, Sanders."

"I'll keep out of sight. It'll be better if I'm there, boss. This is too important to screw up. Parker and Matlock are sharp enough, I guess. But just in case things get sticky, I should be there to ramrod the operation. What'd'ya say?"

"All right." Glen rubbed his forehead. "Yeah, that's a good idea. If that's my Tamara, I'm going to want to do the broad when we snatch the kid. I don't want her taking me back to court to regain custody. Better to get her completely out of the picture."

"We'll have to make it look like an accident."

Glen smiled. "That's your specialty, isn't it, Sanders?"

Chapter 14

Memorial Day weekend, Heath thought grimly, *one of the worst three-day nightmares of the year.* Here it was, only Wednesday, and already the fun had started. The campground looked like a metropolis. Beer coolers and camping gear were strung from here to Christmas, most of it dusty from sitting on garage shelves all winter. Boats of every size and description were down at the boat landing, and all-terrain vehicles were moving up into the surrounding hills in droves. In short, trouble would reign supreme in Wynema County from now until next Tuesday, and where there was trouble, the sheriff had an engraved invitation.

Normally, Heath didn't feel this frazzled until late Sunday evening of Memorial Day weekend, when he'd already survived two days of insanity and was still facing a third. This year, though, he was already in a bitch of a mood before the holiday even began, partly because he knew how grueling the coming weekend would be, but mostly because he'd be working around the clock all this week and well into the next. That would leave him with very little time to see Meredith.

After readjusting his visor to block out the sunlight that slanted through the Bronco's windshield, he resumed the tedious task of filling out a report on the citations he'd just given to two men. *Crazy fools.* What possessed supposedly

mature adults to practice their quick draws in a public
campground? With live ammunition, no less. Give them a
few beers, and some men didn't have enough sense to pour
piss out of a boot with directions on the heel.

"Unit three calling Sheriff Masters." Jenny Rose's voice
boomed over the two-way radio, the transmission unaf-
fected by the range of mountains that lay between Dia-
mondback Campground and Wynema Falls. "Can you
copy? Over."

Heath was tempted not to answer. Five minutes of peace,
that was all he asked, time to sip a steaming cup of coffee
from his Thermos and rest his eyes for a second. There was
no telling why Jenny Rose might be trying to reach him,
the only certainty being that the news would be bad, anything from a shooting to a stabbing to a barroom brawl.

He sighed, grabbed the mike, and keyed it for transmission. "Roger. This is Masters. Over."

"Lower level?" she came back. "Over."

"Affirmative. Over." Heath switched to 7, the frequency
he and Jenny Rose normally used when they wanted more
privacy. He keyed his mike to activate the squelch circuit,
then transmitted again. "Go, Jenny Rose. Over."

"We just had a PC come in for you. I was going to patch
the lady through, but she hung up. Over."

Heath frowned. He seldom received personal calls at the
department, and it was even more rare for Jenny Rose to
patch them through on the air. "What's up? Over."

"She said Goliath bit somebody. Over."

Heath's heart caught. "Come again?"

"She said Goliath bit somebody. No details. She was
pretty upset. Should I send a deputy out that way? Over."

Heath glanced at his watch. It would take him thirty
minutes to get home. If Goliath had bitten someone, the
resultant injury might be extensive. Rottweilers could exert
fifteen-hundred pounds of pressure with their jaws, enough
to snap the humerus in a grown man's arm as if it were a
toothpick.

"Affirmative, Jenny Rose. I'm heading that way. Over."

"The only man I have to send is Moore. Over."

Christ. "That's just great. Isn't there anyone else? Someone who's patrolling out my way or something? Over."

"Sorry, Sheriff. It's been busier today than polka-dots and stripes. Everyone else has his hands full. Over."

He sighed. "All right, send Moore. He's better than a kick in the ass, I guess."

"Roger," she came back. "I'm gone to higher level. Out."

"Ten-four. Out."

Never had the drive home seemed so agonizingly long to Heath. Goliath had bitten someone? Horrible visions filled Heath's head of Sammy with half her face ripped off, or one of her thin little arms mangled. Sweat filmed his forehead, and his hands knotted in rigid fists over the steering wheel. Every awful account he'd ever heard of Rottweilers attacking children came back to haunt him.

He tried several times to make contact by radio with Moore. *No response.* En route, he also talked with Jenny Rose three times, hoping she might give him an update. *Nothing.* So far, Moore hadn't radioed back to inform her of the situation.

"I'm sure it's nothing serious," Jenny Rose assured Heath. "Goliath is a great dog. Why would he suddenly turn mean? Over."

Good question, Heath thought. Still, Goliath was only a dog. Who could say what prompted any canine to bite? Maybe Sammy had poked him in the eye, or pulled his ears, or accidentally stepped on him. Who knew? The possibilities were endless, and with no reports of what had actually happened, Heath's imagination ran wild. Since Sammy and Goliath were nearly inseparable, it didn't take a genius to deduce that Sammy had probably been the recipient of the bite.

What was he thinking? he suddenly asked himself. Sammy could carve that dog into small pieces with a dull knife, and he'd never bite her. Or Meredith either, for that matter. Heath would have bet his life on that. But who else could the dog have bitten?

Her husband. Oh, Jesus. Heath pictured the guy, big and brawny, forcing his way into Meredith's house in a fit of rage. In a situation like that, Goliath might go berserk.

Heath's gut twisted, and nausea surged up his throat. On the one hand, he was glad Goliath had been with Meredith to run interference if there had been trouble, but on the other, all he could think about was the possible consequences.

He whipped the steering wheel hard to the right, turning onto Hereford Lane. Up ahead, he could see the roof of Meredith's house and beyond that, his own. He swiped at the beads of sweat on his brow. *No regrets.* If someone had threatened Meredith or Sammy with bodily harm, it was a damned good thing Goliath had been there. People were more important than animals; that was the bottom line. Especially those two. Heath's heart just broke a little when he considered the price his dog might pay for being so loyal.

As he turned into Meredith's driveway, Heath's first impression was that her yard was packed with vehicles. When he took an actual count, though, he realized there were only three: Meredith's Ford, an unfamiliar blue sedan, and a car from the sheriff's department.

After skidding to a stop, Heath swung out of his Bronco and ran to the house. Standing just inside the living room doorway, Deputy Moore was filling out a report. Heath's gaze swung to Meredith, who sat on the sofa, looking perfectly intact. A short, dark-haired stranger in a badly torn, gray suit jacket paced the floor in front of her, his stormy countenance indicating that he was furious. From somewhere at the back of the house, Heath could hear Goliath snarling and throwing his weight against a door. The sound of Sammy's crying, also coming from the back of the house, added to the din.

"I put Goliath in the bedroom with Sammy," Meredith said in a tremulous voice, her gaze clinging to Heath's. "I,

um . . .'' She gestured at the stranger. ''This gentleman
sells encyclopedias. When he got out of his car, Goliath
just—'' She broke off, lifting her hands. ''It happened so
fast. I was working and didn't even realize anyone was
here.''

The stranger jabbed a finger in the general direction of
Meredith's nose. ''All I did was try to pat your kid on the
head, and that Rottweiler of yours nearly took my arm
off!'' He swung back around to Heath. ''That's all in the
world I did, Sheriff!''

Heath stepped closer to examine the man's arm. Through
the torn layers of the jacket and shirtsleeve, he glimpsed
two puncture wounds. The injury wasn't serious, thank
God, and Goliath had all his immunizations. But even so,
the dog had broken the skin. That was a death sentence for
a retired canine deputy.

Heath felt sick. He glanced at Moore, who quickly re-
arranged his expression to hide the smirk on his face. The
bastard. The only thing the deputy could possibly have
against Goliath was that Heath loved him.

''That's all you did?'' Heath said, turning back to the
angry salesman. ''You just started to pat the child on the
head? It's not like Goliath to bite without reason.''

''Well, he sure as hell did me!'' His dark eyes flashing,
the man held up his arm to drive home the point. ''I didn't
do anything, I tell you. And how the hell do you know the
dog so well? You live around here, or somethin'?''

Heath searched the man's gaze, convinced that he must
have done something more to incite the dog than he
claimed. Something Goliath had interpreted as threatening.

Damn. Heath knew he was grasping at straws. From the
start, Goliath had acted crazy around Sammy. Maybe this
man's trying to pat her on the head was all it had taken to
goad the dog into a rage.

No matter how Heath sliced it, Goliath had broken a
cardinal rule, and there was nothing to do now but face the
consequences.

"Mrs. Kenyon doesn't own the dog," Heath said evenly. "Goliath is a retired deputy."

"A dog cop?" The salesman's gaze dropped to Heath's badge. "He's yours?"

"Officially, he still belongs to the county," Heath explained, feeling as if he were signing Goliath's death warrant with every word he uttered. "I'm his ex-partner and guardian." He pointed toward the living room window. "That house up the road there is mine. Goliath has grown fond of Mrs. Kenyon's little girl, and he spends a lot of time over here."

"A police dog?" the man repeated, as if he couldn't quite grasp it. "I've been bitten by a retired police dog?"

"I'm afraid so, yes."

Here it comes, Heath thought. It wouldn't take the man long to realize the potential for financial gain in a situation like this. A lawsuit, then a big settlement from the county. He'd probably go out for a fancy dinner tonight to celebrate. *Poor Goliath.*

Heath wished he could do something. Anything. If only he could turn back the clock. If he had kept the Rottweiler in his kennel today, maybe this never would have happened.

But it had. And now it was out of Heath's hands.

"I'm very sorry," Heath said. "Goliath has never broken the skin before, not even in the line of duty. I don't know what possessed him."

The salesman ran a hand over his shortly cropped black hair. "Wow." He glanced down at his arm. "A canine cop. I guess I got off lucky. He could have done a lot more damage than this."

That was the heartbreak of it, Heath thought sadly. If a dog like Goliath became vicious, it was a serious liability to the county. That possibility would rest heavily on the minds of the county commissioners when they called a meeting to decide Goliath's fate. They would undoubtedly order Heath to have the Rottweiler destroyed.

"You live right over there?" the salesman asked, leaning

to look out the window at Heath's house. At Heath's affirmative reply, the man glanced down at Meredith. "So you and the sheriff are neighbors then."

Heath drew a card from his breast pocket. "I'll take care of any medical bills you incur. I'm sure you'll want to see a doctor with that immediately."

The salesman flashed a weak smile, looking rather sheepish. He flicked another glance at Meredith and shrugged. "It's just a couple of tooth marks." His smile took hold, spreading across his swarthy face. "I kind of lost my temper, ma'am. I'm sorry for yelling." He ran a hand over his hair again. "The truth is, I should have had better sense. The dog growled to warn me away and I reached toward the kid, anyway."

Heath didn't know what to say. This wasn't going anything like he'd expected. No threats to sue, no blustering. He glanced at Deputy Moore, who looked as nonplussed as Heath felt.

"You really should see a doctor," Heath finally found the presence of mind to say. "A dog bite can become badly infected."

The salesman parted the ripped sleeve of his jacket to peer more closely at his arm. "Nah. A little disinfectant is all it needs. The dog has all its shots, right?"

Heath nodded, not quite able to believe they were getting off this easily. If the man didn't file a complaint, it might make a difference for Goliath when this went before the board.

Moore looked up from his clipboard. "You aren't going to pursue this, sir?"

"I don't wanna get the dog in trouble." The salesman smiled again. "I'm a big fan of dog cops. Watch all the movies about them. And, like I said, it was my own fault. When the dog growled, I should've backed off."

Amazed, Heath turned to watch the salesman move out the front door. Just like that, and the guy was leaving? He hadn't even asked to have the jacket replaced.

Moore stepped to the doorway. "Wait a minute, sir. You never gave me your name."

The salesman stopped halfway to his car to glance back. "Not necessary. Whatever that is you're filling out, just tear it up, okay? As far as I'm concerned, this never happened."

"Did I leave him enough room to get out of the drive?" Heath asked his deputy.

Moore nodded, the frown on his face conveying that he couldn't quite believe the man was leaving. "No figuring people, is there?" he finally said. "Just when you think you've got them pegged, they surprise you."

Heath had to agree. "I guess we shouldn't look a gift horse in the mouth."

"Amen to that." Moore drew the top sheet of paper from his clipboard and crumpled it in his fist. "Well, Sheriff, I guess that settles it. Unless you decide differently, this never happened. Jenny Rose will keep her mouth shut."

The question was, would Moore? Heath was tempted to ask, to even try bribing the younger man. But he quickly discarded the notion. This had to be handled on the up and up. He had taken an oath to uphold the law, not only when it suited him, but always. Oregon had a law governing dog bites. The board of county commissioners had to be notified, and it would be up to them to decide Goliath's fate. Heath could do things no other way and retain the respect of his men.

"It's not quite that simple, Tom. You know it, and I know it."

"Yeah. Goliath's a great dog, though. It's a damned shame."

Heath was surprised to hear Moore say that. Maybe, he decided, the younger man had some good in him, after all.

Tom glanced at Meredith, who had hunched forward over her knees and buried her face in her hands. "Well, I'm no longer needed here. I guess I'll get back to work. Things are hopping today." He touched the brim of his hat. "Nice meeting you, ma'am."

She didn't look up as the deputy left the house. When

the door had clicked shut, she cried, "Oh, Heath, I'm so sorry. Is Goliath in serious trouble?"

As upset as she seemed to be, Heath didn't think it wise to address that issue right then. "It's not anything for you to be worried about, honey."

"What's going to happen?" she asked thinly. "It'll be bad, won't it?"

Heath sighed. "Do we have to get into that right now? Let's just wait to see how things shake out. Sammy's crying. You should go settle her down."

She raised her head, fastening accusing brown eyes on him. "Sammy will be even more upset if something happens to that dog! He could be put to sleep, couldn't he?"

"In Oregon, dogs are allowed only one bite. The second time, they're usually euthanized, yes."

"I hear a 'but' hanging on the end of that."

Heath sighed, resigned to the fact that she wasn't going to let this drop until he leveled with her. "Given Goliath's training, the county may decide the risk is too great to give him a second chance."

What little color remained in her face slowly drained away. "So he'll be destroyed? Just like that? And you'll let it happen?"

"Merry, I don't make the rules, and the decision won't be left up to me."

"Well, that settles it then. You mustn't report this."

Heath felt a monster of a headache coming on. He pinched the bridge of his nose. "I wish it were that easy, Meredith, but it's not. Goliath could be dangerous if he got out of control. His biting someone is a warning signal I can't ignore."

She pushed up from the sofa and started to pace. "He *isn't* mean! You know it."

"I wish I were sure of that. But, goddammit, I'm not. He bit that man. Luckily, he didn't hurt him seriously, but he could have. I can't just turn a blind eye to this and pretend it never happened. The guy did nothing to ask for it. *Nothing!*"

She whirled to face him. "You have to turn a blind eye!"

Heath had the feeling she was about to grab him by the front of his shirt. He gave a humorless laugh. "If this isn't a hell of a note. Not that long ago, you hated that dog and all but accused me of being an irresponsible ass for letting him run loose."

She cupped a trembling hand over her eyes and burst into tears. When Heath tried to reach for her, she pushed his hands away. "That *isn't* fair! Dan's dogs were monsters. It just took me a while to work my way past that."

Heath had no clue who Dan was, and before he could ask, she rushed on.

"I was intimidated by Goliath in the beginning. I admit it. But now I realize how wonderful he is!" She lowered her hand to fasten a tear-filled gaze on him. "Don't you see? This is all *my* fault. I know how protective he is of Sammy. The way he barks every time she's about to do something he thinks may hurt her. The way he watches over her and gets so upset if she seems scared. He loves her so much!"

"Meredith, it's not a question of whose fault it was. Shit happens."

She held up a staying hand. "That dog *knows* how afraid Sammy is of men. He didn't just arbitrarily decide to bite! He was only trying to protect her. You've seen how he acts when she's afraid. Remember the night she had the bad dream? He wouldn't let me near her. It was the same today. She got scared when she saw that man, and Goliath tried to keep him away from her. When the man didn't back off, Goliath bit him. Not *hard*, though. Two little puncture marks. He could have done much worse."

Heath didn't miss the fact that Meredith had finally just admitted her daughter was afraid of men. There had been a time, not so very long ago, when she'd vehemently denied it. On any other occasion, he would have insisted she elaborate.

"Meredith, what exactly are you asking me to do? Lie by omission?"

"What's so wrong with that? There are extenuating circumstances. How do you know that man didn't plan to hurt Sammy?"

"He seemed like a nice enough fellow to me."

"So do serial killers! Little children are kidnapped from their yards all the time. When Goliath worked with you, weren't there times when he alerted you to someone suspicious?"

"Sure he did. But he never attacked anyone unless given the command."

"He isn't a vicious dog."

"In your opinion."

"What does that mean?" she demanded, her voice turning shrill.

"It means I have to think about this. We can justify Goliath's behavior until the cows come home, but it's all just supposition. The bottom line is, I'll be responsible if he hurts someone, and with a highly trained Rottweiler, that's one hell of a lot of responsibility."

"So you'll just let him be put to sleep?" she asked incredulously.

Heath had to clench his teeth to keep from sniping back at her.

Pressing her knuckles against her mouth, Meredith went to the window. She stood gazing out for a long moment. "It's all my fault," she whispered. "If only I'd heard his car. If only I had insisted Sammy play in the house this afternoon."

Heath stepped over to rest a hand on her shoulder. Her body was trembling. "Don't do this to yourself, Meredith."

She gulped and averted her face. "I love him, too," she admitted. "Not as much as you, I know. But I do love him. He's worked miracles with Sammy, and I owe him for that. The thought of him being put to sleep breaks my heart."

Chapter 15

After locking Goliath in his kennel to keep him out of trouble, Heath went into the house, called the department to tell Jenny Rose he meant to take the rest of the day off, and then began pacing the floor. He had a decision to reach, and it wasn't one he could make easily. Goliath wasn't just any dog, but his ex-partner. The Rottweiler had saved his life more times than he could count. Heath could have more easily decided to amputate his right arm than to be instrumental in killing that animal.

Damn. He wasn't sure what to do. A large part of him wanted to follow Meredith's advice and keep this hush-hush. It was tempting. So very tempting.

Finally, as a last resort, Heath telephoned Rich Hamilton, a veteran city policeman and longtime friend who was also providing a home for a retired canine cop. Rich listened quietly while Heath gave him the back story and explained what had happened that afternoon.

When Heath finished speaking, Rich heaved a weary sigh. ''Shit, man. That's a bummer. I can see the dog being protective of the kid. Rambo is so protective of my boy Teddy that I have to keep a really close eye on him. A bigger kid was picking on Ted one afternoon, and Rambo nipped him. Didn't break the skin, but it scared me, all the same.''

Rambo was a great dog, an intelligent, well-mannered

German shepherd. But the dog wasn't another Goliath. The shepherd wasn't as smart, for one thing, and as far as Heath knew, the other dog had never received a single citation.

"I'm so attached to Goliath that it's difficult for me to make a responsible call on this," Heath admitted.

"Hey, buddy, I understand where you're coming from. Rambo is like one of our kids. Diana loves him as much as I do, I think. If something happened and I had to put him down, I'd probably be sleeping on the sofa for six months."

Heath's throat went tight. "I'm going to put you on the spot, Rich. If you were me, would you report the bite?"

Long silence. "Damn. I knew you were going to ask me that." Rich gave a low laugh. "You know what my answer's going to be, Heath. These dogs are wonderful animals until they go bad. Then they're potential killers. If Rambo bit someone, I'd have to report it."

"Even if there were extenuating circumstances?"

"Yeah, even so. There's too big a risk factor to do otherwise. You gotta think of what *could* happen. You know? He's a great dog, and maybe he'll never bite again. But if he does, you don't want it on your conscience. Do you? The guy was just a salesman, for Christ's sake, not a burglar. Maybe then I could say, give the dog another chance. But that isn't what happened."

After a moment, Heath said, "Thanks, Rich. I appreciate your being honest."

"Hey, that's what friends are for, man. If you decide not to report this, the secret's safe with me."

Just as Heath started to hang up, the call waiting beeped. He switched to the other line. "Masters, here."

"Heath?"

He closed his eyes at the sound of Meredith's voice. She was the last person he wanted to speak to right then. "Hi, honey."

"I, um . . . well, I just need to talk to you. About Goliath?"

Surprise, surprise. "Yeah, what about him?"

"I just want to try one more time to convince you that you shouldn't report what happened."

He smiled slightly. Rich thought he might have problems with his wife Diana over Rambo? In Heath's situation, sleeping on Meredith's sofa for the next six months would have been a step up. "I've already made my decision, honey."

"You already turned him in, you mean?"

She made it sound as if he were a Judas. "Not yet. As soon as we hang up."

"Please, don't!"

He clenched his teeth.

"He won't ever bite again. I'm sure of it."

"This isn't going to get us anywhere. I have to do this."

"Why?"

"Because it's the law, and I have to abide by it."

"You bend the law for teenagers all the time. Correct me if I'm wrong, but aren't you supposed to arrest them if they're caught drinking?"

He winced. "That's hitting below the belt."

She fell quiet for a moment. "I'm sorry. I guess it was. It's just—well, you have made exceptions before. All for a good cause, mind you. Isn't Goliath a good cause?"

Her voice squeaked there at the last, and Heath knew she was about to cry. *Christ.* He'd had the occasional relationship over the years, and there had been a few times, none of which filled him with pride, when he'd been responsible for making women cry. But he'd never *cared* this much about any of them.

He felt as if giant hands were grabbing hold of his guts and wringing them like a wet rag. "Merry, sweetheart, please don't cry."

"I'm not."

He knew a sob when he heard one. She was crying, all right, and it made him feel like a jerk. God *damn* it, he didn't need this right now. "Honey, I know you love him. But sometimes we have to set our feelings aside and do hard things. You know?"

"Oh, Heath, they'll put him to sleep! You know they will."

"Maybe not. I'll certainly argue like a son of a bitch against it."

"How magnanimous of you! You know very well they'll still decide to put him to sleep, no matter what you say!"

"Merry, sweetheart—"

"Don't call me 'sweetheart'! You're supposed to be his friend. Some friend!"

With that, she hung up in his ear. After Heath returned the receiver to its cradle, he stood there staring at the phone. He jumped when it suddenly rang again.

When he lifted the receiver, he heard a tremulous voice say, "I'm sorry," before he could even say hello.

"Merry?" Dumb question. How many other bawling females might be calling him to say they were sorry? "Honey, let's not fight, okay?"

"I'm sorry," she squeaked again.

He listened to two sniffs and a gulp, his heart twisting at each sound. "I love him, too, you know," he told her gently. "This is the hardest thing I've ever had to do."

"I know." Gulp, sniffle. "Oh, Heath. I said cruel things. I didn't mean them."

"I know you didn't." He swept a pile of papers off the counter with a vicious sweep of his hand. "I really need you to support me in this. I'm having a tough time."

"I know. I'll try."

"I bottle-fed him. I keep remembering how cute he was. And then all the times he saved my ass. I feel like a bastard."

She made a sound that reminded him of someone sucking air from a whistle. "I support you," she said in a wobbly voice. "I do. I know you're just doing what you feel is right, and I admire you for that."

"Thank you. I need to know that."

"When do you think they'll meet to decide what should be done?"

"Soon, probably. Tomorrow would be my guess. This is

pretty serious business, and they'll get right on it.''

"Will you get to be there?"

"Of course."

"You have to tell them about Sammy, Heath. How protective he is of her. Then, maybe, they'll understand and give him another chance."

"I'll be sure to tell them."

"Promise? Stress to them that he's never offered to bite before."

"I will. I promise."

The whistling sound came again. "Heath?"

He smiled and closed his eyes. Women. Was this what marriage would be like—feeling like a yo-yo on a string? With this particular woman, he wished he could find out. "What?"

"Could you call me when you learn what time the meeting will be?"

"You'll just worry."

"I'll worry anyway. Maybe if I pray a lot while you're at the meeting, they'll give him another chance."

From her mouth to God's ear. If anyone on earth had a divine audience, it had to be her. "All right, I'll call you."

"And when the meeting's over? You'll call me then, too? I'll be pacing the floors, wondering what happened."

"Sure. The first thing I'll do is call you. I promise."

"Don't forget."

As if he could? This lady had taken up permanent residence in his thoughts.

The meeting was scheduled for two o'clock the following afternoon. When Heath called Meredith to inform her of the time, she sounded as if she were talking with a clothespin on her nose.

"So you did it? You reported him."

Son of a bitch. "Yeah."

"Oh."

"Honey, have you been crying all this time?"

"Of course not."

She was a little liar. "It was the right thing for me to do," he said evenly. "You know that, deep down."

"Yes. Now we just have to wait and see what happens. Right?"

"Right."

"It'll be a long night. Won't it?"

"Very." He could think of only one thing that could make it pass more quickly, and she wasn't in the market. "Merry, if you need to talk later, you know my number."

"Same for you."

"I may take you up on it."

"Would you, um . . . well, like to have dinner with us? I fixed plenty."

"I don't think I'd be very good company tonight," he replied. "Thanks for offering, though. I think I'll just spend the evening with my dog. If things go badly tomorrow, this could be my last—well, you know."

"Your last night?" she asked thinly.

"Yeah."

"Oh, Heath. If my car weren't in such awful shape, I'd sneak over there and steal him, then disappear."

She sounded dead serious. Heath smiled. "I don't think that'd be a good idea."

"Don't laugh. I mean it. I've become rather good at doing vanishing acts!"

After Heath broke the connection, he couldn't get the words Meredith had spoken out of his mind. *Vanishing acts?* He felt almost guilty for catching the slip. She was upset right now, not thinking clearly. It really wasn't fair that his law enforcement training kicked in at times like this, enabling one part of his brain to operate on automatic pilot. Otherwise, he might have failed to pick up on what she'd said.

All along, he had suspected that she'd fled from an abusive husband. Now he was certain of it.

Over the years, Heath had seen more women stay in abusive marriages than not, subjecting themselves and their children to hell on earth. He admired Meredith for breaking free. It had taken guts. He had never understood the psychology of battered women. He only knew it was predictable—a characteristic condition and pattern of behavior that led to a mindless sort of resignation and apathy, stemming, he supposed, from relentless fear of reprisal if they tried to leave. Some women did overcome it, but they were in the minority.

No two ways around it, Sammy was a lucky little girl that her mother had found the courage to run.

After bringing Goliath in from the kennel, Heath sat in his recliner, one hand on the Rottweiler's massive head. With every stroke of his fingers through coarse fur, Heath wondered if this would be the last night he ever got to spend with this dog he considered to be his best friend. The thought brought a lump to his throat.

Memories. So many memories. Goliath had once taken a bullet in the shoulder that had been meant for Heath. Another time the dog had saved him from getting his throat slit. There had been other incidents as well. In short, Heath had never had a more loyal friend.

Gazing into his dog's soulful brown eyes, Heath wondered what the hell he was going to do if the board voted to have the animal destroyed.

After tucking under the last flap of the cardboard box, Meredith reinforced the top with wide packing tape. Glancing around her bedroom, she took stock of the few remaining articles of clothing hanging in the closet and lying in the open drawers, the bare essentials she'd left out to wear tomorrow and during the trip.

The word "trip" hung in her mind like a brightly illuminated neon sign. It was a term usually reserved for vacations, and the journey she was about to embark upon was anything but that. Even if the car didn't break down, it was going to be a grueling stint. Nevertheless, she'd been ready to do it to save her own neck and she would do it for Goliath as well. The dog had become like a part of the family, and she loved him far too much to allow him to be destroyed.

Pulling a small duffel bag from the closet shelf, she began packing the toiletries on top of the dresser. In the morning, first thing, she would throw their stuff in the car. No last-minute walks through the house, no grabbing things she nearly forgot. Once she went to the bank to cash out her account, she would be ready to leave town, no looking back.

The car wouldn't hold much, she thought grimly as she left the bedroom and did a slow tour of the house. None of the knickknacks could go or any of the kitchen utensils. Collectively, the whole kit and caboodle hadn't cost that much, but it would still be difficult to replace. The iron and ironing board, the skillets, the coffeepot. She'd spent days combing thrift stores to equip the house, and now she had to walk off and leave everything. It couldn't be helped. What little leftover room there was in the car would be taken up by Goliath.

She had lost her mind, no question about it. First she had kidnapped her child. Now she was planning to steal Heath's dog. But what else could she do? Let Goliath be killed?

No. Over the last six years, there had been a lot of things that happened in her life over which she'd had little, if any, control. But this wasn't one of them, and she was *finished* with not fighting back. That dog had turned her daughter's life around, teaching her to love and trust again, and to laugh when Meredith had despaired of ever hearing her laugh again. Goliath had only been trying to protect Sammy this afternoon. If Meredith let him pay for that with his life, she would hate herself for it until the day she died.

Leaving here had been inevitable, anyway. She'd realized that the first time she saw Heath's Bronco pull into the driveway next door. Living so close to the county sheriff wasn't exactly a healthy situation for a fugitive. True, it would have been better if she could wait. Get the car fixed. Save a little more money. But sometimes life threw a person curve balls, and you did what you had to do and trusted in God.

Somehow, the car would make the trip without breaking down. Somehow, she would get another job and find a place for all of them to stay until she could regain her feet financially. Somehow she'd keep food on the table for Sammy and kibble in Goliath's dish. It wouldn't be easy, and sometimes she might go hungry herself. But somehow she would make it all work.

She moved to the doorway of Sammy's bedroom, her gaze wandering slowly over the contents. Meredith hated to make the child part with all her favorite things again. But better that than to watch Sammy grieve over the death of her canine friend. Toys were replaceable, after all. A dog like Goliath wasn't.

There would be time tomorrow to pack Sammy's clothes and the few small toys that could be stowed in the trunk, Meredith concluded sadly. She would do all the packing on the sly, just in case the board of commissioners surprised her and decided to give Goliath a pardon. In that event, Meredith would slip Sammy's clothes back into her drawers, unpack her own things, and resume the usual routine, with Sammy never suspecting they'd nearly left here.

There was no point in upsetting the little girl unnecessarily.

Not that Meredith believed, even for a second, that Goliath would be forgiven his transgression. Those in positions of judicial power were, in her experience, a blind and dispassionate lot. The law was the law, amen. Even Heath, as kind and caring as he was, had become a slave to his own ethics.

Meredith had revered the law once, almost with awe. And she'd believed in the system, convinced that there truly was justice for all. Acting within the law, she had tried desperately to save her daughter, only to learn when it was nearly too late that Lady Justice sometimes granted her favors to the highest bidder. Since then Meredith's ethics had been dictated by her conscience. She had learned to examine her heart, to hell with the law. Sometimes a person had no other choice.

It wasn't going to be easy for her this time. In leaving Wynema Falls behind, she was also leaving Heath. *Heath*. Oh, God. Until tonight, she'd halfway managed to keep a lid on her feelings for him. Now they were boiling over. Somewhere along the way, she'd fallen in love with him. Head over heels, with all her heart.

It was hopeless, she knew. Today he had proven to her, beyond a doubt, that he was a man of principal. No matter how difficult it might be for him, he would stand behind his convictions, which were intricately interwoven with the law he was sworn to uphold. She was a lawbreaker. All other difficulties swept aside, that one elemental difference was enough to hold the two of them apart.

Thinking back to her childhood and the peaceful summer days she had known as a girl in Mississippi, Meredith wondered how she had ever wound up in a mess like this. She couldn't even contact her parents for fear her calls or letters might be traced. And now she was about to leave a man who'd become as important to her as breathing. Where would it all end?

She imagined moving to another town, trying to create a home in another run-down house, then carefully drilling her daughter on an entirely new set of lies. Mommy's new name, their new past. Trying to explain why Mommy's hair and eyes were suddenly a different color again.

It all seemed overwhelming to Meredith. As she wandered aimlessly through the house, gazing through tears at the bits and pieces of a life she was about to leave behind, she came upon Heath's hammer, lying on the kitchen windowsill.

She closed her fingers over the handle, the wood of which had been polished smooth by the grip of his hand. As silly and sentimental as it was, she decided to steal it, too. A little bit of Heath to take along with her.

Oh, God . . . what had happened to her? How could she care so deeply for a man she didn't dare trust?

*   *   *

Sanders tossed three antacid tablets into his mouth as he lay back against the pillows. As he chewed the chalky substance, he punched 9 on the motel room phone to get an outside line, then placed a credit card call to New York. Glen Calendri answered on the fourth ring, sounding disgruntled and slightly out of breath.

"Have I caught you at a bad time, boss?"

"No." Calendri muffled the phone for a moment, his voice coming through in a hollow rumble as he dispensed with his companion.

While he waited, Allen fingered the fake leather binding on the motel room Bible that lay on the bedside table, idly wondering if anyone had ever actually read the damned thing. In his experience, people came to motels for two reasons, to rest or have sex, not get religion.

"All right, I'm back," Calendri said.

Allen crossed his ankles, his gaze fixed on the toe of one dress sock, which was about to wear through. "We finally got a positive ID on her late this afternoon."

"It is her, then?"

"It's her. No question."

Calendri laughed smugly. "I knew it! We've got the bitch where we want her now. You're positive it's my granddaughter?"

Allen quickly recounted the events of the afternoon. "Delgado's sure. Saw the kid and the woman up close."

"Jesus, why didn't the idiot file charges to get the dog out of the way? They would've quarantined him."

"Too risky," Allen came back. "They could've run a check on his ID, for one. And he was drivin' a rental car. Everybody was so upset over the dog, they didn't check his plates, but they might've if he'd gotten nasty. We'll take out the dog when we go in. Less chance of trouble before the fact that way."

Calendri sighed. Then he chuckled. "The important thing is, we've found the bitch. Right? Now it's just a matter of time till I get my granddaughter back."

Thinking back, Sanders remembered Mary Calendri as she'd been when she first married Dan, fresh out of college, with stars in her eyes. She'd had a smile back then to light up a room. Within a month of her marriage, she'd begun to look like an old woman, her eyes lusterless, her smile strained, her face caked with makeup to hide the bruises. Allen could also remember how nervous she'd been, constantly fidgeting and visibly starting whenever Dan entered the room.

Allen didn't claim to be any saint. Hell, he'd done things that would give other men nightmares. But he drew the line at knocking his old lady around or being mean to his kids. He had pitied Mary Calendri back then and he did now. She'd been incredibly stupid, thinking she could buck Glen Calendri and live. Once you got hooked into this organization, you were hooked for good. There was no way out, unless, of course, you chose to go out feet first.

"How do you want us to take her out, boss? And when would you like it done?"

Chapter 16

After making a quick trip to the bank the next morning, Meredith set her daughter down at the kitchen table to make tissue roses. While Sammy struggled to fashion something remotely resembling a flower with squares of pink tissue and hairpins, Meredith brought moving cartons in from the shed, slipped into the child's bedroom to pack her clothes and then hid the boxes in the closet.

After Sammy went down for her nap, Meredith removed all her nonperishable foodstuff from the cupboards and put it into boxes as well. She left out only two cans of soup, which she figured would suffice as a last-minute meal for her and Sammy before they left town.

When she felt sure Sammy was fast asleep, she began carrying everything to the car, stowing as many of the cartons as possible in the trunk to provide more passenger room up front. When she had finished with that, she checked the Ford's engine oil and transmission fluid to be sure the old car was as ready as it could be for travel.

By then, it was nearly two o'clock. Meredith paced the floors, glancing frequently at her watch to check the time, her nerves raw with anxiety. Heath's meeting with the board of county commissioners would be taking place any minute now. *Pins and needles.* She was so tense that her skin felt prickly.

At least a dozen times, she considered going over to

Heath's house right then and stealing his dog from the kennel. That way, she could be long gone before he even tried
to call her, which would give her a good head start before
he came home this evening and found her gone. The only
thing that stopped her was the remote possibility that the
county authorities might give the Rottweiler a pardon.
Heath loved Goliath, and Meredith couldn't, in good conscience, take the animal away from him unless she had no
other alternative. It would be cruel, both to the dog and the
man.

At around two-thirty, she realized she'd been so busy
doing other things that she had forgotten to pen a farewell
note to Heath. It would be inexcusable if she left without
at least trying to explain why. She spent the next forty
minutes at the table, agonizing over the wording. How did
one say good-bye in a letter? There were so many things
she wanted to tell him, all of which were impossible for
her to express.

She finally settled for thanking him for being such a good
friend to her and Sammy. Then she tried to explain her
reasons for abducting the dog, which struck her as being
more than a little wacky when she put them down on paper.
Maybe it wasn't a responsible decision. If her car broke
down en route, she might even look back and consider it
to have been a crazy one. But she had to do it.

It was ten after three by the time she finished the note
and sealed the envelope. Heath still hadn't called. Meredith
couldn't believe he had forgotten. The man was nothing if
not considerate of other people's feelings, and he had to
know she was pacing the floors, waiting to learn the out-
come of the meeting. She could only presume that the de-
bate over Goliath's fate had dragged on longer than
expected, possibly because Heath was arguing so passion-
ately in his dog's behalf.

By three thirty, Meredith was nearly beside herself. If he
didn't call soon, she'd have no choice but to go get Goliath
and leave. Had he decided to drive home to give her the
bad news?

That thought spurred her into action. If the board had voted to have Goliath destroyed, Heath would undoubtedly do it right away. Waiting until tomorrow would be sheer agony for him. What if he was on his way home right now to tell her the verdict and pick up the dog? She couldn't very well spirit Goliath away with Heath looking on.

She rushed into the bedroom to awaken Sammy, her plan to get the child into the car, drive over to get Goliath, and leave before Heath came home to stop her. Only Sammy wasn't on her bed where Meredith had left her.

"Sammy!" she called as she moved through the house, checking first in the bathroom, then in the other bedroom. "Sweetkins, where are you?"

No answer. Meredith made a quick sweep through the remainder of the house, then went back through each room to check under the beds and in closets. Her daughter was nowhere to be found.

Stepping out onto the back porch, she scanned the yard. "Sammy!" she yelled.

When the child didn't respond, Meredith began to feel the first twinges of panic. Sammy had been fast asleep the last time she checked. Had she woken up while Meredith had been outside packing the car? Meredith thought back. She'd spent several minutes inside the woodshed searching for the oil funnel. Had Sammy come outside during that time, looked in vain for her mother, and then wandered off? Meredith found that difficult to believe. Sammy had never left the yard.

Calm down, she ordered herself. *Even a timid child is likely to wander off sometimes. And here lately, Sammy has been getting much bolder.*

Meredith circled the yard, checking Sammy's favorite hiding places. Nothing. She was about to go back inside and double-check the rooms when her gaze fell on Heath's house. *Goliath.* The dog was in his kennel. Maybe Sammy had sneaked over to see him.

Convinced that was exactly what had happened, Meredith set off up the road. Her heart sank when she reached

Heath's driveway. She could see Goliath lying inside his doghouse, but there was no sign of Sammy.

"Sammy!" she yelled as loud as she could. "Sammy!"

Again there was no response, only the gentle whisper of the afternoon breeze in the surrounding trees. As Meredith turned to go back home, she glimpsed a patch of pink in the cow pasture on the opposite side of the road. *Oh, God.* For a frozen instant, all she could do was stand there and stare, her heart in her throat. What if the child had slipped through the pasture fence? Was that Sammy, lying out there in the grass?

Meredith couldn't believe Sammy had gone anywhere near those cows. But sometimes children grew so distracted that they didn't pay attention to their surroundings. How many times had Meredith read about a child chasing a ball directly into the path of a speeding automobile?

Sammy loved butterflies and sometimes tried to catch them. She might have followed one into the pasture.

Meredith broke into a run, her gaze fixed on that splotch of pink. *Her baby.* The cows in that field were dangerously unpredictable. Accustomed to grazing on open range, the animals were spooked easily by humans. One of them could have trampled Sammy or even gored her.

After scrambling over the fence, Meredith cut across the field. By the time she reached the splotch of pink, her breath was coming in ragged gasps and she had a stitch in her side. *Clover? Nothing but clover?* Meredith couldn't believe she'd run all this way, half crazy with fear, only to find a clump of pink blossoms.

She spun, scanning the pasture around her. Oh, God. She wouldn't be able to bear it if something happened to her daughter.

In the adjacent pasture, which lay directly behind her house, Meredith saw another splotch of pink. Probably only more clover, she told herself. But what if it was her child, lying injured and helpless in the grass? She broke back into a run.

Halfway across the field, she stepped in a burrow. Her

ankle twisted painfully, and she pitched forward, hitting the
ground face first. Star-studded blackness exploded inside
her head. For a moment, all she could do was lie there, her
deflated lungs grabbing frantically for breath.

As her vision began to clear, Meredith pushed to her
knees, her entire being focused on reaching that fence. She
clawed her way erect and staggered forward.

Sharp barbs tore at her clothes and skin as she climbed
over the wire. She scarcely felt the pain. *Running, running.*
Her cheeks vibrated with every impact of her feet against
the ground. When at last she reached the splotch of pink,
she hugged her aching sides. *Clover.*

Doing a slow turn, she saw that the clumps of pink flowers dotted the fields for as far as she could see. Only what
if one of those splotches *wasn't* clover? The cows weren't
the only dangerous creatures out here. There were rattlesnakes as well. If Sammy were injured, she could lie un-
noticed in the grass for hours, possibly even die.

As Heath executed the turn onto Hereford Lane, he was
only half aware of his driving, his thoughts focused on how
best to tell Meredith that the board had voted to have Goliath destroyed. She was going to cry. Hell, he wanted to
bawl himself. And she was also going to oppose the decision. He dreaded that most of all because a part of him
wanted to shake his fist at the commissioners and tell them
to go straight to hell. Goliath had risked his life so many
times in the line of duty that Heath had long since lost
count. It didn't seem fair that the dog should receive so
little consideration in return.

On the other hand, though, Heath knew, deep in his
heart, that the decision was the only one that could have
been reached. The instant he'd seen that salesman's arm,
he'd known. Only a few weeks ago, Heath had seen on the
news where a man who had been arrested for drug posses-
sion was filing a $300 million lawsuit because a police dog
had bitten him while he was in handcuffs. The financial

liability for the county in regards to Goliath could be as-tronomical.

Up ahead, Heath saw someone walking along the road. Pedestrians were a rarity this far from town. As he drove closer, he noted the person's diminutive stature and dark hair. *Meredith?* He tapped the brake, slowing the vehicle to a stop as he came abreast of her. For a moment, she didn't seem aware that he was there, just kept stumbling along the shoulder. Something was wrong, he realized. Really wrong.

When she finally realized a vehicle had pulled up beside her, she whirled to peer in the passenger window. Then, with a glad cry, she circled the Bronco, drawing up outside the driver's door. Heath rolled down the glass, noticing as he did that her face was streaked with dirt and that she'd been crying. The tracks of her tears had formed muddy rivulets on her pale cheeks.

"Merry? What in God's name is—"

He forgot what he meant to say as he locked gazes with her. One of her eyes was the same dark brown he'd come to expect, but the other was a startling sky blue. *Christ.* Heath blinked, thinking maybe it was the sun partially blinding him, but when he looked again, one of her eyes was *still* blue.

Her voice rang in his mind, none of the words sinking in. He was so stunned that concentrating on what she was saying was beyond him. Instead, all he could do was gape, and while he did, he noticed yet another flaw in the picture, that her wind-tossed mane of dark hair seemed to be slightly askew.

It hit him then, like a fist to the jaw, that this woman he had come to care about so deeply had not only been wearing brown contact lenses ever since he'd known her, but a wig as well. Upon closer inspection, he spied a wisp of blond hair trailing from under those sable tresses that he had always so greatly admired.

What else about her was fake?

His gaze dropped to her bust, which had always struck

him as being just a trifle too ample for such a slightly built female. Because she had seemed so wary of men, Heath had tried like hell never to ogle her figure if there was a chance she might catch him, which had been most of the time. He allowed himself the privilege now. What he didn't see filled him with quiet rage. In the coolness of the breeze, her nipples should have been reacting and forming hard peaks. *Nothing*. That had to mean she wore padding in her bra.

An instantaneous sense of betrayal crashed over him. For weeks, he'd been falling slowly and irrevocably in love with her, and all the while, everything about her had been a lie.

Then something she said sliced through the red haze of his anger. *Lost*. Had she just said that Sammy was lost?

"What?" His voice sounded as rough as sandpaper. "What did you say?"

She grabbed the top edge of the door window, her slender fingers turning white at the knuckles. "I can't find her!" she cried. "I can't find her anywhere! Not with Goliath, not anywhere! She's been gone for at least an hour. Maybe even longer. She was taking a nap the last time I checked. That was probably about one."

Heath's heart caught. His anger deflated like a punctured balloon, and he forgot all about her mismatched eyes. He cast a worried glance at the surrounding terrain. Even though they were only a few miles from town, this was hard, dangerous country out here. In addition to the damned cows, the fields abounded with rattlesnakes. And bordering those fields were forests, some of them stretching for miles.

"Over an hour?" he repeated incredulously. "She's been gone that long and you haven't called the authorities?"

"I thought—" She released her hold on the window glass to gesture weakly with a hand. "I tried to find her myself, first. I didn't want to raise a false alarm."

"A false alarm? Jesus Christ, Meredith! It's not like we're in the suburbs where she could be at one of the neighbors. Don't you know what could happen to her out there? What the hell were you thinking?''

At the question, she cupped her hand over her eyes. No answer, just a silent jerking of her shoulders that told him she was gulping back sobs.

Caught between flagging anger and a clawing fear for Sammy's safety that made him feel sick, Heath couldn't take the time to comfort her.

''Get in!'' he barked.

While she circled the Bronco, he radioed the sheriff's department. He was already speaking with Jenny Rose by the time Meredith climbed into the rig. When she saw what he was doing, she turned as pale as milk.

Heath knew then that his first reading of Meredith Kenyon had been dead to rights. She was hiding from someone, undoubtedly a husband. That was the only reason he could think of that she would react this way. She was afraid the authorities might put out an APB. Or, worse yet, flash a picture of Sammy on all the news broadcasts.

For some reason, that realization only made Heath angrier. That she would trust him so little . . . All she had ever needed to do was ask, and he would have done everything in his power to keep the bastard away from her. Didn't she know that?

Hell, no. He was a man, and in her opinion, that meant he automatically had ''jerk'' emblazoned on his forehead. So much for his making headway with his pretty little neighbor. Who the hell had he been trying to kid? She didn't trust him any more now than she had in the beginning.

Feeling like the world's biggest chump, Heath slammed the Bronco into gear and peeled rubber going up the road. After parking in Meredith's driveway, he killed the engine and threw open his door.

''Is the house locked?'' he asked curtly.

''No, why?'' She wrenched on her door handle. ''Shouldn't we keep looking outdoors for her until the other searchers get here?''

"I want to check the house again first."

She piled out of the Bronco and dogged his footsteps all the way to the house, her shrill voice cutting through the unnatural silence. "I told you, she isn't here. I looked everywhere! This is just a waste of time. And for your information, the *only* reason I hadn't already called the police when you came is because I've been out in the fields! She's wearing pink, and there are patches of clover everywhere out there! I kept thinking it was her."

Seeing her stricken expression, Heath started to wish he'd kept his mouth shut out there on the road. He felt like a jerk for snarling at her, and if that wasn't a hell of a note, he didn't know what was. After what he'd just discovered about her, he was nuts to still care this much.

Heath proceeded to check each room. More than once, he'd found a missing child asleep in a small cubbyhole right under a frantic mother's nose. At times like this, most parents got a little hysterical and failed to search as thoroughly as they should.

To Meredith's credit, she didn't simply stand there arguing with him, but began combing the rooms again herself. Heath even heard her go out to check in the Ford. When he found nothing but a few dust balls under the beds, he returned to the kitchen to check unlikely hiding places. Meredith was right; the child wasn't in the house.

Meredith emerged from the bathroom just as Heath reentered the kitchen. He didn't miss the fact that she'd straightened her wig and that both her eyes were once again brown. She had apparently gotten a look at herself in one of the mirrors.

Interesting. She couldn't afford to buy good cuts of meat, but she'd coughed up the money for a spare set of contacts. Heath knew damned well the lenses didn't come cheap. Aside from the cost, it also struck him as odd that she would go to such lengths to alter her appearance. It couldn't be comfortable, wearing a wig all the time, yet he'd never seen her without it. The man she was eluding must be a world-class asshole, he decided. Maybe even a sicko. She was taking no chances that he would find her.

Avoiding his gaze, she pushed nervously at her hair as she moved past him. "Now what? Can we start searching the fields? I'm so—" She broke off and pressed her hands over her face. "I'm so afraid she's lying out there somewhere, hurt."

Heath didn't doubt her sincerity. She was scared to death for her daughter, no question about it. He just wasn't blind to the fact that Sammy's well-being wasn't the only thing she was worried about. *The little fool.* She was hoping and praying he hadn't noticed the slightly crooked wig or the missing contact.

Fat chance. Right now simply wasn't the time to confront her. Finding Sammy had to take precedence.

"I'm going to get Goliath," he told her. "He'll be worth ten men out in those fields."

Heath didn't add that they might have to comb the surrounding woods as well. As a lawman, he was accustomed to sometimes having to be less than honest with parents. It wasn't easy to keep one's cool when a beloved child was missing. In fact, for the first time in his career, he was getting a taste of just *how* difficult it was.

He loved that little girl. God, how he loved her. But facts were facts, and there was no one to act as a buffer for him so he didn't have to face them. It would be fully dark in about three hours. If he and his deputies hadn't found Sammy in half that time, he'd have no choice but to call in the state police.

They couldn't leave the child out there alone after the sun went down. The high desert temperatures dropped sharply at night, which would increase Sammy's risk of suffering from exposure. And, thanks to recent legislation that restricted hunters from using dogs, there were also a considerable number of cougars in the area.

Heath stepped over to look out the window, his gaze fixed on the fields and forests. Five years ago, he wouldn't have been concerned about a cougar attacking a child, for the large cats weren't naturally inclined to prey on humans.

But now that the cougar population had exploded, the younger males had been forced closer to towns to find their own territories. In this day of depleted game, each adult male cougar now required fifty square miles of hunting ground just to stay alive. That equated to hungry cats, which led to their attacking pets and livestock on a regular basis, and occasionally the unwary human. A child Sammy's age would be extremely vulnerable.

Heath turned to meet Meredith's frightened gaze. "My deputies will come here instead of to my place. Can you wait here for them while I go get my dog?"

She hugged her waist, looking so shaken and lost herself that Heath was tempted to hug her. All that held him back was knowing those big brown eyes of hers were as fake as a counterfeit bill.

Once at his place, Heath alighted from the Bronco in a run, heading straight for Goliath's kennel. When he reached the gate, he saw that the latch had been lifted. His gaze shot to Goliath, who lay inside the doghouse. There was no sign of Sammy, but she'd obviously been here. If the Rottweiler had lifted the latch, he would be long gone.

"Goliath, come here, buddy," Heath called.

The dog thrust his massive head out the opening of the doghouse, but made no move to get up. Heath stepped inside the chain-link pen.

"Goliath?"

The Rottweiler whined and pushed up on his haunches. Heath hunkered down to peer past the dog's stout body and saw a bit of pink in the shadows. *Sammy.* Heath nearly hooted with joyous relief. Of course the child had come here. She'd probably overheard her mother speaking with him on the phone last night and had understood enough of the conversation to get upset.

Heath grabbed his dog by the collar and tugged him from the enclosure. Sammy lay curled up on Goliath's blanket, deeply asleep. When Meredith had come here looking for her earlier, she hadn't searched thoroughly enough. *Typical.*

Heath had seen other parents do the same thing a hundred times, darting here and there, screaming in panicked voices, hysteria clouding their thinking. In their terror, they seemed to forget their kids might be asleep and not hear them yelling.

Retracing his steps to the Bronco, Heath radioed the sheriff's department again to tell Jenny Rose that a team of searchers wouldn't be necessary, after all.

"So, she's safe and sound? Over."

Heath chuckled and keyed the mike. "Yeah. Having a nice little nap. Over."

Jenny Rose laughed. "I'll call off the troops, then."

"Thanks, Jen. I'm gone. Out."

Still grinning, Heath returned to the kennel and dropped to his knees in front of the doghouse to gaze at Sammy. In one limp hand, she held what appeared to be three hairpins with pieces of pink toilet paper clumped at the ends. The unfurled fingers of her other hand revealed a dime and three pennies resting on her grubby little palm. Gently, Heath gave the child a shake.

"Sammy," he called softly. "Wake up, sleepyhead."

The little girl blinked and yawned. As she sat up, she dropped the coins on the blanket and immediately began picking them back up. "Hi, Heef."

"Hi, yourself. What are you doing here, Sammy? Your mommy is really worried."

She thrust the hairpins at him. "I brung you flowers." Rubbing her eye with the fist that held the money, she peered at him as if to gauge his reaction. "I made 'em for you all by myself with hardly any help."

A lump lodged in Heath's throat as he accepted the gift. *Christ.* He was getting choked up over globs of toilet paper on hairpins. What the hell was the matter with him? He held up the offerings to admire them. After studying them from all angles, he still couldn't tell what kind of flowers the bedraggled clumps were supposed to be.

"Wow. These are the prettiest flowers anyone has ever given me." That wasn't a lie; they were the *only* flowers he'd ever received. "And you made them all by yourself?"

"Yup. Do you like that kind?"

Heath nodded. All of a sudden, dirty pink was his favorite color. "I *love* this kind."

She pursed her small mouth. "I bet you can't tell what kind they are."

Somehow, he had known that question was coming. Thinking fast, he said, "I can so." Then, catching sight of his barbecue grill, which he'd set under the eave of the pole barn, he quickly added, "They're *hitachi paperondus.*"

Her expression went from expectant to disappointed. "Nope. They're roses. I guess I di'n't make 'em very good."

Heath twirled one of the tattered blobs on its stem. "Oh, no, sweetheart. These are the most beautiful *hitachi paperondus* I've ever seen." He winked at her. "That's an inveigler's name for roses. Didn't you know that?"

"What's a"—she wrinkled her nose—"inbeggler?"

"An expert of sorts." Heath was definitely an expert at spouting bullshit when the occasion called for it.

And since Merédith had moved in next door, he was also becoming an expert at dealing with females. He had a sneaking suspicion he was being buttered up by this little lady. Sweetly, to be sure, but buttered up all the same. As a kid, he had been particularly nice to his dad whenever he wanted something, serving him coffee, fetching his slippers. He had a hunch Sammy's roses were a version of the same strategy.

What did she want? That was the question, and Heath didn't really have time to find out. Meredith was still pacing the floors, and he needed to get Sammy home.

"Well, sweetcakes. Let's go see Mommy. She's been looking all over for you."

"Not yet," Sammy said, her expression slightly mutinous. "We gots to talk first."

"We do?" Mutiny coming from Sammy was an unexpected turn. Heath could see that whatever was on her mind was extremely important, at least to her. "What do we have to talk about, honey?"

The determined glint in her big blue eyes should have been fair warning.

"I wanna buy G'liath from you." She thrust out her hand, palm up, to display the thirteen cents. "If that's not enough, I'll pay you a bill every month like my mommy does the 'lectric comp'ny."

Heath wasn't sure what to say. He stared down at the coins, which were apparently a small fortune, in her estimation. "Well, now. That's quite an offer."

"I been savin' for a Barbie outfit. But I 'cided I gotta buy G'liath instead."

Heath searched for some way to explain that Goliath couldn't be sold. Technically the dog was the property of the county.

"Gee, honey. That's a tough one. You see, I can't sell Goliath. Not to anyone."

"You gots to. I don't wanna hurt your feelings, but G'liath needs me to buy him."

"He does?"

"Yup. So's I can be the boss over him. Not nobody else. Just me."

"I see," Heath said. Only, of course, he didn't see at all.

"If *I'm* G'liath's boss, I won't *never* make him go asleep."

"Ah." The lights were starting to come on.

"I know what 'going asleep' means. It's what grownups say to little kids when somebody dies. My daddy went asleep, and so did my par'keet, and both of 'em got covered up with dirt afterward. My fish went asleep, too, but I guess that don't really count. Fishes just get flushed."

Heath wished he'd brought Meredith. He was way out of his depth.

After regarding him for a long moment, Sammy continued. "A real friend is s'posed to be a friend for always, no matter what. Did you know that?"

Heath bit back a smile. "I think I've heard that a time or two."

"I heard it from my mommy, and she's most always right."

"I imagine she probably is."

Sammy leaned forward. "I'm not mad at you or nothin'."

He was relieved to hear that. "You're not?"

"Nope. Mommy says it isn't always easy to be a friend. That's how you can tell your real friends from the pretend ones, 'cause the real ones stay your friends no matter what." She touched her small hand to his. "Sometimes 'no matter what' is somethin' real bad, Heef. Like when a dog bites somebody." Her chin started to quiver and her eyes filled with tears. "G'liath shouldn't have to go asleep and get covered up with dirt for biting that man. He wasn't a nice man. G'liath was just trying to be my 'tector, is all."

Pinned by her gaze, Heath found himself thinking that he'd never seen eyes so incredibly blue, or so large and guileless. A man didn't stand a chance.

"Hasn't G'liath always been a good dog up till now?" she asked. "He saved little kids, and he always minded what you said. Now, just 'cause he's done *one* bad thing, you're gonna make him go *asleep*! Haven't you never done a bad thing?

Heath had definitely made his share of mistakes, and Sammy's lecture was making him realize how close he had come to making another one. In the state of Oregon, all dogs were allowed one bite that broke the skin. Didn't Goliath deserve the same fair shake? *Lawsuits, rules, following orders.* He'd gotten so wrapped up in the legalities and risks that he'd lost sight of what really mattered.

Looking over at Goliath, Heath recalled all the times the dog had been his friend "no matter what," and he knew, deep in his heart, that Sammy had just hit the nail on the head. Goliath would go up against insurmountable odds to save Heath, and if Heath wanted to be able to live with himself, he could do no less in return. Screw the risks, and the technicalities, and the state's goddamned rules. It would result in a nasty battle, but Heath owed it to the dog to fight for him. He only regretted that he had needed a child to remind him of it.

Heath tucked the roses into his pocket and patted his thigh. "Come here, Sammy."

Clutching her money, she crawled from the doghouse. Heath deposited her on his knee. She turned to place her little hands on his cheeks. "Please, Heef? Don't make him go asleep."

"I won't," he said, wanting to get that concern out of the way immediately. "You're right, sweetheart. I have to be Goliath's friend, no matter what."

"Do you promise?"

Heath hesitated. If the county insisted that the dog be euthanized, he could end up in court, and even then a judge might rule against him. What did he plan to do then? Appeal, he guessed. And fight like hell. "Yeah," he said gruffly. "I promise."

She beamed a smile at him and planted a kiss on his chin. "See, G'liath? You don't gotta go asleep for a long, long time."

Heath smiled and reached over to pet his dog. Goliath whined and moved closer, licking Sammy's face then Heath's hand. It was almost as if the Rottweiler understood.

"About your buying Goliath," Heath said. "You understand, don't you, that he's a retired canine deputy?" At Sammy's nod, Heath continued, "Well, that means he isn't really my dog. I'm just his guardian, and I can't sell him to anyone. If I could, though, I can't think of anyone I'd rather sell him to than you. You love him a lot, don't you?"

Sammy nodded solemnly, then spread her arms wide. "I love him *this* much."

"That's a lot," Heath agreed.

"Yup. That's how come I wanna buy him, 'cause I don't want him to go asleep."

"You can trust me to be sure that doesn't happen." He studied the child's upturned face. "Sammy, since I can't

sell Goliath to you, how would you feel about being his
honorary guardian?''

Her eyes filled with bewilderment. ''What's that?''

''Well, you'd be like me—sort of his owner, but not
really. In an unofficial capacity.''

''Does that mean I can be the boss over him?''

Heath couldn't hold back a grin. ''You could give me
advice and be number two boss. How does that sound?''

''Can I 'cide things? Like if he's gotta go asleep?''

''You can help me decide.'' At her look of disappoint-
ment, Heath quickly added, ''You helped me decide today.
And you're not even his honorary guardian yet.''

''Would I be 'portant?''

Gazing down at her, it almost frightened Heath to admit
exactly how important. After learning what he just had
about Meredith, he knew that caring so deeply about
mother or child wasn't exactly the smartest move he'd ever
made. ''Absolutely,'' he said, his voice gone husky with
emotion. ''More important than you'll ever know. Taking
care of a dog is a lot of work, and sometimes it requires
time I really can't spare. Until I get this matter about his
biting that man settled with the county, I'll have to leave
him in his kennel while I'm working. He'll need looking
after. It'd be a big load off my shoulders if I had a helper.
Someone to check his water and play with him and take
him for walks on his leash. Or to take him to her house for
a visit so he doesn't get lonesome. You could tie him in
your backyard while you were outside playing.''

''Yup. I can do that.''

He thrust out his hand. ''Shake with me on it?''

''What's shaking do?''

''It cements the deal. An extra kind of promise.''

She put her small hand in his. ''I promise.''

Heath made a great show of pumping her arm up and
down. ''Now it's official. You're Goliath's unofficial honorary guardian.''

''For always?''

''For as long as you live here, anyway.''

"What if we gots to go 'way?"

Heath prayed to God not. Gathering Sammy into his arms, he pushed to his feet. "We'll cross that bridge when we come to it, sweetcakes. Right now, I have to get you home. Your mommy is probably beside herself." As he left the kennel, Heath whistled for his dog. "Come on, you mangy mutt. If I'm going to buck the county, I may as well go all the way and let you out of jail for a few hours."

On the way back to Meredith's, something Sammy had said slammed into Heath's mind like a hollow-point slug. *My daddy went asleep.* And afterward, the man had been covered up with dirt. That had to mean Meredith's husband was dead.

Heath's hands convulsed into throbbing fists over the steering wheel. *Dead?* If that was true, then who was she hiding from? All of a sudden, he felt as if he had swallowed live snakes, a cold, slithering sensation low in his gut. *Oh, Christ.* He remembered back to that first night and the feeling he'd had that he'd seen Meredith and Sammy before. And later, how he'd scoffed at himself for entertaining the notion, however briefly, that he might have seen their likenesses at the department.

What if Meredith was wanted for something? Was it possible he'd had a fugitive living down the road from him all this time and never suspected it? Glancing at Sammy, Heath didn't want to believe such a thing or even explore the possibility.

As the sheriff of this county, he didn't have a choice.

Chapter 17

Meredith was so overjoyed to see Sammy that she dashed past Heath as if he weren't there. Falling to her knees on the patchy grass, she clasped her sleepy-eyed child in her arms, sobbing and laughing. Goliath, who had leaped from the vehicle after Sammy, barked and horned in on the re-union, licking Meredith's tear-streaked face and butting her shoulder until she looped an arm around his neck.

Watching the trio, Heath got a lump the size of a golf ball in his throat. He forced himself to turn away. He had to keep his head on straight, dammit. Maybe Meredith was as inno-cent of any wrongdoing as a newborn babe. He hoped to hell she was. But until he knew for sure, he couldn't afford these feelings. If push came to shove, he could find himself having to arrest her.

Finally Meredith released her daughter. Giving the dog a final pat, she pushed to her feet. "Are you going back to work?" she asked.

"I missed most of the day. I really should go in and check on things. When the cat's away, and all of that. It's a crazy time right now. Memorial Day weekend is coming up." He glanced at Sammy and the dog. The child was planting kisses on the dog's snout, her small face twisting in distaste when Goliath's tongue got in the way. He smiled and inclined his head at the pair. "Sammy gave me a talking to, by the way. As a result, I've come to my senses and decided to fight the county's decision.''

''They ordered Goliath to be euthanized?''

''As of today. But just because I'm given an edict, it doesn't mean I have to abide by it. I'm in the mood for a good fight.''

Her gaze jerked to his. He could tell by her expression that his double meaning hadn't been lost on her, and that she was wondering what he'd meant by it. Two bright spots of color flagged her cheeks. ''After all you've been through this last twenty-four hours, I guess you have a right to be in a bad mood.''

''A real *bitch* of a mood.''

The sudden rush of color drained from her cheeks. She knew. He could see the wariness in her eyes. What had she thought? That he hadn't seen what was right in front of his nose? One blue eye was a little hard to miss. And what did she expect him to do now? Pretend he hadn't noticed and just go on as if nothing had changed? He didn't appreciate being made to look like a stupid ass.

It occurred to Heath that his alluding to the wig and contacts might be a mistake. If she was wanted for something, she just might run. He almost wished she would. Maybe then, some other poor son of a bitch would have the honor of arresting her.

''I have to go,'' he spat out.

She just stood there with her hand pressed to her throat and her heart shining from her eyes. A silent plea for him to pretend he didn't know, maybe? He stared into her eyes, thinking of all the times he had felt as if he were drowning in them. *Lying eyes*. They were blue, not brown. And that wealth of dark hair was fake as well.

''Good-bye then,'' she said softly.

Had that been a note of finality he'd heard in her farewell? Heath hoped so. Now that he thought about it, he wanted her to run. Preferably as far away as that rattletrap old car of hers would go before breaking down.

God help him, if there was a warrant out on her, he didn't know if he could bring himself to arrest her.

After collecting his dog, Heath drove straight from Meredith's house to the sheriff's department. His computer system there was linked to a nationwide law enforcement network. On a regular basis, he imported and exported information on criminals, keeping in constant contact with the FBI, the state boys across the country, and with myriad police departments, both metropolitan and jerkwater. If Meredith was wanted, for anything, he would be able to find out. Oh, it might take him a few hours, maybe more than a few, depending on how broadly he had to search to find data matches. That was all right; he was a patient man.

Once he was closeted in his office, Heath was driven nearly to distraction by Goliath, who paced the confines of the small room, whining and jumping up on the door.

"Damn, Goliath, stop it. I'm trying to concentrate," Heath groused as he scrolled.

As the minutes passed, the dog grew more nervous, his whines taking on a frantic edge. Back and forth, he paced. Heath wondered if there was a female dog in heat close by. Except for the night Goliath had met Sammy, he'd never acted this way.

Thinking perhaps Goliath needed to go, Heath escorted him outside. The dog made a beeline for the Bronco. Heath called him back.

"Just lie down and be quiet," he ordered as he resumed his seat at his desk.

The dog stayed down for about five seconds, then began pacing again. Heath glanced up, beginning to feel uneasy himself. About what, he wasn't sure. He eyed the telephone, tempted to call Meredith to make sure that she and Sammy were okay.

Craziness. As fond as Goliath was of Sammy, he didn't have telepathic communication with the child. No question about it, there had to be a female dog in the neighborhood. As for Heath's uneasiness? Nerves, he assured himself. The possibility that Meredith could be running from the law had his imagination kicked into high gear.

Settling back down to work, Heath began scrolling through the computer files again. After about an hour, his eyes started to burn. He kept searching.

If the woman he'd believed himself to be falling in love with was wanted for a crime, he had to know, the sooner, the better. The truth was something he could deal with. It was the not knowing and being lied to that he couldn't handle.

Meredith stood at the stove, stirring a pot of soup. *The last supper*, she thought nonsensically. As soon as she and Sammy had eaten, they were out of here. After what had happened this afternoon, she had no choice. Heath had noticed the missing contact and the wig as well. There had been no mistaking that glint in his eyes when he told her good-bye. He was going to learn the truth now. It was only a matter of time. And when he did, he would have no choice but to arrest her. That was his job.

Tears burned at the backs of her eyes. She blinked them away. Letting Sammy see how upset she was would only make their departure more difficult for the child.

"Are we ever gonna come back, Mommy?" she asked in a tremulous voice from where she sat at the table.

"Maybe. Probably, sweetheart." Glancing over her shoulder, Meredith flashed a stiff smile. "While the soup's heating, why don't you run into your room and choose one great big toy that you'd like to take with you. Hmm? I'll make room in the backseat."

Sammy pulled a glum face. "A toy won't make me feel glad."

"Sweetkins, I've explained over and over why we have to go. Heath saw me without my contact, remember?"

"Don't he like blue eyes?"

"Sammy, if we don't leave, Heath will find out who we really are sooner or later. When that happens, the police will send you back to New York. Is that what you want?"

The little girl's eyes grew large. "No. I wanna stay here."

"We can't, punkin. I wish we could, too. But to keep you safe, we have to go. Sometimes life doesn't give us any choices." She forced a smile. "We'll have each other. It won't be so bad. You'll see. Now go and choose a toy to take along. Make sure it's your very favorite big one. We only have room for the one."

As the child ran to her bedroom, Meredith returned her gaze to the stove. Oh, God, how she wished they could return someday. But that would only come about if a miracle happened. Like for instance, if she could somehow iron out the legal wrinkles back in New York. Or, maybe, if Glen died. He was getting older. What was he now, sixty-six? There was always a chance he might keel over with a heart attack.

Meredith no sooner entertained the thought than she scoffed at herself. Glen's death wouldn't bring an end to her problems. Who was she kidding? They'd be after her for the rest of her life, no matter who was at the helm.

Still, it was nice to think that someday she might return here with Sammy. That she would be free to fall in love, make commitments, and build a future.

The thought made her smile bitterly. *Right.* Heath Masters, her hero. He was probably trying to get the goods on her this very minute, and as soon as he did, he would sell her down the river. Is that what she wanted? Another man who would turn on her?

From the start, she could never trust him. His career meant too much to him. Which would he choose, her or law enforcement? His work with kids was an atonement for Laney's death. To give it up, he'd have to forgive himself first, and so far, he hadn't.

After supper, she had to get Sammy out of here. Before leaving town, she'd stop at a store and get several cans of cheap spray paint to hide the color of her car. She could do that at one of the less popular recreation parks. Once the car was painted, she'd drive through the suburbs and exchange license plates with another car.

When she left, she could leave no trail. Kidnapping was no misdemeanor. The minute Heath learned why she was wanted, he'd be furious. A child stealer, the lowest of the low. It would stick in his craw that she'd slipped through his fingers. He'd be riding high on anger and never stop to ask himself *why* she'd taken her child. He would react first, and think later. The law was the law, amen. And she had broken it, big time.

Luckily, it would take him a while to learn who she was, even with a computer network at his disposal. Before he could find her on the system, he had to know what he was looking for. Right now, all he had to go on was a physical description. Worst case scenario, he'd stumble onto information about her tonight. More than likely, though, he wouldn't find anything until tomorrow. Either way, she'd be on the road, in a different-colored car with someone else's license plates. They'd play hell trying to find her.

Soon, she and Sammy would be in a new place, starting over fresh. And next time, she promised herself, she wouldn't let herself care about the neighbor man.

What did she even want with a man, anyway? She hated having sex, and to even consider marrying for financial security would be a very bad trade. Dan had been wealthy, filthy rich, in fact. Beautiful houses and clothing. Oh, yes, while married to Dan Calendri, she'd had it all. Only the beautiful houses had been high-security prisons.

She was finished playing Russian roulette with her life. No man was ever going to have control over her again or have the right—legally, morally, or otherwise—to lay a hand on her daughter again. And she would never, *ever* trust again.

It hurt too badly when the person let you down. . . .

The tears Meredith had been holding at bay rushed to her eyes. She swiped angrily at her cheeks, furious with herself for having fantasized about a future with Heath in the first place, or to care this much. *Men.* They were all the same, a faithless, unreliable lot. So what if he cared more for his precious career than he did her?

"I'm sad, Mommy. I really, really, really don't wanna leave."

"Don't feel sad." Meredith tapped the spoon on the edge of the pot. "I'll tell you what. When we get settled in our next house, how would you like a puppy?"

"I want G'liath! He's my friend, and I love him *this* much."

From the corner of her eye, Meredith saw Sammy spread her arms wide. She stifled a weary sigh. "I know you do, sweetie. But we *have* to leave. So, let's think happy thoughts. A puppy will be lots of fun."

The ceiling light blinked out. Meredith scowled. "The electricity just went off." Glancing out the window, she saw that the sun was setting over the mountains. Twilight would come fast, as it always did at higher elevations. "Fantastic. I guess this old joint is going to have the last laugh."

Sammy moved closer. "It's kind of dark in here."

"Not so dark we can't see to eat." Meredith grabbed bowls from the cupboard. "You want to get the spoons? Let's hurry, or we'll be drinking soup in the dark."

While Meredith served the soup, Sammy fetched the silverware. In short order, they were seated at the table, eating their meager meal. Meredith soon found herself wishing she hadn't put their jackets in the backseat of the car. It was cool enough this evening that she would have turned on the furnace if they'd been staying the night.

By the time they finished eating, it was nearly dark. Worried that Sammy might get chilled, she pushed up from the table and said, "Okay, punkin, let's go."

"Aren't we gonna wash dishes?"

Meredith smiled as she stepped over to get her purse off the top of the refrigerator. "We're leaving, remember? Tonight, we don't have to clean the kitchen. Mr. Guntrum can pay to have it done out of my cleaning deposit."

Sammy climbed off her chair, her small face looking

forlorn in the shadows. "I wish I could tell G'liath bye."

"I wish you could, too, swee—"

A loud crash in the utility room cut Meredith short. She whirled just in time to see a man enter the kitchen. Even as Meredith fell back a step in startlement, she felt a vague sense of recognition. As the man stepped closer and she was able to discern his features, she saw why. Their intruder was none other than the encyclopedia salesman Goliath had bitten yesterday. Another man pushed into the kitchen behind him.

"What are you doing here?" Meredith demanded in a shaky voice. She cast a frightened glance at her daughter. "Sammy, sweetie, go to your room."

"No, Tamara, don't," the salesman said softly. "You stay right where you are. If you're a good little girl and do as you're told, we won't shoot your mother."

Tamara? Meredith's gaze dropped from the man's shadowy features to his hand. *A gun.* Her heart lurched, skipped a beat, and then felt as if it simply stopped, quivering at the base of her throat like a blob of gelatin. A watery sensation ran down her legs.

In stunned disbelief, she looked at the man who had entered the room behind the salesman. *Tall, slender, and blond.* She remembered him instantly. He was the man who had approached her in the supermarket parking lot, asking for directions. The one Goliath had growled at so viciously. *Oh, God.* Glen had found them.

Meredith didn't know how long she stood there frozen. By the time she jerked into motion, the dark-haired salesman was upon her, his stocky body knocking her off balance. As she staggered to keep her feet, he grabbed her left wrist and wrenched her arm behind her back. Pain exploded in her shoulder. The next instant, she felt the cold barrel of the gun pressing against her temple.

"Not one sound, bitch!" he snarled.

Meredith had no intention of screaming. Even if Heath had been at home, which he wasn't, he wouldn't have heard her.

"Sammy, run!"

The child just stood there, her small body quaking, her fear-widened eyes luminous in the dimness.

"You shut up!" The salesman thumped the gun barrel against Meredith's temple in warning. "Not a word, I told you!"

"Run, Sammy!" Meredith cried again. "Run!"

Sammy spun in a panic, her sneakers squeaking on the linoleum. The blond man grabbed her by the hair. The child wailed and clamped her hands to her smarting scalp.

"Take your hands off of her!" Meredith yelled. "You animal! Don't hurt—" The words snagged in Meredith's throat as the salesman twisted viciously on her arm. "Ahhh!" She gulped back the rest of the scream, not wanting to give him the satisfaction of knowing he'd caused her pain. "Let *go* of her hair, damn you! She's just a little girl!"

Instead of releasing the child's hair, the blond dragged Sammy across the room and lifted her onto a chair. The child shrieked in pain. If Meredith could have broken free at that moment, she would have attacked him with her bare hands. The man holding Meredith jerked up on her arm and shoved her toward a chair across from Sammy. Meredith's teeth snapped together when he slammed her down on the cushion.

Oh, God . . . Oh, God. That was as far as Meredith could get with a prayer.

The salesman released Meredith's arm, then drew a tablet and pen from under his jacket and slapped them onto the table in front of her.

"You're going to write a letter to Glen," he informed her. "I'll tell you what to say. Date it two weeks ago. Top right corner."

Meredith couldn't remember what month it was, let alone what the date had been two weeks ago. She picked up the pen, shaking so badly she wasn't sure she would be able to write, not to mention that the light was so poor she doubted she'd be able to see. "It's May twenty-second now,'' the salesman snarled at her. ''Date it May eighth.''

The tip of the pen quivered against the paper, making the letters she wrote look as if they'd been fashioned by someone with palsy.

''Damn you! Do it right, or I'll blow your kid's brains out.''

Meredith gulped and took a ragged breath, willing her hand to be steady.

After she'd written the date as he'd instructed, the man said, ''Now write, 'Dear Glen.' ''

As Meredith wrote Glen's name, the horror of what was happening began to sink in. A loud ringing started in her ears. Numbly, she wrote the letter exactly as she was told, informing Glen that she had decided Tamara should be in his custody. Money was tight, she was ordered to say. It was impossible for her to properly support her daughter, and she had concluded that the child would be better off and far happier living with her grandfather. She was instructed to end the letter by asking Glen to please make arrangements to come for Tamara as quickly as possible.

''Very good,'' the swarthy man said, retrieving the tablet and putting it back inside his jacket. ''Now, get up.''

Meredith pushed to her feet, her gaze clinging to her terrified child. She yearned to circle the table and gather Sammy into her arms, to tell her not to be afraid, that everything would be all right. Only, of course, that would be a lie.

The salesman thrust the gun against Meredith's spine, shoving her along in front of him as he moved from the kitchen to the living room. Meredith craned her neck to see what the other man was doing to Sammy until the dividing wall blocked her view. Sammy immediately began to scream. The child's cries nearly broke Meredith's heart.

''Left!'' the man barked at her, giving her a hard shove.

Meredith turned, dimly registering that he was taking her to her bedroom. ''Wh— What are you going to do?''

He just kept shoving her along ahead of him. When her legs connected with the mattress, he planted a hand in the center of her back and pushed her face down on the bed. Then he wrenched her hands behind her back and bound her wrists. Next he bound her feet. All the while, Meredith could hear Sammy screaming.

"Please, my little girl. Don't frighten her like this, please."

Even in the near darkness, the salesman's teeth gleamed eerily as he smiled. He drew something from his jacket pocket. Squinting, Meredith saw it was a syringe.

"You're going to take a little nap," he informed her in a voice that made icy rivulets trickle down her spine. "After you're asleep, we'll untie you and make a few adjustments on your gas furnace so the pilot light goes out. Then we'll turn on the gas valve."

Meredith stared up at him. *They're going to kill me*, she thought stupidly.

"By the time your boyfriend stops by to check on you, you'll be in never-never land." He unsheathed the hypodermic needle, pointed it upward, and slightly depressed the plunger until a bit of clear liquid spurted. "It'll look like an accident. People will think you got chilly, turned on the furnace, and fell asleep without smelling the gas."

The chill of dread along her spine radiated outward to form knots in her stomach. Glen had found a way to kill two birds with one stone, she realized. He would not only get permanent custody of his granddaughter by killing her only surviving parent, but he would eliminate the threat Meredith represented because she knew too much.

"You're crazy! You'll never get away with this."

She tried to wrench her wrists free, realizing as she struggled that he'd bound her with velvet cord. Horror seeped into her brain. These men had thought of everything. Velvet wouldn't abrade her skin as noticeably as regular rope.

The man leaned over her, the needle poised near her upper arm. "This won't hurt," he assured her. "You'll just feel a little prick."

Meredith rolled to evade the injection. "I'm telling you, they'll know it's murder!"

He gripped her shoulder to hold her still. "Relax, Mary. You'll just go to sleep."

Meredith threw her head and kicked with her bound feet, striking him across the knees. "Goddammit, be still! I told you, it ain't gonna hurt!"

That her death would be painless was little consolation. *Sammy.* She couldn't die and leave her little girl. Not with a man like Glen. *Please, God, not with Glen.*

Just as the needle started to prick Meredith's skin, the man in the kitchen yelled, "Delgado, come quick! The kid's getting away!"

Delgado swore, tossed the full syringe onto the bed, and raced from the room.

The men's footsteps echoed through the house. A door crashed against a wall, the sound cutting through the air like a rifle shot. Terrified for her daughter, Meredith jerked her arms and twisted at the waist, trying to free her wrists. Her struggles sent her toppling, the corner of the nightstand jabbing her shoulder as she fell. She landed on her side, her stomach convulsing with nausea that surged in hot waves up her throat.

Trying not to vomit, she lay there panting. In the stillness of the twilight, she could hear the men's angry curses from outdoors. *Run, baby, run.* Never in all her life had she felt so horribly helpless.

"Heath! Help us! Heath!"

Even as Meredith cried his name, she knew it was useless. He was still at the sheriff's department. He couldn't possibly hear her. If only he could.

Chapter 18

Trying to ignore Goliath's continuous pacing and whining, Heath stared at the computer screen. He didn't want to believe what he was seeing. *Pay dirt.* He had found his man. Or, in this case, his woman. *Mary Calendri, kidnapper extraordinaire.*

Except for the facial structure, the photo of her scarcely resembled the Meredith he knew. Shoulder-length honey-colored hair, streaked with blond. Big, blue eyes, just like Sammy's. She'd done an incredible job of altering her appearance. He'd give her that much.

Acid indigestion rolled up the back of his throat like liquid fire as he scanned the file on her. *Holy shit.* There was no way to whitewash this. In defiance of a court order, she had removed her child from the state of New York while a custody suit was pending. The charges against her were mind-boggling. No penny ante stuff for this lady. Abducting a child and then crossing the state line was a serious crime.

No wonder she'd gotten so upset when he'd started calling her Merry. Merry and Mary, exact soundalikes. The first time he'd used the shortened version of her alias, it must have scared the hell out of her.

Heath's initial reaction was rage. Jabbing the arrow keys on the keyboard with a rigid finger, he scrolled back and forth through the information. Talk about being made to look like a fool! How could he have been so blind? From the first, all the signs had been there, and he had ignored them, so taken in by her big brown eyes and vulnerable mouth that he had refused to consider she might be wanted by the law.

And she had realized, damn her. She had known he was falling in love with her, and she had allowed it to happen.

Even as he thought that, he knew it wasn't fair. One thing he couldn't accuse Meredith of was leading him on. Everything about her had screamed, "Don't touch." She'd never given him any signals that she wanted to get more friendly. If anything, she'd done the opposite, always shying away when he got too close.

After rereading the file, Heath turned to pick up the telephone, intending to collect on a few favors and get more information, not necessarily official. In his experience, a law officer could learn a lot more from scuttlebutt than official reports. He didn't know any cops in New York, but he knew a cop who did. By working through that contact, he'd be able to connect with officers who could tell him what he wanted in the know.

Why had Meredith run with her child? That was the first question he intended to ask. If her husband was dead, how in the hell had she ended up in court, fighting for custody? Who had filed suit against her? A relative? If so, how was that person related to Sammy, and what had been the motivating factor? As far as Heath could tell, Meredith was a wonderful mother. Why on earth would anyone want to take her child?

As Heath started to dial the phone, Goliath hurled himself against the office door, coming dangerously close to connecting with the window glass in the top half.

"Goliath!" Heath lunged across the office, catching hold of the dog's collar barely in the nick of time to keep him from jumping again. "What the hell has gotten into you?"

Goliath barked and threw his head. For the second time that evening, Heath was reminded of the first night Goliath had ever seen Sammy. The dog was in the same sort of frenzy now. It was almost as if the child were in the next room and in grave danger.

The hair on Heath's nape prickled. He'd learned a long time ago never to ignore Goliath when he behaved this way. The one time Heath had, he'd found himself staring into the barrel of a sawed-off shotgun a few seconds later.

Tugging Goliath along, Heath returned to his desk and dialed Meredith's number. The phone rang endlessly.

"Dammit." He slammed the receiver back in its cradle, his sense of uneasiness increasing. Turning his gaze back to the dog, Heath stood there for a moment, his rational side at war with his instincts. "You're trying your best to tell me something's wrong, aren't you, buddy?"

The dog lunged against Heath's hold, trying to reach the door.

Heath sighed. "Give me a break, Goliath. I'm in the middle of some important stuff, here. And Sammy's ten miles away."

Emitting a ferocious growl, Goliath reared up to plant his large front feet on Heath's chest. Heath glanced back at the phone. Meredith wasn't answering at her end, and that wasn't like her. Chances were that she had hightailed it. But just to be on the safe side, it wouldn't take him all that long to drive home.

"All right. If you say something's up, let's go check it out."

En route to the door, Goliath circled Heath's legs. Once they gained the outer office, the Rottweiler made a beeline for the front exit, sideswiping a deputy.

When Heath got outside, he shook his head at the way the dog jumped at the Bronco's doors. Even so, the dog's sense of urgency was contagious. Heath picked up his pace. Goliath never acted like this without a reason. At the door of the vehicle, Heath dropped his car keys and had to search for them in the dim light of the parking lot, an endeavor made all the more frustrating by the Rottweiler bumping against him.

By the time Heath got into the Bronco, his patience with

the dog was wearing dangerously thin, and so was his patience with himself. *Admit it, man. The real reason you're dragging your feet is because you dread having to face her.* His duty was clearly defined. Meredith was wanted on criminal charges, and if he saw her again, he would have to arrest her. No ifs, ands, or buts.

For the first time, the thought of having to do his job made him cringe.

Terror. The taste of it was metallic at the back of Meredith's tongue. Full darkness had descended now, and the rest of the house was as black and silent as a tomb. Faint shimmers of moonlight came through the window above her, providing the only light. Shadows shifted and reached toward her. She strained to listen. Had Sammy gotten away? On the one hand, Meredith prayed she had. On the other, she feared for the child's safety. Had she slipped under the pasture fence? Was she hiding out there in the field, even now, her small body concealed by the tall grass?

Oh, God. There were snakes out there, and those half-wild range cows. She didn't know which was worse, the creatures who might harm her child, or the men who were chasing her. Either way, Sammy was in terrible trouble. And Meredith couldn't help her. Trussed like a calf for branding, she couldn't even help herself.

Thrashing and twisting to free her wrists, Meredith rolled onto her side, grinding her cheek against the floor. Something got in her mouth. She sputtered and pushed at it with her tongue, then tried to spit it out. *Goliath hair.* A sob tore up her throat and tears filled her eyes, for thinking of the dog made her yearn for Heath as well. The phone had rung a few minutes ago. Had it been Heath calling?

Oh, God, please, let him realize something's wrong.

Not knowing what was happening to her daughter was torturous. Meredith lost all sense of time. How long had Sammy been out there? Ten minutes? Twenty? She imagined her little girl, alone somewhere in the dark, frightened and sobbing.

Suddenly the house erupted with noise. Doors slammed and footsteps resounded. Barely audible above the din, a shrill mewling trailed eerily through the rooms. *Sammy.* Heartsick, Meredith realized the child was crying, "G'liath! G'liath!" Over and over again, the summons tolled in the darkness, a futile invocation. The dog wasn't going to hear, and he wasn't going to come. Not this time.

"This time, Nelson, put the little shit in the bathroom and keep her there until I finish with the woman!"

The salesman's voice, she thought, then wondered why she continued to think of him as a salesman. If the man peddled anything, it was death. She glanced at the hypodermic needle that awaited her on the bed. Then she heard footsteps coming toward her room. He'd kill her now. Was she just going to lie here and accept that?

No. Why make it easy for them? In the darkness, maybe she could hide.

She looked wildly around. The moonlight seemed brighter now, reaching farther into the room to pool like molten silver. Even if she rolled into a corner, they'd see her.

The bed. She wasn't sure she could fit under it with her arms tied behind her back and adding extra thickness to her torso. She rolled onto her stomach and flattened herself against the floor. By pushing with her feet and rocking her shoulders, she wiggled under the bed frame, barely getting her legs out of sight before Delgado burst through the doorway. She heard him stop. Silence. Then heavy breathing.

"God *damn* it! Now the woman's gone!"

The bed frame shook. She guessed that he'd kicked it. Furniture scraped the floor. Then she heard the closet door swing open and crash against the wall.

"Son of a bitch!"

"Wasn't she tied up?" Nelson asked from somewhere near the doorway.

"Hell, yes! What d'ya think I am, stupid?"

Yes, Meredith thought. The first place she would have looked was under the bed. She bit her lip to hold back panicked laughter. She heard them searching the other rooms, kicking in doors, shoving aside furniture. Their angry curses rang through the house. Then she heard them coming back toward her room.

"She's gotta be here. I tied her up good, I tell you! She couldn't have gone far."

The other man, Nelson, said, "Delgado, if we screw this up, the boss is gonna have our heads. How hard can it be for two men to handle a woman and a kid?"

"Shut your trap! It's not my fault you let the kid get loose!"

"She bit me!"

"Oh, my heart bleeds."

Meredith couldn't imagine Sammy fighting back that way. She had bitten the man? *Good for you, Sammy! Good for you!* Not so very long ago, the child would have huddled in a corner, frozen in terror. Meredith knew whom she had to thank for the change. Tears stung her eyes again. *Heath.* And, of course, Goliath. The two of them made an incredible duo, and they'd given Sammy things Meredith had been unable to provide, namely a sense of security and the inner strength that came with it.

Meredith only wished they were here now. So powerful was the yearning that she nearly began sobbing Heath and Goliath's names as she'd heard Sammy doing.

"You check under the bed?" Nelson asked.

Silence. Then, "Hell!" The next second, a dark hand shot under the dust ruffle. Meredith shrank away, trying to evade the groping fingers. No chance. The man closed his hand over her arm and grunted with satisfaction. "Got her!"

The next second, Meredith's shoulder exploded with pain as she was dragged from under the bed. Her left arm scraped the underside of the frame. *Good.* She was glad for the pain. They had hoped to make her death look like an accident. Well, they could think again. Bruises would be a dead giveaway to the coroner.

"Don't rough her up!" Nelson cried, almost as if he'd read her mind.

In his anger, Delgado flung Meredith onto the mattress with such force that she bounced. Something clattered onto the floor.

"Shit! The syringe!"

Like foraging rats, the two men began scurrying around the room. On the one hand, Meredith prayed they wouldn't find the needle. On the other, though, she wondered how they might kill her if they didn't. At least going to sleep was painless.

Light suddenly flooded the room, a bright, blinding glare that swung in a wide arc over the walls. For a second, Meredith thought that one of the men had turned on a flashlight. But then she heard the squeak of automobile brakes.

"Fuck! It's a car!"

The two men dashed to the window to look out. Meredith took advantage of their distraction to roll off the bed again, not caring and scarcely feeling the pain when she collided with the nightstand a second time. *Heath.* Who else would be pulling into her driveway? Terrified that he would walk into a trap, Meredith screamed to warn him.

"Heath, be careful! Be care—"

Delgado whirled, drew back his foot, and kicked Meredith in the stomach. "Shut up, you stupid cow!"

Drawing up her knees, Meredith gulped desperately, her breath making short whistling sounds in her windpipe. *Oh, God.* She couldn't breath. A swirling, star-studded blackness blanked out her vision. Finally, her lungs expanded, the indrawn breath catching in her throat and making her gag.

In the twin beams of the headlights, Heath saw two men outlined against Meredith's bedroom window. What the hell? One man held something in his hand that flashed like a mirror. Heath's gut clenched. *A gun.* He no sooner thought that than he heard a scream.

Heath grabbed for the radio, elbowing Goliath aside to

reach the mike. After keying for transmission, he said, "Masters, calling unit three. Urgent!"

Sarah Brewer, the swing shift dispatcher, came back. "Yes, Sheriff? Over."

Goliath lunged across Heath's lap to claw at the door. Heath hooked one arm around the dog's neck and shoved him back onto the passenger seat. "I've got a B and E at 1423 Hereford Lane. Two men, both armed. I'm going in and need backup. Out."

"Sending backup, 1423 Hereford Lane. Out."

Heath didn't cut the engine or douse the headlights. The glare would blind the other men and provide him with at least some cover. He threw open the door, using it as a shield as he swung from the Bronco. Goliath leaped out and lunged past him.

The dog looked surreal in the lights, a hundred and fifty pounds of black fury bounding toward the house. Before Heath could even move, the Rottweiler leaped and went airborne, clearing the porch and hurtling himself through the bedroom window. The glass shattered, the shards catching the light and imploding like silver rain into the room.

Like a cannonball, Goliath plowed into the chest of the man standing closest to the window, the force of impact carrying the man backward. The semiautomatic flew from his hand and struck the floor, a bullet discharging with explosive report.

The house suddenly seemed a hundred miles away. Instead of taking a direct path to the porch, Heath hunkered down, circled out from the Bronco into the darkness, and then veered back, giving the lights a wide birth. He felt as if he were running against a headwind. By contrast, his brain was racing, his thoughts a tangle of half-formed perceptions—that of men, of guns, and Meredith screaming. He had no idea who the men were. Or why they were there. He only knew they had weapons and deadly intent.

With each running step, Heath took in details. There was no strange car in the driveway, which meant the men had come in on foot. Judging by the sound of Meredith's cries, she was somewhere in the bedroom. He saw no sign of Sammy.

Thank God he hadn't ignored Goliath's strange behavior. The dog had known. Somehow the dog had known.

Images ran fleetingly through his mind as he reached the porch. Of bedraggled paper roses and a little girl's quivering mouth. Of a woman with a smile so sweet it made his heart catch. Less than thirty minutes ago, Heath had been shaking with anger at Meredith. Now none of that seemed important. Not any of his questions, nor any of her possible explanations. All that mattered was getting her and Sammy out of there.

Heath's first instinct was to rush into the house right behind his dog. His training took over where common sense failed him.

A confusing cacophony of sound erupted from the bedroom. Male voices, crying out in angry surprise, then in fear. Goliath's snarls, deep and frenzied—the crazed battle cry of a dog attacking to kill. The dull thud of a body hitting a wall. Objects crashing to the floor. Dislodged furniture scraping the linoleum.

Gun drawn and ready, Heath plastered himself against the side of the house. *Never rush in blind.* As difficult as it was, he had to force himself to think. He had no backup yet. If he screwed up, there wouldn't be any second chances.

Meredith. Oh, God. Meredith was in there someplace.

Heath slipped in the front door, any sounds he made drowned out by the ruckus. Back to the wall. In a firing stance. Weapon ready. He knew the drill, had executed the moves a thousand times. He shoved his concern for Meredith to the back of his mind. No room for mistakes, no time to let emotion cloud his judgment.

Guarding his back because he had no idea how many other intruders might be in the house, he slid along the wall toward the bedroom doorway. *Count one.* He dragged in a deep breath and unlatched the safety on his gun. *Count two.* He stepped out from the wall and pivoted to face the doorway, his arms extended, elbows locked, the gun in his hands rock steady. *Count three*. He burst through the doorway, squinting against the blinding glare of his Bronco's headlights.

"County Sheriff! Freeze!"

Heath burst through the bedroom doorway like a tornado, ready to take out anything in his path. Meredith had never been so glad to see anyone in all her life. Wrists locked, weapon ready to fire, he stood with his feet spread and his legs slightly bent, swinging first to the right, then to the left.

She felt as if she were watching a divided television screen, the blur of motion and noise coming at her so fast she couldn't focus on any one thing. Delgado, roaring in pain and trying frantically to get away from Goliath. The dog, snarling horribly and jumping Delgado from behind. The blond man, Nelson, who had been crawling around on the floor to find the gun he'd dropped, leaping out of the darkness to hit Heath broadside. Heath, staggering sideways and loosing his grip on his gun. The two men, pummeling each other, then falling backward, Heath striking his head on the wall.

In the movies, the cops always won. Didn't they? *Oh, God*. Stunned from the blow to his head, Heath slid down the wall and slumped on the floor, a dazed expression on his face. Taking advantage of his opponent's momentary incapacity, Nelson leaped to his feet and began kicking Heath, the blows making muted thudding sounds as the toe of his shoe connected with flesh. Having just experienced the pain of being kicked herself, Meredith's body convulsed with every strike.

Straining at the cord on her wrists, she cried, "Heath! Get up! Oh, God, get up!"

He shook his head, then struggled to his knees. Like a vulture swooping down to tear at carrion, Nelson descended again, delivering a stunning blow to Heath's jaw that sent him reeling backward. Nelson began kicking him again.

"Stop it! Oh, God! Don't!"

Meredith thought sure Heath would never get back up. With one kick to her stomach, she'd been unable to breathe, let alone move, and Heath had been kicked a dozen times. He angled an arm over his mid-section, groaned, and tried to sit up. Nelson laughed and leaned over him, grabbing him by the front of his uniform shirt to haul him to his feet.

"Looks like the big, tough sheriff ain't so tough!"

Arms hanging limply at his sides, his boots set wide apart to keep his balance, Heath swayed and shook his head again, senseless from the blows. Nelson rammed a fist into his belly, knocking him back a step. Heath's lungs expelled breath with a low *whoosh*, but he staggered to stay erect. Nelson advanced on him again.

"Don't! Stop it! Please!" she cried, knowing even as she pleaded that these men didn't know the meaning of the word mercy.

Nelson only laughed. Terrified for Heath, Meredith managed to sit up, but that was all she could do. No matter how she jerked or twisted her arms, she failed to break the cord on her wrists. Only a few feet away, Goliath still struggled with Delgado, his snarls a throaty harmony to the man's hoarse curses and shouts.

As Nelson stepped close to strike Heath again, Heath moved with a suddenness that took both Nelson and Meredith by surprise. Not senseless, after all, she realized. Far from it. Heath grabbed Nelson by the hair and butted the other man in the face with his forehead. Nelson roared and grabbed for his nose, only to have Heath butt him again before he could get his hands up. The blond staggered backward when Heath released him.

"Not so tough, hey, city boy?" Heath grabbed Nelson by the front of his jacket and buried a fist in the man's stomach with such force that Nelson's feet parted company with the floor. When Heath hit him again, Jensen crumpled, his knees cracking loudly against the floor as he fell. "Out here, we call it playing possum, asshole. Lesson number one: when you're kicking the shit out of country boys, don't get cocky.''

Nelson slumped onto his side in a fetal position, blinking to clear his vision, his nose and mouth streaming blood. Sitting only a few feet from him, Meredith wished with all her heart that her hands were free so she could thump him a good one herself. She would never forget or forgive the way he had dragged Sammy around by her hair.

Heath stepped around Nelson to retrieve his semiautomatic. Just as he bent to pick up the gun, Nelson made a grab for it as well. This time, however, he didn't have the element of surprise to give him an advantage. Heath came down on top of him, and being the larger and stronger of the two, he quickly pinned Nelson and gained control of the weapon.

Just as Heath started to roll Nelson over onto his stomach to cuff him, the room exploded with the report of a gun. Heath jerked and whirled toward the sound. Only a few feet away, Delgado writhed on the floor, trying frantically to pry Goliath's jaws loose from his wrist. A mere inch beyond the man's reach lay his gun, which had evidently gone off accidentally while he struggled with the dog.

With the heel of his hand, Heath slid Delgado's weapon well away from him. ''Hold him, Goliath!''

The Rottweiler released Delgado's wrist to seize him by the throat. The dark-haired man went still, stark terror contorting his features.

Heath reared up on his knees over Nelson and went suddenly still himself. Meredith drew her gaze from Delgado and Goliath, wondering what was wrong. Then she saw the blood pooling on the floor under Nelson's head.

''Oh, God,'' Heath said softly. ''He's dead.''

Meredith couldn't believe it. Heath leaned forward to check for a pulse. At his touch, Nelson's head lolled sideways, turning his face toward Meredith. Blank, blue eyes stared at her. Her stomach convulsed, and her bile rose.

''Got him in the back of his head,'' Heath said.

Meredith couldn't stop staring at the blood. It was

spreading out from Nelson's head like a small lake, obscenely crimson against the speckled linoleum.

Heath didn't seem as affected by the gore as she was. Moving away from the body, he quickly checked something on his gun and pushed unsteadily to his feet. For a moment, he seemed to have difficulty standing. The punishment he'd taken from Nelson had taken more of a toll on his body than he'd let on, she realized.

Awash in the blaze of light that poured in the window, his dark face revealed no emotion. He simply stood there for a moment, as if regathering his strength. Then, swinging around, he aimed his semiautomatic at Delgado.

The man still lay in a motionless sprawl. Every time he so much as breathed too deeply, the Rottweiler snarled and bit down over his throat a little harder.

"I should let him rip out your jugular," Heath said as he stooped to pick up Delgado's gun. He winced and pressed his arm to his abdomen as he straightened. After tucking the weapon under his belt, he said, "All right. Off, Goliath. I've got him."

The Rottweiler whined and backed slowly away. Delgado pressed a shaky hand to his neck. "He could've killed me!" he cried in a voice gone weak with fright.

"If he'd wanted to kill you, you'd be dead," Heath retorted. "Roll over, face down, arms behind your back! Give me any trouble, and I'll let him tear you apart."

The instant Delgado turned over, Heath planted a knee in the center of the man's back, then holstered his gun.

"Easy!" Delgado cried. "Take it easy. You trying to snap my spine? I'm gonna sue! Unnecessary force! There are laws, man. You can't treat people like this!"

It looked to Meredith as if Heath pressed down even harder with his knee. Then he removed the set of handcuffs from the pouch on his belt and snapped one of the bands closed over Delgado's wrist, the other over the footrail of the bed frame. The moment the cuffs clicked closed, Goliath raced from the bedroom. Meredith suspected the dog had gone to find Sammy.

Sammy. Tears rushed to Meredith's eyes. What kind of state might the child be in? She had to be all right. She just had to be. Thanks to Heath and Goliath, Meredith had survived Glen's second attempt to kill her. Before he could try again, she and Sammy would be far away from here, leaving no trail so Glen might find them again.

For now, it was over. She and Sammy were safe. Where there was life, there was hope, and that was what she needed to focus on.

Heath pushed to his feet. As he turned toward her, the lights of his Bronco struck him full in the face. His dark features were set in grim lines, his mouth narrowed, a muscle along his jaw twitching. As he moved toward her with slow, deliberate steps, his gaze flashed like quicksilver in the glare of the headlights, seeming to scorch her everywhere it touched.

Not over, she realized. Without his saying a word, she knew he had discovered the truth about her. It was written all over him, from the measured way he moved to the glitter in his eyes.

Back when she'd first met him, Meredith remembered thinking that having to deal with this man when he was angry wasn't an ordeal she wanted to experience, and even after she'd come to know him better, she'd always been careful never to make him mad.

Well, she'd done it now. The laser-hot blast of his eyes could have pulverized rock.

Chapter 19

Heath had never been so furious. Walking away from the man on the floor without killing him was the most difficult thing he'd ever done. Then he saw a dark splotch of blood on the sleeve of Meredith's white shirt, and his rage went from barely restrained to atomic, erupting in a cloud of heat that seared a path to his face.

She was hurt. The sons of bitches had hurt her. Heath knotted his hands into fists, struggling against the urge to strangle the one surviving man with his bare hands.

Meredith jerked away as he knelt beside her. When he touched her shoulder, she flinched. The fear he saw in her eyes would have taken him to his knees if he hadn't already been there. She thought his anger was directed at her.

For a moment, he couldn't think why she would believe that. Then he remembered how furious he had been earlier when he'd learned there was a warrant out for her arrest. That was an issue he had no choice but to address, but he'd worry about it later. Right now, he had more immediate concerns.

"Are you all right?" His voice came out gruff and strained. "You're bleeding."

She glanced down at her sleeve. "It's nothing. A scrape, is all." Her teeth began chattering as she spoke, and then her body began to shake. "Just a scrape."

Concerned that she might be going into shock, Heath

touched his fingertips to her throat to take her pulse, which was elevated but within normal range. Her skin felt dry, rather than cold and clammy, which was a good sign as well.

"Where's Sammy?" he asked gently.

At the mention of her daughter, she began to jerk futilely to free her arms. "Have to go. Find her. Please." A stricken look came over her face. "Oh, God, that man—her hair." Her voice broke. "Jerked her around—up onto a chair. She ran a—away!"

"Merry, calm down." Heath bent to untie her. "Do you know where she went?"

"Outside. They ch—chased her. Brought her back. She *bit* him!" A hysterical little laugh erupted from her. "Bless her heart. She bit him and got away. I have to go find her. I have to! Please, Heath?"

She was tearing so frantically at the cord on her wrists that he was afraid she might hurt herself. "Merry, stop it!" he ordered harshly. "Hold still so I can get at the knots. That's a girl. Just calm down. We'll find her, all right? I'm sure she's fine. She's a tough little nut."

That was a lie, of course. Sammy was a fragile child, those blue eyes the biggest thing about her. As Heath struggled to free Meredith's wrists, his concern for the little girl's safety mounted. "Do you think they hurt her?"

"Her hair," she repeated. "He grabbed her hair, picked her up, jerked her around!"

Heath had thought he'd never feel more furious than when he saw the blood on Meredith's shirt. Wrong. He wanted to put his fist through something, preferably the salesman's face. He finally succeeded in untying the cord that bound her wrists, then the one at her ankles.

The instant she was free, she scrambled to her feet and raced from the room. Heath ran after her, finding his way in the darkness by memory and hoping with every step that he didn't trip over something and break his neck. He came to a stop just behind Meredith in the bathroom. Moonbeams spilled through the window, gilding the small enclosure with silvery light.

Sammy was huddled in the bathtub with Goliath, her thin little arms wrapped around the dog's neck, her face buried against his fur. She didn't look up when she heard footsteps. For that matter, she didn't move. It was as if she were frozen in one position, clinging to Goliath for dear life.

"Oh, God," Meredith whispered raggedly as she dropped to her knees beside the tub and leaned over the rim to lightly touch her child's hair. "Sammy?" she called softly. "Hey, sweetkins, it's Mommy. Are you okay?"

When the child didn't respond, Meredith sat back on her heels and clamped her hands over her mouth. In the dimness, Heath saw her shoulders jerking and knew she was gulping back sobs. Alarmed by her behavior, he went down on one knee beside her and reached for Sammy himself. The instant his hand settled on the child's back, she shrieked and shrank closer to the dog, who growled and bared his teeth in warning.

"Hey, Sammy," Heath said softly, ignoring Goliath's snarls. "Are you all right, honey?"

At the sound of his voice, Sammy's head came up and she whipped around, giving a joyous little cry. Before Heath could even react, she launched her small body at him. Wincing at the pain that lanced across his bruised rib cage, he caught her close, horribly aware of how violently she was trembling.

"Heef!" she squeaked. "It's you!"

Heath realized then that she'd heard him enter the bathroom behind her mother and believed he was one of the other men. A searing sensation washed over his eyes as he cupped a hand over her head and jostled her against his chest to get a better hold. One of her bony little knees jabbed a sore spot on his abdomen.

"Of course, it's me, sweetcakes. Goliath wouldn't let anyone else get this close to you."

She hugged his neck so tightly that Heath could scarcely

breathe. "I thought they made you go asleep!" she cried. "The gun banged, and I thought they made you go asleep!"

Imagining how terrified she must have been when she heard the gunshots, Heath gathered her even closer. No child her age should have to go through something like that. "No, honey, no. I'm fine. All of us are fine."

Rubbing Sammy's back, Heath glanced over at Meredith. She still sat on her heels with her hands clamped over her mouth. In the moonlight, her eyes looked like glistening splotches of black water.

"I think your mommy needs a hug, Sammy," Heath whispered.

The child gave his neck another fierce squeeze before turning to reach for her mother. With a broken sob, Meredith caught Sammy in her arms and began rocking back and forth. "Thank God," she whispered. "Thank God. It's going to be okay now, punkin. It's going to be okay."

Heath wasn't certain whom Meredith was trying to reassure, the child or herself.

Goliath whined and reared up onto the edge of the tub to nudge Sammy's back. The little girl twisted at the waist to hug the dog's neck again. The Rottweiler bathed her face, whining and growling, almost as if he were speaking to her.

"You came, G'liath. I knew you would." The child rained kisses over the dog's nose. "I called and called, and you heard me, huh? I knew you'd come. I *knew* it. And you bringed Heef to help save us!"

Meredith laughed, the sound shaky and tearful. Releasing her daughter, who was still clinging to the dog, she said, "I heard you calling him."

"I did!" Sammy said with an emphatic nod. "I called him real loud. And he heard me, Mommy!"

A shivery sensation raised goose bumps on Heath's skin. Had the dog heard her? The possibility defied rational explanation, and yet there was a part of Heath that believed it had happened just that way. The strangest part was that Sammy seemed to take the telepathic communication for granted, as if Goliath's "hearing" her were the most natural thing in the world.

Watching the dog and child interact, Heath decided maybe it was. There was surely no sweeter or purer devotion than this. Just love, in all its simplicity, with no barriers or complications.

Still watching her daughter and Goliath, Meredith pushed to her feet, one arm hugging her waist. Heath rose beside her. When she turned toward him, her face was so pale it glowed like iridescent porcelain in the moonlight. She met his gaze evenly, hers dark with uncertainty.

"Well," she said shakily.

There was a wealth of meaning behind that one word—a question with no easy answers. No matter how they circled it, she was wanted on criminal charges.

He had backup on the way. At any moment, his deputies would arrive. He should be arresting her right now—reading her her rights, slapping cuffs on her wrists.

"Meredith," he said huskily, "talk to me. What the hell's happening here?"

Heath wasn't sure what he expected. For her to start crying again, maybe? To give him an explanation, surely. There was a dead man in her bedroom, for Christ's sake.

She moved to the toilet and sat down as if her legs were about to give out. In a voice shaky with fear, she whispered, "He won't stop with sending only two men. More could be coming, even now, and they won't give up until I'm dead."

He'd already determined that this had been no random B and E, that those men had come here with a specific aim that was somehow connected to Meredith. But murder? "Did you say *dead*?"

She wrapped her arms around herself and shivered. "That's why they came," she said, pitching her voice so low that Heath had trouble making out the words. "To kill me. They were going to inject me with a sedative, make me go to sleep. Then they were going to douse the pilot light on the furnace and turn on the gas. It was supposed to look like an accident.'' She kept her gaze fixed on the wall, not looking up at him. ''If you don't believe me, the syringe is in there on the floor someplace. And the letter they made me write is in Delgado's—the encyclopedia salesman's—jacket.''

He leaned down to meet her gaze. ''Have I got this right? You're telling me that those two men actually came here to *kill* you? No figure of speech. No exaggeration. As in six feet under, *dead*?''

She glanced toward the bathtub, where Sammy and Goliath were still making over each other. ''Keep your voice down,'' she said softly. ''I don't want her upset.''

''Upset? Two gunmen just broke into your house, and you don't want her *upset*?'' Heath straightened and shoved a hand through his hair. ''Jesus. You tell me two men just tried to kill you, and you don't expect me to raise my voice? I can't believe this.''

''Believe it. If Sammy hadn't run away, I'd be dead,'' she whispered. ''They were delayed by having to chase her, and then you came.'' Her shoulders lifted in a hopeless shrug. ''He won't stop. He'll just send more men. He'll never stop. For all I know, he could have sent more than just two this time. Knowing how he does things, probably.''

''He? He, who?''

''Glen.''

Heath had no idea who the hell Glen was. Or why he wanted to kill Meredith. And until his backup arrived, he couldn't take time to find out. Not if there was a chance more men might be out there somewhere, watching the house.

He drew his weapon and left the bathroom to make a stealthy tour of the rooms, peering from each window to check the yard and adjoining fields for any sign of movement. *Nothing*.

A few seconds later, he heard the kitchen floor creak. The hair stood up at the back of his neck. After all the work he'd done on this place, he knew every inch of that floor. Someone was walking in there. He crept back the

way he'd come, his pulse slamming. The kitchen lay be-
tween him and the bathroom. If there was another intruder,
Heath would have to get past him to reach Meredith and
Sammy.

Damn, it was dark. He crept through the blackness, his
ears tuned to catch the slightest noise. He heard another
creak, this one near the utility room door. He moved that
way, ready to shoot first and ask questions later. Then, in
the moonlight that came through the window over the sink,
he saw a flash of white.

"Merry?" he whispered.

He heard a faint gasp. As she whirled to face him, she
moved more fully into the moonlight. Heath relaxed and
flicked his weapon back on safety. "For God's sake, what
are you trying to do, get shot?"

She gave no reply, just stood there with one hand on the
knob of the utility room door. Sammy and Goliath stood
beside her.

It was then that Heath realized they had been about to
sneak out. Anger streaked through him. Measuring off the
distance between them in three long strides, he clamped a
hand over Meredith's wrist. "Oh, no, you don't."

Even in the shadows, he could see the appeal in her eyes.
"*Please?*"

Just that one word, whispered to him like a prayer.
Please.

Heath knew she had intended to run, that she was begging him to turn a blind eye and let her go. He tightened
his grip on her wrist, acutely conscious of the fragile network of bones under his pressing fingers.

The next instant, he heard cars skidding to a stop out
front. A dizzying play of blue and red light danced over
the walls.

"My deputies," he explained. "Before I came in, I radioed for backup."

"Oh," she said faintly and let her eyes fall closed. "I
see."

No, Heath thought, she didn't see. He was the sheriff.

He wasn't allowed to have personal feelings, not if they interfered with his job.

His job. Never had it cost him quite so dearly to execute his duties. To do what he had to do, he found himself blocking out reality and performing by rote. Directing his deputies. Calling for an ambulance. And, finally, arresting the woman he had come to love. Reading her her rights. Drawing her arms behind her back and securing her wrists with handcuffs.

The entire time, Sammy stood off to the side, softly crying, her huge blue eyes filled with accusation. With every word and every action, Heath knew he was destroying the trust he had worked so hard to establish between him and the child. And that was to say nothing of the damage he was doing to his relationship with Meredith.

Heath drew the line when it came time for the prisoners to be taken into town. Under other circumstances, he would have stayed on at the scene, allowing someone else to provide transport. Not this time. He took Meredith in himself, flaunting regulations by putting her up front in the passenger seat instead of at the back behind wire mesh. He told himself it was because the seats in the storage section, where he usually hauled prisoners, were so uncomfortable. But the truth was, he couldn't bring himself to subject her to any more humiliation.

En route to the department, he wanted nothing more than to talk with her. To his way of thinking, he damned well deserved an explanation for all of this. But Sammy was in the backseat with Goliath, able to hear every word that was said. Discussing any part of this mess in front of her didn't strike him as a wise idea. Meredith seemed of like mind, for she uttered not a word during the whole trip.

Once at the department, Heath turned Sammy over into the care of Deputy Helen Bowyer. The mother of four, Helen had a wonderful way with kids, and Heath trusted her to make this ordeal as easy for Sammy as possible.

Tugging uselessly against the restraints on her wrists, Meredith blanched when Helen came to take her child away. She turned an imploring gaze on Heath. "Please," she whispered so Sammy wouldn't overhear. "She'll get so upset."

The way Heath saw it, Meredith should have thought about how her daughter might react to this separation *before* she broke the law. "She'll be fine."

As gently as possible, he grasped Meredith's arm and forced her into a walk. Even then, she hung back, craning her neck to keep her daughter in sight.

"She'll be all right, Meredith. For right now, Goliath's with her."

Once inside his office, Heath locked the door and drew the blinds so they had some privacy. After depositing Meredith on the chair in front of his desk, he stepped around to face her. Folding his arms, he locked gazes with her, giving no quarter.

"I think it's time you start talking. Sammy can't hear you now. No excuses."

Meredith gulped, the sound making a hollow plunk at the base of her throat. She was so nervous that she wasn't sure she could talk, even if she could figure out what to say. At the best of times, Heath Masters was a lot of man to contend with, well over six feet tall, every inch of him roped with muscle. And right now, there was no mistaking that he was coldly furious.

He stood with his booted feet set apart, his arms folded over his broad chest, his body so rigid that in places his khaki shirt was stretched tight over bunched tendons. The stormy expression on his face, coupled with the stare of his relentless blue-gray eyes, made her mouth go dry.

"What, exactly, do you want to know?" she asked, stalling for time. She had no idea how to begin. The story sounded crazy, even to her. He would probably never believe it.

A muscle began to tick along his jaw. "Goddammit, Meredith, don't play games with me. I want to know it all, from start to finish."

He grabbed a straight-backed chair and dragged it over

to her. When he sat down, he was so close, he would have
been nose to nose with her if he hadn't been so tall. He
corrected that problem by leaning forward and bracing his
arms on his knees, the position thrusting his face so close
to hers that she jerked away. Unfortunately, the back of her
chair only allowed her to retreat a scant few inches.

"Start talking."

She tried to moisten her lips with a tongue that felt like
parchment. "I, um . . . I'm not playing games. Honestly. I
just don't know where to start."

He narrowed his eyes, clearly not convinced she was
being up front with him. With her wrists handcuffed behind
her back, she felt vulnerable in a way that brought back
memories she'd tried hard to forget, and suddenly she
found it difficult to breathe.

After regarding her relentlessly for a moment, he reached
up, jerked off her wig, and tossed it on his desk, his firm
mouth thinned into a sneer. Then, with a harsh glint in his
eyes, he hooked a fingertip under the strap of her bra, tracing its length to the cup where he tested the thickness of
the padding. Meredith did stop breathing then, her heart
pounding at the base of her throat.

The dread that Heath saw in Meredith's eyes stopped him
cold and forced him to take stock of what he was doing.
He glanced down and stared at his hand, feeling as if it
belonged to someone else. His fingers were plunged inside
the cup of her bra, his knuckles pressed intimately against
soft flesh, the only barrier between his skin and hers the
well-worn cotton of her shirt. *Christ.* She was in restraints,
her arms angled sharply behind her back. He shouldn't even
be touching her.

He jerked his hand away. Rubbed his face. Rocked back
in his chair. When he had regrouped and felt in control, he
leaned forward again to brace his arms on his knees.

"Everything about you is a lie," he whispered. "One
great big lie, from start to finish. Why don't you start with
that? Has there been any honesty at all between us, Meredith? On your part, I don't think so. I found you on the

computer tonight. I know everything, your real name, that you blatantly disregarded a court order and left New York, that you're wanted for kidnapping. I'd like some kind of explanation. I think I deserve at least that much.''

When she didn't speak, he sighed.

''Start with—what was his name?—Ben? Who the hell is he, and why would he send those men to kill you?''

She just sat there, staring at him, her platinum-streaked honey-colored hair forming a shimmering tangle around her face, which was still as pale as wax. Dimly, Heath wondered why in the hell she had chosen to wear a wig instead of dying her hair. Probably, he decided, because she'd had no idea how long she might be able to stay in Wynema Falls.

As if it mattered? He was losing it. Really losing it. He'd just shoved his hand inside her bra, for Christ's sake. And now his thoughts were racing, none of them making sense. He'd always prided himself on being level-headed, on keeping his emotions in check. Not so tonight. He wanted to shake her, and judging by her pallor, she knew it.

She fixed her gaze on the floor, her posture rigid. No tears. More importantly, no explanations. Just an awful, brittle self-control, as if she were barely managing to ward off hysteria. Her resolute silence frustrated him.

''Meredith, for God's sake, talk to me. How can you expect me to help you, if all you do is lie to me? Has it gotten to be second nature for you, or something? Lie, lie, lie? I have to know what the hell is going on.''

With a suddenness that startled him, she looked up, her eyes blazing. ''I *lied* to you, yes! No honesty, from the very beginning. Just one lie right after another. If you want to condemn me for that, go right ahead. I did what I had to do to protect my daughter. Nothing more, nothing less! As far as I'm concerned, Sheriff Masters, you can take your sanctimonious attitude and go straight to hell!''

This, from the lady who wouldn't say ''shit'' if she had a mouthful? Heath was so startled by her outburst that he blinked. Nothing changed. She was still glaring at him with a fierceness that was totally uncharacteristic, her small chin thrust forward, her cheekbones flagged with angry color.

"As for my being wanted for kidnapping? I hate to tell you this, but your precious judicial system isn't always fair! And neither is life. Do you think I *asked* for any of this? That I made choices, hoping that one day I'd be sitting here, about to be put in prison? I'm going to lose my *child*, damn you!" She gestured toward the door with a swing of her head. "She's out there, right this minute, scared to death! Not *just* because she's been separated from me, as you seem bent on believing, but because she knows what's in store for her if we can't get out of here!"

Her voice broke at the last, and she sank her teeth into her bottom lip. The pain he saw etched into every line of her face was no lie. He would have bet his life on that.

"Then talk to me. Let me try to help you. If you don't tell me everything, Meredith, how can I do anything, except my job?"

Her shoulders shook. For a moment he thought she was sobbing. Then he realized she was laughing. "Help me?" she finally said. "You just don't get it, do you? Those men who broke into my house weren't your dime store variety burglars. They were professionals. Thugs, for want of a better word. They do stuff like this for a living."

"Thugs," he repeated. "And they work for this guy, Ben?"

"*Glen!* Glen Calendri, my *esteemed* ex-father-in-law. He's an international union official. He has criminal connections."

Heath couldn't believe he had heard her right. "Criminal connections."

"Organized crime, for want of a better word."

For a moment, all Heath could do was stare at her. "Meredith, the term 'organized crime' is generally used only in reference to widespread and very sophisticated crime rings."

"I realize that."

"Then don't use the term loosely."

She looked up, her eyes shimmering with tears. "I'm not. That's why you can't help me. No one can."

Heath saw that she was serious. He raked a hand through his hair. "Organized crime," he repeated. "Your father-in-law?"

"Yes," she said faintly.

"How in the hell did you get tied up with people like that?"

"I did an incredibly stupid thing."

"What?"

"I got married."

"Married? Millions of women get married."

She let her head fall forward, her hair forming a curtain that hid her face. "I guess you could say I have lousy taste in men."

"So your husband had criminal connections?"

"Yes."

"And you married him?"

"I didn't know when I married him. I found out soon after, but then it was too late."

"You expect me to believe you married a guy, and you had no clue he was a slimeball?"

"I honestly didn't."

"That's a little hard for me to swallow. You sure as hell didn't have any trouble being suspicious of me."

"Yes, well, I've learned a lot since then. I don't trust as easily as I once did."

That was an understatement. "So you *accidentally* married a hoodlum," he capsulized. "What then? How did you get from wedded bliss to kidnapping your own child and being a target for murder?"

"It was *never* wedded bliss," she said bitterly. "It was a nightmare, from start to finish! And I *didn't* realize! Get that right out of your head. I would have had to be crazy to marry him if I had. Until after the wedding, I thought he was wonderful!"

Heath could see that he'd poked at a real sore spot. Knowing her—hell, maybe she actually had been that naïve. He couldn't count the times that he'd sensed she felt out of her depth with him, and he would have wagered his last dollar that she had little experience with men.

"Hey, look," he said gently. "I'm sorry. That was a rotten shot for me to take. Of course you didn't realize."

"I honestly didn't. The only other man I knew well was my dad, and he's so—" Her voice caught, and she looked up again, her expression softening. "He's so *good*. You know? Kind and honest and God-fearing. I thought *all* men were like him. Now I know better. Every other man I've ever met has been a skunk in one way or another."

"Ouch."

"I don't mean you."

He could hope. "So you were very sheltered growing up, in other words."

"On a farm in Mississippi. And not sheltered, exactly. It's a world apart down there. A sleepy little place, where neighbor helps neighbor. My parents didn't shield me. There was nothing in their little world to shield me from."

"How about television and public school? It's a little difficult to be all that insulated from the harsh realities these days."

"Not down there. We were poor. A television was a luxury we couldn't afford, and the school was small, all the kids there just like me, with folks who were poor dirt farmers. Up until November, none of the kids wore shoes. I had one store-bought school dress. My mother made everything else, when we could afford material. I was sixteen before we ever had a refrigerator. I dipped my milk from a bucket in the ice box."

Heath tried to imagine a place so completely segregated from his reality and couldn't. "It sounds sort of backward."

"It *was* backward. Is still is. It's also wonderful. I miss it."

That last admission was so heartfelt that Heath knew she really did miss it. Meredith, the lady with no VCR. "You don't strike me as backward. In fact, I've thought more than once that you must have quite an education under your belt.''

''I do. Computer programming.''

''No refrigerator or television, and you're a computer expert?''

''My dad never got past the sixth grade, so he worked himself half to death to send me to college, thinking he was doing me a big favor. I attended Old Miss.''

''So what happened at Old Miss? No boyfriends to clue you in?''

She met his gaze, hers reflecting bitterness. ''Forget it! Just lock me up. You're not going to believe anything I say, so why bother?''

''That's not true. I do believe you. I'm just trying to get a picture of who you are, Meredith. And how you landed yourself in such a hell of a mess.''

''I was an ignorant hillbilly. Does that synopsize it clearly enough for you? I thought *everyone* went barefoot until the rainy season, all right? As for boyfriends, I didn't have any. They were probably afraid I'd belch and pick my nose in public. Just put me in a cell and leave me alone! I've lied to you about everything else. Why should you believe me now?''

Heath leaned back in his chair and crossed his arms. ''Not until I hear the story. And don't try to snow me, honey. There had to be guys who panted after you in college. I sure as hell would have, and I wouldn't have been put off by cultural differences.''

She avoided his gaze. ''I didn't choose to date very much. All right?''

''Why? You've never liked men, I take it?''

''I liked them fine. *Then!* It was only later I developed what you might call an avid distaste.''

''Avid distaste'' didn't say it by half. Heath couldn't count the times when he'd entered a room and sensed that she couldn't wait to get away from him. ''So why didn't you date back then?''

''It didn't seem right to goof off when I knew how hard

my dad was working to pay my tuition. And my mother went without. One month, she didn't fill her blood pressure prescription to buy one of my text books. How do you think that made me feel?''

''Not very good. And obligated to study. I guess I would have been a bookworm, too. It sounds like one hell of a set of parents you have.''

''The salt of the earth. They would die for me.'' She blinked. ''I can't even call them now. I'm afraid the connection will be traced. I know they must be worried. But all of this is so far beyond them, they could never comprehend. Knowing Dad, he'd drive to New York in the hay truck and knock on Glen's front door. He's not very savvy, my father.''

''And consequently, neither were you.'' The pieces of the puzzle were starting to fit together for Heath, and the image of the younger Meredith that was taking shape in his head nearly broke his heart. Unknowingly, her father had sent her out into a world she had been completely unprepared to deal with. ''It must have been one shock after another, discovering that your home place in Mississippi didn't represent the whole of humanity.''

''I got a few shocks, yes. Dan used to say I still had straw in my hair when he gave me my first job.'' The corners of her mouth trembled. ''He thought I was stupid, and sometimes I wondered if he wasn't right.''

''You're not stupid, Meredith. Far from it.''

''I believed everything he told me when we were dating! That was pretty stupid.'' She got a distant look in her eyes. ''I think I was dazzled by it all—his wealth, the glitter, getting to ride in a limousine. He bought me beautiful presents. Clothes and jewelry. It was like in a fairy tale, and I was Cinderella with her prince.''

Heath tried to imagine what it must have been like for her, a naïve young woman who'd gone barefoot nearly half her life meeting a man who probably wore three-thousand dollar suits and was chauffeured around in a limousine. ''Only he didn't turn out to be a prince?''

Her expression conveyed that she was still lost in the past. "When we went to his townhouse that night, and he started acting so mean, snapping his fingers at me and ordering me around, I thought—" She gulped and shrugged. "I thought he was joking and that it was funny—right up until he hit me."

Heath's gut knotted. "What night was this?"

"Our wedding night."

"He hit you on your wedding night?"

Rationally, Heath knew that a man's striking a woman was unacceptable on any occasion, but for some reason, his doing it on their wedding night seemed even worse. His mind shied away from the pictures her words evoked. Meredith, young and naïve, with stars in her eyes, thinking she'd found her one true love, only to have the bastard turn on her. He couldn't conceive any man hitting her. Those fragile facial bones, the slightness of her build. Heath felt fairly certain he would break her jaw if he even so much as slapped her.

"Ah, honey." Rescinding his vow not to touch her, he cupped a hand to her cheek. "What kind of a man was he, anyway?"

"He was horrible." She turned her cheek into his palm, looking as if she might loose control and start to weep. That she managed to hold back the tears told him just how much steel that Mississippi upbringing had put in her spine. "He was—horrible."

Like scatter spray from a shotgun, the rest of the story erupted from her then. The sadistic games Dan had liked to play. Siccing his Dobermans on her. Terrifying her, just for the hell of it. The beatings he had meted out to her on an almost daily basis. The threats he made on her life. His shady union dealings. His father Glen's connections with higher-ups in a crime syndicate. The arranged killings. Her fear that she might end up dead herself.

"I couldn't go home," she whispered shakily. "Or even tell my dad what was happening. He would have gone to New York loaded for bear. I know he would have. And he would have ended up dead. So I just stayed. I didn't know what else to do. It was—like a nightmare that never stopped, and I couldn't see a way out.''

Heath's heart caught at the anguish he saw in her eyes, and it took every ounce of self-control he had not to take her into his arms. ''Yet at some point, you did divorce him?''

She hauled in a deep, shaky breath and gazed at the ceiling for a moment. ''Yes. Right after Sammy was born.''

''I'm surprised you wanted to bring a child into a mess like that.''

''I didn't. Dan flew into a rage when he realized I was using birth control.'' She laughed, the sound empty and strained. ''He wanted a son to carry on in the family business. Can you believe it? He threw my pills away, and after that I was never allowed to go out alone, so I couldn't get more. Once I realized what he was like, the *last* thing I wanted was to get pregnant, but I did. Within just a couple of months of our wedding.''

Heath wondered if Dan had continued to be abusive during her pregnancy. He wasn't sure he really wanted to know, so he didn't ask. ''And after Sammy was born?''

''When she was four days old, he nearly smothered her with a pillow to make her stop crying. A baby girl wasn't what he'd yearned for, he wanted nothing to do with her, and her crying was annoying his important guests.'' Her mouth twisted, trembled. ''I, um . . . stopped him. He warned me to keep her quiet. 'Babies just stop breathing sometimes, you know.' That's what he said to me. 'They'll think she died in her sleep.' I knew then that I had to get her out of there. I was her mother, and it was my duty to protect her. If he found me and killed me—well, I still had to try. So I ran. And the next morning, I went directly to a lawyer and started the proceedings to sue for divorce.''

''And he never came after you?''

''I knew too much. To protect myself, I drafted a letter with dates and times and details of activities that would have put both him and his father behind bars if it ever went to the authorities. My attorney kept a copy in his office safe, I put another in a safe deposit box with instructions that, in the event of my death, it was to be sent to the district attorney's office. My lawyer also sent copies to Dan and his dad. Dan was afraid to come after me or harm me, for fear he'd go to prison.''

Heath sensed there was far more, that she'd left out the more intimate aspects of her marriage. Judging by her timidity around him, Heath could only guess at the things Calendri might have done to her.

Carefully continuing the questioning, Heath learned that the divorce decree had awarded Dan child visitation rights, and that during those weekend visits, the man had badly abused Sammy, causing her serious emotional trauma. Terrified for her child, Meredith had taken Dan back to court, hoping to get his visiting privileges revoked. Dan had filed a countersuit for sole custody of the child, claiming Meredith was an unfit mother.

After Dan's death in a car accident, Glen Calendri took up the litigation where his son had let off. At that point, Sammy was Glen's only living heir, and he was determined that she would be raised as a Calendri. He brought in paid witnesses who swore under oath that Meredith used illegal drugs, engaged in lewd conduct, and that she frequently left her child unattended. It was nothing but bald-faced lies, but Glen was waging war, no-holds-barred, and Meredith found herself losing at every turn.

The court battle came to a premature end when Meredith's attorney died suspiciously of a heart attack, and she subsequently learned that the exposé letter she had written had disappeared, both from his office safe and from her safe deposit box.

"I knew Glen had had my lawyer killed," she whispered. "And shortly thereafter, I was nearly run down by a car. It wasn't an accident. With the letters gone, there was nothing to stop them, and they were going to take me out."

"So you ran," he said softly.

"You understand, don't you? That I had no choice? I

couldn't let Glen have Sammy. I just couldn't.''

"Ah, Merry,'' he said, his voice gravelly with regret. "Why didn't you tell me all of this sooner? Didn't you trust me to help you? If it hadn't been for Goliath's weird behavior, I might not have rushed home tonight. Where would that have left you? Do you realize you could be dead?''

"And if I had told you?'' She shook her head, her eyes aching with sadness. "There were times when I wanted to, I admit it. Times when I wished with all my heart that I could. But it was just wishful thinking. I knew that.''

"Why?''

She gazed at him for a long moment, a world of hurt reflected in her expression. "I knew your job was the most important thing in the world to you. That you needed it, like I need air to breathe.''

"My job's not *the* most important thing, Meredith.''

"Isn't it?'' Her eyes filled with tears. "It seems to me that tonight has proved it is. Here I am, arrested and in handcuffs, my daughter and I sitting ducks for Glen's thugs.''

"That's hitting below the belt. What choice did I have?''

"None, I guess. But by the same token, this isn't exactly what I call help, either, Heath. I'm not safe here. And when I'm sent back to New York, which I will be, you'll be signing my death warrant. Is that your idea of helping me?''

He pushed up from his chair and began to pace. After taking several turns around the room, he stopped to regard her. She looked damned uncomfortable with her arms twisted behind her back, and she continually chafed at the bracelets.

"Are those cuffs bothering you?''

"Does it matter?''

He cursed under his breath as he walked toward her. "You're trying your damnedest to put me on a guilt trip, aren't you?'' He quickly unlocked the cuffs, removed them, and returned them to the pouch on his belt. "Do you think you're being fair?''

"All's fair," she said simply, rubbing her wrists. "My daughter's future is at stake. Dan didn't turn out the way he did by accident. He was raised by Glen Calendri and learned to be what he was from his father. I'll do anything to keep Sammy safe from Glen. Cheat, lie, steal. Anything. If that means playing dirty, I won't hesitate."

"Putting me on notice, Meredith?"

She met his gaze head-on. "Yes."

Heath smiled in spite of himself. All along, he'd wanted honesty from her; now he was getting it. "I'm going to step out for a minute. I have a phone call to make."

She looked startled. "And leave me alone?"

At the door, he turned to grin at her. "You won't be going anywhere. Not without Sammy, and she's surrounded by deputies."

Heath went to the pay phone outside to place his call. Dumb of him, he guessed. But he didn't want anyone overhearing his conversation, especially Meredith. It had been a hell of a long time since he'd contacted his father to ask for help.

As he dropped a coin in the slot and punched out the phone number, Heath braced himself for a proverbial kick in the teeth. His father was a self-absorbed jerk, always had been. Unfortunately, Ian Masters was also the most knowledgeable man about the law in Heath's acquaintance. The last Heath had heard from Skeeter Pope, his dad's ranch foreman, Ian was taking a two-week hiatus at the ranch. Heath just hoped to God he was still there and hadn't already returned to Chicago.

On the fourth ring, Ian answered. "Masters, here."

The way his father answered the phone reminded Heath of himself. *Damn.* He hated to think that he was like his dad, in any way. "Dad? It's me, Heath."

A long silence. Then, "To what do I owe this honor?"

The sarcastic bastard. Heath clenched his teeth. He could do this. For Meredith and Sammy, he could do it. "I, um, need some advice."

"You're calling *me* for advice? This is a new twist. You've never listened to a damned thing I've said in thirty-eight years, and now suddenly you want my advice?"

Heath almost slammed the receiver down. Almost. He undoubtedly would have if a picture of Meredith's pale face hadn't flashed through his mind. For her, he would eat humble pie. By the shovelful if he had to. "I need legal advice, and there's no one I know who holds a candle to you. Are you going help me, or not?"

"What the hell have you done this time?"

That almost made Heath grin. In his dad's mind, he was still a nineteen-year-old kid with a wild hair up his ass. "You'll be relieved to hear it's not me with my tit in a wringer. I'm calling for a friend."

"What kind of a wringer?"

As briefly and concisely as he could, Heath told Ian the story. "Anyway, I'm thinking about taking her and the child into protective custody."

"My God, son, look at the facts, here. This woman is wanted. The charges against her are serious. Everything she told you could be a pack of lies."

"I don't think so."

"It's not your job to decide that. If her life's really in danger, let them worry about it back in New York."

"With organized crime involved? She may never reach New York, and if she does, they'll just have her killed in prison. It's done all the time, and from what she told me, she knows too much for them to let her live."

"You don't know that. And it isn't up to you to play judge and jury," Ian reminded him. "If you try to help this woman, it may be the dumbest move of your life! A blatant flouting of the law that may jeopardize your career. Do you have any authorization to take her into protective custody?"

The way Heath remembered it, his father had never held his career in very high regard, anyway. "No. It would be my call."

"A call you would make without knowing all the facts." Ian snorted with disgust. "Use your head, Heath. You have no idea what this Meredith Kenyon could be involved in. Drug trafficking, for all you know! There are any number of reasons why those two men may have tried to kill her. The smart thing for you to do is extradite her. If you had any sense, you'd be making the necessary calls to set the wheels in motion right now. There's such a thing as obstruction of justice, remember. You shouldn't take her into protective custody on her say-so alone. You show me a criminal who *admits* to committing the crime, and I'll put in with you. They always have a sob story.''

As much as he hated to admit it, Heath knew his father was right. ''So basically what you're saying is that my career could go down the tubes if I help her.''

''And you could end up serving time. This is serious stuff! Kidnapping, and a man is dead. If you get involved, your ass could end up being grass, a judge the lawn mower. With a child mixed into the equation and a warrant out on the mother, how long could you keep them in protective custody, anyway? The authorities in New York are going to demand her extradition and that the child be turned over to her legal guardian. What're you going to do then? Tell them to go screw themselves? You do that, and you'll find yourself in more trouble than you can handle. Sheriff or not, at that point, *you* would be an accessory, not just to kidnapping, but possibly other criminal offenses you aren't even aware of. Is that what you want? To serve time over this?''

''No, of course not.''

''Toughen up. Just do your job. I've been there a couple of times. I know it tugs on the heartstrings when a woman plays on your sympathy. But, hey, the Don Quixotes of this world always get screwed. She isn't worth it.''

Heath sighed. ''Well, thanks for the advice.''

''What are you going to do?''

''What I have to do,'' Heath said hollowly. ''You're right. I know that. I guess I just needed to hear you say it.''

Chapter 20

As Heath reentered the building, the sound of a child crying drew him to an inner office where he found Helen attempting to soothe an inconsolable Sammy. When the little girl saw Heath, she struggled down from the female deputy's lap.

"I want my mommy!" she said, sobbing as she hugged Heath's leg. "Please, I want my mommy!"

Goliath trotted over, whining in concern and nudging Sammy's back. Heath hunkered down to loop an arm around the child. "Hey, there, sweetcakes. Why all the fuss? You've got Goliath here."

"We *both* want my mommy!" she cried, rubbing her eye with a fist. "Where'd she go?"

"She's in my office."

Heath cupped the child's small face in his hands and rubbed at her tears with his thumbs. It was hard to say no to those big blue eyes. Besides, he asked himself, what could it hurt to allow mother and child a short visit? Soon, they would be separated for a very long time, possibly forever. Sammy's grandfather might never let Meredith see the child again after she was released from prison.

"I guess I can take you in for a short visit."

Sammy immediately brightened. "Can G'liath come?"

"Sure."

After leading the child and the dog to his office, Heath

stood just inside with his back to the door, numbly watching Meredith comfort her daughter. Within him, a gamut of emotions were at war for supremacy, not the least of which was his affection for this woman and child. He knew what he had to do. The badge he wore on his chest demanded it of him. But that didn't mean it was easy.

Meredith's whispered reassurances to Sammy drifted to him like accusations. *It's going to be all right, sweetie. I won't let anything bad happen to you, I promise.* Despite the avowals, there was an underlying note of uncertainty and terror in Meredith's voice. Heath squeezed his eyes closed, trying to block it out. As his father had so succinctly pointed out, it wasn't up to him to play judge and jury. Meredith could be lying.

All's fair, she'd told him. She had as good as said that she would lie to him and use him, that he shouldn't trust her. Maybe her being so honest with him on that score was what made him believe so strongly that she was telling the truth about everything else.

More importantly, though, Heath was impressed by the fact that she had other weapons at her disposal that she still hadn't used. The stakes in this were high, the woman wasn't stupid, and yet she wasn't playing her one trump card. She had to realize how deeply he cared for her, yet she hadn't tried to use that to her advantage. No tearful avowals of love for him, no offers of a sensual nature, no sobbing and pleading with him to save her.

Heath knew that many women, in similar circumstances, would have played this hand out differently. Far differently. Hell, he'd had female prisoners come on to him in every conceivable fashion, offering him whatever he wanted in exchange for his dropping the charges against them. He'd been kissed, felt up, and afforded the dubious pleasure of seeing women strip and play with themselves in an attempt to entice him.

Not that he believed seduction would come easily to Meredith. In fact, he had a feeling she abhorred the thought of sexual intimacy. But, unless he was reading her totally wrong, her own fears and aversions would take a second seat to her daughter's welfare. She would probably do almost anything, make any sacrifice, to save her child, even if it meant having sex with him.

Funny, that. Having sex with her would be his dream come true. He wasn't sure he'd be able to walk away if Meredith Kenyon slipped out of that shirt and gazed up at him with a come-hither look in her eyes. Even the thought tied his guts into knots. Yet she hadn't used that against him. The fact that she hadn't told him more about her than she could possibly know.

Heath took a deep breath. *Christ.* He felt as though he were standing on a high dive and about to jump.

He focused to find Sammy gazing across the office at him. *Friends are s'posed to be friends, no matter what,* she'd told him that morning. God, that seemed like a lifetime ago. And yet the words rang in his mind as clearly as if she'd just said them.

He smiled at her. Clinging to her mother, the child gazed soberly back at him. She was a tiny replica of Meredith. The same fragile build and delicate features, the same big eyes. Someday even her hair would probably turn the same color as her mother's, a rich honey color streaked with gold. She'd be a heartbreaker, too, no question about it.

Right at the moment, Heath wasn't entirely sure who he loved the most, Meredith or her daughter. He only knew he did love them, each in a different way, and that even if it *was* the dumbest move he'd ever made, he couldn't sacrifice either of them on the altar of the law.

He'd already had to endure one lecture from Sammy today. Maybe he needed another one. Sure, performing his duty, keeping his oath, and being honorable were important. Until now, he had lived by those tenets. But there were other things that were equally important. Right at the top of the list was being a loyal friend, no matter what.

The whys and wherefores didn't matter. Meredith needed him. The truth of that was there in her eyes, a tug on his heart he couldn't deny. Brown eyes, blue eyes. It didn't matter. It was the essence of her that he had come to love, and right or wrong, he couldn't turn his back on her.

Barely aware that he had moved, Heath strode across the room. He grasped Meredith's arm and drew her to her feet. "Come on. We're getting out of here," he told her gruffly.

She gave him a startled look. "What?"

"We're leaving. I'll take you someplace where you and Sammy will be safe until I can iron all this out and decide what the hell to do." He drew her arms behind her back to put the handcuffs back on her wrists. "At least it will buy us some time."

She threw a frightened glance toward the window. Heath knew she was thinking of the dangers that could be lurking out there. She obviously didn't feel entirely confident that she could count on him to protect them. Hell, to be honest, he was none too sure of it, himself. Taking on thugs who were affiliated with international union leaders and organized crime was pretty scary stuff.

"Look, Meredith," he said softly. "I'm won't railroad you into this. And I can't promise we'll come out of it in one piece."

Her gaze clung to his, the expression on her face one of stark fear. Heath wished he could tell her he was one tough son of a bitch, that he could take on the mob with one arm tied behind his back and still kick ass and take names.

"I guess you put it best," he said. "I'm a big fish in a little pond—the sheriff of Podunk, Oregon. This mess you're in is way out of my league. I'm liable to get my ass kicked nine ways to hell, and take you and Sammy down with me. On the other hand, taking a chance with me is better than no chance at all."

"Wh—where will you take us?" she asked shakily. "Are you sure it'll be safe there? That they won't find us?"

"I'm not sure of anything," he admitted. "I wish I were." He sighed and ran his hand over his face, feeling suddenly tired and old beyond his years. "The way I see it, our best chance is for me to stick with what I know. They're big city. If they follow us into a wilderness area, they won't know their asses from holes in the ground.''

"A wilderness area. Out in the middle of nowhere, you mean?"

Looking down at her, Heath began to wonder if the threat from Glen Calendri's thugs was her only worry. In the wilderness, she would be completely dependent upon him for everything. She'd trusted a man once, and just look where that had gotten her.

"Well?" he pressed. "It's your call, sweetheart. But don't take all night. If we hang around here too long, my deputies will start to wonder what the hell's going on. I should have you processed by now and be locking you up."

"Is it legal for you to do this? I mean . . . is there any chance you could get in trouble?"

"I'm the sheriff, aren't I? I answer only to the county commissioners. If I deem it necessary, of course I can take a prisoner into protective custody." Heath didn't add that the safest place for a prisoner was usually in a cell. If he kept Meredith here, the New York authorities would demand she be extradited as soon as they were notified she was in custody. He couldn't let that happen until he knew for sure that she'd be protected. "I know what I'm doing, Meredith."

Hope flickered in her eyes. "Well, then, of course, I'll go. It's just—"

"Just what?"

"It's just so frightening. A wilderness area? I know nothing about the woods in this part of the country, and—"

"You don't need to. You'll have me." He caught her chin with the crook of his finger and lifted her face. "Merry, you're going to have to trust me. After hearing the story about Dan, I know it's probably not easy for you, and I don't fault you for that. If anyone ever had reason to keep her guard up, it's you. But, sweetheart, you don't have a choice. I promise you, I'll do the best I can to keep both of you safe."

Her eyes clung to his, as if she were searching for things he'd left unsaid.

"I'm right. You know I'm right," he whispered. "If you don't go with me, you'll be sent back to New York, and Glen will get custody of Sammy. Like I said, this will buy us some time. I've got some connections. I might be able to do some finagling at this end to minimize the risks when you are sent back, and maybe I can cast enough doubt on Glen's character that they'll make Sammy a ward of the court until he's been more thoroughly investigated."

"Do you really think so?"

Heath didn't know. He just didn't know. "What can it hurt to try?"

Leaving the sheriff's department turned out to be far easier than Heath anticipated. Everyone in the outer office stared at him in stunned perplexity when he informed them that he was taking Meredith and the child into protective custody. But in the past, Heath had always demanded absolute compliance with his orders and decisions, and he took full advantage of that mindset now, using his authority to forestall any questions.

Taking Deputy Bailey aside, Heath said, "I'm leaving you in charge, Charlie. I'll keep you posted by radio."

The older man rubbed the top of his bald head, looking concerned. "You sure you know what you're doin', Heath? Where are you takin' 'em?"

"I think it's safer if I don't tell you that. I have reason to believe the mob has its finger in this, Charlie. The woman's life is in serious peril. Once I reach my destination, I'll even drive several miles away from there to contact you by radio. I don't want to take any chance on their zeroing in on our location."

"The mob? Holy shit."

Keeping it short, Heath filled Charlie in on the story Meredith had told him.

"Those mob boys play rough, son," Charlie warned. "Keep your head down and your asshole puckered. And, for God's sake, be careful with that radio. They have more technical gadgets than a hog belly's got freckles." Charlie leaned closer. "I seen a show the other night where they aimed a little gadget at a house and could hear everything folks said inside. From clear out on the street! And they tapped into the phone line from out there, too."

Heath smiled to himself. Charlie was a good deputy and a loyal friend, but his perception of the world was similar to Meredith's down in Mississippi, very cloistered, the only difference being that Charlie watched television. "I'll be careful. Count on that. The lady's important to me."

Charlie nodded. "For a hundred and six pounds, she's put together real nice. Not much of a rack, though." The paunchy deputy shrugged. "Hell, who notices? You know? My Mabel's ain't much bigger than skeeter bites, but I wouldn't trade her for a dozen busty women. She keeps me cool in summer and warm in winter. What more can a man ask?"

Heath chuckled. His life was turned upside down, he might find himself surrounded by thugs shortly after he left this building, and Charlie was talking about his sex life? The man was obsessed. As if anyone could determine Mabel's breast size? The woman weighed 350 pounds.

Heath rested a hand on the deputy's shoulder. "Charlie, you keep your nose out of the girlie magazines. You hear? I need you to look smart and keep your eyes open for trouble. I have a feeling we may get a dose."

"I don't look at the pictures. Mabel'd slice my bacon and slap it on a hot griddle." He scratched his nose. "I only read them articles. They're real informational, you know. Written by educated fellows."

"My ass." Heath punched Charlie's arm. "Don't educate yourself while I'm gone."

"I won't. You know you can count on me."

"If I didn't, I wouldn't be leaving you in charge."

Once Heath had gotten Meredith and Sammy safely inside the Bronco, he climbed in under the wheel, started the engine, and backed from the parking space.

"Meredith, get your head down," he ordered brusquely,

patting the molded plastic console between them. "Lie across here."

"Why?"

He flashed her a look that had her obeying him even before he replied. "I don't want you to be seen. If Glen sent more than just two men, they may have followed us here from your place."

"If they did, and they're watching, won't they know I'm in here with you?"

"With the hedges at each side of the lot, they can't see the front of the building from either direction if they're parked on the road." He reached over to adjust the volume on his radio. "They'd have to park in that empty lot straight across from us, and no one's out there."

"Mommy! I wanna go to bed. I'm sleepy."

"I'm tired, too, punkin. But we aren't going home to our house tonight. We're going someplace special."

"Where?"

"It's going to be a surprise," Meredith replied. "Why don't you lie down and take a little nap so you won't feel as tired when we get there. That's a good girl. Are you comfy?"

"G'liath's tummy makes gurgles." The child giggled. "He's a noisy piddle."

Heath guessed Sammy meant "pillow" and smiled. She was obviously lying on the dog. Was there nothing Goliath wouldn't do to please that kid? Evidently not. Glancing down at Meredith, Heath decided maybe he shouldn't be pointing the finger. He and his dog both had it bad.

The plastic console was slick, and with her hands secured behind her back, Meredith had no way of anchoring herself. Heath knew that had to be a strain, as well as uncomfortable, but she didn't complain or ask him to remove the cuffs. He admired that about her. *Christ.* Why didn't he just start a Meredith Kenyon fan club? He liked *everything* about her.

He saw her struggle to keep from sliding backward off the console as he accelerated the vehicle. He curled his right hand over her shoulder to keep her from falling. Even the warmth of her skin through the shirt seemed delicate, he thought. Somehow less than his own body heat. It was as if their thermostats were set differently, hers on gentle warmth, his on high with all the propulsive fans going. And she felt so slight. The joint of her shoulder felt itty-bitty with hardly any meat to pad it. He could encircle her upper arm with his hand, his fingers overlapping by a good margin. Even her collarbone felt fragile where it sloped up to her shoulder.

Aware of her tension, he sought to reassure her. "I don't see any cars parked on the road. That's a good sign."

She still didn't relax.

"Merry, stop worrying. If anything happens, I'll handle it, all right?"

Meredith had a feeling that from here on in, he would be handling everything, including her if the casual way he'd laid his hand on her shoulder was any indication. His fingers were large and strong, the warmth of them radiating through her shirt.

As the minutes passed, she tried to tell herself she was being idiotic, that he was only holding her so she wouldn't slide off the console. But it didn't quite wash. The moment he touched her, he had begun making gentle circular motions over her skin with his fingertips. The thin cloth of her shirt felt almost nonexistent under the searing caresses. To make matters worse, he had long fingers that enabled him to make light passes over the side of her breast without moving his hand from her upper arm.

Was he even aware of what he was doing? Meredith wanted to believe he wasn't, that he had so many other things on his mind, he was preoccupied. But, somehow, try as she might, she couldn't quite convince herself of that. In the past, he had always been a perfect gentleman, never so much as looking at her in a way that might have been interpreted as lustful. Now, all of a sudden, he was touching her intimately, as if it were his right.

What had changed? The balance of power had shifted.

That was what had changed. Quite simply, he had her over a barrel.

Stop it, Meredith. Just stop it! How can you even think such a thing of him?

Ah, but she could, more was the pity. Once burned, twice shy. It was all too easy for her to believe that the wonderful Heath Masters she had come to know might be nothing more than a façade. That the minute he felt in control, he might show his true colors. Without him, she and Sammy were sunk. She knew it, and he knew it. By accepting his help, she'd given him carte blanche.

From here on out, he no longer had to be a gentleman or play by her rules. He could make them up as he went along. She was his prisoner and in restraints. Even if she filed a complaint against him later for his conduct, who was going to believe her?

She clenched her teeth to keep from saying anything, a part of her knowing that her thoughts were crazy and that she was being entirely unfair. Heath Masters had been nothing but kind to her and Sammy, and now he was going to great lengths to protect them. He'd done nothing, absolutely nothing, to deserve this from her except rest his hand on her shoulder, and here she was, reading all kinds of vile meanings into it. Had Dan completely stripped her of all ability to trust?

Yes. God help her, yes. She had trusted practically everyone once, and that trait had sucked her into the worst nightmare of her life.

"I'll scratch your back if you'll scratch mine." That had been Dan's favorite saying, and he'd applied it to every aspect of their marriage. He had fed her, clothed her, and provided her with shelter. *"Nobody gets somethin' for nothin', doll face,"* he'd often reminded her. In exchange for all that he gave her, Dan had felt that he owned her. On their wedding night, he had put their marriage certificate in a picture frame and hung it on the wall next to his Dobermans' pedigrees. *"Mary, Gretchen and Otto,"* he'd said smugly, and then had begun her obedience training. Up

until that moment, Meredith had believed that, next to her dad, Dan Calendri was the gentlest, most wonderful man she'd ever met.

Staring fixedly at the multicolored lights on the dash, she tried to block out Heath's touch. During her marriage, she had become very good at that little trick, but evidently she was out of practice. Heath Masters' touch was hard to ignore. He traced the shape of her arm, ran his fingertips along her bra strap, gave her shoulder an occasional gentle squeeze. He was definitely staking his claim, she decided. No one could tantalize so many of her nerve-endings without being aware of what he was doing.

Tears sprang to Meredith's eyes. Angry tears. The dash lights began to swim in a dizzying blur. At that moment, she hated herself. By distrusting Heath, she was not only doing him a disservice, but she was, in effect, still letting Dan shape her thoughts and control her life. When was she going to get past this? Never?

Trust. Heath was right; it didn't come easily for her. Yet she had begun to trust him, little by little, one painful inch at a time. And right now, she needed desperately to believe he was every bit as wonderful as he had always seemed—a real life hero, rescuing two fair damsels in distress. Trust was a decision, wasn't it? So why couldn't she just decide, for once and for all, to put her complete faith in this man? No doubts. No vile suspicions slithering into her mind every time he innocently did something that reminded her of the past. Just absolute and unconditional trust. After all, if she couldn't trust Heath Masters, who in the world could she trust?

His fingertips trailed down her bra strap again, then followed the edge of the cup where it curved under her arm. Light touches, and ever so gentle, barely seeming to graze the cloth. Why, then, was she letting them fill her with such a crushing sense of betrayal?

Heath had one thing on his mind: getting to hell out of town as fast as he could make tracks. He had to stop at

Meredith's and his place first. It was risky, but he had no choice. She and Sammy would need clothing where he was taking them, and he had to get his weapons, his ammunition, and what little cash he had stashed in his closet safe. While there, he decided he might as well pack what food he had in the cupboards.

En route, Heath was as jumpy as a frog on hot cement, watching his rearview mirror, sweating when he saw headlights. He was glad Meredith was lying down. She'd been through enough hell for one night. And this was no picnic. Every time he saw a car coming up fast on his back bumper, he felt the jolt as surely as if he'd stuck his finger in a light socket.

Sammy was already asleep in the backseat, still using Goliath as a pillow. Her sweet, little-girl snores made him realize exactly how much was riding on him. Her safety. Her future. *Friends, no matter what.* God help him, he couldn't let her down. Or Meredith, either, for that matter. She was putting all her faith in him by doing this, and he knew that couldn't be easy. Not after everything that bastard, Dan Calendri, had put her through.

He had done the right thing, he assured himself. All else aside, it couldn't be wrong to protect them. No matter what he had to do, or what it cost him, it couldn't be wrong.

As he turned onto Hereford Lane, Heath radioed in to speak with Charlie. "I'll be heading out in just a few minutes," he told the deputy. "So far, everything's copacetic at my end. How about yours? Over."

"No real problems. That Delgado character demanded that we let him make a phone call. Knew his rights. This ain't his first time in the hoosegow, that's for sure. Over."

"Did you let him use the phone? Over."

"That's an affirmative. Over."

"Did you monitor the conversation? Over."

"Negative. I went and stuck my nose in a girlie magazine."

Heath chuckled. "Who'd he call?"

"Somebody in *Noo* York. Before I could shove a sock

in it, he blabbed that you left with the woman and kid. How the hell he knew that, I don't know. Somebody yackin' in front of him back in the cell block is my guess. Sorry. I didn't know he knew. Over.''

''No problem, Charlie. The word was bound to leak, and I'll be gone before reinforcements can arrive from New York.''

''Keep your head low. I don't like the look of that dude, Delgado. He's a mean son buck. Eyes like a lizard. Over.''

Heath keyed the mike. ''You've got him pegged. Unless I encounter trouble, I probably won't call back in until tomorrow afternoon.''

''Take care. Watch your back. Over.''

''I will, Charlie. Hold down the fort for me. Masters, out.''

Once at Meredith's place, Heath was none too pleased to learn that all their clothing was already packed in the trunk of Meredith's car. Along with other items, her purse had been confiscated by his deputies as evidence and taken to the department. Her car keys were inside it.

''What are we going to do?'' she asked, struggling to sit up.

''*We* aren't going to do anything. Just stay down!'' he ordered. ''I'll take care of it.''

He opened the trunk with a tire iron. By the time he had accomplished that little feat, he was damned glad he hadn't chosen street crime as a way to make a living. He would have starved to death. He pried, jerked, pushed, pulled, and cussed, tearing the trunk lid all to hell, but still not getting it open. In the end, he resorted to wedging the tire iron under the latch and jumping on the handle with both feet. When the trunk finally popped open, he was sweating like a horse.

After rummaging through the boxes, he took only those that looked as if they held clothing. From Meredith's place, he went directly to his, making short work of gathering his guns, the ammo, and what food he had on hand. When he got everything stowed in the back of his Bronco, his rig looked like something straight out of *The Grapes of Wrath*. Hell, he'd even tossed in dog food and dog dishes.

"How long do I have to stay down?" Meredith asked shortly after he got back out on the road. "I'm getting a crimp in my side."

Heath felt bad for having snapped at her when she tried to sit up. But, *damn*. If she was right, and Glen Calendri actually had organized crime connections, the men chasing her were real bad asses. He couldn't take a chance that she might be seen. Against rapid-fire automatic weapons, his guns in the back of the Bronco would be about as effective as peashooters.

"Not too long now." He reached down to cup his hand over her shoulder again. "I'm sorry I jumped down your throat back there. I know lying on that thing can't be very comfortable. You can sit up just as soon as we hit the highway. All right? Once we're on the outskirts of town, the chances that you'll be seen will be next to zero."

"Thank goodness. Every time you stop and start, I almost go flying."

He chuckled. "I've got you. Just relax."

She didn't.

Fifteen minutes later, Heath drove past the sheriff's department en route to the highway exit. Everything looked quiet. He saw no cars parked near the facility to indicate it was being watched. That was definitely a good sign.

The headlights that had been hanging back about a mile behind him weren't. He wasn't sure exactly when the vehicle had fallen in behind him. He only knew it had stuck with him through three turns and was still holding fast.

Probably nothing, he assured himself. Hell, there was nothing suspicious about another car being on the road. Right? At this time of night, the highway to the mountains didn't normally have that much traffic, but there was always some, and the count increased at this time of year when people began flocking to the lakes. Because of the steep grades and sharp curves, most folks drove up before dark, but there were always the exceptions.

At the turn-off, Heath helped Meredith to sit back up. She sighed with relief at no longer having to lie twisted across the console, and he guessed he couldn't blame her.

"There's a recreation park about fifteen miles from here," he told her. "I'll pull over there and take off those cuffs."

She leaned against her door, her face glowing like a pale mask in the light from the dash. Huddled there that way, she looked like a young girl, a very frightened young girl. "You mean I'm not going to have to wear them? I thought—well, I understood that I was still arrested and your prisoner. Aren't you supposed to keep me in restraints?"

"It's regulation, something we're all trained to do as a safety precaution. Keeps a prisoner from taking an officer by surprise." He glanced over at her and winked. "Under the circumstances, though, I think we can dispense with the formalities. If you get squirrelly on me, I think I can handle you."

"I'll appreciate not having to wear handcuffs. Thank you."

He nodded toward the radio. "I've been keeping an ear open, and I haven't heard anything from Charlie. No problems at his end yet. Try to relax, why don't you? When we get the cuffs off, maybe you can get a little rest."

She was silent for a second. "Do you think we're home free?"

He didn't, but judging by her pallor, she needed reassurance. He was worrying enough for both of them. "It sure looks that way."

"Where, exactly, are we going?"

"An old high school buddy of mine has a hunting cabin up near Emerald Lake."

"What's it like up there?"

"Beautiful country, open for as far as you can see. The cabin's nothing fancy. Two bedrooms, a kitchen, and a sitting area. No electricity. But it does have indoor plumbing.

Gravity fed. I've gone up with him and know where he puts the key.''

"Tell me the truth. Do you think we'll be safe there?''

"As safe as we can get. Like I said, it's way to hell and gone out in the middle of nowhere. Nothing but a rutted, dirt road leading in to it. I doubt a two-wheel drive would even make it, and it'd be a hell of a trek on foot.''

She turned her face toward her window. "There aren't many houses out this way, are there?''

"No. And they'll get scarcer. A few miles farther up the road, there are only vacation homes, mostly around the lake, some peppering the forests. It's a popular hunting and fishing area up there.''

The isolation up at the cabin would be both good and bad, Heath thought. On the one hand, unexpected visitors would be unlikely. On the other hand, though, there was always the possibility someone might find them, and in that event, they would be a long way from any kind of help.

He clenched his hands on the steering wheel, trying to sort and organize everything Meredith had told him. Organized crime, mob killings, vicious Dobermans. Some of it sounded almost too fantastic to be true. But, by the same token, he remembered reading an article recently about union corruption and links between top officials and organized crime.

Heath knew next to nothing about large-scale crime networks. He'd seen enough movies about them to know they existed and that men in the ranks—thugs, goons, soldiers, or whatever else you wanted to call them—were shrewd, well-trained, and merciless in the execution of their orders. When Heath thought about battling it out with dudes like that, it scared the piss out of him. But, then, he figured he'd have to be nuts not to be a whole lot scared.

The highway narrowed to two lanes as they climbed into the sharp mountain curves. Heath devoted his full concentration to his driving and watching the rearview mirror. Every few minutes as he brought the Bronco out of a curve, he glimpsed headlights coming into the turn behind him.

He increased his speed and began watching for a side road, preferably a dirt logging route. The Bronco was a high-clearance, all-terrain, four-wheel drive, and he could take it places a car couldn't follow. If he dropped off the main highway, cut his lights, and drove like a bat out of hell, he could probably lose anyone trying to tail him. If, of course, it *was* a tail. Maybe he was just being paranoid. But the way he figured it, better to be safe than sorry.

Unfortunately, they were into the sharp curves, and there were no cut-offs. At least not any that he saw. What he did see were headlights coming up fast behind him. *Too fast.* He tromped the gas pedal.

"Wh—What are you doing?" Meredith asked.

"Is Sammy still buckled up?"

She glanced back. "Yes, but she has the belt loose to lie down. Why?"

"Tighten the slack."

"I can't."

He remembered the handcuffs and swore under his breath. He hadn't buckled Meredith into her seat because he'd wanted her to lie down. "Then all you can do is brace yourself. Get your feet up under the dash and push back as hard as you can against the seat. I think we may be in for a rough ride."

"Why?"

Before he could reply, the car rammed into them. The jolt knocked the Bronco's back end sideways just as it nosed into a curve, and the vehicle went into a broad slide, the tires squealing.

"Damn!"

Heath had barely managed to regain control when the other car rammed the Bronco again.

Chapter 21

"Oh, my God!" Meredith cried as the Bronco crashed against the guardrail. "Heath? Heath! Don't let them roll us! Oh, God, don't let them roll us!"

She twisted in the seat, trying to see Sammy. The child had awakened with a start and was shrieking in terror. "Mommy! Mommy!"

Meredith would have given anything to be in the backseat holding her daughter. But in handcuffs, she couldn't even reach for her. Through the rear window, she saw the headlights coming up fast again on their back bumper. In the nimbus of light, she was able to tell that the other car was a light-colored, full-sized sedan.

"Watch out!" she screamed. "They're coming at us again!" The Bronco jerked at the impact. She fell hard against the door, cracking her head on the window. For a second, all she could see was black spots.

"Get your feet under the dash, dammit! Brace yourself!"

Meredith knew Heath was right. She would be of no use to Sammy if she went through the windshield. She turned in the seat and pushed hard against the floorboard with her feet. In the backseat, Goliath began to bark, the sounds nearly drowning out Sammy's pathetic wailing.

The expression on Heath's face was frightening. The glow of the dash lights etched his features with an eerie green iridescence and reflected off his tousled dark hair.

His lips were drawn back from his white teeth in a snarl. He darted glances at the rearview and side mirrors, his hands clenched on the steering wheel as he fought for control of the vehicle. He seemed to know instinctively what to do, turning sharply into the direction of the slide, then correcting to bring the rear of the Bronco back around.

"All right, you sons of bitches!" he said as he righted the vehicle. "You wanna play rough? Come and get it!"

He slammed on the brakes. The sedan behind them was forced into the opposite lane to avoid the unexpected collision. As the automobile came alongside the Bronco, Heath swung the steering wheel hard to the left, careening into the other lane and knocking the car off the road. Meredith watched in horrified astonishment. In the darkness, the sedan's headlights appeared to be unattached orbs, bouncing crazily through the blackness, illuminating trees and boulders in dizzying, erratic flashes.

Then she realized the force of the sideswipe had sent the Bronco careening to the right and into a skid. Just as Heath managed to regain control, the four-wheel drive's right rear tire lost traction on the gravel shoulder, and the vehicle began to fishtail. Meredith thought sure they were going to crash, but with impressive driving skill, Heath brought the Bronco to a stop just inches before it plunged sideways into a deep ditch at the edge of the road. The engine coughed and died.

Meredith tried to peel herself off the door, but the Bronco seemed to be leaning sharply in her direction. Evidently, they'd come closer to going off the edge than she cared to consider.

Dead silence. Even Sammy and Goliath had fallen quiet. Heath sat there, gripping the wheel and staring, as if he couldn't quite believe they were stopped. Then the faint sound of a voice drifted through the night to them. He swore, depressed the clutch, and turned the ignition keys.

"We have to get out of here!" he said, his speech clipped and agitated.

Meredith nearly wept with relief when the engine roared

back to life. Heath was right; they could waste no time in getting away. At least one of those men had survived that wreck, and he could come running across the road at any moment with his gun blazing.

Heath shifted into first and tromped the gas. A shrill, whining sound filled the interior of the Bronco. "God*dammit!*"

"What?"

"Mommy! Mommy!" Sammy wailed.

"It's all right, sweetie!" Meredith cried, unable to tear her gaze from Heath.

"A back tire is off in the ditch," he said. "We're high centered."

"You mean we can't go?"

He leaned down to shove and jerk on the shorter of the two floor shifts. Meredith didn't know what he was doing, and her heart was pounding too hard to ask. He tromped the gas again. This time, in addition to the squealing of the back tires, the front wheels grabbed at the gravel shoulder for traction. She realized then that he had put the vehicle into four-wheel drive. The Bronco heaved, then fell back, heaved, then fell back. Meredith rocked forward with it, hoping the transfer of weight might help. But despite all her efforts and Heath's, they didn't go anywhere.

"Christ!" He shut off the headlights and everything else on the dash, including his police radio, which had been emitting occasional bursts of sound and static. Then he pressed a lever to roll down the back window, jerked off his seat belt, and threw open his door to leap from the vehicle.

"Get down on the floor. Both of you!" he ordered in a hushed voice as he closed the door almost soundlessly.

Meredith twisted in her seat. Through the side windows, she glimpsed his silhouette against the moonlit sky as he ran to the back of the rig.

She leaned over the console, straining to see him in the darkness through the wire mesh. "Heath?" She heard the rasp of gunmetal, the unmistakable sound of a rifle action, and then the click of a bullet being jacked into the chamber.

"Oh, dear God," she cried. "Don't go out there after them! They'll kill—"

"Meredith, shut up!"

His voice cut through her panic like a sharp knife. She jerked and gulped.

"Your voice will carry! You don't want to draw their fire. Get Sammy down on the floor! And then get down there yourself! *Now!* Keep Goliath here with you."

She saw the shadowy flash of his outline as he loped away into the blackness.

After that, there was only an awful quiet. Meredith felt her teeth chattering and bit down hard. She had to think. Through the side window, she could see the other car's headlights, tipped at a crazy angle. It looked to her as if the sedan had slammed into a pine tree. She couldn't tell how badly the car was damaged or if it was likely that more than one passenger had survived the collision. She only knew that if more than one of Glen's men was out there, Heath was outnumbered and seriously outgunned.

She seriously considered opening her door and making a run for it with Sammy. If they went deeply enough into the woods, maybe those men wouldn't find them. Only it was dark, so horribly dark. And the terrain around here was undoubtedly rugged. Wearing handcuffs, she wouldn't be able to carry Sammy or even hold her hand to help her keep her footing.

"Sammy, get down on the floor, sweetie."

"Mommy?" the child squeaked. "I'm scared!"

"Don't be scared, sweetkins. Heath will take care of us," Meredith assured her as she slid off her seat onto her knees. "See? I'm getting down on the floor. Be Mommy's big girl, okay? Let's show Heath how good we can follow directions."

"I don't want to."

A burst of gunfire rent the silence, an awful *rat-a-tat-tat*, the sound so loud and explosive that Meredith nearly wet her pants. Sammy shrieked. Then another lethal burst of

noise erupted through the night, followed by several ping-
ing thuds that vibrated through the Bronco. *An Uzi*, Meredith thought nonsensically. *That gun sounds just like
Dan's Uzi.*

Goliath whipped toward the noise and leaped at the window, snarling and baring his fangs. Sammy was still huddled on the seat. If she didn't get down, one of the bullets
might hit her next.

"Sammy!" Meredith angled her body over the console
to bring her face closer to her daughter's. "You get your
little fanny down on the floorboard. *Now!* Do you hear
me?"

The child mewled and blubbered, but she unfastened her
seat belt. As she slid off onto the floor, another shot exploded through the darkness, the *ka-boom* of a high-
powered rifle.

Meredith leaned over to watch Sammy lie down. "All
the way. Flat against the floor, Sammy. There, that's
good."

Goliath followed the child down onto the floorboard,
placing his paws on each side of her legs to stand over her.
By the animal's stance, Meredith knew he would die before
he let anyone touch her. Meredith could only pray it didn't
come to that.

"Mommy?"

"What, sweetie?"

"Don't go 'way."

Meredith pressed herself as close to the console as she
could. "I won't, punkin. I'm right here. If you reach up,
you can feel me."

Sammy twisted an arm up behind her back and touched
Meredith's hair. "You stay, okay?"

"Wild horses couldn't drag me away."

Eternity. Meredith knew the meaning of that word now,
and it wasn't measured by mere units of time, with centu-
ries passing into millenniums that stretched to infinity. Eternity was a state of mind in which every breath you drew

took a thousand years to expel, the rasp of your lungs re-
sounding against your eardrums, the loud thuds of your
heart spaced a hundred years apart. It was living forever in
a black time warp, with gunfire exploding all around you
and not knowing, from one heartbeat to the next, if your
heart would ever beat again. It was lying only inches away
from your child, yet unable to see her clearly in the shadows, your terror mounting because she lay so still and
didn't seem to be breathing. It was staring at the faint glim-
mer of blond curls, searching for red-black splotches of
blood, until your eyes burned in your skull like smoldering
coals.

Eternity was knowing that your life, pathetic though it
had become, rested entirely in the hands of one man who
had loped off into the darkness to do battle against impossible odds. It was seeing him in your mind, memories flashing in a colorful blur like the rapidly turned pages of a
picture book. *Heath*. Looming, bigger than life, his body
strapped with muscle. His skin as coppery brown as old
bronze. His sable hair, always in need of a trim, trailing in
lazy, wind-tossed waves over his high forehead, the gleaming thickness of it furrowed from the habitual raking of his
fingers. It was remembering his eyes and how they changed
with his moods, gunmetal gray when intense, a twinkling
slate-blue when he laughed, and as turbulent as a stormy
sky when he grew angry or worried. It was recalling his
hands, which could look as large as supper plates when his
long, blunt fingers were splayed, the palms as thick and
leathery as sun-dried slabs of meat. It was remembering the
touch of those hands, how they radiated a comforting
warmth, and how gentle they'd always been despite their
bruising strength.

Eternity was remembering how he had cupped your
shoulder with one of those hands, and how easily you'd let
your faith in him be shaken. Eternity was the guilt you felt
because you knew he was out there in the darkness somewhere, possibly dying for you, and that if he survived, as

grateful as you might be, there would still be a part of you that feared him.

And, lastly, it was hating yourself because you knew your feelings were wrong. Horribly wrong. It was knowing that you had become a sick, twisted person, trapped in the maze of your own emotions, some pure and good, others dark and evil. It was knowing that no matter how hard you tried, you would never claw your way free of the memories or overcome the unreasoning fear. Your rational thoughts and your twisted ones chased after each other inside your mind in endless circles—the hateful and fearful side of you always winning.

Eternity was lying across a console until your breasts felt flattened and your ribs crushed, with your eyes streaming tears and your lips whispering soundless prayers for your child, and for yourself, and for a man whose survival had become inseparably linked with your own. It was begging God to protect him, your heart breaking at the thought of his getting hurt or losing his life, and knowing on some level that you were hopelessly in love with him, whether you wanted to be or not.

Eternity was realizing with a start that you'd become so lost in your churning thoughts that you hadn't noticed the sudden silence. No gunshots. Just an awful quiet that made the darkness close in around you, blacker than black.

Meredith lifted her head, holding her breath to listen. All she heard was the night wind whispering in the towering pine and fir trees, the mighty trunks occasionally creaking and groaning as they swayed in the gusts.

"Mommy?" Sammy whispered shakily. "Where's Heef?"

Meredith straightened to peer out the window. The headlights across the road had gone out. Now there was only darkness for as far as she could see—a whispering, shifting darkness filled with black shadows that seemed to move toward her when she stared at them.

"Quiet, Sammy."

She heard a footstep in the gravel and flattened herself

against the console again, her limbs turning to water. Goliath whined and growled.

"*Quiet!*" she rasped.

Another footstep. Someone was coming. The question was, who? Craning her neck, Meredith stared, her eyes dry and bulging from their sockets. In her temples, she heard the rhythmic *swish* of her own blood.

In that moment, she wanted to scream at the injustice of it all. Heath had gone out there and died for them. Oh, God. And now those men were coming. She couldn't run. Not without being able to carry Sammy. All she could do was lie there, waiting to die herself. And afterward, poor little Sammy would probably wish she were dead, too. Glen would get his hands on her. If Sammy survived the years of abuse with her little mind still intact, she would emerge into adulthood as crazy and spiritually decayed as her father had been.

The black, hulking outline of a man appeared at the opposite window. She heard the latch of the driver's door click. Cool air rushed in as the door swung wide, the hinges giving a metallic *clunk*. Meredith tried to brace herself for a spray of lead, knowing that the man could cut loose with an Uzi at any moment. Only none of her muscles would tense. Terror had short-circuited the signals from her brain.

"Are you all right in here?" The deep, masculine voice was pitched to a panicky alto. The barrel of his rifle smacked against metal as he propped it in the crack of the door and came scrambling over the seat to grab her. "Son of a *bitch*! Meredith? Oh, Jesus, no!"

Big hands. They seemed to be everywhere on her body, patting, pressing, checking her clothes. Still numb from fear, the silent screams locked behind her larynx, Meredith couldn't speak. She just lay there like a beached fish grabbing for air.

Heath. He wasn't dead. He was here, running high on adrenaline and shaking like a leaf. But *here.* "H—heath," she finally managed to gasp. "Oh, Heath!"

"Are you hurt? Did the bastards hit you?"

"N—no. Fine, I'm fine."

He dropped her like a hot potato. Still unable to control her limbs, Meredith landed hard on the floorboard in front of the passenger seat, her rump smacking the rug between her spread feet. Pain lanced up her thighs from the twisted angle of her knees.

Heath dove his shoulders through the opening between the seats. "Sammy?" He shoved Goliath out of the way with such force that the dog thumped against the vinyl wall. Then he plucked Sammy up from the floorboard, handling her as if she were an oversize rag doll. "Sweetcakes?"

"Heef."

Meredith could only sit and watch as Heath twisted down onto the driver's seat and clamped Sammy to his chest in a fierce hug. He didn't speak, just held onto the child as if determined to squeeze all the breath from her tiny body. Meredith heard his breath catch. When he inhaled again, the sound was jerky and ragged.

After a few moments, he gently deposited Sammy on the backseat again, then left the vehicle. Meredith could barely discern his outline in the darkness as he paced back and forth along the edge of the road. He didn't want them to see him right now, she thought. He'd been frantic, thinking they were hurt, and now he was trying to walk off the panic.

When he finally came back to the Bronco, he seemed calm. Meredith wished she were. But she kept searching the darkness, expecting a man to emerge, his gun spitting orange flame. She assumed that Heath had eliminated the danger. But he hadn't said as much. And in a situation like this, she found it difficult to relax on the strength of an assumption.

"Are you all right?" she managed to ask.

"I'm fine. Not a scratch."

"Wh—what happened?"

Thrusting his arm through the opening between the driver's seat and the door frame, he patted his dog and ruffled Sammy's hair. "Hey, there, sweetcakes. How's my best girl?"

"Fine," Sammy said thinly. "I was real scared while you were gone, though."

"Me, too." He drew his arm free and propped it on the back of the driver's seat, his head and shoulders delineated against the moonlit sky behind him. For a long moment, he just stood there, leaning as if he were exhausted. Then he said, "It's all taken care of."

Just that? It was all taken care of? "H—how many were there?"

"Three," he replied softly. "Man, I want a cigarette."

A cigarette? She hadn't realized he smoked. "Three? Are they all—?"

"I took care of it," he repeated, cutting her off and glancing toward Sammy as if to warn her to watch what she said.

The encroaching blackness seemed filled with menace to her. "Are you s—sure? That you took care of them *all*, I mean?"

"Positive." He made an odd sound that resembled a laugh, but wasn't quite. "I went over and checked."

He sounded so confident that Meredith stopped searching the darkness for movement. They were safe. For now. Her heartbeat slowed, the limp heaviness of her body growing even more leaden.

He strode around the front of the Bronco to open the passenger door. She felt his hands at her wrists. A second later, the handcuffs fell away. Her arms were achy, yet numb, and hung from her shoulders like stiff stumps. She flexed her fingers, wincing at the needle pricks of sensation.

"Thank you," she said softly.

"Yeah, well. Better late than never." He opened the glove compartment and rummaged around. A moment later, a lighter flared, and she heard him drag in a raspy breath. The smell of tobacco smoke curled in tendrils through the darkness. "Sorry, but when shit like this comes down, I need a cigarette afterward."

The smell of the smoke made her think of her father and his pipe. Oh, how she would love to be sitting by the stove with her dad right now, a world away from this, watching the pipe smoke wreathe around his gray head.

Using the heels of her hands on the seat, she pushed up to get her feet under her rump. The pain eased in her knees and thighs. She turned to gaze at Heath.

He took another drag from the cigarette, the tip glowing orange and casting a glow over his dark, sharply chiseled face. As he exhaled, he chuckled drily. "Keeps me from heading for the bushes. Not very macho, I guess, but there you have it."

Meredith peered through the shadows at him, not entirely sure what he meant. Then she realized he must be feeling squeamish. On the tail of that thought, she turned her gaze into the night beyond the Bronco windows, wondering what horrors the darkness concealed. Three men. All taken care of. And now he was smoking to keep from vomiting. As a girl, she'd once gone hunting with her dad, and she had seen the damage a high-powered rifle could do to a deer. The result was probably the same with a man.

Her stomach lurched, and the blood drained from her head. *Three men, all taken care of.* Oh, God. He had just *shot* three men. And then he'd gone over there to make certain they were dead. He'd had to look at them, touch them.

Not very macho? He'd gone to face them with only a rifle and a police-issue semiautomatic against at least one Uzi and God only knew what other weapons. Only a stupid man would have been unafraid, and Heath wasn't stupid. He wasn't one to strut, or flex his biceps, or wear his shirt unbuttoned to show off his chest. But when push had come to shove, he'd stood his ground, and he'd put his life on the line. In her book, that was about as macho as macho could get—the very best kind—understated until it counted.

He tossed down the cigarette and ground it out under his boot. "I need to call this in." He shut her door, came back around the vehicle and swung up onto the driver's seat. Leaning forward, he turned on the dash lights and then the radio. After adjusting the squelch, he brought the mike to his lips. "Masters, to unit three. Come back."

Almost immediately, a man's voice came over the air. "Boss? I been tryin' to get you. Thank Christ you called. The shit's rollin' downhill, and we're up to our eyebrows."

Heath glanced over at Meredith. "What do you mean, Charlie? Over."

"We got the Feds breathin' down our necks, and three county commissioners are sittin' in your office, pissed off royal. You gotta bring her back in. Over."

"The Feds? What're you talking about?"

"The FBI! How in hell they got wind of this, I don't know. We ain't contacted nobody. But they sure as shit know! We got big trouble, son. There ain't been but one call made from here tonight, and you know who made it. Now, suddenly, we got the friggin' Feds on their way out here to transport your lady friend back east. Over."

In the glow from the dash, Heath's dark face went stony. He keyed the mike. "The son of a bitch has FBI agents in his pocket. Over."

"Go to the head of the class, over," Charlie replied.

Heath swore and punched the steering wheel with the side of his fist. Meredith's stomach convulsed as if he'd hit her. "I can't turn her over to crooked agents, Charlie. If Delgado made the only call out of there about this, it doesn't take a genius to figure out that he called Calendri. Now the Feds are suddenly involved? Those agents have to be on his payroll. If they take her into custody, she'll never see a courtroom."

"You don't got a choice. Game's over. If you don't bring her back in, you're screwed. Over."

Meredith leaned back against her door, hugging her waist. Heath just sat and stared at the radio. "I can't," he finally said.

"Masters?" The male voice coming over the radio belonged to another man, and he seemed to be yelling. "Is that you, Masters? This is Roy Fergusson. Do you hear me?''

Heath sighed. ''Christ. The district attorney?'' He keyed the mike. ''I hear you, Roy. Stop yelling so loud. Over.''

''You get that Calendri woman back here. Immediately. Do I make myself clear? You've got six hours. I don't know where the hell you are, but you'd better make the most of them. If she isn't back on these premises and inside a cell where she belongs in six hours, you can kiss that badge of yours good-bye.''

''Roy, her life is in danger. Her father-in-law, Glen Calendri, is tied in with a big crime ring. Over.''

''Oh, bullshit!'' The radio blasted static, making Meredith jump. Then Fergusson came back. ''Would you listen to yourself? Organized crime? Get real. What you've got is trouble on your hands. She's fed you such a line of malarkey, I'm surprised you fell for it.''

''It's not malarkey, Roy. I just found that out, up close and personal. Three men just tried to run me off the road. When they piled out of their car, it looked like the Fourth of July. I danced real pretty to the tune of nine-millimeter slugs, sprayed from Uzis, and I damned near sold the ranch. No malarkey to it. Over.''

''Son of a— Don't tell me! I don't want to hear it! You took them out, didn't you?''

''What do you think? They would've sprayed me so full of holes I'd've looked like a colander. Over.''

''Oh, shit.'' There came an awful racket at the other end. Then Fergusson said, ''Do you have *any* idea what you've done?''

''Saved my ass. Over.''

''You probably just killed three FBI agents!''

Heath sighed. ''Roy, FBI agents don't run people off the road and then start shooting without even showing their badges. Besides, I checked. None of them were packing ID, FBI or otherwise. Over.''

''You listen to me!'' Fergusson roared. ''You get her back here. You got it? Six hours, Masters. That's it. No further discussion. None of us want trouble with the Feds, and if you make any, we'll crucify you before we take any of the heat ourselves!''

Heath replaced the mike in its bracket and turned off the radio. Meredith was uncertain what to say. As if anything she said would make a difference? His career was on the line. He had no choice but to take her back to town. If he didn't, he would be in horrible trouble. As it was, it sounded as if he'd have to do some fast talking.

He folded his arms over the steering wheel and rested his forehead on his wrists.

''I'm so sorry, Heath.''

He gave a weak laugh and straightened. ''It's a hell of a mess. I'll say that.''

Meredith swallowed. ''I, um . . . I really appreciate all you've done. I'll never forget it. Except for my dad, no one's ever stood up for me like this. Not even my dad, actually. I wish I knew how to—to thank you. And I truly am sorry about the trouble you're in.''

''Mommy, why is Heef in trouble?''

''For being our friend,'' Meredith said softy. ''He has to take us back to town, punkin, or they're going to take his badge away.''

Sammy leaned her elbows on the console, peering up at Heath. ''It's shiny. You like it a lot, huh, Heef?''

He tucked in his chin to gaze down at the badge. After a long moment, he removed it from his shirt and held it up to the moonlight. The look on his face was incredibly sad and empty, making him seem like a lost little boy for a moment. Then, as if he were flipping a bottle cap, he sent the badge spinning out his open door and into the darkness. A second later, a distant *clink* drifted back to them.

Meredith felt as if her stomach had dropped down around her ankles. He turned his gaze on her. Then he looked down at Sammy, his teeth gleaming eerily in the gloom as he smiled. ''I don't like anything in the whole world better than you and your mommy, sweetcakes.''

"Heath," Meredith interjected. "We need to discuss this."

"There's nothing to discuss. I'm going to need your help getting us out of here. Can you handle a stick shift?"

She'd learned to drive in a hay truck. "Yes, but—"

"No buts." He climbed from the vehicle. "We can't stay here like ducks in a shooting gallery. The keys are there, in the ignition. Start her up. When I holler, pull forward. If you hear a racket and you feel the back end drop, don't worry about it."

As she crawled over into the driver's seat, he leaned back in to add, "Just don't run off and leave me." Then he chuckled and slammed the door.

As if she would leave him? She hadn't the vaguest clue as to where she was, and she knew nothing about surviving in these woods. In addition to that, he'd just saved their lives and might again before this was over.

She heard him pawing through the stuff in the back of the vehicle. Then heavy metal clunked and grated. With each grating sound, the Bronco lurched. He was jacking up the rear axle to give the front tires traction.

"Okay, go!" he yelled.

She shifted into first, hit the gas, and simultaneously let out on the clutch. Gravel flew, pelting the underside of the vehicle. Then the Bronco lunged forward, its back tires hitting the earth with such force that the shock absorbers bottomed out. She slammed on the brake and clutch, gearing down into neutral.

Heath put the jack back in the rig, then came around to the driver's door. After setting the hand brake, she moved over into the other seat so he could drive.

He didn't stay on the highway for long. About two miles up, he turned onto a side road and soon took another turn off of it. From the console, he withdrew a spotlight and connected the clips at the end of the wire to something under the dash. Then he dropped the Bronco's speed to a crawl and began spotlighting both sides of the road. When they came up on a cabin, he looked it over carefully before he drove on. Meredith had no idea what he was doing.

"Have you forgotten where it is?" she asked, thinking perhaps he'd lost his way to his friend's place.

He cast her an odd look. "No, I'm just doing a little shopping."

Shopping? Meredith settled back. Several miles and at least a half dozen cabins later, Heath spotlighted a small log house back in the trees. Under a makeshift carport, she glimpsed an old red truck. "This'll do. No one's been here for months. Last hunting season would be my guess. They probably only come up a couple of times a year."

"Are we going to stay here?" she asked.

"Hell, no. I'm gonna swap cars," he said as he cut the light and the engine. "This rig's gotta go. They'll have an all-points-bulletin out on it by morning, and the sheriff's department insignia will be too easy for Glen's thugs to spot."

He was going to *swap* cars? He made it sound as if he planned to have a nice little chat with the people who owned the truck and strike a deal with them. "Tell me that you're *not* going to steal a car."

As he shoved open his door and swung out of the seat, he threw her a warning look, then glanced back at Sammy. "I'd never steal anything. It's a very bad thing to do. I just plan to get us another rig at a five-finger discount."

For several seconds, Meredith watched him walking away, his tall frame illuminated only by moonlight. He was about to steal a truck, and not in the line of duty. He'd kissed that good-bye when he sent his badge spinning into the darkness.

Oh, God. If he did this, he would be going well beyond the point of no return. Grand theft. Haboring a criminal. Obstructing justice. Aiding and abetting. Possibly even an accessory to kidnapping. Ever since hearing his conversation with the district attorney on the radio, Meredith had been battling with her conscience, trying to convince herself she didn't care what happened to Heath or anyone else, just as long as Sammy was safe.

But now the voice of her conscience could no longer be ignored. If she didn't stop this, right now, his life was going to be ruined, his career down the toilet. He'd be giving up *everything* for them. Everything. There would be no turning back.

The ramifications of it all began to sink in. Back at the sheriff's department, Meredith had been so scared for herself and Sammy that she hadn't really considered the consequences for Heath if he helped her. Not like this, from beginning to end.

She opened her door and piled out. "Heath! Wait!" She ran toward him. "You can't steal a car! It's madness!"

Well into the trees, he wheeled around, planting his hands on his hips. "Would you keep your voice down?" he asked in a loud whisper. "Sammy will hear you. I don't want her thinking I'm a thief."

Meredith pitched her voice low. "What, exactly, do you think you'll be if you steal a truck? Law enforcement officer of the year? We have to talk."

"About what?"

When she reached him, she grabbed the sleeve of his shirt. "You can't do this. You're the *sheriff*! It's your whole life! I can't let you throw it all away."

His expression turned incredulous. "This is a hell of a time to start worrying about that. Like I've got a choice? I can't take you back, Meredith. If something happened to you, I—well, I just can't, that's all." He waved a hand. "And those guys back there were shooting real bullets! Our asses are on the line, here. We've got to get another vehicle. This is perfect. Chances are, the people who own that truck won't come back here for months to report it missing. Maybe I'll even be able to return it before they know it's gone."

"And if they come up here tomorrow? Or in a couple of days? You're playing roulette with your future."

"I've got to do it."

"Listen! Listen to me, please? We have other options."

"Like what?"

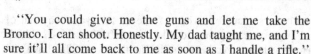

"You could give me the guns and let me take the Bronco. I can shoot. Honestly. My dad taught me, and I'm sure it'll all come back to me as soon as I handle a rifle."

He chuffed and shoved his fingers through his hair.

"It's workable," she cried. "We could make it look like I overpowered you. That'd work. I, um—" She made a fist in her hair, trying frantically to think. "I'll hit you on the head. Not hard enough to hurt you, of course, but give you a lump. You could tell them I knocked you out and that I escaped!"

He stared down at her. "And then what?"

"I'll run. Disappear. I've done it before, I can do it again."

"In a sheriff's vehicle? With every cop in the country watching for you? The minute I reported that you escaped, they'd have roadblocks up on every major highway. You had the element of surprise in your favor when you left New York. That's not how it works when the cops are after you. They'd nail you before you drove a hundred miles. And off to New York you'd go. Huh-uh. I won't have that on my conscience. No way!"

He jerked his sleeve free and strode away from her. She started to run after him, but Sammy shrieked in terror. "Mommy, don't leave me!"

She threw an agonized glance back at the Bronco. "I won't, sweetkins. I promise." Then she turned to gaze at Heath's retreating figure. "Come back here!" she cried softly, half afraid he might be mistaken about the cabin being unoccupied. "Heath!" When he didn't stop, she picked up a small rock and threw it at him.

He jerked and spun, rubbing his shoulder. "I can't *believe* you did that!" He came back toward her, his boots scuffing the dirt. "Three inches up and you would have hit me in the head!"

"We *have* to talk!"

"Christ Almighty! Talk, then," he said, still rubbing his shoulder.

"I can't let you dig yourself in any deeper! You're already in so far now, you may never talk your way out of it! Now you're going to add car theft to the list? *Think*, Heath, please! We have to find another way. This has gone too far.''

"That's right. 'Gone'! Past tense! Meredith, I just blew away three men with a 30.06 rifle. Registered to me, I might add. Talk my way *out* of it? There *is* no *out*, honey. Not now. Fergusson wasn't kidding. If I don't take you back, my ass is in a sling for sure.''

Meredith pressed her hands over her face. "Take me back then.''

"*What?*''

"Mommy?'' Sammy whined from one of the open Bronco windows. "It's dark in here, and I'm scared. You said you wouldn't go 'way!''

Meredith drew her hands from her face. "I'll be right there, punkin.''

"Go take care of your daughter.'' His eyes glittered in the moonlight. "I'm a big boy. I know what I'm doing.''

"Trashing your whole life?'' she whispered. "That's what you're doing!''

"Yeah. Well, what the hell did you think would happen, Meredith?''

That was most awful part. She hadn't thought. He had been her way out, and she hadn't cared about anything but saving herself and Sammy.

"You asked me to help you. Remember? You said I'd be signing your death warrant if I sent you back. Did you really think I could help you *without* trashing my life?''

Meredith's legs were shaking. Everything was shaking. For some reason, she'd thought they could simply drive off into the darkness, covering their tracks, and that Glen would never find them. Now Heath was destroying himself, right before her very eyes, systematically slicing away big chunks of who he was.

"I guess—I guess I didn't think!'' she cried. "Oh, God, Heath, I'm sorry. I just didn't think!''

He cupped her face between his hands. "Merry, sweet-

heart . . . don't do this, all right? I shouldn't have said that.
It was my decision to make. No one else's, and I would
have made it, no matter what you said.''

''What have I done?'' Her voice came out in a squeak.
''If you do this, you can't ever go back. Oh, God, what
have I done?''

''Nothing, honey. Nothing. I don't have to do this. I want
to.''

''I let Dan destroy me. And then I let him destroy
Sammy. Now, he's reaching beyond the grave and I'm letting him destroy *you*! Where does it stop?'' She hauled in
a breath, held it, and then released it in a shaky gush. Jabbing her finger toward the ground, she said, ''Well, I've
decided. It stops right here! Right now. I won't let him ruin
your life. It's bad enough what I let him do to mine and
Sammy's.''

''You didn't *let* the son of a bitch do anything. You're
here, aren't you? And you're still fighting back.'' He lifted
her face. ''As for what's happening to me, *I'm* responsible.
Not you. I've thought this through, Meredith, and I know
exactly what I'm doing. And you know what?''

''No, what?''

''I think I'm making a damned good choice.''

Chapter 22

The pickup truck Heath hot-wired was a rattletrap, four-wheel drive Ford pickup that had once been red but now had more dings and dents than it did paint. It ran good, though, and had a king cab with a full-sized backseat for Sammy and Goliath. It also came with five cans of gas, which the owners had stored at one end of the carport. The refillable cans and the fuel might come in handy before this was over. Heath didn't like the truck's long wheel base. It cornered wide, and he feared the undercarriage might high center on rough terrain. But beggars couldn't be choosers. It was transportation.

After moving Sammy and Goliath and the Bronco's contents into the stolen truck, he wasted no time in getting out of there. He had Meredith follow him in the Bronco back to the spot where the shootout had occurred. Once there, he radioed in to report the fatalities and requested clean-up of the site as well as an ambulance to transport the bodies back to town. That done, he got his walkie-talkie and spotlight out of the console, then hustled Meredith to the pickup, afraid they might be caught if they lingered.

"I don't understand why we came clear back here," she said.

"Number one, I can't leave dead bodies lying along the road. Call it crazy, but some old lady might find them and have a heart attack. Number two, if we'd left the Bronco anywhere near where we got the truck, we may as well have put up a sign saying, 'Stolen Vehicle.' This way, the trail stops here.''

''You think like a criminal.''

''I think like a cop. That's why we're such a menace when we turn crooked.''

On the way to his friend's cabin, Heath frequently took side roads and doubled back to the highway to throw off any pursuers. Only after he felt sure that no one was tailing him did he head in a direct route to their destination. Even though he'd called in to report the location of the three bodies, he felt confident no one would think to look for him at Mike's place. He hadn't been up there in years and seldom even saw Mike anymore. The highway continued across the mountain and tied in with Interstate 5, which was undoubtedly where law enforcement would believe he had headed. Most fugitives tried to get as far away as possible, never realizing that the safest hiding place might be right under the local cops' noses.

There was no doubt in Heath's mind that there would be a search launched for him now. His badge could only protect him to a point, and he had stepped way beyond it when he ignored Fergusson's warnings. Meredith felt responsible, he knew. He wished he could think of something he might say to relieve her mind. There was nothing. The bottom line was, he hadn't done all of this for the hell of it, but for her and Sammy. To claim otherwise would be an outright lie, and a transparent one at that.

Dog and child asleep in the back, they traveled for quite a while in silence. A tense, brittle silence. He was worried about her. She hugged the passenger door, for one thing, putting as much distance between them as possible. And she was gripping the armrest so hard that her whitened knuckles almost glowed in the dark. She was still extremely upset, no question about it, he supposed because he'd just added grand theft to his list of crimes. He thought about reminding her that this was a life or death situation, not a joy ride. When it came to staying alive, a man did things he might never do otherwise. But he figured she knew that already.

"Meredith, can you talk to me? Maybe you'll feel better if we hash this out again."

In response, she just shook her head.

Heath couldn't let it go at that. "You're feeling responsible because I'm tanking my career. Correct?"

"It's that, and I'm also upset because—oh, it's nothing! I'm just—" She broke off and shook her head again. "It's nothing."

"You know damned well it's something. You haven't said a word in forty miles."

"I can't think of anything to talk about."

"Don't think. Just talk. You're stewing about something. I want to know what."

She threw up her hands. "It's just everything, Heath. All you've done for us. All you've sacrificed for us. It's way too much!"

"I was starting to hate the job, anyway."

"That's baloney. Working with teenagers. Saving lives. Remember? It's your atonement for what happened to Laney. Do you think I don't know that it means everything to you?"

"Honey, let's leave Laney out of this. All right?"

"The point is, you're throwing *everything* away. And you could end up in prison."

"Like I said. That's my decision to make, isn't it?"

"Maybe, but it makes me feel really uneasy."

"Uneasy?" He'd expected her to say she felt guilty. *Uneasy*. He didn't like the sound of that. "In what way?"

She waved her hands again, a telltale sign of just how agitated she was. "It's so hard for me to put it into words. My thoughts are going in circles, and I don't want to blurt something out and make you upset with me."

Heath had been there a few times. "You don't have to be guarded about what you say to me, honey."

"I don't?"

He chuckled. "Of course not. Just tell me what you're

thinking, and we'll sort through it together.''

She looked hesitant, but she hauled in a deep breath and said in a tremulous voice, ''Well, right now I'm thinking that you're the very best friend I've ever had, and that I don't know what I would have done without you, not just tonight but all along. And it frightens me to think of what may happen to Sammy and me if we lose you.''

Heath's heart caught, and a lump came into his throat. ''You aren't going to lose me, Merry. You can count on that.''

''Not even if I make you so angry you hate me?''

''What could you ever do to make me hate you? Nothing.''

In a thin voice, she said, ''Not even if I have trouble living up to my part of the bargain?''

''What bargain?''

She waved her hand to encompass them both. ''*Our* bargain. Neither of us has actually verbalized it, of course, but I'm not so obtuse that I believe you've done all this for nothing. You surely have certain expectations, and I know in my heart that I owe you that and more. I could try for the rest of my life and never be able to repay you for all you've done tonight.''

''What sort of expectations do you think I have, Meredith?''

''Well, you obviously care very deeply for me, and for Sammy, too. I mean, well, a man doesn't go to these lengths for just anyone. Right?''

''This isn't exactly the moment I would have chosen to profess my feelings for you, but, yeah, I care. One hell of a lot. For you and for Sammy. And, no, I wouldn't have done all this for anyone else. So what's your point, precisely?''

''I'm just—concerned. When it comes time for us to— well, you know—I'm worried that you'll get really angry if I—well, if I'm less than enthusiastic. In situations where I feel cornered—''

''Cornered?''

"I guess that's not the right word, exactly. Um . . . jeez. It's so hard to explain." She flashed him a glance. "Sort of trapped?"

"Trapped." He rolled the word over his tongue, bitterness washing his mouth.

"When I feel like that, my head gets all crazy, and it isn't *now* I'm thinking about, but *then*, and I get this claustrophobic feeling. I can't breathe and I kind of—panic inside. Needless to say, I've avoided the situation since my divorce. But now I can't, and I'm—well, very concerned because I'm not sure I can control it, and if I can't, I may be uncooperative. And I'm afraid you'll—get really angry with me. Justifiably so, of course. You understand?"

He understood, all right. He just couldn't quite believe that was how her thoughts were running. After all he had done to gain her trust—all he was *still* doing—and she had his motivation narrowed down to one thing, a hard-on. Even worse, she obviously believed he'd be a jerk if she refused him. *Less than enthusiastic?* She couldn't be thinking that he might force her. Surely not. Yet he had a feeling—a really bad feeling—that she sure as hell was. The thought made his blood boil.

"No, I guess I don't understand," he lied. He'd be damned if he'd let her get away with being vague while she ripped his character to shreds.

She gazed at him in bewilderment. "You don't?"

"No. Spell it out for me."

She pressed a hand to her chest and began fiddling with her shirt buttons. "You do understand, and now you're angry because I've been worrying about it."

"I am not angry." Timid little women, frigid schoolmarms, humorless nuns, and panty-waist priests got angry. He went straight past angry to totally pissed off.

"Please, Heath. Don't be angry. You did say I didn't need to be guarded."

He *had* said that. "I told you, I'm not angry."

"Why is your jaw ticking, then?"

He pried his teeth apart. "When I'm intent on a conversation, I sometimes grind my teeth a little.'' And rip steering wheels off their columns. And drive ninety miles an hour. And fantasize about wringing a certain pretty lady's scrawny little neck.

She inhaled deeply and sighed. ''After Dan, I guess you might say I'm more than a little hesitant about having another relationship.''

''I can certainly sympathize with that.'' He really, really wished Dan Calendri were alive so he could murder the bastard.

''And the thought that another relationship may be imminent—well, it makes me rather uneasy.''

As she spoke, the hand she gestured with was shaking visibly. She called *that* rather uneasy? In his books, it was better described as scared spitless. He started gritting his teeth again, reminding himself, without much success, that it was a dumb thing to do. He'd once gotten so pissed off and bitten down so hard that he cracked a molar.

She pressed her lips together and stared out the windshield. He glanced at her, then back at the road, until his eyes began to feel like swivel bearings. In the lights from the pickup dash, he saw that she'd knotted both fists on her lap.

''I will, of course, try my very best not to be difficult,'' she said softly.

''*Difficult?*''

''Yes. You have every right to expect me to cooperate.''

''Meredith, just to clarify, are we talking about sex?''

She threw him a startled look. ''I'd really rather not get graphic, if you wouldn't mind.''

Graphic? He had an awful urge to laugh. Only he was too furious. ''Can I take that as an affirmative, that we *are* discussing sex? You and me, getting intimate. And that you're not too hot on the idea?''

''That's a good way to define it, 'not too hot on the idea.' Only, um . . .'' She worried her bottom lip. ''Only it's more a *whole lot* not too hot on the idea.''

''And you're worried that I'll be a butt about it.''

Her expression turned horrified. "Oh, *no*! I can't imagine you ever being a butt about anything!"

Heath relaxed slightly, damned glad that he'd asked. He could handle her being worried about it. Hell, he could handle her feeling terrified, even. God knew, she probably had reason. What he *couldn't* handle was her thinking he'd done all this with that reward in mind, and that he'd demand it as his right, even if she resisted. *That* was a low blow.

"I never meant to imply *that*!" she went on. "I think you're—" She gulped and got tears in her eyes. "You are, without question, the finest man I've ever known. I think you even outshine my dad, and for me, that's saying something."

Heath was starting to feel sheepish and very relieved that he hadn't given in to his urge to lace her up one side and down the other. "Thank you, Meredith. That's quite a compliment." He flashed her an understanding smile, thinking as he did that a man with a truly admirable character should be humble. "But I gotta say your dad sounds like quite a guy, a real hard act to follow. I've got a few faults you probably haven't seen yet. I am only human, so don't put me on too high a pedestal. I may disappoint you."

"I know." She blinked away the tears. "That's why I'm so concerned."

Red alert. He got locked in on his driving course so he could spare her another long look. "What do you mean?"

She shrugged, her expression conveying that she felt utterly miserable. "It's not in a man's nature to be very patient when it comes to—well, you know." Her hands were still knotted into fists. She turned an imploring gaze on him. "Could we like, maybe, strike a deal? That I will try really, really hard not to be difficult, and in exchange, you'll try equally hard not to lose your temper with me?"

Heath felt sure he'd just flattened one of his six-hundred-dollar dental caps. "I don't know if I can agree to that. Right now, I'm very, *very* close."

"To what?"

"Losing my temper!" Her eyes went wide. He tried to modulate his voice. He honestly did. "I don't force myself on a woman. No matter how much I might want her, or how much I might love her. Never, period. And I don't expect or demand sexual paybacks just because I do a woman a few favors, even if they are big ones. And you know what else? I find it *extremely* insulting and offensive that you think I'd ever even consider treating you like that."

"Oh," she said faintly.

"So here's the deal, all right? The only one I'll agree to, at any rate. I won't so much as *touch* you. Got it? So you can stop worrying. If the time ever comes that you have a strong urge to get laid and want me to do the honors, you just whistle. Goddamn fool that I am, I'll probably come running."

He turned his gaze back to the road. *Glared* at the road, to be precise.

"I didn't mean to offend you," she said in a quavery voice.

"I'm finished discussing the subject," he replied with biting finality. "Rule number one, when you piss me off—which you seem to be gifted at doing, I might add—is to shut up while you're ahead."

"I'm sorry."

He heard a catch in her breathing and narrowed his eyes on the road. "Don't you *dare* start crying, Meredith. I mean it. In my rule book, that's dirty pool, and tears don't work with me."

"I'm not. I hardly ever cry, and certainly never to manipulate someone!"

"Good. It'd be a waste of your energy."

He kept glaring at the road, hoping she believed him, because he knew he'd be all over himself apologizing if she shed one tear. And right now, he didn't want to apologize. He was royally pissed off, had every right to be, and he needed some time to work his way past it.

Sex. That was what she thought he had on his mind. No

wonder she had been clinging to her door and looking so tense. She was dreading the grand event. *Christ.* As if he was that desperate. He didn't even *like* blondes, dammit. Especially not a short one with great big eyes, the personality of a rug, and a figure like Popeye's girlfriend. What was her name? Olive Oil. Or was it Olive Oyle? Hell, what did it matter? The point was, Mary Calendri, a.k.a. Meredith Kenyon, didn't have what it took to drive him to rape.

His hands slippery with sweat on the steering wheel, Heath kept driving. At this point, it was way too late to turn back. As if he would have, even if he'd had that choice. No, what he really wanted to do was strangle her.

As for what he expected as payback, maybe he should take his cue from her and be the bastard she obviously believed him to be, he thought furiously. Far be it from him to disappoint a lady. Her words kept slamming into his brain, making him madder and madder. Never once had he *ever* given her cause to think that of him. Just the opposite. When he recalled all the times he had practically glued his eyeballs to the floor to keep from ogling her figure, all the times he had wanted to kiss her and didn't, all the times he'd fantasized about screwing her brains out and made no moves on her . . . *Damn!* Maybe he should have just copped a few feels when the mood struck. He sure as hell hadn't earned any Brownie points by behaving like a gentleman.

A few minutes later, he noticed that Meredith's head was starting to nod. That *really* pissed him off. He felt like reaching over and pinching her awake. Wasn't that just like a woman? She got a man so furious he was snapping at his own tail and then she took a nap.

Glancing at his illuminated watch dial, he decided she was probably exhausted. It was after midnight, and she'd had one hell of a day. Unlike him, she wasn't accustomed to pulling double shifts and going without rest. Nor had she learned to insulate her emotions when all hell broke loose.

Hell, the fact that she'd fallen asleep was proof of how tired she was. For all she knew, he might pull over at any

moment to start collecting on all those sacrifices he'd made
for her.

His mouth twitched at the corners. The fact that he was
about to smile made him all the more furious. Who was
crazier, her or him? He had it bad. No question about it.
He was Stetson over boot heels in love with her.

Stetson?

He glanced around the truck. Son of a bitch. His *hat*!
Where the hell had he left it? He had already thrown his
badge away. His career was destroyed. The future looked
so grim, even speaking of it was tantamount to saying the
''F'' word. Was it too goddamned much to ask that he at
least get to keep his hat?

He shot a glare at Meredith. *Sleeping beauty!* It was one
thing to screw up his whole life for her. But, by God, a
man's hat was another matter. She sure as hell did owe
him. Big time.

Her head lolled against the door, her neck twisting toward her shoulder. She was going to get a stiff neck. And
why the hell did he care? Right now, she was lucky he
didn't have his hands around her throat. His Stetson. God,
he was going to miss it.

He glanced over at Meredith again, then sighed and
reached across the truck to grab her shoulder and straighten
her posture. Her head lolled back over the top of the seat,
her lips sputtering on a feminine snore.

He smiled slightly, then caught himself and scowled.
Damn. Even when he wanted to kill her, all it took was
one look at her, and he got soft in the head.

And hard elsewhere.

Maybe she was right, and his motivation all boiled down
to one thing: sex. She was one extremely expensive piece
of ass, if that was the case. His Stetson had cost him a
hundred and ten bucks.

The cabin was nestled high on a mountain amongst a stand
of majestic pine and fir trees. In the beam of the flashlight
Heath carried when he entered the cabin to light the lan-

terns, Meredith saw that the structure was fashioned from logs with a red aluminum roof. When she went inside moments later, she took a quick tour to discover that the furnishings were sturdy and practical. The floor plan could best be described as compact and functional, with two bedrooms, one small with a double bed, the other hardly bigger than a closet with a child-sized cot.

After tucking Sammy into the cot for the night, Meredith scotched all thoughts of joining the child there later. Goliath immediately snuggled down beside the little girl, taking up what little extra room there was, and she didn't think he or Sammy would appreciate it if she ousted him. That left one remaining bed, and two individuals who needed a place to sleep.

In an attempt to block that worry from her mind, she applied herself to the task of helping Heath unload the pickup. She tried to ignore his angry scowl and the fact that he barely spoke to her, but that was difficult. He was so big. And so furious. She felt as if she were locked in a cage with an unpredictable gorilla.

After they had carried everything inside, she busied herself putting the food away while he sorted his ammunition on the kitchen table and systematically began loading the weapons. He scarcely looked in her direction, but when he did, there was no mistaking the angry glint in his eyes.

It was just as well that he was ignoring her, she thought, as she sank wearily onto a chair across the table from him. Watching him handle the guns made her head swim with memories of Dan, especially when he picked up the handguns, Dan's choice of weapon. To this day, the smell of gunpowder made her feel queasy, and if Heath looked at her, he was bound to notice she was turning a little green.

As if he would care. He was mad at her, and she couldn't blame him. She'd never intended to offend him earlier. In fact, she'd tried her best to avoid discussing her feelings entirely. But, oh, no. He had insisted. And just look where honesty had gotten her. Now he looked as if he were chewing nails, and try as she might, she could think of no way to mend her fences.

Stupid, so stupid. Half the time, that had been part of her trouble with Dan, saying something to set him off.

"Heath?"

He slapped the semiautomatic's loaded magazine into its niche, the gunmetal making that unmistakable rasp that always made her skin crawl. She jumped with a start.

"What?"

Dark head bent, his expression stony, he fairly spat out the word. Meredith swallowed, hoping to steady her voice. Fat chance. Being around a furious man made her hair stand on end, and no amount of swallowing and taking deep breaths was going to cure the problem.

"I, um . . . want to try to explain about what I said in the truck."

"No need. You made it pretty clear."

"No, I mean explain *why* I said it." She hugged her waist, which was tender from where Delgado had kicked her. "My, um . . . anxieties. They aren't—well, they have nothing to do with you, and you shouldn't take them personally."

He shot her a frosty look. "Nothing to do with me? And I shouldn't take it personally? Pardon me all to hell. I think sex is pretty damned personal. Coercing a woman to have sex, in any fashion, is tantamount to rape. At least, in my books. It isn't in yours?"

"Yes. No! I mean—" She rubbed at her temple. "Of *course* it is! But—"

"And you're concerned that sex is my price for helping you. Correct? So, in effect, you think I'm the kind of man who would *force* a woman? Right?"

"No!"

"Explain it to me. Which part didn't I get right? My price? Are you saying you *weren't* worried about my demanding sex from you?"

"No, I—" Meredith realized she was staring at him through a blur of tears, and for once, she wasn't weeping for herself or Sammy. She had hurt this man, badly, and he, of all men, didn't deserve that from her. "Please, will you just be quiet and let me explain?"

He shrugged. "You'll think I'm a goddamned stump. Talk away."

"I *don't* believe you would ever force me," she began. "And yet I do."

He snorted. "I feel better already."

"You said you'd be a stump."

He shot her another look, this one as searing as the other had been frosty. "Sorry. It's just difficult to keep my mouth shut when my character is being denigrated."

"It's *not* about you! Can't you understand that? It stems from my past. My rational side knows that I'm being absurd. But there's this little voice at the back of my mind that keeps whispering, 'Be careful. Don't trust blindly. Don't make the same mistake twice.'" She held up her hands and leaned forward in her chair, pleading with her gaze. "Only I can't be careful. This situation hasn't given me time to breathe, let alone think. Things are happening so fast! Just like before. I trusted Dan with all my heart, believing him to be everything he pretended to be, and look where it got me!"

The glint in his eyes reminded her of flint sparking off steel. In that moment, he seemed gigantic to her, all hard muscle and raw masculinity. His dark, collar-length hair was wind-tossed, his steely blue eyes contrasting sharply with the burnished cast of his features. Tension knotted the tendons along his jaw and drew his mouth into a thin, uncompromising line.

Setting the loaded gun aside, he pushed up from the chair to pace back and forth for at least a full minute. When he finally stopped, he turned to regard her. Meredith had no idea what to expect when he sauntered toward her, his gait lazy and unhurried. When he reached down to cup her chin, she tensed. To her surprise, he hunkered in front of her. Looking into his eyes, she saw tenderness mixed in with his anger now, the latter disappearing entirely as his sensual mouth tipped into one of those grins that always managed to make her knees feel weak.

"I think I'm the one who should be apologizing," he told her huskily. "After what you've been through, I guess you have every right to be a little gun-shy, and I had no business getting pissed off because you were honest with me about it."

"I never meant to hurt you," she said shakily.

"And that's it, isn't it? I got my feelings hurt." His mouth curved up at one corner again. "And instead of admitting that, I got mad."

"I'm so sorry. You're the last person on earth I would ever try to hurt."

"I shouldn't have let it hurt. In fact, I feel like a jerk. You have a problem, and you wanted me to help you deal with it, and instead, I blew up at you. I wish I hadn't."

"It's all right. Really. It's a stupid problem."

"It is *not* stupid."

He sounded so emphatic that it emboldened her. "I feel so mixed up inside. It's like I've got two of me running around in there."

"God forbid. One of you is all I can handle."

Meredith laughed in spite of herself, and yet she had an awful urge to cry. After what he'd said in the truck, she was terrified she might. "I think maybe I need counseling. My feelings aren't—right. They're twisted and sick." She looked into his eyes. Those wonderful blue-gray eyes, and she remembered her thoughts of him in the Bronco when she'd been afraid he might die for her. "I'm—I'm in love with you, you know."

He said nothing for an endlessly long moment, rubbing his thumb over her bottom lip. "I've been hoping you might be. It'd be a hell of a note if you weren't. I've never loved a woman before, so I don't have a measuring stick, but I'd say I'm about as far gone as a guy can get."

Meredith already knew that. He had said it with his actions so many times, most eloquently tonight. Lots of men claimed to love a woman enough to die for her. Heath had never boasted that; he'd just gone out and put his life on the line. That's why she knew her fears were irrational, the twisted reasoning of an emotionally sick person. She had *nothing* to fear from this man. Nothing. And yet the thought of his touching her intimately made her quake.

"So you see my problem?" she asked him shakily. "I should *want* to be with you. I need professional help."

His eyes went dark and molten. "You need to be loved, Meredith. And I don't mean sex, so don't get claustrophobic." His mouth curved up at the corners. "That will come. Right now, you just need to be loved, with no expectations, by a man who's willing to listen and help you deal with all these feelings. As it happens, I know a fellow who might volunteer for the job."

"How can *you* help me? You're my problem!"

He narrowed one eye at her. "I am not your problem. Old baggage with Dan Calendri's name on it is your problem. You need to talk to me about that. Get it out of your head and in the open. I can testify to the fact that it helps. Talking to you about Laney got a lot of the demons off my back."

"I'm glad. But it won't work for me. Talking? I can't talk about Dan. I just can't! I'm so *ashamed*. If I told you all of it, you'd *never* look at me in the same way again."

"Ashamed? You? Why, for God's sake? It was Dan's shame, not yours."

Meredith felt the tears welling. An awful ache centered in her chest and at the back of her eyes. "I'm sure you've read about women like me or heard discussions on talk shows. The victims! Pathetic creatures who stay in abusive situations, who somehow *need* to feel dominated and be humiliated. Or else they're so weak and scared, they can't find the courage to help themselves. The last, that was me. I *stayed*, Heath. I stayed and *let* him victimize me! And then I let him victimize Sammy. When I remember, I'm disgusted with myself, and if you knew what I allowed him to do to me, you'd be disgusted, too."

"Honey, no."

"Yes!" Meredith heard her voice going shrill and felt the tears spilling over her lashes, but she couldn't stop herself. It felt as if a volcano was about to erupt inside her. "The things I did. You have no idea. Horrid things. Degrading things. And I just—" She threw up her hands, a tearing pain going through her abdomen. "I just did them. I was afraid of him. So afraid! If he snapped his fingers and said, 'Crawl,' I dropped to my knees. Once when there were *people* there. He was drunk and thought it was funny."

She held her breath for a moment, trying to regain her self-control. Then she looked at Heath, saw the horror reflected in his eyes, and felt the tears rushing up again. He would never have any respect for her now. After seeing what he had done tonight, she couldn't imagine his ever giving way to anyone out of fear. He would never bend or break, and he would certainly never crawl. He'd never be able to understand that she had.

But wasn't it better this way? At least he would know now what kind of person she was. A non-person. A spineless coward who would have done anything, no matter how demoralizing, to keep her skin intact.

"Once," she managed to say, "when I was crawling, he told me to bark. He had this notion that a wife was—" Her throat closed off, and for a moment, she couldn't breathe. "He had Dobermans. Very expensive, well-trained Dobermans with German pedigrees. He used to tell me my bloodlines were pathetic by comparison, that I was a mongrel hayseed. So you see, it wasn't only that he considered me to be no better than his dogs, but *less* than." The pressure at the back of her throat became almost painful. "And that day when he ordered me to crawl and bark, I knew that he was—that he was right. If he went too far, beating on the Dobies, they fought back. I didn't." She looked Heath directly in the eye, even though his dark face looked as if it were swimming. It was the hardest thing she'd ever done, saying those last words. "I just—did what he told me to do."

His hand tightened on her chin. "You barked?"

The disbelief in his voice made her feel so ashamed that she closed her eyes, and as she did, the sob she'd been trying to hold back erupted from her, and it was quickly followed by another. And another. She couldn't stop them. Horrible, heaving sounds like those of a sick dog.

She wanted to stop. Tried to stop. But she couldn't.

"Meredith, for God's sake. Just let it out." He slipped an arm around her waist and drew her head down to his shoulder. "Don't, honey. You're going to break something down in there."

Feeling his strong arm around her was Meredith's complete undoing. She was surprised he could even bring himself to touch her. She started to weep then, and once the tears started to come, she couldn't make them stop either. Not even when Heath startled her half to death by lifting her from the chair and into his arms. Oh, God, he was every bit as strong as she'd always feared.

"That just makes it easier for me to hold you," he rumbled as he carried her from the kitchen. "Nothing more. I swear it, honey."

With a sense of horror, she realized she'd spoken the thought aloud.

He jostled her in his arms, then turned sideways to go through a doorway. She saw the bed, a dizzying blur of colorful crazy-quilt patches. Her first thought was to get out of there, away from him, and that only made her cry harder.

"Sweetheart, it's just a bed. It won't bite you, and neither will I."

Oh, God! She was babbling out every thought that went through her mind. She had to shut up. He was going to hate her, and she wouldn't blame him. She was disgusting, pathetic and paranoid. Why couldn't she get Dan out of her head? Was she going to let him destroy what remained of her life?

He sat on the mattress with his back against the lodge pole pine headboard. Shifting her on his lap, he clamped her head to his shoulder with one hand and rubbed her back and her scraped arm with the other. "Sweetheart, I don't hate you," he said gruffly. "And I never will. And you're not disgusting, pathetic, *or* paranoid. You're sweet and wonderful, and I love you. Do you hear me? And Dan Calendri is *not* going to ruin the rest of your life. You've got me now, and we can get past this. I promise you, we will."

He felt so solid and warm. Meredith couldn't resist the draw and turned to loop an arm around his strong neck, her face buried against his shirt to hide her tears. She stopped fighting them, and just let them come. Rivers and rivers of them. She cried until she was hoarse. Until she was weak with exhaustion. Until she ran the well dry. And then she just lay against him, shuddering.

In the aftermath, she became aware, measure by measure, of Heath. Of the way his hands moved over her back, kneading away the tension one moment, then lightly caressing. She made fists on his shirt, clinging to him. He felt like a wall of muscle, so hard and invincible, yet wonderfully safe. The masculine smell of him surrounded her, a pleasant blend of cotton and starch, musk aftershave and sweat, leather and gun oil.

She remembered how she had prayed for him to come home earlier that night, how she had wanted to follow Sammy's example and scream his name when she was afraid. How could she care so much for a man, trusting him so implicitly in so many ways, yet still quake at the thought of his having any sort of power over her?

"Can I talk for a minute now?" he whispered near her ear. At her nod, he said, "First of all, you aren't a victim. You were victimized, yes, but there's a hell of a difference. I've seen the victims, honey. They stay for years. Year after year after year. They never fight back, and they never find the courage to run. Not to save themselves. Not to save their kids.

"You left Dan when Sammy was four days old. Correct?" When she nodded again, he said, "That means you stayed less than a year. You were in a hell of a mess, much worse and far more dangerous than for most battered women. It wasn't just Dan, but organized crime you were up against. For Sammy, you found a way out. A rather creative way out. It took intelligence to outwit the bastards at their own game, and it took courage. A lot of courage. They might have killed you, and you knew it. But for Sammy, you ran anyway.'' He made a fist in her hair. ''I think you're a very brave lady.''

''Oh, don't....'' She pressed her face harder against his shoulder. ''Don't.''

''Don't what? Speak the truth? You've got guts, Meredith Kenyon. Or would you rather I started calling you Mary?''

''Mary is gone, and I don't want to be her anymore. I want to be someone new, and I want to pretend that the other me never existed.''

''She'll be a hard act to follow,'' he whispered. ''Mary Calendri was some lady. As for pretending none of it ever happened, you can't. It'll stay in your head all your life. You have to deal with it. And the only way to do that is strip it bare. Admit it to yourself. Take it all out and face it. You can't run fast enough or far enough to get away from it.''

''I can't tell you any more of it. You have no idea, Heath. I just can't.''

''You're right,'' he said huskily. ''I have no idea. Don't you think it's about time I did?''

Chapter 23

Heath felt the rigidity return to Meredith's body, and by that he knew just how difficult it was for her to talk about Dan. He'd carried his own secret shame, buried deep inside, for years. Lacerating himself with guilt, punishing himself with the memories, hating himself for making a mistake that had cost his sister her life. One bad decision, and he'd paid dearly for it, in his dreams and while he was awake, for almost twenty years. Somehow, talking to Meredith had purged him. Since that evening in her yard when he'd spilled his guts to her, he hadn't had a single nightmare, and during the day, when the guilt slammed into him like a brass-knuckled fist, he had begun to shove it away, no longer accepting it. It was over. He had grieved. He had been punished enough. Beating up on himself for the rest of his life was not going to bring Laney back.

Like him, Meredith had made only one bad decision, and she had been paying for it ever since. Even worse, she seemed to believe that because her bad decision had thrust her into a life-threatening situation, the things she had done to survive were unforgivable. She had crawled, and for that, she couldn't forgive herself.

The very thought of Meredith being reduced to that, of her actually getting down on her hands and knees for the bastard, nearly made Heath gag. She was such a sweetheart, this woman. For a man to treat her like that, and for her to have believed, even for an instant, that she had sunk lower than the bastard's dogs was almost beyond his comprehension. Even more heartbreaking was his suspicion that she still hadn't told him the half of it. The knowledge that he would have to force her to tell him weighed on his chest like a boulder.

"Merry," he said softly, "why are you so afraid of handguns?"

At the question, she stopped breathing. Agonized seconds passed before he felt her chest rise and fall again.

"Out at the table," he went on. "You turned white when I was cleaning and loading my handguns. Can you tell me why?"

He thought she meant to ignore his question. But then she stirred against him, her silky hair brushing lightly against the underside of his jaw, the strands catching on his day's growth of beard. "Dan," she said. "Remember, I told you he liked to frighten me. He was especially fond of doing that at night when we—when he—well, you know."

Heath pictured himself at sixty, still referring to sexual intercourse as, "you know." Somehow, right then, it didn't strike him as being very funny. That awful ache still hung there in his chest. And it kept getting worse, making him wonder if, instead of it being heartbreak, he was about to have a coronary. "When you had sex, you mean? He frightened you then? With a gun?"

"Yes."

"How?"

She made fists on his shirt. "He—he kept a revolver in the nightstand drawer. It had one of those little wheel things with holes for the bullets, and he kept only one in it."

Christ. He *was* having a coronary. The ache was worse, and it had moved into his throat, the thud of his pulse so hard and loud that he thought he could feel the bed shake. Oh, God, he knew what she was going to say. And he could *not* calmly sit here and *listen* to her say it. He needed to step outside. Find a tree. Pretend it was Dan Calendri, and pulverize the bastard with his fists.

If he felt this way, just from hearing the story, how in the hell did she feel? He wanted to run. She couldn't get away. It was there, inside her head. *It was never wedded bliss*, she'd told him at the department. *It was a nightmare.* And God forgive him, he had yelled at her in the truck when she'd tried to tell him how nervous she was. What a prince he was. All he'd been able to think about was the insult she'd dealt him, never stopping to consider what the hell had happened to fill her with such dread.

Well, he wasn't going to let her down again. He would stay, and he would listen, and somehow, he would deal with it and help her to deal with it.

"What did he do with the gun, Meredith?"

"You *know* what he did!" she cried.

He also knew she had to say it. "Tell me."

Anger was interlaced with the pain in her voice when she cried, "While he was—doing that—he held it to my head! And when he was going to—you know—he pulled the trigger. I never knew if the gun would fire, so every time, I thought I might die. I was so terrified. Sweating. Couldn't breathe. When you think a bullet is about to explode into your brain, your whole body tenses. He—liked it that way."

Heath realized he was hugging her so hard he was about to squeeze the life out of her, but he couldn't unlock his hold. To his surprise, she wrapped both arms around his neck and pressed even closer, clinging to him as if she were about to plunge to her death and he was her only salvation.

"Ah, Merry. I always sensed my weapon made you nervous. Now I know why." He smoothed her hair, aching for her. "Is it bothering you that I'm wearing it right now? I really shouldn't take it off, you know. Chances are, no one will come up here, but—"

"It's all right, Heath. My rational side knows you'd never hurt me with it."

He wasn't asking about her rational side. Bless her heart,

no wonder she was skittish. He'd seen war veterans who got the shakes if an explosive sound startled them. He'd seen abused women and kids who ducked or flinched every time a man gestured with his hands. Her fears really weren't anything personal against him, but instinctive reactions she couldn't control. *I'll do my best not to be difficult.* God, he'd been such a jerk, and he was damned lucky she'd forgiven him for it.

"Never is right," he whispered, his voice throbbing. "I'd rather cut off my arm than hurt you or frighten you, Merry girl. I'm so sorry if I ever have."

"Oh, Heath, I love you." She shuddered and clung to him more tightly. "I didn't want you to know about the gun. Not ever. I was afraid you'd be disgusted."

He was disgusted, all right, with some of his fellow men. "I think you're the most wonderful lady I've ever met, and nothing you ever tell me will change that."

The entire story poured from her then. Every nightmarish, sordid detail. For some reason, the point that lingered with the most clarity in Heath's mind was about the spiders, probably because it was so representative of Dan's cruelty. The man had to have been insane, his mind diseased. No normal human being would do such things.

Meredith had always been afraid of spiders, the phobia dating back to childhood, and good old Dan loved to torment her with them, putting them under her pillow or between the sheets, perching one on her shoulder when she was preoccupied, sometimes slipping them into her clothing before she dressed. If she did something to displease him, that had been one of the ways he punished her, with spiders.

"To this day, I can't crawl into a bed without checking it first," she whispered. "Not even if Sammy's watching. I'm so ashamed of that. A good mother doesn't set that kind of example or risk making her child afraid of something silly. But I can't stop doing it. I've tried, and after I get in bed, I think I feel them crawling all over me."

"Merry, you're a fantastic mother. Sammy's not phobic about spiders. I think she understands it's something you can't help. You've taught her to be compassionate." Repositioning his arms around her, Heath buried his face in her hair, not speaking for a while. When he finally did, he asked, "Where the hell did Dan get so many spiders?"

"He bought them by the dozen at a pet supply store. They came in little cardboard containers, sort of like Chinese take-out." She laughed tremulously. "Needless to say, I never eat Chinese take-out. One look at those white boxes, and I lose my appetite. He used to have—sex with me while spiders crawled over my skin."

Heath cursed under his breath, the shock in his voice unmistakable. Meredith heard revulsion in his voice as well and tried to move off his lap. His arms tightened around her like steel bands.

"No way," he whispered.

She pressed her face against his shoulder again. She had no more tears left to cry, so she simply lay there against him, her emotions oddly numb.

"Oh, sweetheart, I'm so sorry." His hands moved over her as lightly as butterfly wings. "I wish I had known you then, that I had been there to help you."

Meredith could detect no note of disgust in his deep voice, no harsh judgments, only a heartfelt regret that she had faced it all alone. It was the most beautiful feeling. A shimmery, warm glow that moved all the way through her. He loved her. He truly did. A no-matter-what kind of love, the kind that would last a lifetime. It made her feel so incredibly good and safe. His strong arms. The steady thud of his heart. The heat of him surrounding her. She kept her eyes closed and wished she could melt into him, that she would never have to move away, that she could just be absorbed by his strength and never be alone again.

"What would you have done?" she asked. "Tell me, like in a story, and after this, whenever I remember, I'll pretend it happened just that way, that you came and made it all stop."

His chest rumbled as he spoke, the vibration moving through her body, the deep, gravelly timber of his voice soothing her like a healing balm. He spun a tale, much like the ones she told Sammy, of him coming to New York and walking the streets until he found Dan's house where she was imprisoned. Of him kicking down the front door, storming in to find her, and encountering Dan as he searched the rooms.

Meredith thought that was going to be her favorite part of the story because Heath kicked Dan's butt. Pummeled him, and made him crawl. She really, really *liked* that part.

"And then what?" she caught herself asking, just as Sammy did when she paused for breath while telling her a story.

Heath sighed. "Well, then, I went up the stairs." He looked down. "Were there stairs?" At her nod, he continued. "And I searched all the rooms until finally I opened a door, and there you were, so beautiful and sweet that I stopped dead in my tracks and just stared."

She giggled.

"Hair the color of honey shot through with sunlight. Skin like fresh cream. Lips the faint pink of new strawberries on the vine. And the most gorgeous brown eyes I had ever seen, the color of chocolate caramels."

Meredith pinched him. "Blue! My eyes are blue."

"Shit." He tucked in his chin to scowl down at her upturned face. "They *are* blue, aren't they? Those damned contacts go. Right now. A man's got a right to see his woman with her real eyes on."

She pushed up, using her elbow against his chest for leverage, which made him grunt. After she popped out the contacts, he took them from her palm and tossed them on the floor. Then he framed her face in his big hands and gazed at her for an endless moment. "Gorgeous blue, rimmed in red."

She gasped. "That's not romantic!"

"Neither is a red nose, but I still think you're pretty damned cute." He patted his shoulder. "Back down here. I'm just getting to the good part."

She snuggled against him again, keeping her head tipped

back so she might watch his dark face and the changing expressions that flitted over his features. He got a distant, tender look in his eyes and a half smile played upon his lips.

"Anyway, there I stood, frozen to the spot. She was so beautiful, I couldn't stop staring. A little lady, the biggest thing about her these gigantic blue eyes and a belly that stuck out like a twenty pound watermelon."

"Heath!" She pressed a hand to her waist. "It *doesn't*!"

"It did *then*! You had to have been pregnant most of the time you were with the asshole. We're in the happy ever after part of the story now."

"You're going to make me pregnant?"

He glanced down at her and raised his eyebrows. "Can I?"

She made a face.

"Anyway, I just stood there, totally hypnotized by this beautiful little lady with a great big whopper of a belly." She giggled. "Once I recovered from my initial disbelief, I stepped closer. And with every step, I got a stronger feeling that there'd never be any turning back, because I loved her. So I swept her up into my arms and carried her down the stairs to the—"

"On the way out, let me stop and punch Dan," she inserted.

"—living room," he continued, barely missing a beat, "to let my lady fair punch Dan Calendri's lights out."

"I want to kick him, too."

He threw her a startled glance.

"Well? If I'm going to refer back to this story, I want to remember myself getting even!"

He grinned. "After she punched his lights out, she kicked him, over and over again, from his head to his shoulders, until he was lying there on the floor, a bloody pulp. And then I gave her my knife and she whacked off his—"

"Ear!" she injected.

He chuckled. "Ah, come on. I want some satisfaction,

too.'' When he saw her expression, he grinned. ''Oh, all right, his ear, then. She whacked off *both* his ears and fed them to the Dobermans. Before we left, I belted him one more time, just for good measure, and then made him crawl over to my lady fair and beg her forgiveness for every mean thing he'd ever done to her.''

''And she refused.''

''And she refused. She was a very bitter lady, and a little bloodthirsty, too. But I didn't care because she was so gorgeous. So I swept her back into my arms and carried her off into the Oregon sunset, where we had a baby girl who looked just like her, and we named her Samantha, which she never learned to spell.''

Meredith laughed and sighed, thinking that was the end. But Heath looked down at her, his eyes a dark, intense blue gray, his expression one of absolute tenderness. ''And I loved them both for the rest of my life,'' he said huskily, ''keeping my vow to protect them from any kind of harm and doing everything in my power to make them happy.''

Meredith touched her hand to his lean cheek. ''I know you will, Heath.'' As he had done to her, she moved her thumb lightly over his lips. ''That's a beautiful story. Like my own little fairy tale. Whenever I start to remember, I'll think of that instead.''

''You do that,'' he whispered. ''Because if I had known you then, that's how it would have happened. Only I probably would have killed him.''

Under the pad of her thumb, his lips felt like warm silk. They fascinated her, and she fixed her gaze on his mouth. ''If I ask you to kiss me, will you stop if I hate it?''

''You asking?'' When she nodded, he smiled. ''You're not going to hate it, but, yeah, I'll stop.''

As he bent his dark head, she gazed up at him, committing to memory his expression, the blur of his features as he moved closer, the smell of him, and then the way it felt as his lips settled over hers. For those first few seconds, she remained separate from it all, more observer than participant, testing the feel of his strong shoulders under her

palms, noting the way his hard chest tantalized the tips of
her breasts when he shifted, absorbing the incredible feeling
of his arms cradling her and his hands moving on her back,
his fingers curling over her ribs and learning the shape of
her waist and hips. It was like being traced, his fingertips
the charcoal that lingered over each line and angle. Her last
thought was that she was being recreated with every gentle
touch, that Mary Calendri truly had ceased to exist and a
perfectly new person was taking her place.

Then all she could do was feel. Drowning in golden sensation, melting into it, surrendering completely to it. His
mouth was like warm, wet silk. He was hardness, then heat,
and then fire, igniting her body with a yearning she'd never
experienced. A trembling need pooled with electrical intensity in the pit of her stomach. She knew he felt it, too. With
her backside on his lap, she could feel his hardness thrusting against his jeans—a throbbing pressure, like pulsating
steel, against her softness.

For the first time in her life, she *wanted*. She wasn't sure
how, but somehow she opened his shirt. She ran her hands
over his chest and shoulders, dived her hands down his shirt
sleeves to discover the muscular bulges of his upper arms.
His skin felt like satin over hard, mounded padding. Resilient. She pressed in with her fingers, testing the strength of
vibrant tendons. With her fingertips, she followed the outline of his collarbone and then acquainted herself with the
corded muscles in his neck. He was hers, all hers. Even his
heart belonged to her. And she gloried in the experience of
exploring him, marveling at the power she felt moving under her hands and wondering how on earth he could be so
incredibly gentle.

As if he had magic in his fingertips, her shirt fell open.
She hadn't felt him unfastening the buttons. He was
breathing hard, fast, his chest shuddering. With a push of
his hands, he swept the cotton off her shoulders and down
her arms. Then he settled his hot mouth over the pulse at
the base of her throat, drawing hard on her skin as if he
meant to imbue himself with the very essence of her.

Reaching behind her, he unfastened her bra. His palms slid up her back, his calluses like fine sandpaper and tantalizing her flesh, his fingers slipping under the cotton straps and lifting them away.

The next instant, she felt his arms coming around her, one at her waist, the other behind her knees, and before she could blink, she was flat on her back with Heath Masters looming over her like a broad canopy of oiled bronze. His eyes were storm dark, the glint of them like spikes of lightning, and she felt the shock as his gaze settled on her breasts. Her nipples went instantly hard and started to throb with every pulse beat.

His arms braced on each side of her, he held himself high, his chest heaving as he grabbed for breath. It looked to her as if every muscle and tendon in his body tensed. Suddenly he closed his eyes and clenched his teeth, his firm yet full lips drawn back over gleaming white. The drawn, agonized expression that contorted his burnished features frightened her.

With a raspy curse, he shoved against the mattress and sprang erect beside the bed. Not sparing her another glance, he began pacing the floor, brutally shoving rigid fingers through his dark hair. With each stride, he hauled in a ragged breath, blowing afterward like a surfacing whale.

Meredith grabbed her shirt and bunched it over her naked front, stunned, embarrassed, and alarmed. Whenever he dropped his hands from his hair, he knotted them into fists. Huge fists. And he looked like a man in a rage.

When his breathing began to slow, he finally stopped pacing to rub his palm over his face. When he finally looked at her, his eyes were still shooting sparks. "I promised you I wouldn't do that," he said huskily. "I'm sorry for breaking my word."

"It's all right." Her voice sounded faint, nothing like her own.

"It isn't all right, Meredith." He jabbed a finger at her. "I told you, when you're ready. And I'll by God keep my promise. I apologize for losing it like that, and I won't again.''

He scrubbed at his face, then *whooshed* out air, making her jump. Then he strode over to the bed. "It's late. Let's get you settled for the night." He bent, grabbed the quilt, and jerked it back until the weight of her rump got in the way. "Up you go."

Meredith scrabbled off the bed like a startled crab, grappling to keep her shirt over her breasts. When she was standing, he started ripping the bed apart as if it had committed a crime punishable by death. Meredith stood frozen, gaping at him, wondering if he'd lost his mind, then concluding that he obviously had. He tore off the quilt, jerked off the sheets, stripped the cases off the pillows. When the mattress was bare, he grabbed the corded edge, heaved upward, and flipped it over. Then he picked up the bottom sheet and snapped it in the air, the crack of the linen so loud she fell back a step.

Why was it, she wondered, that it was always her misfortune to pair up with lunatics? He turned the cases inside out, shaking them like a terrier shakes a rat, then reversing them to stuff the pillows back inside.

When the bed was completely remade, he straightened and flashed her a strained grin. "Can you sleep all right now?"

"What?"

He gestured at the bed. "Spider free."

It took her two heartbeats to register the words, and then tears sprang to her eyes. She'd forgotten all about telling him of her phobia. That was why he'd attacked the bed. He wasn't a lunatic, after all, but the sweetest, most wonderful man on earth. She couldn't believe he'd done all that, just for her. Or that he loved her so much that he'd bother.

He stepped around the end of the bed to her, bending his head as he drew to a stop to plant a light kiss on her forehead. "Goodnight, sweetheart. Have sweet dreams, all right? I'll stand watch until morning, just to be safe, and you can spell me tomorrow so I can grab some shuteye.''

He moved past her to the nightstand to huff into the open chimney top of the lantern, dousing the flame. Amber light from the sitting room streaked the dark shadows that swooped down over them. "Don't be nervous. I give you my word, nobody will get past me."

With that, he left, softly shutting the door behind him. Meredith stood there in the blackness, still hugging her shirt. She'd neglected to tell him she was also afraid of the dark and had to have at least a night-light burning so she could go to sleep.

Tossing, turning. Onto her back. Onto her stomach. Hugging the pillow. Pushing it aside and lying flat. No matter what she tried, she couldn't go to sleep. Maybe, she decided, she'd dozed for too long in the truck.

Liar! a little voice whispered inside her mind. *You're a spineless coward. If you had any backbone at all, you'd go after him.* Unfortunately, she didn't have a backbone. She was a pathetic fraidy-cat, phobic about spiders, frightened of the dark, and terrified of having sex. It had been easy not to feel scared with Heath's strong arms around her. But now? The thought of going out there and asking him to make love to her made her stomach quiver.

Stupid, stupid, stupid! He loved her. He truly did. With all his heart. He would never hurt her. Never. And the very fact that he'd torn her bed apart like a lunatic gone berserk should have been proof enough that he'd never get his kicks by scaring her. *She* was the lunatic, huddling here in the dark, clinging to a pillow. She trusted him. She did. Absolutely. She could strip off naked and walk out there, bold as brass. That was how much she trusted him. Being in his arms had been wonderful. Fantastic, even. What in her wildest imaginings was there to be afraid of? Nothing, absolutely nothing.

She swung out of bed. Stood there, debating. Then she stripped off her shirt. Bare as a newborn baby, she groped her way to the door, then stood there grasping the knob. She would just walk out there. Smiling would be a good idea, of course. And then she would simply say, *Heath, I love you. Would you please come back and make love to me?* And he would sweep her into his arms, carry her back to the bedroom, and make love to her so gently that she'd never worry for a second about going through the ordeal again.

She tightened her hand on the knob, urging herself to open it. When that didn't work, she counted, determined to throw the door open on three. At ten, she scuttled back to the bed and searched frantically for her shirt. When she finally found it and got it on, she was panting as if she'd run six miles.

Oh, God. She hated herself. She was a human jellyfish. Lower than low. Despicable. She kept remembering that lost-little-boy look on his face just before he threw away his badge. And then the agony in his expression a few minutes ago as he'd pushed himself away from her. After all the times he'd been there for her when she needed him, the one time he had needed her, she'd let him down.

The rich aroma of freshly brewed coffee filled the small kitchen. Heath stood at the front window, the handle of a stout porcelain mug hooked by his finger, the steam from the piping hot coffee drifting up to move over his face. Shifting his shoulder against the window frame, he searched the darkness beyond the glass for any sign of movement. He didn't actually expect company. He'd taken every precaution to cover his tracks in coming here. No one was ever going to find them, not even by helicopter, because they wouldn't recognize the vehicle.

Standing watch was just something to do. God knew he couldn't sleep. He was as horny as a three-pronged billy goat and feeling twice as cantankerous. Trapped inside jeans that suddenly felt eight inches short at the inseam and a couple of sizes too small, Old Glory was as rigid as a steel pipe, bent almost double, and throbbing like a son of a bitch. Heath was tempted to strip down to his boxers and let the poor old guy poke through the opening of the fly.

If he hadn't been afraid Meredith or Sammy might catch him, he would have.

Taking a careful sip of the boiling hot coffee, he smiled slightly, picturing himself scrambling frantically for his britches, looking like a maniac who was water-witching the kitchen with a short stick. Well, not *short*, exactly. Impressively stout.

Not a good plan. Sammy was of tender years, and Meredith would probably drop dead of cardiac arrest. He would just have to suffer. It wasn't as if it was his first experience with the problem, after all, and he'd lived through it. Hell, how many times? Since knowing Meredith, he'd taken more cold showers than he ever had in his life. He remembered comparing her to Popeye's girlfriend when he was pissed off and grinned. No resemblance. For a little gal, she had plenty of everything and was perfectly proportioned. A body to die for, in miniature.

Against the glass, he envisioned her, standing before him naked. The longer he stared, the more detailed the image became. Her body gilded by the amber glow cast by the lantern. Her hair falling in tousled, golden-streaked ribbons of rich butterscotch to her alabaster shoulders. Breasts just large enough to fit a man's cupped palms, the hardened tips the same delicate rose as her parted lips. A waist he could easily encircle with his hands. A thatch of honeyed curls at the apex of her slender thighs. Cute little knees with dimples in them.

The hair stood up at the back of his neck. *Knees?* He had a vivid imagination, but *knees*? He blinked. *What the hell?* And just about then, he heard a tremulous little blowing sound coming from behind him. He whirled, slopped scalding hot coffee over the back of his hand, and swore, ripely and loudly. When he jerked at the burn, he lost his grip on the handle. The mug dive-bombed, hitting the floor in an explosion of sound. Shattering porcelain and hot coffee shot upward like a geyser. Meredith leaped like a startled gazelle.

"Jesus H. Christ!" Moving toward her, Heath swiped at

the searing damp spots on his pants. "Honey, did it get you?"

She crossed her arms over herself, trying without much success to hide everything with her splayed hands. "No-o-o. I'm f-fine."

She'd been trying to whistle. Bless her heart. She was so nervous, he could see her shaking. *Just whistle, and goddamned fool that I am, I'll probably come running.* Instead, he had slopped hot coffee all over both of them, and she was standing barefoot in shards of porcelain. If it had been someone other than Meredith, it might have been funny. He could have said something witty, like, "Leave it to me. I could screw up a wet dream without half trying." And they could have moved past it. But she wasn't someone else, even though she was trying very hard to be.

That was what got to him, way down deep, knowing what it had cost her to come to him like this. And she thought she had no courage.

"Mommy!" The plaintive cry came from the rear of the house.

Meredith's eyes went wide with horror. She whirled and bounded across the kitchen to the bedroom. Heath couldn't pry his gaze from her sweetly rounded backside, the jiggle of those dimpled cheeks mesmerizing him.

She'd been trying to *whistle*! Son of a bitch. She'd been standing an arm's length away, offering herself to him, and he'd screwed it up. The sweetest gift anyone had ever tried to give him, and he'd *totally* screwed it up! He wanted to run after her. As a matter of fact, he felt as if he were attached to her by invisible strings. But Sammy was wailing. He had to go settle her down first.

He let himself into the small bedroom then moved toward her bed in the semidarkness. "Hey, sweetcakes? What's the matter?"

As he sat on the edge of the mattress, Sammy rose onto her knees and hugged his neck. *She'd been trying to whistle*, he thought as he gathered the child close. He needed to get his ass in there before she changed her mind, or even worse, started to think he found her undesirable.

"I heard a loud noise," Sammy said groggily.

"I'm sorry, honey. I dropped my coffee cup. I didn't mean to wake you."

"Now I'm scared."

Please, Sammy, don't be scared. Give me a break, all right? "You are, huh? There's nothing to be afraid of, sweet cakes. Goliath and I are both here, and we'll keep you safe."

She patted his hair with a little hand. "I love you, Heef."

"I love you, too, sweetheart. Great big, as far as my arms will stretch."

"That's lots."

"It sure is." He rubbed her back for a moment, the entire time his brain screaming at him to dump the kid and go find Meredith. Before the mood fizzled. Before she covered that gorgeous body with clothing and buried it under a pile of blankets and vowed never to humiliate herself like that again. "I love you and your mommy a whole lot."

"Heef?"

"Hmm?"

"Will you tell me a story?"

No! Not on your life. No how, no way! "What kind of story, honey?"

"Cin'erella."

Cinderella had mice in her attic, went for a ride in a squash, wore glass slippers, fell in love, the end. Heath sighed and moved his fingers through her baby-fine curls. The writing was on the wall. At times, fatherhood was going to be a real bitch. But, hey, how long could a story take. Right? He'd just tell her a shortened version.

"Once upon a time," he began, "there was a beautiful girl named Cinderella who wanted to go to the dance."

"You forgot the mean, wicket stick mother and the ugly stick sisters! And she di'n't want to go to a dance. It was a boil ball."

"A what?"

She leaned back and peered at him through the shadows.

"Your mommy died and di'n't never tell you this story, huh?"

He knew someone else who was in perilous danger of losing her life at an early age. "My memory's rusty, for sure. A boil ball?"

"Yup. At the tassle where the king lives. He gots a crown and he has a boil ball so the prince can pick a boil bride."

"Royal, you mean?"

"That's what I said, *boil*."

It took Heath thirty-five minutes to get the story told to Sammy's exacting specifications.

By the time Heath could go find Meredith, she had lighted the lantern and was sitting cross-legged on the bed, dabbing at her shins with a cotton ball and hydrogen peroxide, which he guessed she'd found in the medicine cabinet. When she heard him entering the bedroom, she swung her legs over the edge of the mattress and wedged the tails of her shirt tightly between clamped thighs. He nearly wept. Hope springing eternal, and all of that, he closed the door and locked it before he moved toward her.

"I'm sorry I didn't come running faster, sweetheart." God, he was *so* sorry. "But I was telling Sammy a story."

She smiled slightly, her face flushed crimson. "That's all right. I'm just disinfecting a couple of nicks before I call it a night." Her lashes fell to shadow her eyes. "It was a really dumb thing to do, anyway. Bad timing. Bad stage set. Bad everything."

"No, it wasn't." Was that him? He sounded like a choir boy whose voice was changing. "It was perfect timing. And I particularly loved the props."

Her face flushed an even deeper shade of crimson. She bent forward, pretending to be intent on her shins.

"Here, let me." As he knelt before her, she gave such a start that he could have sworn he saw daylight between her fanny and the mattress. He curled his hand around a slender ankle, the texture of her skin reminding him of satin. "I'm sorry I hurt you."

"Oh, it's nothing!" She tugged, trying to free her foot. "I can get it. Really."

"I insist." The foot first, then the slender shapely calf, then the dimpled knee. He was going to kiss and nibble every sweet inch, straight up the inside of that silken thigh to the cache of honey-colored curls she was trying so frantically to hide. He plucked the cotton ball from her fingers, dabbing carefully at the two little spots. "No slivers that I see."

"No."

He lifted her slender foot, pretending to check the sole for pricks. Like hell. He had the side vision of a horse. The shirttails parted slightly. "Hmm."

"Are there fragments?"

He lifted her foot just a little higher. *Perfect.* "Hmm."

She leaned forward slightly to look. "How many are there?"

Dozens. Beautiful little corkscrew curls. Oh, yeah. "Not many." He dabbed at her heel like a blind man. "There. No fragments, I don't think. Just little glimpses of pink."

"Glimpses?"

"Spots!" he amended quickly, tossing the cotton ball in the general direction of the nightstand. He ran his thumb along her instep. "Has anyone ever told you how beautiful your feet are?"

"My *feet*?"

"God, yes. I've never seen such a perfect—foot." He bent to kiss the inside depression just below the protrusion of her anklebone. "Cute toes with little pink tips."

He suckled the big one, then nipped its tender underside. "You are *so* sweet."

She tugged and tucked her shirt, trying to hide the triangle of curls, which was nigh unto impossible with her leg hiked in the air. Those curls gleamed in the lantern light like a treasure trove of tiny gold nuggets.

"Heath?" she said in a squeaky voice. "You're embarrassing me to death. I need a bath, and I'm sure my feet smell.''

He went to work on the next toe over, speaking to her between nibbles. ''Sweetheart, don't you know that civilized man has been deprived of the natural feminine scent?''

''The what?''

''Soap and deodorant and perfume and powder. All that junk disguises a woman's natural essence, which a man finds extremely arousing.''

''You're *aroused* by my smelly feet?'' She jerked her leg again. ''Please, don't suck my toes. Oh, my God—*not* the bottoms. I *walk* on them. I—that tickles!'' She tugged again and gave a startled giggle. ''*Stop!* It—oh, lands!— that feels so—oh, please, I'm so embarrassed. Heath?''

''I'm stopping.''

He kissed and nibbled his way up her calf, pretending he didn't notice when she made fists in his hair, the desperate grip of her fingers making his scalp sting. He didn't care if she snatched him bald, just as long as she kept her hands in his hair and nowhere near those shirttails.

''Wh—what are you doing now?''

Dumb questions inspired dumb answers. ''Nothing.''

He reached her knee and propped her calf on his shoulder, anchoring it there with the grip of his hand. With her leg up and nearly straightened, he was afforded the most glorious view that God had ever created, prettier than sunrise or sunset and everything in between. He concentrated on the bend of her leg—the backside, of course, so he had to lift her leg *just* a little higher—lightly nipping the sensitive flesh then soothing it with tickling strokes of his tongue. She jerked as if he'd stuck her with a pin.

''I—oh, my—you—oh, dear.''

He moved to her silken inner thigh, teasing and kissing until she began to tremble. ''You are so sweet, Merry, so incredibly, wonderfully sweet. I want to taste every inch of you.''

''D—do you really think this is a good idea?''

It was the best idea he'd ever had, even if he did end up bald. "Doesn't it feel nice?"

"Oh—well, yes. No! What are you?—where are you?—not so *high*!"

"I won't go too high."

"You won't?"

"Absolutely not."

He raised his shoulder, forcing her leg higher. She gasped and fell back, her tightly fisted hands tugging his head forward in a direct line to goal. She immediately started to shove, of course, but she was too late. She bleated like an orphaned fawn when he nuzzled those curls.

"No! This is—*don't!* Heath?"

He settled his mouth over glistening sweetness and delved deep with his tongue. She bucked with her hips, he presumed to escape, but succeeding only in thrusting herself more firmly to his mouth. He drew gently, finding the tender flange with his tongue, laving it with light strokes that made her body jerk.

"Oh, my *gaw—ww—d!*" she cried.

"Shhh," he managed to say without drawing away. "Sammy'll hear."

She gasped at the rush of his hot breath and the vibration of his voice. Her reaction was so satisfying, he considered serenading her with the recurring chorus and all the verses of "God Bless America." Sure as hell, if he did, Sammy would wake up, though, and he didn't want to get stuck telling any more stories.

He settled for a low-pitched vibrant sound of appreciation. "*Mmm—mm-mm.*"

Her entire body convulsed. "Oh, my God—oh, my God—oh, my God."

She hooked her leg over his shoulder to catch him under the arm with her heel, as if she were afraid he might get away. *Now, they were getting somewhere.* Her hands stopped shoving and jerked him closer, and she arched her hips in unmistakable invitation, even though she kept whispering, "You can't! Oh, Heath, you *can't!*"

He could, and he would. And he did. Until she sobbed and her body convulsed in the throes of pleasure. And even then, he stayed to tease her to climax twice more. Only when she lay limp and trembling did he rise to kneel on the mattress edge, where he unfastened her shirt and then his own, kissing her belly and her ribs between buttons. She watched him with unmistakable wariness as he removed his gun, wrapping the belt around the holster before he laid it on the nightstand.

He nearly said, "Don't even think it." But that would have been defensive, not comforting. Instead, he said, "It's a semiautomatic, sweetheart, and fires with every pull of the trigger. No sick games, I promise."

"I know that, Heath. No matter what kind of gun you have, I know better."

Yes, she knew better. And yet she didn't, a part of her simply reacting. Earlier this evening, her admission of that had made him furious. Now he just felt sad. No one should have to live through what she had, especially not someone gentle like her. He kicked off his boots, then peeled off his shirt, jeans, and boxers. Old Glory sprang up like the high end of a seesaw.

Looking into her eyes, he could tell that seeing the gun had upset her. He moved over her to kiss her breasts, determined to take all the time needed to reassure her and rekindle her need. She clutched frantically at his shoulders when she felt his hardness nudging against her center. He gently removed her shirt, then bent to lave her nipples with teasing strokes of his tongue. Almost instantly, her tender flesh responded, swelling and thrusting in eager rigidity. He captured one peak between his teeth, rolling it to make it even harder and tormenting it with drags of his tongue. Then he switched to the other breast until she moaned and arched, begging for the hard pull of his mouth.

"Heath?"

"I'm here, honey." He gave her what she wanted, suckling each nipple to make her mindless as he coaxed her thighs apart to accommodate his hips. Once in position, he rose above her, trying to tell by her expression if she was ready. Her features were drawn, her pupils dilated— whether from passion or fear, he wasn't sure. "Are you okay?" he asked. "You're not afraid, are you?" *Please, God, don't let her say yes.* "I'll stop if you want."

"Yes," she said in a thin voice. "Please."

With Old Glory lunging at the gate, Heath froze. Every curse word he knew, a considerable collection, went through his mind. He *could* stop. It was a simple matter of prying himself away from her and walking to the nearest wall, where he would pound his head against one of the logs until he was pronounced brain dead.

"Does that mean yes, you want me to?" he asked in a strained whisper. He would *not* strangle her. Nor would he yell. He was going to be patience itself—immediately after he located a waist-high knothole. "Merry? Sweetheart, answer me."

"Yes," she replied in that same reedy tone.

Hope no longer sprang eternal. Only Old Glory. Heath drew back, swallowing the roar that tried to blast from his throat. He was *not* pissed off. He loved her with all his heart, and he understood. He truly did. It was just that certain parts of him had no reasoning power.

She clutched at his shoulders, her eyes going cloudy with confusion. "Where are you going?"

"For a walk." The choir boy with the changing voice had returned. "Just around the house, so don't be scared. I just—need a breath of fresh, pine-scented air."

She blinked at him like a contented little owl. He really *was* tempted to wring her neck. "Does that arouse you, too?" When he didn't answer, she asked, "Are you coming back when you get done?" She smiled softly. "If you like pine-scented air, why don't I come with you? We can take a blanket and finish under a pine tree."

Finish. He loved the ring of that word. "You mean you want to?"

"Sure." She started to sit up. "I'll have to throw my shirt and jeans on so—"

He planted a hand in the center of her chest and flattened her against the mattress. "Not the damned *pine* tree, Meredith! Do you want to finish?"

She blinked again. "Don't you?" A hurt look came over her face, and she cupped her hands over her breasts. "Oh," she said faintly.

He went down on his elbows, vised his fingers around her wrists, and anchored her hands above her head. As he rained kisses over her breasts, he said, "Of *course* I want to finish. I thought you'd changed your mind."

"Why would I do that?"

That was a good question. He'd answer it later.

He eased his way into her, jolts of pleasure shooting through his starved body as her tight, moist heat sheathed him. She quickened at the invasion, the velvety walls of her femininity closing around him. The wary look vanished completely from her eyes.

"Oh, my . . ."

She was ready for him, and he was well past ready. He drove home, hard, pushing her a ways across the quilt with each thrust until he feared she might scoot right off the bed. He caught her behind the knees and lifted.

"Put your legs around me," he urged.

She did as he asked, crossing one ankle over the other to lock the position. He plunged deep, his tempo hard and fast. She clung to him, absorbing the thrusts, little moans catching in her throat, begging for more and urging him on. Her cries grew more shrill and rapid as he pressed her closer and closer to another climax. When it came, he sought his own as well. It crashed through him with the force of a nitro blast. A kaleidoscope of blinding colors exploded inside his head. Seconds later, Old Glory dwindled to limp exhaustion and Heath collapsed, barely managing to shift his body so he wouldn't crush her as he sank to the mattress.

She turned into his arms, snuggled closed, and almost instantly went to sleep. His feet dangled over the end of the bed. He didn't care. He threw one leg over both of hers, gathered her close, and sank with her into total blackness.

Two hours later, he awoke to the feeling of velvety lips trailing kisses over his chest and arms. He cracked open one eye. Meredith pushed up on an elbow and smiled dreamily. Then she leaned closer, lightly grazing the stubble along his jaw with her nipple. The tip went as hard as a little rivet, and she dragged it over his cheek to tease the corner of his mouth, then the crease of his lips. He managed to pry open his other eye. God help him, that was all he had the energy to do.

"Are you too tired?" she asked sweetly.

"You are so beautiful, I'll *never* be too tired," he lied. *Urgent SOS to God. I need a miracle.*

There was a blush on her cheeks. Her smile was shy. He had a feeling she had never initiated lovemaking with a man in her entire life. He had failed miserably to react appropriately the first time. If he was unable to rise to the occasion this time, she might never approach him again.

Where *was* God, anyway? Vacationing in the Bahamas? *SOS signals to Saint Peter or Luke or John—whoever the hell was on duty up there.* As seldom as he prayed, he would have thought *someone* would snap to attention.

She trailed her fingertips lightly down his chest to his belly, then even lower. Praise God and all the saints, Old Glory responded with no help from his brain, and by the time her small hand curled over him, at least *something* had snapped to attention.

He made love to her again, outshining even his first attempt, which in his opinion had been pretty damned spectacular. At the finish, his arms hung from his shoulders like overcooked spaghetti noodles, and if he had legs, he couldn't feel them. She curled around him like tendrils of silk and buried her face against the slope of his neck. He opened one eye when he felt her tongue tracing circles under his ear.

"I never knew," she whispered throatily. "I never had any idea."

"About what, sweetheart?"

"That it could *be* like that. It's so wonderful, Heath. I want to make love with you all night."

Somehow—maybe it was God finally getting back to him—he managed to open both eyes and paste what he hoped was a reasonably awake and cognizant expression on his face. He found himself gazing into the most beautiful, *expectant* blue eyes he had ever seen.

He had created a monster.

God help him. He was thirty-eight years old, hadn't slept in almost twenty-four hours, and the last time he had, he'd tossed and turned all night, worrying about his dog. Since then, he'd been scared nearly to death three or four times, kicked, pummeled, shot at, and chased. He'd driven all night. He'd stolen a car. He'd tossed away his life. And he'd lost his hat. He just wasn't as young as he used to be. Old Glory was at half mast, and a whole regiment playing trumpets wasn't going to revive him. Only who could say no to those huge blue eyes? Not him.

Luckily, and just in the nick of time, God finally answered his SOS. As Heath kissed Meredith, he made a mental note to be sure and thank Him.

Later . . . much later.

Chapter 24

When Meredith woke up the following morning, sunlight filtered through the white cotton curtains at the bedroom window, and the cheerful singing of birds drifted to her. She lay alone in the bed, a depression in the pillow beside hers the only sign that Heath had slept with her. She rolled over and yawned, listening for movement in the other room. She heard the faint *clink* of a spoon against glassware and then the tread of a man's booted feet. She smiled. Knowing he was there made her feel sleepily content and completely safe, even though, in the back of her mind, she knew it couldn't last. Glen was still out there, as ruthless as ever. The danger wasn't over. But, if all ended badly, at least she'd been granted this one fragment of time with a man whose very touch filled her with wonder.

The only trouble was, now that she'd had a taste of what it was like with Heath, she wanted a lifetime with him. Love and laughter. She couldn't help but hold the hope close to her heart that maybe, just maybe, this time she would come out a winner.

Slipping from the bed, she rummaged for a change of clothes in the cardboard box Heath had set in the corner. Wrong box. These were her old things, stuff she'd brought with her from New York but had never worn in Oregon. Knit tops, blouses, dress slacks, two bras from her pre-padded days. At the bottom, she found two pairs of designer jeans, both far too formfitting to provide any camouflage.

Disgruntled, she closed the box and went searching for her shirt, thinking that she'd slip it on and go find the other boxes of clothing. Just as she shoved an arm into one sleeve, it occurred to her that her wig and contact days were over, at least for the moment. Here at the cabin, she needn't worry about wearing baggy clothes or padded bras. She went back to the box, tugged out a red knit top, jeans, and underwear.

When she stepped out of the bedroom, Heath was sitting at the kitchen table with a cup of coffee cupped between his hands. When he glanced up at her, he did a double-take then smiled and ran his gaze from the top of her head to the tip of her toes, whistling appreciatively. Meredith felt a flush rise up her neck.

"Wow." He leaned back in his chair and made a circular motion with his hand. "All the way around. Let me look at you."

She almost made a U-turn back to the bedroom for her baggy shirt and jeans. She had small breasts and big hips. Pear-shaped best described her. What if he measured her against women he'd known before and found her lacking? All this time, he'd believed she had a much more generous bust than she actually did. Some men were really hung up about that sort of thing. Weren't they?

A horrible, frightened feeling attacked her stomach. If he didn't like how she looked, what was she going to do? If she lost him, she wouldn't be able to bear it. She would die inside and never be the same again.

He said nothing as she turned in a circle for him. Why? she wondered miserably. Oh, God, he was disappointed. He'd discovered she had a fat butt and no top. He probably liked tall, slinky women with big breasts. As she came back around to face him, Meredith prepared herself for the worst.

He just sat there, rocked back in his chair, staring at her. She lowered her gaze to the planked floor, wishing she could dissolve and disappear through the cracks.

"I can't believe my eyes," he finally said.

All and all, she truly didn't think she was *that* bad. She looked up and met his gaze, which was twinkling mischievously.

"Christ! Have I ever got my work cut out for me. Sammy's going to be the spittin' image of you. I'll have to run the boys off with a shotgun." He crooked a finger at her. "Come here."

Her feet had grown to the floor. "You mean you think I'm—? Well, you know."

"Do bears shit in the woods? Sweetheart, you're gorgeous. I can't believe you had all of that covered up with those tents you wore."

"Tents?"

"Those God-awful britches! The legs in those buggers would swallow me."

"If you hated the way I looked so much, what made you feel—interested in me?"

He winked. "I have vision that can peel paint off walls. Whenever you weren't watching, I stripped away layers."

"You did not. You were always a perfect gentleman."

"Have I ever got you fooled. Polite, maybe, but not stone blind. Besides, it wasn't your body that hooked me. It was that fantastic hair and those great big, beautiful eyes."

Both of which were now a different color, she thought dismally, and a horrible urge to cry came over her. She absolutely would *not* give in to it. He'd start to think she was a big old bawl baby. That might be the final draw for him, considering he'd fallen in love with a dark-eyed, larger-breasted brunette who didn't exist.

"I'm sorry," she said.

His brows swooped together in a scowl. "For what?"

"For—for not being all you thought I was."

He held her gaze for a long moment. "Meredith, you were pretty before. Now you're beautiful. Talk about hiding your light under a bushel. You've got a figure that makes my eyes nearly pop out of my head. And that hair. Whenever I look at it, I want to get my hands in it. And those eyes—I think they're the most wonderful eyes I've ever seen. When you walked out of that bedroom just now, I almost swallowed my tongue.''

Flattery to *that* degree was highly suspicious. She searched his dark face. He *knew* she felt self-conscious, and he was trying to make her feel better. And, oddly, she did. Not because she believed, even for a second, that she could ever make him swallow his tongue, but because he loved her so much. He didn't care if she had big hips and no breasts. Or hardly any, anyway. He loved her just the way she was.

She moved toward him, and when she reached him, he grabbed her and jerked her across his lap, kissed her until she felt dizzy, and then began nibbling along the neckline of her top, growling like a bear. Meredith didn't feel alarmed until he dragged her top down with his freshly shaved chin to plunge his tongue under the edge of her bra cup. Somehow, he coaxed her breast out, and right there, in the middle of the kitchen, in *broad* daylight, he began suckling and worrying her nipple with his teeth.

''We can't—you can't do—Heath? What about—?''

She meant to remind him of Sammy, but somehow, the words never got out. He caught the sensitive tip of her between his teeth, tugging and dragging with his tongue. She felt as if all her bones melted, and she couldn't quite recall her daughter's name.

He teased her until she wanted to pull him to the bedroom by his hair. Then, with a satisfied glint in his eyes, he stopped and tugged her clothing back into place. ''Good morning,'' he said huskily. ''Would you care for a cup of fresh coffee?''

''That's it? After that, and all I get is coffee?''

He tweaked her other nipple through the layers of her clothing. ''Feels like I have all your nerve-endings fully awake. That little sweetheart is standing at attention and begging for attention.''

She bent to kiss him. He laughed and evaded her. ''Nope. You gotta wait.''

"Until when?"

"Tonight," he whispered. "No time for that today."

"That is *so* mean!"

"Mean? Nah. This way, you'll think about it all day. By tonight, when I finally get around to it, you'll be putty in my hands."

"I'll be putty right now."

"Nope. We have to talk and take care of business." He set her off his lap to go pour her a mug of coffee. As he returned to the table, he said, "I've been thinking, and I believe I've come up with a way to get you out of this mess."

"You have?" That news made Meredith forget about going to the bedroom. She cupped the steaming mug between her palms. "How?"

He sat down across from her, planted his elbows on the table, and leaned toward her. "Ever since I woke up, I've been mulling it over, thinking there has to be a way to outsmart Glen Calendri and do battle with the mob on our own terms. And there is, I think. Remember the exposé letter you wrote? I want you to tell me everything you can recall that was in it, along with anything else you can remember that might be evidence against Glen or any of his associates."

"Why? What good will that do?"

"Just humor me. I'd like to hear all of this before Sammy wakes up."

Meredith settled in her chair, cradling her mug and taking sips of coffee as she let her mind drift back in time. "There was a man named Peter Caldwell that I'm almost certain—" She stopped and met his gaze. "Well, actually, I *know*. They had him killed." She stared into her coffee for a moment. "I told you last night, I have a lot to be ashamed of, Heath. How are you going to feel about me when you hear all of this and realize I did nothing—not to stop it from happening or to report it to the police?"

"What could you have done to stop it?"

"I don't know. Something! Instead, I pretended I hadn't overheard them."

"What would Glen and Dan have done if you'd called the police? Would Dan have known for sure you had done it?"

"Of course. I was the only person who could have known. When they had discussions like that, they planned ahead of time and gave the household staff time off. I always knew when something was up, because everyone, from the cook and butler down to the maids, got an afternoon or evening off with pay."

"So they would have known you snitched. What would they have done to you?"

"Dan would've killed me! That's why I didn't have the courage to do anything."

"Courage? You were how old? Twenty-five."

"I was twenty-three when I married, almost twenty-four when Sammy was born."

"Very young, in other words, and scared to death. Get past it, Meredith. Forgive yourself. When you're in a no-win situation and you know one wrong move will mean your death, it's your instinct to survive. You were young, pregnant, emotionally and physically battered. What were you supposed to do? Take on a brutal husband, all the corruption and the mob as well? Singlehandedly, of course."

"You make it sound so understandable! I let people die. That haunts me."

"You know, sweetheart, I know this may sound really cold-hearted, but most of those people who got knocked off were probably white-collar criminals. When they decided to play ball with Glen Calendri, they knew they'd be screwed if things went sour. They *asked* for it. Now, you tell me. Why should an innocent girl and her baby have to die to save men like that? When you feel guilty, you look at your daughter. And if you can honestly say you should have let her die to save some crooked bastard, then by all means, beat your breast and punish yourself with guilt for the rest of your life."

"It's just that I used to think I was the kind of person who would always do the right thing, no matter what. Someone brave. That I'd run in front of a car to save a child, or leap off a bridge to save someone from drowning. Now I know that I'd only stand there. It isn't a good feeling. It makes me feel so ugly inside."

"Merry . . . that isn't true. Remember that first night you met Goliath? You were terrified of him, but when I got there, you were about to take him on barehanded to save Sammy. And leaving New York? If that didn't take guts, I'll put in with you. Reacting on impulse to save someone in a dangerous situation is easy. You have no time to feel scared. You just do it, and people call you a hero. You were terrified of dogs *before*, but you stood your ground. You must have been scared when you left Dan, and again when you fled from New York, but you did it. You'd be amazed at how many people wouldn't have. I think you're quite a lady.

"You did what you had to do to protect yourself and your baby. You weren't responsible for Glen and Dan's actions, and you weren't elected to save the world. You couldn't have, not without dying yourself. I want to hear you say it. 'I wasn't to blame.' Come on. Say it!"

"I wasn't to blame," she said faintly.

"Louder. And look at me. Don't hang your head as if you're ashamed."

She raised her chin. "I wasn't to blame! Is that *loud* enough?"

He grinned at her. "It'll do. Now, back to Peter Caldwell. He got knocked off, you knew and didn't do anything, thank God, amen. Now give me details."

She laughed in spite of herself and drank in his smile. It was the most wonderful feeling, to have him here with her. She felt safe and happy for the first time in so long that she couldn't remember when.

There had been times in her life when she had wondered why so many bad things had happened to her—if, perhaps, she'd done something wrong, and it was all some kind of punishment. Now she realized that all along she'd been on a journey—sometimes a terrible journey—but every step she'd taken had been leading her to this man. It seemed so clear, in retrospect, that nothing had been left to chance. Something—or someone—had guided her in every move she made. She'd chosen to go to Wynema Falls by closing her eyes and stabbing her finger at a map of Oregon. Out of hundreds of towns, somehow her fingertip had landed on *his* town, in *his* county. And because of financial difficulties, she'd rented a rundown old house on a deserted country road, with only one other house in sight, *his* house. God, fate, *something* had arranged it all. They were meant to be together, had always been meant to be together.

Heath Masters was the one man in the world for her, the *only* one. He filled her up where she was empty, and he healed her where she was wounded, and he was strong for her when she was weak. *Home.* Oh, how she had yearned all these years to be able to go home. And now, thousands of miles away from where she'd always believed home was, she had finally gotten there. Not back to the old farmhouse where she'd grown up, where the shade of the oaks cast lazy shadows over a world that moved in slow motion. Not back to her dad, with his pipe and his coveralls and his great big hugs. Or to her mom, with her loving smile and her dingy house dresses and a kitchen that always smelled of fresh baked bread. Home wasn't a place at all.

"Meredith? Hey, there? Come back down to earth."

She smiled. "I'm here." She straightened in her chair. "Back to Peter Caldwell."

Five hours later, after a tense and grueling trip from the cabin to his father's ranch on unpaved forestry roads, Heath parked the battered old pickup in a thick stand of pines about three-quarters of a mile from the main house. He had elected to avoid the more frequently used highway turn-off that led to the ranch, just in case law enforcement or Calendri's thugs were keeping it under surveillance.

Jerking loose the hot-wiring under the dash, he grinned

at Meredith. "Ain't it great? I don't have to worry about where I left my keys."

She didn't smile back. "Heath, please, won't you change your mind? I'm not too hot on this idea, anyway. And I really hate for you to ask your father for anything. I know you wouldn't do it for yourself. Why for me?"

"You're better lookin'." He threw open his door and jumped out. As he reached to open the rear door to get Sammy and Goliath, he said, "My mind's made up, Meredith. So stop arguing and start walking. It's a bit of a hike to the house."

As Heath and Meredith set out on the road, Sammy and the dog ran ahead. Meredith gazed after them, her heart squeezing at the sound of her daughter's laughter. "What if the things I know aren't enough to convict any of them?" she asked. "What if we contact the FBI, they talk to me, and then they say, 'Think again, lady. You're going to jail, and your kid's going back to her grandfather.' It's been almost five years. Maybe it's too late to even do anything!"

"There's a seven-year statute of limitations on some crimes, but they track down murderers twenty years after the fact all the time and arrest them."

She trudged along beside him, her sneakers turning red from the powdery dust. "And the FBI? How do I know I can trust any of them? I heard what Charlie said last night on the radio. Glen has agents in his pocket! If I contact the bureau, tell them I'm willing to testify in exchange for getting the charges on me dropped, I might be calling the very men who have orders to kill me!"

He spun to a stop and planted his hands on his hips. "Do you trust me?"

She rolled her eyes. "Yes, of course, I do!"

"Then trust me," he said more gently. "Do you think I haven't thought of all that? Merry, my dad is one sharp son of a bitch. He's got connections coming out his ears, all across the country, *particularly* within the government. He'll find out the names of the agents in Glen's pocket. He'll be able to find out which men are safe. And if he isn't absolutely positive you know enough to bring about convictions, he won't call anyone.''

"How will he find out who's in Glen's pocket? Call good old Glen?''

"Of course, not! It's fairly elementary, sweetheart. Those guys called the department and threw their weight around. We've got 'em nailed. We keep records of stuff like that, and from the way Roy was shitting green apples last night, I'm sure they leaned on him, too. Getting their names will be a piece of cake.''

Sammy and Goliath came running back along the road just then. Meredith glanced around just in time to see her daughter catch the toe of her shoe on a rock and pitch face first in the dust. The child came up squalling, her tears making muddy red trails on her cheeks. In a shrill voice, she cried, ''Son of a bitch!''

Meredith gasped. Heath froze with a dumbfounded expression on his face. He couldn't have looked more shocked if a fire-breathing dragon had appeared before them.

Meredith collected herself first. After checking her daughter for injury and finding only a scratch on the child's chin, she hunkered down. ''Sammy, you mustn't ever say that word again. It's a very bad word, and sweet little girls shouldn't say it.''

Heath came walking up just as Sammy said, ''How come? Heef says it.''

Meredith angled a glare at the man who loomed over her. Then she pushed to her feet, turned to him with a sugary sweet smile, and said, ''I'll let you handle this, Mr. Masters. I'm a firm believer that people should clean up their own messes.''

He looked down at Sammy as if Meredith had just asked him to solve a nuclear physics equation. He rubbed his jaw and gazed off into the distance for a moment. Finally, he redirected his gaze at the child. She was watching him with an indignant expression on her muddy face, obviously convinced he was going to inform her mother that the word

she'd said was perfectly acceptable. Meredith was fully prepared to kick him if he dared.

Looking like innocence itself, he asked Sammy, "Are
you *sure* you've heard me say that bad, icky, really *awful*
word?"

Sammy poked out her bottom lip and nodded emphati-
cally. "Lots!"

He arched one eyebrow. "Well, I'll be da—" He
coughed and scratched beside his nose. "I'll be a horn-
tailed tooter. You did? Lots?" He squatted and set Sammy
on his knee. "Well, sweetcakes, I owe you an apology.
That's not a nice word at all, and if you ever hear me say
it again, I want you to wash my mouth out with soap. Is it
a deal? 'Cause that's a bad habit I need to break."

Sammy wrinkled her nose. "Heef, soap doesn't taste
very good."

"Did you taste it?"

She nodded again. "Made me urp! Mommy had to run
all new baff water."

"Well, even if it tastes bad, it's about the only way I
know to clean up a dirty mouth. I guess I'll just have to
try not to swallow any." He tweaked her nose. "Same goes
for you. Say that word again, and I'll scrub *your* tongue."

She shuddered. "I won't never say it!"

"Good girl." He set her down. As she ran off again with
Goliath, he called, "Pick up your feet!" Glancing at Meredith, he said, "Damn. Are all little kids that accident
prone?"

"Do you like soap? I certainly hope so. You're going to
be eating *lots*!"

He looked sheepish. "That bad, huh?"

"Only every few words."

"Every few words? Oh, come on. That's bullsh—" He
broke off as if a fly had just flown in his mouth. "Bull-
corn."

They laughed and fell back into step to follow the child
and dog. Heath gazed after Sammy, a thoughtful frown on
his face. "How is it that she mispronounces pillow, saying

'piddle,' and elbow, saying 'ubble,' and bath, saying 'baff,' and royal, saying 'boil,' but when she yells, 'son of a bitch!' she enunciates it as clear as polished crystal?''

"Children pick up unsavory language very easily for some reason, possibly because the words are said with such emphasis, and they seemed to know, without being told, that they're 'bad' words, maybe because their mothers never say them."

He chuckled again. "Don't miss an opportunity to get your jabs in."

She winked at him. "If I had all the answers, I'd write a book and be a millionaire. The truth is, kids are a puzzle."

"They sure as hell are."

"That's two. Do you prefer Dial? Or Ivory?"

He winced. "*Christ!* I really have a problem, don't I?"

"That's three. We should probably get one of those hypoallergenic brands, the clear bars. They might cause less irritation in your stomach and intestinal track. Taking the Lord's name in vain is a more serious offense, punishable by two washes."

"Thank God. I thought you were gonna say punishable by death!"

"That's four, and another double wash, I'm afraid. Shall we buy soap by the case?"

"My ass! I've heard *you* say 'God.' " He jabbed a finger at her. "Be fair!"

"You may wash my mouth with soap if you hear me say it again. And that's two more, a single and a double."

He fell silent for several minutes, stomping along beside her, his boots raising clouds of red dust. "Am I going to make it?" he suddenly asked her.

"To where?"

He turned worried slate blue eyes on her. "As a father."

Meredith stopped and looped her arms around his waist, making him stop as well. "Are you applying for the job?"

He narrowed one eye. "I've already been hired and have OJT. She's *mine*. And so are you. Don't you ever forget it.

I love you both—so much.'' He ran a hand into her hair. ''I'm gonna need help, though, Merry. She doesn't come with any instructions.''

Meredith gazed up at him through a blur of tears. ''Heath, even if you never break yourself of cursing, you'll still be a sensational father. What you say isn't nearly as important as what you *do*. You've been so good for her that I can't begin to tell you. You've made her feel safe and loved, and you've helped her to forget. She isn't timid and frightened anymore, and she's learning to trust again. Have you any idea what a wonderful gift that is? She'll remember you and Goliath and your love for her for the rest of her life. In the bad times, she'll think of you, and it'll be like a hug to comfort her. Believe me, I know. In the really bad times, the one thing that kept me from believing the whole world was evil was remembering my folks. You're going to be a wonderful father. The very best.''

His eyes darkened. ''*Going to be?* Meredith, why do I get the feeling you're telling me good-bye. Sammy won't have to remember me when things get rough and she needs a hug. I'll be there to give her one.''

''Oh, Heath, I hope so.''

''What do you mean, you *hope* so? Don't you love me?''

''Oh, yes. It's just—''

''Just *what*?''

''Haven't you stopped to think, Heath? You said if I testify to put Glen and his associates behind bars, that the government will protect me from retaliation by entering me and Sammy into the Protected Witness Program. That we'll be given new identities and relocated where the mob and Glen will never be able to find us.''

''Yeah. So?''

She pressed her face against his shirt and clung to him. ''You won't be able to go with us.''

She felt his body snap taut, and his arms vised around her. ''Like hell,'' he said gruffly. ''We may be apart for a while, honey, but not forever. I'll find a way, I promise you.''

With all her heart, Meredith wanted to believe that. Even as he made the promise, though, she felt a tremor run through him, and by that she knew he was as worried about what the future might hold as she was.

Ian Masters was an older and more refined version of Heath, tall, well-muscled, and darkly complected, with professionally styled, salt-and-pepper hair. Just back from horseback riding, he was wearing a denim shirt, Wrangler jeans, and dusty saddle boots, which made him look oddly out of place in the expensively furnished house. His hands were broad and thick through the palm like Heath's, but Meredith saw no calluses to indicate he did any physical labor. She also noticed straightaway that his nails were neatly manicured and shone as if they'd been buffed, possibly even polished. She suspected that he usually dressed in rich casual while at home, sharply creased slacks, an expensive polo shirt, and spendy knock-around loafers. In the professional sphere, he was undoubtedly an icon of success who made semiannual flights to Hong Kong to be fitted for custom tailored suits and shirts. The cost of a pair of his shoes would probably feed an entire family in Africa for six months, if not for a year, with a large chunk of change left over.

Oh, yes. She had known Ian Masters' kind, and she was extremely glad to have left that world behind her.

When Heath introduced Meredith to him, Ian's steel blue eyes seemed to miss nothing as he looked her over. He didn't reply in kind when she said she was pleased to make his acquaintance. He simply turned his back and led the way to his study, glancing icily at Sammy when she and Goliath dared to run ahead of him. Meredith's heart caught when she saw a Chinese vase perched on a spindle-legged table farther up the hallway, her child barreling directly toward it.

"Sammy, be careful!" she cried.

At the last second, the child veered around the obstacle. Heath smiled. "Merry, don't worry about it. If she breaks something, I'll pay for it."

Meredith wondered if he had any inkling how much the vase was probably worth. Thousands was her guess. She'd mixed with the affluent for less than a year, but in that time, she'd developed an eye for fine things. If that vase was a reproduction, she'd eat the shattered remains. As she thought that, she remembered this was Heath's childhood home, the man leading them along the hall, his father. Heath was surely as aware of the vase's value as she, if not more so.

Once in the study, Meredith collected her daughter and sat stiffly on a proffered leather chair that felt as cold against her skin as its owner. The tension in the well-appointed room was almost palpable, sparks bouncing back and forth between the two men as they stood, feet spread and arms akimbo, facing each other.

"I heard the news on the radio," Ian said. He sent Meredith a searing glare. "I hope you realize what you've done to my son, Mrs. Kenyon. His career is shot. He may go to prison before it's all said and done. How does it make you feel, knowing you've destroyed a man's life?"

Until that moment, Meredith had been playing judge and jury, and she'd found Ian Masters sorely lacking—a cold, self-centered man who was incapable of really loving anyone, even his children. But when he turned on her and she searched his face, that wasn't what she saw at all. His expression looked exactly as Heath's had last night when he scrambled into the Bronco, believing she or Sammy might have taken a bullet. Fear, panic, bitter rage. The man *loved* his son, and very deeply. He obviously hated Meredith for what she'd done to him. She couldn't blame Ian for that. When she thought about it, she even hated herself.

"Dad, please, don't attack Merry. I didn't come here to get in a pissing match, and that's a damned good way to start one."

At Heath's warning, Ian spun back, his face contorting.

"A pissing match? I swear, if you were a kid again, I'd beat you within an inch of your life and lock you in your room until you were thirty! After all the sacrifices, and the worry, and working my tail off for you, and now you're tossing it all away. It's the height of stupidity."

A muscle along Heath's jaw began to tick. "I'm asking you, Dad. Please, don't do this."

Ian's jaw muscle began to work as well. "Do what? Tell it like it is? She's using you, and you're too stupid to see it. My God, Heath. For once in your misbegotten life, stop and *think*."

Heath stabbed his fingers through his hair. "I can't believe this. Is it an allergic reaction you have to me or something? All it takes is for me to be in the same room with you, and you start hurling insults. Why don't *you* stop and think. Do you realize how long it's been since I've darkened your doorstep?" He shook his head. "You were yelling and calling me names when you threw me out, and now, after all this time, you're taking up where you left off. Aren't you even glad I'm here?"

"If I thought for a minute that you came only to see me, I might be glad. But that isn't the case, is it? Like always, you want something."

"I have called you every Christmas and Father's Day. I've never missed."

"Oh, yes, your obligatory phone calls. An icy greeting, comments on the weather, and a curt farewell. Thirty-eight one-minute conversations."

"At least I called."

"And now, suddenly, you're here in the flesh. What is it you want this time? Money?" Ian glanced at Meredith again. Then he held up a staying hand, laughing bitterly. "Oh, no. Don't say you want me to represent her. She can't afford me, I assure you, and I'll be damned if I'll do it free of charge."

Meredith's predicament was the last thing on her mind at the moment. Her stomach twisted as she darted her gaze back and forth between the two men. *Such pain.* Two phone calls a year, divided into thirty-eight, equaled nineteen. That couldn't be right. A father and son who loved each other as much as these two obviously did couldn't possibly cling to old hurts and not see one another for *nineteen* years. It was absolute madness.

Heath hauled in a deep breath and let it out slowly, as if he were silently counting to ten. "I don't think it's entirely fair for you to immediately assume I want something. I haven't asked you for a red cent since I left, or for any kind of help. That's half of my life, *all* of my adult life. It's not as if I've been a habitual moocher."

Ian folded his arms and smiled. "So you didn't come here for help?"

Heath raked his hair again. "Dad, I'm sorry I haven't come to see you, all right? If I had thought you wanted me to, I might have. But you told me never to come back. Remember?"

"I never said that!"

"You certainly did! You said if I stepped foot on this land again, you'd kill me. That you couldn't bear to look at me."

"Give me a break, Heath! I can scarcely remember what I said that night. You had just *killed* my little girl! And hours later, you were still staggering drunk. With her *blood* all over you, for God's sake. She wasn't cold on the slab yet, and you were already slugging more beer. At that moment, I *wanted* to kill you."

Heath's face went white, his eyes like dark splotches of water flecked with moonlight. For a moment, Meredith thought he might go to his knees. She couldn't let this continue. The two men needed to iron this mess out, no question about it, but not like this, with Heath pulling his punches, afraid of alienating Ian because he was their only hope. Heath was literally laying himself out as a sacrifice to appease the man, as if he were a vengeful God.

She gathered Sammy close and pushed to her feet. "Excuse me," she interjected. "I'm leaving now."

Heath blinked and jerked his gaze to her. "Merry, no. He's your only way out."

"The price is too steep," she said shakily.

"Meredith, I'm all right. Sit back down."

"No," she cried. "You're not all right, and I can't watch you do this. Not for me."

"It's *not* just for you. My life is at stake, too."

She sank back down on the chair. "That's not playing fair."

"This is too important to just walk away. We need his help, and if his price is hurling insults, we've got to pay it. We can't afford not to."

Ian chuckled, looking Meredith over. "Very good! I take it he falls for this?"

Heath groaned. "Jesus, Dad! I can't believe you. Look at her! Is she your typical *femme fatale*?"

"They come in all shapes and sizes. In my profession, I've seen them all."

"So have I," Heath shot back, "and she doesn't fit the stereotype."

"You've seen the Wynema Falls variety," Ian replied. "This one has more class. And I don't mean that as a compliment," he said to Meredith. "You're a master at the craft, and you're playing him like a three-string banjo. If you were only taking his money, I might feel less hostile. But you're destroying everything that he is."

"Dad, I think I'm capable of judging the lady's character without your input. You don't know her. I do. And I'm telling you, this isn't a snow job, I'm not making decisions with the lower half of my anatomy, and she's nothing like you *think*!"

"A sterling recommendation, coming from my son, the screwup."

"*Screwup?*" Heath repeated tautly.

"You always have been, always will be. Sometimes I wonder how such a bull-headed, impulsive and uncontrolled *idiot* could possibly have sprung from my loins. I *told* you to get rid of her! To let someone else handle this. What the *hell* were you thinking?''

Slate blue eyes clashed over a distance of seven feet, both sets identical in color and glinting with the same stubborn, indomitable pride. The creases in Ian's lean, burnished cheeks were deeper than Heath's. He had more crinkles at the corners of his eyes. His skin had aged on his neck, taking on the texture of crepe. But otherwise, father and son looked enough alike that they might have been cast from the same mold.

If Ian's barbed comments hurt, Heath didn't reveal it. His jaw muscle relaxed, his stance went from tense to lazy, and he flashed his dad a cocky grin. ''You're such a cold, unaffectionate son of a bitch, my mother probably got knocked up by the postman.''

Ian doubled his fists. ''You little bastard. Why I was hoping you might have grown up, I have no idea! Don't you *dare* speak of your mother with disrespect!''

''The disrespect wasn't aimed at her. I've heard men refer to their wives as their better halves. My mother was far more than that. She must have been the glue that held your humanity together because it's sure as shit scattered on the wind now.''

''You're the same wild, unpredictable smart ass that you always were,'' Ian tossed back. ''And you still don't have a lick of respect for me. Do you?''

Meredith had wanted Heath to fight back, but now that he was, she felt extremely uncomfortable. They were squared off like two men about to exchange blows. Just the *thought* terrified her. Approximately four hundred and eighty pounds of muscle-packed masculinity, out of control, and she and Sammy might be caught right in the middle of it.

''Mommy, Heef said it.''

''Shhh, sweetie.''

''But he *said* it!''

Meredith wished she had a sock to stuff in her daughter's

mouth. Sammy turned bewildered blue eyes on her. "They're saying *lots* of bad words, huh?"

"Sammy, please," Meredith whispered. "We'll talk about it later."

"Is 'bastard' naughty?"

Meredith's heart was starting to slam. She stared at her daughter. There wasn't a trace of fear in Sammy's eyes. She seemed totally unconcerned that the two men in the room appeared to be mere inches away from violence. So did Goliath. The dog had plopped beside her chair, his massive head resting on his paws. Occasionally, he opened one eye when the male voices went from loud to wall-shaking, but otherwise he just lay there, seeming to snooze.

Heath answered Sammy's question. "Yes, Sammy. My dad said some bad words, and so did I. I'm sorry, and when we go home, you can wash my mouth out. If I say any more, you be sure to count them."

"Okay." Sammy fixed her gaze intently on the two men. With a hand resting on her knee and one small finger extended, she looked very like a miniature umpire keeping track of fouls at a ball game. "Just remember, Heef. Soap'll make you urp."

Heath had already returned his attention to the quarrel. Sammy's warning seemed to take the starch out of his spine. He stared at his dad, his face relaxing. After a moment, he shifted his gaze back to Sammy, his expression going tender and his mouth quirking at the corners. He finally smiled.

"You know what, sweetcakes? You're right. This isn't worth having to eat soap."

He looked at Meredith. "I'm sorry, Merry. I shouldn't have brought you here." He extended his hand toward her. "The price *is* too steep. Let's get going."

Meredith started to stand. At her movement, Ian whirled on her, his face so twisted with anger that she started and fell back in her chair. For an awful moment, she thought he might leap at her. He advanced on her instead.

"What have you got, pure gold between your legs? He's

lost his ever loving mind! And *you!* Oh-hh-h! You have the act perfected, don't you? The timid little woman who needs a big, block-headed man to fight her battles for her. I know your kind. A cold-hearted, manipulative bitch, that's what you are.''

Goliath lifted his head and snarled. Ian reeled to a stop.

''Heath, get your goddamned dog under control.''

''He is under control, Dad. You're the one who's lost it. You don't even see them, do you? Not really. You're so used to making snap judgments and weighing the evidence, all they are to you is a couple of bodies. Look in their eyes. Really look. Meredith is scared to death of you, and Sammy thinks you're rude. *Most* people exclude little kids from a disagreement—offer them a tablet to scribble on, maybe some milk and cookies—anything to make it clear to them they aren't in the line of fire. You didn't even ask Sammy's name or how old she is, the usual accepted behavior when you meet young children. Why am I not surprised? The fact is, you can look into her big blue eyes and not give a shit what happens to her. You just want me to do the smart thing and sacrifice her, *and* her mother, on the altar of the law. Well, Dad, *screw* you! As for your help? Forget I asked. We'll find another way to save our bacon.''

Keeping excellent track of Heath's language, Sammy poked out two more fingers. There were now three counts against him.

''I'm four,'' she told Ian. Then she tipped her head questioningly. ''Do you want me to count bad words for you, too? You're sayin' lots of nasty, icky ones. Heef says it's a really bad rabbit he oughta break.''

Ian stared down at Sammy as if she were an alien from another planet. ''Excuse me?'' he said in that haughty tone he had probably perfected in the courtroom.

Sammy sniffed. ''Did you farfle?''

''*What?*''

Sammy leaned slightly toward him. ''You know, from your bum? My mommy says you gots to always say 'scuse me, 'cause it's not p'lite.''

Ian's eyes darkened, and his color rose. Looking exactly like his son, he jabbed his fingers through his hair and blinked, totally ruining his professional styling job. "No, young lady, I did *not* 'farfle.' "

Sammy's expression saddened. "I bet your Mommy died when you was real little, huh? Just like Heef. That's how come you don't got any manners. Right? 'Cause you di'n't have her to teach you nuffing. Can you say your letters?"

Ian took a turn around the room, raking his hair as if he'd suddenly discovered it was infested with vermin. Glancing at Meredith, he said, "While you're teaching your daughter manners, Mrs. Kenyon, you might remind her to respect her elders. I don't appreciate having my behavior criticized by a four-year-old."

Meredith pushed up from the chair again, juggling Sammy on her hip. "Until we met Heath, I didn't feel any of my daughter's elders, aside from myself, had earned her respect. If she has offended you, I apologize. But even you have to admit, this hasn't been a very pleasant visit."

Heath covered the distance to Meredith and scooped Sammy from her arms. Then, taking her elbow, he said, "Come on, sweetheart. I'm sorry I subjected you and Sammy to this. I thought—well, never mind what I thought." He snapped his fingers. "Goliath, come."

"Heath, wait a minute!" Ian called from behind them. "What did you mean when you said your life was at stake, too? Was it an exaggeration, or are your lives actually at risk?"

Heath continued walking toward the study door.

"Dammit, Heath! I asked you a question. If the situation is really that serious, of course, I'll help you. All else aside, you're my *son*!"

Heath stopped, handed Sammy to Meredith, and said, "Sweetheart, wait for me on the porch, okay? I'll be right there." Then he turned toward his father. His eyes glistened with a suspicious brightness. "I'm not your *son*. I've been many things to you. An inconvenience. An embarrassment. A trial. Your cross to bear, definitely. But *never* your son."

Meredith knew she had to get Sammy out of there. She backed away as far as the doorway, but then she couldn't seem to pry her feet from the rug to go any farther. She knew Heath thought she'd gone, but she couldn't leave him. Not when he had that stricken expression on his face that told her how badly this confrontation was hurting him. She would stay, and Sammy would stay, because Heath would have stayed for them.

Chapter 25

I'm not your son. The words hung there in the room, seeming to echo. Ian looked as if Heath had struck him.

"Think about it," Heath cried raggedly. "Nineteen *years*, Dad. Sure, I screwed up. God forgive me, I screwed up really bad. But I was only a kid. And you *spat* on me. Do you remember that? You called me a murderer, told me to never defile your home with my presence again, and you spat in my face. I had five dollars and some change in my pocket. You didn't even give me my clothes or a jacket. You just shoved me off the porch at six in the morning and washed your hands of me."

"You were staggering drunk. I'd just been to the morgue. And you were responsible for her death! Do you think I was thinking clearly? I wanted to rip you apart."

"You have no idea how many times I wished you had," Heath said softly. "Because you were right. I had killed my little sister. Do you *know* how much I loved her? With you gone so much, she was my whole world, and she was the last person on earth I ever would've hurt." The tendons along Heath's throat stood out. "I was the one who found her under the truck. The one who stayed, trying with everything I had to lift it off of her. And when the cops got there and finally did get her out, I was the one who tried to resuscitate her. Her head was crushed. You just *think* about that. Mouth-to-mouth, Dad. *That's* why I had so much blood all over me, damn you!''

Ian locked his knees and closed his eyes, his face turning ashen. He looked like a man taking brutal body blows. Meredith's heart nearly broke for him. The great Ian Masters had failed miserably at being a good father. She didn't doubt that. But she could also see very clearly that he had cared about his children.

''Oh, God, Heath, please,'' he whispered, ''don't do this to me. *Please.* I can't bear it. Not the details, please.''

''Do this to you?'' Heath retorted. ''What about what you're doing to me? You thought I was *drunk* when you saw me? You'd come in from Chicago, for Christ's sake! *Hours* later! They had sedated me!''

Ian's head came up and a stricken anguish came into his eyes. ''They would've *told* me,'' he said raggedly. ''You're lying. Making excuses. They would've told me!''

''*Jesus*, Dad! Would you look at me? I'm not a kid anymore. Lying? Why would I bother? To save our relationship? What a joke! And I'm sure as hell not afraid you'll kick my ass.''

''You just can't admit the truth to yourself,'' Ian accused.

''Not true. I've *lived* with it all these years. Seen her face, not as it was in life, but as it was when I was trying to—'' Heath's chest heaved and tears tracked his leathery cheeks. ''I kept thinking I might be able to save her—if I just tried hard enough. Remember how she always came running to me when she got hurt?''

Ian made a strangled sound and nodded.

''After Mom died, I was the only one here to make it better. When she was younger, it was scraped knees. When she got older, she'd come to me when some boy broke her heart. That night, all I could think of was that I could make her better if they'd just leave me alone with her for a while.'' Heath heaved a shaky sigh. ''I was stupid drunk when I rolled that truck. I admit it. I take complete responsibility for that, and I'll carry the guilt with me to my grave.

But I never touched another drop of beer *after* the wreck, and when you saw me later, I was *not* still drunk.

"I was a two hundred and twenty pound linebacker! I wrestled bulls and rode broncs in my spare time. When they tried to put her in the ambulance and wouldn't let me get close to her, I went berserk, and once I reached her, they couldn't get me away from her. A bunch of them finally tackled me and held me down while a paramedic jabbed me in the arm. End of story. I wasn't *drunk*! I had been drugged. And I'm sorry, but I can't believe they never told you that. By Oregon law, I was still a minor."

His arms rigid at his sides, Ian shook his head. "I can't remember anyone telling me that, Heath. But, then, it's all a blur. I went on automatic pilot. Got the charges against you dropped and all reference to them taken off the accident report. Identified the body. I don't remember half of what was said to me."

Heath's face went taut with bitterness. "You might have asked me, given me the benefit of the doubt. But you didn't, did you? Back then, you never had an ounce of faith in me or bothered to listen to anything I said, and you still don't."

Meredith couldn't bear to watch this any longer. Heath was tearing his father apart. "Heath, that's enough."

Heath spun toward the doorway, his gaze shooting to Sammy. "Merry, I asked you to get her out of here."

"I couldn't leave you."

"Well, you're right. Enough is enough. Let's go." He came to the doorway, encircled her with an arm, and propelled her down the hallway with such force that she felt like thistledown in the wind. "I just never learn. You'd think by now I'd know he doesn't give a hoot about me, and that he never has! But, oh, no. I had to come back for one more kick in the teeth."

On the porch, Meredith dug in with her heels, set Sammy down, and turned toward Heath to grab him by the front of his shirt. "Heath? I've changed my mind. I'm afraid this may be a bad mistake."

"What is?"

"Leaving like this. If you walk away now, you'll never come back."

"Damned straight, I won't!"

"I can't let you do it. You'll only be hurting yourself if I don't stop you."

"I hate his guts. He has no power to hurt me, period. And the feeling's mutual."

"Oh, Heath. How can you be so blind? He loves you. It's written all over him. He just doesn't know how to say it! This is destroying him."

"Oh, for God's sake! He looked pathetic for a couple of minutes. Big deal. He isn't destroyed, Meredith. You have to care to be destroyed."

"You go back in there. Please, Heath. I'm not leaving until you do."

"And say what? That I'm sorry for what I said? It was the truth."

"Why has he stayed here?" she demanded to know. "He works out of Chicago. Why did he come here in the first place?"

"He'd promised my mom he wouldn't raise us in the city. What difference does it make?" He stepped off the porch. "I know you mean well, but you have no idea what you're talking about." He started up the circular drive. "You saw what he's like. The man even turned on you."

"Yes," she admitted. "In defense of you. He believes everything he said to me. That I'm just using you. He's *furious*, Heath. And fighting for you with everything he's got. He's a mess as a parent. I won't say he isn't. But look past it. It's not that he doesn't love you. He's just—inept."

"There's a good word, inept. And he calls *me* a screw-up."

"He stayed here because of you, Heath!" she called after him. "You have to know that. What else is here for him? An empty house? Long plane trips? He stayed to be near you!"

Not looking back, he kept walking. She sat down on the porch. He covered several feet, realized she wasn't behind him, and turned. When he saw her, his face flushed to an angry red, and he stomped back toward her.

"What in the hell are you doing?"

"I'm having a sit-down strike," she replied calmly.

Huffing air into his cheeks, he glanced over at Sammy and Goliath, who stood on the gravel drive. "You're taking my father's side against me?"

"No, of course not. I'm taking your side. I'll always take your side. It's just that I know you love him, and you've been so hurt. Please, go back in. Give him just one more chance. Don't carry this around inside you for the rest of your life. Please?"

"I don't *like* the jerk."

"He doesn't like you, either. I don't think you even know each other. But you love each other. And you're both dying inside."

He set his jaw. "I appreciate your concern, all right? If he were normal, I might even agree he deserves another attempt. But he isn't, and I don't. So get your little butt up from there. We're leaving."

"You've done so much for me, Heath. Let me do this one thing for you."

He snapped his fingers and pointed at his feet. "We're leaving!"

Last night, Meredith had believed she'd seen him angry. Now she realized he had been only perturbed by comparison.

"Don't push me, Meredith!"

She gazed up at him—approximately six feet five inches of outraged male, every muscle tensed. He was snapping his fingers and ordering her around, looking fully capable of slapping her silly if she didn't obey him. Yet she didn't feel the least bit intimidated. It was the most glorious feeling in the world.

"Heath," she said softly. "Would you look at yourself? You're acting like Dan."

His face went redder. "Jesus! Don't compare me to Dan. I don't goddamn appreciate it!"

"Then, please, don't snap your fingers at me. It makes you look silly."

"Silly?" He moved his lips but no sound came out. Finally, he managed to sputter, "You'll *think* silly! And I'll snap my fingers if I want to! I won't spend the rest of my life being compared to good old Dan."

"I'm *not* comparing you to Dan. For Dan, I would get up!"

That gave him pause. "If *that's* not a hell of a note, I don't know what is! You'd hop to for him, but not for me?"

"I was afraid of Dan."

He leveled a finger at her. "Meredith Lynn, get your ass up off that goddamned porch!"

"Mommy? Are you and Heef fighting?"

Meredith glanced at her daughter, who stood a few feet away with her hand curled over Goliath's collar. "No, sweetkins. We're having a discussion."

"This is *not* a discussion," Heath corrected. "It's a fight, and your mother is about to find out what will happen if she pushes me too far."

"Is Mommy winning?"

Again Heath seemed incapable of speech for a moment. He tugged on his earlobe, then swiped a hand under his nose. "No, she is *not* winning. She seems to *think* she is, but she's about to learn she's not." He gave Meredith a measuring glance. "No contest!"

Meredith sighed. "You're going to feel so awful about this once you calm down."

"I am not."

"Yes, you are. You're beside yourself right now, and you can't see how badly you're behaving."

"Badly? Excuse me, but from my side of the fence, I'd say—"

"But you will later," she rushed on, cutting him off. "Do you know what's happening here, Heath? You're doing just what you did last night when I hurt your feelings, only this time it's your dad. Blowing up doesn't make the hurt go away. It just covers it up for a while."

He planted his hands on his hips, walked in a tight circle, and huffed like a surfacing whale. She'd seen him do that last night as well and realized it must be his way of taking timeout.

When he finally stopped pacing, he crossed his arms, his stance more relaxed. After regarding her for a moment, he sighed, a twinkle replacing the glint of anger in his eyes. He didn't smile, but Meredith knew he was struggling not to. "You do realize I could jerk you up from there, throw you over my shoulder, and paddle that cute little fanny of yours all the way back to the truck."

"That sounds like it might be fun." She dimpled a cheek at him. "But you have to wait until *after* you go back in. Then, no matter how it turns out, I promise to be putty in your hands."

"You should be putty *now*. I wear the pants in this family. Don't forget that."

"Mommy gots pants on, too!"

Heath narrowed an eye at the child, who stood knee-high to him. "Mine are bigger."

Sammy regarded the long legs of his jeans. "Yup. Lots bigger."

Heath looked at Meredith. "You see? Don't mess with the bull. You might get him by the horn." He strode slowly toward her, then drew up and hunkered in front of her. Catching her chin in his hand, he gazed into her eyes. "He'll just get a few more licks in. You do realize that. I'll do it. For you. But it isn't going to work."

She caught his wrist and kissed his palm. "The two of you have hashed out every old hurt, avoiding the elementary truth, as if to admit it would be losing face. Tell him, Heath. Before you leave, please, won't you tell him? A big, strong man like you. You can handle saying three little words. Let them fall where they may, but know you've said them. If he isn't man enough to do the same, then that's his problem."

He rubbed his thumb over her lips. "You owe me for this one."

Shortly after Heath reentered the house, Meredith had cause to wonder if he would ever forgive her for insisting he speak with his dad again. The front windows seemed to vibrate, they were yelling so loudly, every word of their argument carrying to her on the porch. To keep Sammy from listening, Meredith directed the child to go play on the lawn with Goliath. Never had Meredith heard such a vicious exchange.

Heath aired old grievances against Ian for becoming an absentee father after Heath's mother died. Ian confessed that after his wife's death, burying himself in his work had been all that had kept him from falling apart. Heath pointed out that in Ian's opinion, Heath had never done anything right, that he'd been constantly criticized by his father and never once praised for any of his accomplishments. Ian fired back with lethal rounds of *more* criticism, claiming that Heath had always scorned everything Ian was and all that he had stood for, that Heath had patterned himself after Skeeter, the ranch foreman, instead of after his own dad. Heath struck back by saying that the reason he'd hero worshiped Skeeter was because the wiry old cowboy had been more of a father to Heath than Ian ever had.

On and on it went, until Meredith wished she had left well enough alone. Toward the end of it, Heath informed his dad that he had returned to the house to tell him only one thing, then angrily bellowed, "I love you! God knows why, but I do!" After that, she heard nothing more.

For a few minutes, Meredith expected Heath to come storming out of the house. When he didn't, she decided the two men must still be arguing, but at a lower pitch. When a quarter of an hour passed, she sighed with relief and gave herself a congratulatory pat on the back. For the first time in nineteen years, father and son were finally talking instead of yelling.

She didn't kid herself. Heath and Ian weren't going to heal all the old wounds with one conversation, nor would this talk bridge all the chasms that yawned between them. And she sincerely doubted either of them would ever put the heartache of Laney's tragic death completely behind them.

But this was a start. Where there was communication, there existed hope for some kind of relationship between them, even if it wasn't a perfect one.

Three hours later, Ian rejoined Meredith and Heath in his study. He tossed a notepad down on his desk. "I placed a few phone calls, talked with people in the know. Glen Calendri and some of his associates are already under investigation."

"They are?" Meredith pressed a hand to her throat. "That's good news, right?"

Ian smiled. Since his second talk with Heath, he had not only apologized to Meredith and Sammy for his earlier behavior, but had been a model of cordiality and good manners. He'd also refrained from cursing.

"Well, it means Calendri is operating under a cloud of suspicion. So far, they can't get anything to hang him with, so it's unofficial and doesn't help you out much. However, if the information you gave me checks out satisfactorily, there's every possibility that you can send your ex-father-in-law and a few of his friends to the pen for a very long time. I've also been assured that in exchange for such testimony, the government would be willing to enroll you and the child into the Witness Protection Program.

"With a phone call, I can set the wheels in motion. From this point forward, things should move along nicely. Whether I make that call is entirely up to you, Meredith. If you give me the go-ahead, you'll have to return here to the ranch in three days to give an official and detailed statement to the proper authorities. They will, of course, check out the information between now and then. Names, times, dates, the crimes that you allege were committed. If they meet you here, the interview will be a mere formality."

"What then?"

"You'll be called to testify before a grand jury. If all goes well, that first go-around will result in indictments. If so, Glen and his associates will be arrested and held for trial, with you as the primary witness." He sighed and looked at her sadly. "Now, for the downside. Once you give your statement in three days, the ensuing investigation will take time, anywhere from several days to possibly months. Meanwhile, you may be in grave danger. That will necessitate your being taken into protective custody immediately. You and Sammy will reside in what they call a 'safe house' until you've finished testifying, at which time you'll both enter the witness program. In short, after this initial three days, you'll live in seclusion, with no contact with anyone from that point forward until the trials are over. The entire process, from beginning to end, may take months, or possibly even years."

Meredith listened to this news with numb acceptance, keeping her gaze carefully averted from Heath's. *Three days*. After that, she might never see him again. As a protected witness, she would assume a new identity. God knew where she and Sammy might end up after the trials, the only certainty being that Heath wouldn't be there. Tears threatened. She blinked them away. This was the answer to her prayers. A way out, an opportunity for her child to have a normal life.

Magic and miracles and fairy tale endings. Only last night, she'd dared to believe that maybe this time she would come out a winner. Now all hope for a future with Heath was being quashed. It hurt. She couldn't even think of telling him good-bye. But for Sammy's sake, she would have to.

"It's tough, I know," Ian said solemnly. "On a bright note, if your testimony checks out, Heath's decision to take you into protective custody, and his actions later to protect you, will be justified. If he wishes, I'm sure he can have his job back."

Meredith nodded. "That *is* a bright note." She smiled at Heath. "Maybe your whole life won't be tanked, after all."

Heath regarded her silently, his mouth pressed into a grim line. Then he said, "Make the call, Dad. We don't have any choice."

Three days. That was all they had, only three very short days, and both Meredith and Heath longed to have a lifetime. Given Oregon's three-day waiting period, they discussed making a quick trip to Reno so they might be legally married, which would make Heath's enrollment with her in the Witness Protection Program automatic. But in the end, Heath scotched the idea because the long drive to Nevada would put Meredith's and Sammy's lives at risk. Glen Calendri's men were still out there somewhere, and their bullets were still just as deadly. They had to stay on the mountaintop, where there was at least some margin of safety.

"I'll find another way, Merry," he told her shortly after making love to her in the moonlight. "Somehow, some way, I'll be waiting for you when you've finished testifying. We'll have a whole new life, and we'll be together until we die. I swear it."

Meredith knew Heath meant that, from the bottom of his heart. But she also knew he was only one man and that some things were beyond his control. This was probably going to be it for them, just three short days to last them a lifetime, and by unspoken agreement, they were determined to live each second as if it were their last.

It hurt. In all her life, Meredith had never felt such pain. In so short a while, this man had become her world. So many times, she caught herself watching him through a blur of tears as he interacted with Sammy. *Merry, will I ever make it?* he'd asked her. In Meredith's opinion, he had already surpassed excellence and was the most fantastic father in the world. She committed the moments to memory, promising herself she'd recall every little thing so she might share it with Sammy in stories after he could no longer be with them. When Sammy remembered her father, Meredith wanted her to think of Heath Masters. He was love and honor and strength and courage, all rolled into a wonderful package, the perfect gift to her child. And she wanted Sammy to have that gift forever.

The incident that particularly touched Meredith and stuck in her mind was when she found Heath and Sammy in the bathroom. Heath was stooped over the vanity, his elbows braced on the edges of the sink. He was gagging. Sammy sat cross-legged beside him on the counter, waiting with the bar of soap until he recovered enough to open his mouth again.

"I'm sorry, Heef. I told you, soap makes you urp."

Heath shuddered, filled his mouth with water, and made a shrill, sputtering sound. "It's not your fault, sweetcakes," he managed to say. "Nobody controls my mouth but me." He lifted his head, stuck out his tongue, and made inarticulate noises. "*Wah id ahin.*"

Making a horrible face, Sammy rubbed the bar of soap back and forth over his tongue. With one stroke, she went farther back than she intended. Heath's eyes bugged, and he jackknifed forward, shoving his head into the sink to wretch. When he drew breath, he croaked, "Jesus, Sammy! Not down my *throat!*"

"I'm sorry!" she cried. Then she made a gasping sound. "Uh-oh, Heef. You done it again!"

"What?" He gagged and sputtered. Sammy leaned over to whisper the word he'd said in his ear. He groaned, gagged, raked his teeth over his tongue, spat, and then said, "Oh, Christ . . . I'm not—going to survive this."

Two scrubs later, he said, "Sammy, are you *sure* you counted *ten* bad words?"

At this point, Sammy was starting to gag just watching him. "I think so," she said faintly. "Maybe I made a 'stake, though. We can stop now, Heef. I know you're sorry."

Meredith figured Heath should be grateful the child only had ten fingers. Past that, Sammy hadn't yet learned to count. He hauled in a bracing breath, squared his shoulders, and stared into the sink for a moment. "No," he finally said. "If I cussed twelve times, it's not right to skip washes. What will that teach me?"

"Ten times," Sammy corrected.

"And then the two just now," he reminded her.

Sammy sighed. "I'm all the way teached." She shook her head. "I ain't never gonna cuss again. I don't like to urp."

Seconds later, she got sick watching Heath and did just that. He swore—Meredith was becoming convinced he would never break himself of the habit—and held Sammy's head, wiping her little face with a wet cloth. When Sammy recovered, she asked in a squeaky little voice, "Heef? Can't you just sit in the corner?" Heath gratefully agreed.

Over the next few days, he spent quite a bit of their remaining time together with his nose pressed to the wall, and every second made Meredith love him just a little more. On one occasion while he was outside playing with Sammy and Goliath, she heard him yell, "Oh, God!" He quickly followed it up with, "Love me!" Then, in a voice he undoubtedly pitched low so Meredith wouldn't hear him, he told Sammy if was all right to say "God" if he was praying, and asking God to love him was definitely praying. Meredith figured the request was entirely unnecessary. If God didn't already love Heath Masters, then He hadn't been keeping tabs on the folks in Oregon.

Making love all night . . . Taking snoozes along the creek bank in the warm sunshine while Sammy and Goliath played . . . Picnics under the fir trees . . . Feeding the squirrels . . . And making love again. In the next three days, they made a thousand memories, reality intruding only when Meredith noticed Heath's shotgun and rifle, which he carried everywhere. Being with him. The four of them, a family. Lying in his arms at night. It was all Meredith's sweetest dreams come true.

Sadly, like all wonderful dreams, it ended far too soon.

On their last night together, Heath took her for a walk in the moonlight after Sammy fell asleep. They couldn't wander far from the house, so they circled it, keeping to the same path through the trees. In a small, moonlit clearing Heath drew to a stop and dropped to one knee in front of her to ask her to marry him. Meredith tearfully said yes, clinging to the hope that his proposal might come to fruition and that one day, she would be joined with him forever in the eyes of God and the law.

As Heath pushed back to his feet, he whispered, ''Let's do it, right now.''

Meredith felt a tearing pain in her chest, for she knew he would only ask that if he believed they might never get a chance to say the words for real. He braided her a wedding ring with blades of grass, its setting a tiny white wild flower. Then he took her hand, and together, they made their marriage vows, God in heaven their only witness. When Heath slipped the woven grass ring onto her finger, Meredith clung to him and started to weep. She expected him to chide her and reassure her, saying that they were only going to be parted temporarily, that one day soon, they'd be together again.

Instead, he held her locked in his strong arms, his body shaking with the intensity of his emotions. Shortly before he finally released her, Meredith believed she felt a single tear slip from his lean cheek to trail down her neck. She knew then . . . beyond a shadow of a doubt . . . that he feared they might never see each other again.

The next morning, all of them were quiet during the ride back to town. There were a thousand things Meredith wanted to tell Heath, yet she couldn't seem to put any of them into words. How could she tell a man that he had been her salvation, that by loving her, he'd healed her? She no longer felt fearful. The shame and constant guilt that had dogged her for so long had disappeared. She was whole again. More importantly, he had taught her to respect herself again. The thought of facing the rest of her life without him tore her apart, yet deep inside, in a secret place, she knew she would survive, not because she didn't need him, but because his love had made her strong enough to stand on her own and face whatever came her way.

When they reached Ian's place, Meredith was whisked away to the study by two strange men in suits. She was closeted with them for hours while she gave her statement. When she was finally finished, they allowed her only a few minutes in private with Heath to tell him good-bye.

He was waiting for her in his dad's den, his folded arm braced on the fireplace mantel, his head bent to gaze into the firebox. When he heard the door lock click, he spun around. Meredith ran to him, and he caught her up in his arms. Neither of them spoke. What was there to say that hadn't already been said? Instead, they communicated with only their bodies, she clinging to him and wishing she never had to leave, he holding her as if he wished he never had to let her go.

There were no words. How could they talk when their hearts were shattering?

Finally, at the very last, Heath whispered, "I'm already checking into ways that I can go into the program with you, Merry. There are stumbling blocks, big ones. I won't lie to you about that. But there must be a way to work around them. There *has* to be."

Somewhere along the way, Meredith had tucked her hope for that away, and it had died a final death last night when they had shared wedding vows in the clearing. She leaned back in his arms, struggling not to cry and make this harder for him, her gaze fixed on his dark face. Dear God, how she loved him. He was like the hero in one of Sammy's fairy tales, everything about him somehow finer and on a larger scale than anyone in real life. She truly didn't know how she would be able to bear being apart from him, or how she was going to find true meaning in her life without having him beside her.

When Sammy and Goliath entered the den, the child grew frantic when Heath gently told her good-bye. She clung to Heath, then to Goliath, sobbing her heart out.

"Hey, sweetcakes?" Heath pried her loose from the dog and cradled her in his arms as he paced back and forth across the room. "Why all these tears? You're acting like you're never going to see us again."

"I'm n—not!" Sammy cried. "Please, Heef, don't go 'way. Stay with me and my mommy. Please? I want you to be my daddy!"

Meredith stood with her fists knotted at her sides. The anguish she saw in Heath's eyes made her want to collapse and weep right along with her daughter. Oh, God, this hurt. It was like having her heart carved from her chest with a dull knife.

"Hey . . . hey . . ." Heath rubbed the child's back, jostling her against him. "Listen to me, sweetcakes. You listening?"

She buried her face against his neck. "'Kay. I'm listenin'."

"I *am* your daddy. Got it? You have to go with your mommy for right now so you can keep her company and take care of her. But the minute she's done testifying, Goliath and I are going to be waiting for both of you. We'll have a brand-new house, and we'll all live there together. How does that sound?"

"Do you promise?"

Heath locked gazes with Meredith. His dark face had grown taut, the cast of his skin tinged with gray. "I promise, sweetcakes. Have I ever broken a promise to you?"

"No."

"Well, then." He looked deeply into Meredith's eyes. "God willing, I won't break this one. I'll be there. Goliath will be there. There's no reason for you to feel so sad."

The message Heath flashed to Meredith was as clear as if he'd spoken it aloud. *God willing.* He wanted her to remember and explain to Sammy that he'd qualified the promise, just in case he wasn't waiting for them.

Somehow Meredith held herself together. She had to, for Sammy's sake. Standing off to one side, she smiled as if her heart wasn't breaking while the child told Heath and Goliath a final good-bye.

Ian took Sammy from the room to allow Heath and Meredith a few last seconds together. The moment the door closed, Meredith knelt to put her arms around Goliath. From the first, this silly dog had been the unbreakable link between her and Heath. In the end, Goliath's love and devotion to Sammy had been instrumental in saving Meredith's life. He wasn't just a dog to her, but one of the best friends she'd ever had, loyal to the end. Knowing him had taught her a great deal—about giving and receiving love, and about commitment. Goliath's was complete, and without condition.

Then the inevitable moment came. Barely managing not to break down, Meredith ran into Heath's arms for one final embrace. Then before she burst into sobs in front of him, she raced from the room.

Men were waiting just inside the front door to take her and Sammy into custody. After nudging her daughter out onto the front porch, Meredith hesitated on the threshold to look back down the hall. Heath stood there, his body taut, as if braced for a blow. Tears filled her eyes, but she forced a smile, for that was how she wanted him to remember her. Then she turned and walked out.

It was the longest walk of her life, but for Sammy's sake, Meredith forced one foot in front of the other. Four men flanked her and her daughter, guiding them to a nondescript, white sedan parked on the circular driveway. She and Sammy were hustled into the backseat, two of the agents sitting up front. The other two men climbed in a separate vehicle, their plan evidently to ride shotgun behind the sedan.

As the car executed the loop and eased down the driveway, Meredith craned her neck to look back at the ranch house. She saw Heath standing on the porch, one hand lifted in farewell. In those last heart-wrenching moments, she remembered the fairy tale he'd made up especially for her, about his carrying her off into the Oregon sunset and devoting the rest of his life to keeping her and Sammy safe.

He had kept his promise. She and Sammy would be protected now. But what about the "happily ever after" part of the story?

Knowing in her heart that she would never see Heath Masters again, she pressed her tear-streaked face against the window glass, her gaze clinging to him until, at last, he faded completely from sight.

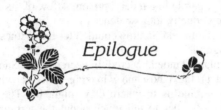

Epilogue

Somewhere, USA
Eighteen months later

The thud and clanking of landing gear resounded through
the cabin of the small, government-owned jet as it circled
and nosed down into its final descent. Through the small
window, Meredith could see the airport that lay below
them, a tiny municipal with only two hangars, an office
building, and a dime-sized parking area. Like a satin rib-
bon, the gray-black stretch of runway shone with wetness,
probably melted snow. Judging by the drifts that lay over
the fields around the airport, there would be a lot of snow-
fall here in the winter. But for now, as if in welcome, all
forms of precipitation had given way to the relentless
gloom of a November afternoon.

Meredith was exhausted, and she felt sure Sammy was
as well. Though the flight itself had been slightly less than
five hours, their emotions were running high, and neither
of them had slept soundly last night. After a quick breakfast
at dawn, they had been transported under armed guard to
a similar small airport in upper state New York. This plane
had been awaiting them there.

At long last, it was over. Meredith was finished testifying, and now, even though two of the trials weren't yet
concluded, the nightmare for her and her daughter had

reached an end. Glen Calendri was now serving a life sentence without parole in a federal prison. A few of his chums were serving equally long sentences.

Now, Meredith and Sammy could enter the Witness Protection Program.

As the plane landed, Meredith peered over Sammy's blond head at the landscape whizzing past the window, seeking some clue as to where they might be. The snow was too deep for her to tell much about the terrain. This was *awful*, she thought, and if it was difficult for her to handle, how must it be for Sammy? They had no idea where they were, or even what their new last name would be, only that a house had been procured for them in a rural area outside an unknown city. The government had also secured Meredith a position of employment in computer programming, if she chose to take it. As if she had a choice? She would supposedly be allotted enough money to make a fresh start, but once that ran out, she and Sammy had to make it on their own.

Though it had been a seeming eternity since Meredith had last seen Heath, she still thought of him as the plane coasted to a jerking halt on the wet tarmac. Months ago, she'd received word through a U.S. marshal that Heath had been absolved of all criminal charges right after she left Oregon and that he had resumed his duties as the sheriff of Wynema County. Goliath's death sentence had also been rescinded, given the fact that the man he'd bitten had been a dangerous criminal.

Meredith knew Sammy was thinking of Heath as well. In one hand, the little girl clutched a bouquet of paper roses she'd made, a gift she insisted was for Heath when she saw him again. Meredith had tried to explain to Sammy that Heath might not be able to keep his promise, that she shouldn't count too strongly on his being there when they got off the plane, but her daughter refused to listen. Heath had promised, and for eighteen months, Sammy had clung to that hope like a lifeline.

Oh, how Meredith wished Heath were here, even if it

were only for a moment. She so wanted him to see Sammy. In eighteen months, the child had sprouted up a foot. She was six now, almost seven—a gangly little hoyden with a tangle of golden curls, big blue eyes, and more length of leg than she could easily coordinate while in motion. *Definitely* an accident waiting to happen. Meredith smiled and smoothed her hair.

"Mommy, don't!" she said crankily, shrugging away from Meredith's touch. "I fixed it special for Heath!"

I'll be there waiting.

Meredith's heart caught as she watched Sammy press her nose to the window. "It's been snowing," the child said firmly. "He's waiting for us in that building, I bet."

Meredith sighed. "Sammy, love? Remember, I told you, don't get your hopes up too high. Heath said he would be here if God was willing. Sometimes, God answers our prayers by saying no."

"Not this time, Mommy. He's my daddy! He said. And he'll be here. You just wait. You'll see! And I'm going to tell him you didn't think he'd keep his promise. He'll be mad at you."

As they were ushered from the plane and down the steps, Meredith had to catch Sammy from tripping and pitching headfirst to the tarmac. The child was too busy searching for Heath to watch where she was going. Meredith even found herself glancing everywhere, her heart in her throat, her stomach twisting. She would have given anything to see a tall, dark-haired man in faded jeans and riding boots standing near one of the buildings. He would shout and wave, then come running toward them. And they'd fairly bound down the remaining steps, straight into his strong arms.

Only he wasn't there. . . .

Once on the tarmac, Sammy stumbled to a stop. She had insisted on wearing a pretty dress, a pink, frothy creation with a layered skirt, the hem of which rode a bit too high above her bony knees. Below the edge of her gray wool coat, the ruffles billowed out like the edge of a fluted bowl.

She stood in a puddle of water, her black patent leather shoes and lacy white ankle socks getting soaked.

"He's not here," she said hollowly. "He promised me! And he's not here! He *lied*!"

"Oh, Sammy, no!"

In a fit of anger, Sammy threw down the bouquet of paper roses and leaped on one to grind it under her shoe. "He lied. He tricked me so I wouldn't cry! I *hate* him."

Meredith bent to rescue the other flowers. As she straightened, she grabbed her daughter by the arm and gave her a slight shake. "Shame on you! Don't you *ever* say that, Sammy. I won't have it. Heath *loves* you. He would walk every step of the way in his bare feet to be here with us. You know that. And you can bet his heart is breaking because he couldn't come."

Sammy sobbed and threw herself into Meredith's arms. The shoulder strap of Meredith's purse slid down the sleeve of her coat, the bag plopping on the wet tarmac. For the moment, Meredith didn't care. She just held her daughter close and let her cry.

After the storm had passed, Meredith bent low to look Sammy in the eyes. "Sammy, love, we have each other. Everything's going to be all right." She tucked the damp paper roses into the child's hand. "You save these. I may be able to send them to Heath for you, through our agency contact."

Sammy wiped away her tears, forced a tremulous smile, and tightened her fingers around the flower stems. "You know what, Mommy? I bet he's waiting at our new house! That makes sense. Right? Maybe dogs can't come to airports."

Meredith's heart squeezed, but she managed to smile. "Maybe so, sweetkins. But don't get your hopes up too high. All right?"

Two men in trench coats escorted Meredith and Sammy to an awaiting yellow cab. Behind them, another pair of men hobbled along, carrying their luggage. As the cabby assisted to stow the suitcases in the trunk, Meredith was presented with a large, sealed manilla envelope by one of her escorts. Inside, she would find all the necessary documents and identification papers for her and Sammy to begin their new life.

After climbing into the cab after her daughter, Meredith gazed at the four U.S. marshals as they returned to the plane. Once it was refueled, they would make their return trip to New York, never knowing for certain where they had landed to drop her and Sammy off. Only the pilot had that information, and he hadn't been told who Meredith was.

The cabby waited impatiently for Meredith to tell him her destination. With shaking hands, she opened the envelope and withdrew a sheaf of papers, the uppermost of which bore her new address. "2437 East Shriver Road," she told him.

The driver grunted and set the car into motion. Meredith settled back in the seat with her daughter.

"Where is Shriver Road, Mommy? Did they send a picture of our house? Is my school near there? I'm gonna have my own bedroom, right? What city is this?"

Meredith could only answer one of the questions. "We're in a place called Trad, Wyoming. It's a small ranching community. The town is only about thirty thousand."

Meredith would have greatly preferred being relocated near a large metropolis, but she guessed beggars couldn't be choosers. Still, didn't Wyoming get lots of snow, even blizzards? Why on earth had they settled her and Sammy so far from a large city? Gazing out the windows at the largely rural landscape, she decided Nowheresville, Wyoming, had probably been the government's safest choice. If anyone ever found out where she was, which was highly unlikely, they'd probably have to dig their way through a snow bank to get to her. Most thugs were city boys and unaccustomed to the rigors of undeveloped terrain.

As the car wove along the winding rural roads, Meredith glanced up from the paperwork occasionally to look out the window at the countryside. Though it was a dreary day, with deep drifts of snow in many places, she could imagine how lovely the wooded hillsides and rolling stretches of grassland would be in the spring and summer.

"Oh, Sammy!" she said, trying to put some enthusiasm into her voice. "Aren't we going to *love* it here? We'll go for picnics and go swimming. Won't that be fun?"

Sammy gazed forlornly out the window. "I hate it."

Realizing that it was going to take far more than a note of enthusiasm in her voice to make Sammy feel better, Meredith quickly went through the remaining documents. Her new name was Meredith Middler. It made her think of the singer, Bette Middler, and with that thought, she recalled the song about the stubborn rose that springs to life under the deep winter snow. Meredith just hoped she and Sammy could be as resilient.

Once again, she thought of Heath. If only he'd been able to keep his promise, she thought wistfully. With him beside her, she wouldn't have felt so alone, or so frightened. But he wasn't here. She and Sammy had to face that, and accept it. And somehow they had to pick up the pieces of their lives.

She imagined Heath back in Wynema Falls, driving around in the white Bronco with Goliath in the bucket seat beside him. The picture was oddly comforting, something for her to hang onto in the midst of so much unfamiliarity. She wished she could write to him, but any contact with people from her past was strictly forbidden.

"Yuck, Mommy! It's way out in the fields and trees here!"

Meredith wasn't pleased at the distance they had come from town, either. It was going to cost a fortune for gas going back and forth to her job. *Men*. They should have had a woman choose the house. In the winter, the roads would be covered with snow and ice. She'd never driven on ice in her life and would undoubtedly half kill herself learning how.

Miles farther from town, the cab slowed, turned sharply

right, and drove under an impressive brick archway. It looked like the entrance to a large-scale ranch of some sort. In the distance, Meredith could see cattle eating from mounds of hay in the snow-covered fields. In another pasture, she spotted horses.

"Did they get us horses, too?" Sammy asked excitedly.

"No, sweetie. Of course not. I can't afford to feed horses."

At just that moment, the cab drew up before a huge, rambling brick ranch house.

"This is it!" the cabby told them as he opened his door and climbed out.

"Wow, Mommy! We're rich!"

"No, Sammy, we're not rich. This can't be right." Meredith rechecked the address in the envelope, and it matched the numbers on the house. When the driver opened their door, she called, "Are you sure this is *East* Shriver Road? I did specifically say east."

"This is it, lady," he assured her, then went around to open the trunk.

Meredith peered out the window at the house again. "There must be a bungalow on the property somewhere." On the way in, she'd seen a number of buildings, including the large red barn slightly to the right and rear of the house. There could be a smaller house behind it. "That must be it, a bungalow. I could never afford the heat in a place that size, let alone the mortgage payment. And I'm sure they didn't just *buy* it for us."

Bewildered, Meredith climbed from the cab, stuffed the envelope in her purse, and then looked around while the driver unloaded their baggage and set it on the grass beside the drive. A cattle ranch? She took Sammy's hand, half afraid the little girl might wander off and get trampled. Anger laced up Meredith's spine in a hot zigzag. Of all the crazy moves, locating a woman and child clear out here in the back of beyond?

Sammy's fingers felt rigid and cold against Meredith's palm. *Nervousness*. Meredith knew the feeling. Should they knock on the front door? Or go traipsing through the mud and slush, and possibly through the snow, to see if anyone was working outside who might direct them? From where Meredith stood, she could see one half of the barn's front doors. She thought she glimpsed movement. Hopefully, someone had seen the cab and was coming out to meet them. She was wearing two-inch pumps, for pity's sake, not exactly the thing for wading through snow. Her stockings would be ruined, not to mention her dress, and it was a nice one she hoped to wear for work.

God help them, she couldn't quite believe this was happening. She dug in her purse to recheck the address. Then she fixed a panicked gaze on the cabby. He was closing the trunk. Any moment now, he'd drive away, and they would be stranded here. He turned from the car to regard her. "That'll be thirty-three fifty, lady."

Meredith gaped at him. That seemed like highway robbery to her. Nonetheless, she drew out her wallet, found three tens and a five, and handed it to him. "Keep the change as your tip."

"Hey, thanks."

The sound of a barking dog punctuated his words. Meredith glanced up and saw a streak of black racing toward them from the red barn. A very *large* streak. The cabby took one look and leaped for the driver's door of the taxi. "Shit! A Rottweiler!" He leaped into the vehicle, slammed the door, and took off without looking back. Meredith and Sammy were left to face the charging dog by themselves, the receding sound of tires crunching on gravel the only sign that the car had ever been there.

Suddenly Sammy jerked her hand from Meredith's grasp and let out a shriek that would have done a banshee proud. "Goliath!"

"Sammy, no!" Meredith dashed after her daughter, trying frantically to catch hold of the back of her coat. "Honey, it can't be Goliath. It's a strange Rottweiler, and he may not like our being on his property!"

Sammy wasn't wearing two-inch heels, and she bounded

beyond Meredith's reach like a long-legged baby gazelle. "Goliath!" she cried again.

The Rottweiler's snarls and barks changed to high-pitched whines and growls that seemed laced with eagerness. Child and dog collided in an open area that was more mud than grass. Sammy toppled. The Rottweiler straddled her and began licking her face.

Meredith stood frozen about ten feet away. When Goliath spotted her, he left Sammy for a moment to come see her, bumping against her numb legs and licking the backs of her hands. Meredith was too stunned to return his affectionate greeting, and after a moment, the dog raced back to Sammy.

I'm dreaming, Meredith thought dizzily. *I'm still back in New York, snuggled under the covers and sound asleep, waiting for the bedside alarm to go off. The plane trip here was nothing but a wishful fabrication, and in a few seconds, I'll jerk awake and wish with all my heart that it could really happen just this way—that Heath might be waiting for us at journey's end.*

"I *knew* you'd come. I knew it!" Sammy cried, wallowing around in the mud, trying to cling to the excited Rottweiler's neck. "Oh, Goliath! I *love* you!"

A movement caught Meredith's eye. Dazedly, she shifted her gaze toward the barn to see a tall, long-legged man emerging. Western boots, faded denim jeans, a brown Stetson. That loose-jointed stride was one that she would have recognized anywhere. Her heart soared and her stomach leaped. She couldn't credit her eyes.

"Heath!" Sammy screamed. "Oh, Heath!" She scrambled to her feet, ran a few steps, and then circled back to snatch up the paper roses she'd dropped in the mud. She didn't seem to notice that they were ruined. As she raced toward the tall man in the sheepskin jacket, she yelled, "You came! I *knew* you'd keep your promise. I *knew* it!"

Heath bent to catch the child in his arms. He obviously wasn't prepared for the weight Sammy had packed onto her frame, or for the additional inches. She threw herself at him, plowing into his chest like a small cannonball, the top of her head catching him squarely on the chin. He staggered back a step, laughing.

"Hey, there, sweetcakes! How's my best girl?" He swung her high in the air and circled around, making Sammy squeal. "Jumpin' Jehoshaphat! You're so pretty, you knock my eyes out! And you're all grown up!"

As he completed the circle, he came to a stop facing Meredith again. For a long moment, he buried his face against Sammy's curls and hugged her as if he never meant to let her go. Sammy finally squirmed free.

"I made these special for you," she said, handing him the paper roses.

Heath shifted her to one hip and accepted the flowers almost reverently. He gazed down at them for several long seconds, his expression solemn. "Thank you, sweetcakes," he finally said. "I'll keep them forever."

Sammy hugged his neck. "You didn't lie. You really are my daddy, and we're gonna live here. All of us together! Right?"

"All of us together," Heath assured her. "Nothing on earth could've kept me away."

Goliath was circling and barking, clearly eager for another hug from the child, so Heath finally set Sammy down. As the child danced around him with the dog, Heath fixed a somber gaze on Meredith. For some reason, she couldn't make her feet move, and she was afraid to let herself believe he was actually there.

She drank him in with her eyes. The dark face, those strong, chiseled features, the shock of dark hair that trailed over his forehead beneath the brim of his brown Stetson. He flashed that crooked grin that she remembered so well, tucking the paper roses into his jacket pocket.

"I promised you I'd find a way," he called to her in that same husky voice that had whispered to her so many nights in her dreams. "I'm sorry I wasn't at the airport. They wouldn't tell me what day you might arrive."

Tipping his hat back, he set out toward her, his loose-hipped, lengthy stride and the shift of his broad shoulders under the heavy coat making her pulse quicken. In sheepskin, he looked so *big*.

As he walked to her, he said, "It took some doing to manage it, I'll tell you. But like they say, 'Where there's a will, there's a way.' I'll tell you all the details later." He drew to a halt about five feet from her, his twinkling, slate blue eyes caressing her face as if to commit every detail to memory. "Right now," he told her in a voice gone gruff with emotion, "all I really want is a hug. Unless, of course, you're not happy to see me."

The love that shone in his eyes was unmistakable. Barely feeling her feet move, Meredith dropped her purse and ran toward him. He met her halfway, catching her around the waist and lifting her into the air, much as he just had Sammy. Sobbing, Meredith wrapped both arms around his neck.

"I c—can't believe you're h—here!"

"Of course, I'm here. I promised you I would be." He cupped a hand to the back of her head, his warm, strong fingers furrowing through her hair. "Sweetheart, don't cry. Oh, honey, don't. I can't stand it when you cry."

His big, wonderful hands. Meredith had thought never to feel them touch her again. She clung to him with an almost desperate yearning, unable to stop sobbing or turn loose of him. "What about your house? And your job?"

"I sold the house and quit the job. It was time for some new blood in Wynema County. I'm kind of hoping Tom Moore takes over as my replacement."

"Tom Moore?" Meredith repeated incredulously. "The one who caused that accident and was constantly arresting the old lady?"

Heath smiled slightly. "He's grown up a lot. And I'm a firm believer that a man who's made mistakes and is haunted by them makes a better lawman. Tom learned a hard lesson, and over time, it shaped him into a pretty good deputy. Believe it or not, he went to bat for me over the recall issue. Even called in his daddy, the big gun, to argue my case. He always had the passion for law enforcement. Now it finally has some direction.''

He hunched his shoulders and cradled her close, his arms feeling like heaven around her. ''From the time I was a kid, I always dreamed of having my own ranch. By pooling my money with Dad's, I finally managed to get one. I've got all the credentials I'll need to return to law enforcement if I ever want to. For now, though, I just want to run the ranch and be a husband and father. We'll do well here financially, so you don't need to worry.''

Meredith didn't care about the money. As long as they were warm and had food to eat, that was all that mattered. Gazing up at him through tears, she asked, ''Is that a proposal, Mr. Masters?''

''Middler,'' he corrected, then winced. ''It doesn't quite work, does it? Heath Middler. Makes me sound like a damned candy bar.'' He looked good enough to eat to her. He arched an eyebrow, his grin mischievous. ''As for the proposal, that's one of the details I mentioned. We're already married. Dad has a good friend who's a judge. After hearing about my dilemma, he pulled a few strings and falsified the marriage documents, dating them before you left Oregon. I forged your signature. It wasn't precisely legal, given the fact that the bride was absent, but it looked good enough on paper to satisfy the government. They had to let me come. A husband has an inalienable right to be with his wife.''

''Bless your father's heart! He must have decided I'm not so bad after all!''

Heath chuckled. ''You could say that, yes. He's here, you know. I fed them a cock-and-bull story about his health being fragile and his needing me.'' He winked. ''I've never told so many whoppers in my life.''

''What about his practicing law?''

''He's already past retirement age. He wants to try his hand at being a dad and grandfather in his golden years.''

Meredith could scarcely take all of this in. ''So your dad's here? And I got married without even being there?''

"Well, I admit, it was sort of an underhanded way to get a woman to marry me," he said with a chuckle. "But since you'd already made the vows, I figured you probably wouldn't mind if I handled the paperwork. If you do, I guess we can pretend we're not legally married and set a terrible example for our kids."

"Kids. Plural?" She teasingly grasped his coat collar. "Who wears the pants in this family, anyway? It sounds as if you've been making a lot of decisions without me."

"Look around you, half pint. You're smack-dab in the middle of Podunk, Wyoming! No question about it, I'm wearing the pants." He clamped a hand over her backside and worked her coat up to feel the clingy slickness of her dress and slip. His eyes darkened. "Proof in point, you're not wearing any at all. What do you think you're doing, dressing like that when I'm not around?"

Meredith giggled. "It's just a dress."

"That is *not* just a dress. That's pure heaven, lady," he said huskily.

They gazed into each other's eyes, their emotions high as the reality of being together again began to sink in. Then he leaned down and settled his mouth over hers in a deep kiss that set her head to spinning. When he came up for air, he whispered, "Remember the fairy tale I told you? I got a couple of details wrong. It's Wyoming, not Oregon. And I left out the part about carrying you to the nearest bed and raping your sweet ass. Is that gonna be a problem?"

Meredith started to laugh and cry, both at once. She arched back in his arms to look up at his darkly handsome face. "We can't. We have Sammy."

Heath startled her half to death by throwing back his head and bellowing, "Dad! Come get my daughter!"

The barn doors swung open and Ian poked his head through the crack. "You need a babysitter *already*? Give the lady a chance to get her bearings, son!"

Heath bent and caught Meredith up in his arms. "She's with me, Dad. That's all the bearings she needs for now.

Show Sammy the foal and pups. All right? And when she gets bored with that, let her choose names for all thirteen. Not just any old name, either. I need at least an hour.''

Ian chuckled, shook his head, and gave his son a mock salute. Then he beckoned to Sammy. ''Come on, honey. Your folks want some time to chat, and I want you to meet Goliath's kids. They're all twelve ornery, so take your time picking out the one you want to keep.''

Heath wheeled back around. ''*Dad!* Are you out of your mind? I don't want three Rottweilers!''

Ian and Sammy had already disappeared into the barn. As Heath redirected his steps toward the large, brick house, Meredith heard her daughter's delighted giggles and knew Sammy would be happily occupied with the puppies for quite some time.

''Three Rottweilers?'' She looped her arms around her husband's strong neck. ''Goliath and one puppy makes two. What am I missing here?''

''I got a female, the mama of the pups. Her name is Sassy.'' He hit the back steps, shoved open the door, and stepped inside to kick it closed behind him. ''You'll love her.''

Meredith was dimly aware of a cheerful yellow kitchen with rich oak cabinetry, but mainly all she could focus on was Heath.

He let her slide slowly down his body, kissing her every inch of the way. She was breathless and dizzy when he finally broke off to begin unfastening her coat, pushing her backward across the room as he slipped the buttons free. The coat was tossed on the floor, and then he went to work on the tiny bodice buttons of her dress, all the while nudging her along in reverse. They moved from the kitchen into a hallway.

''Where are you taking me?''

''Straight to bed.''

''You're not even going to show me the house?''

He pushed the front of her dress open as he backed her through another doorway. He paused only long enough to lock the door after he closed it, then turned toward her and started stripping off his clothes. His coat, his hat, his shirt. The man seemed to be raining garments. He hopped around on one foot in front of her, trying to tug off a boot, which stubbornly refused to part company with his person.

"Strip!" he said.

Meredith felt a little embarrassed. She'd made love with him before, of course, but only for a stretch of three days, and it had been an endless eighteen months since then. "Wouldn't you like to talk just a little?"

"You're gorgeous."

"That's it?"

"I love your eyes." He got the boot off. It hit the wall with a thud. As he bent to jerk off the other one, his broad shoulders rippled in a muscular play of bronze. "Your mouth drives me crazy. And God, I love your hair." He got rid of the second boot and crossed the room to her, wearing nothing but tight denim jeans that sheathed powerful, incredibly long legs. "You're not stripping, Meredith Lynn."

"It just seems a bit—" Her breath caught as he somehow coaxed the lacy cups of her slip and bra away from her breasts. His hot mouth settled over a nipple and he drew sharply on her sensitive flesh, arching her back over his arm. "Oh, my God! Heath? Talk to me. Just for a few minutes. I—it's been so long. Can't we spend just a little time getting reacquainted?"

"We can't," he said breathlessly, trailing his lips up to her throat. "We made plans for later, and if I don't make love to you right now, I won't get another chance until late tonight."

"Can't you and your dad change your plans? It's my first night here."

He groaned and nibbled at her ear. "Trust me, Merry, you won't want the plans to be changed. They involve you and Sammy. It's a surprise."

Her eyes drifted closed. As many times as she'd dreamed of being in his arms again, her imaginings had never come close to being as wonderful as the reality. She'd nearly forgotten how he made her feel—as if she were melting. Sighing blissfully, she asked, ''What kind of surprise?''

''After we make love, I'll tell you. Not before. You'll take off like a shot and leave me standing here with only half my clothes on.''

After feeling his silken lips and warm breath on her skin again, she couldn't imagine leaving him. ''No,'' she whispered. ''Nothing could drag me away.''

''Do you promise?'' He kissed his way from her ear to the corner of her mouth. ''If I tell you now, you'll stay right here and make love with me before you go.''

He was crazy. For eighteen months, she'd ached to be with him, and now he was convinced she might leave him. ''I'm not going anywhere, period. I promise.''

Setting her senses afire, he retraced his path back to her ear and whispered, ''Your folks are here.''

Meredith's eyes flew open. ''What?''

She felt his lips curve in a grin. ''Dad bought the spread next door. There are two houses over there—really nice ones. We took a page out of your book. Changed our looks, flew to Canada under assumed names, then took a flight out of Ontario to Mississippi. Dad stayed down there to help them sell their farm and make all the necessary arrangements. Got them new identification, social security numbers, a car that couldn't be traced. They're right up the road. Have been for eight months.''

Meredith shoved at his shoulders and reared back to stare up at him. ''My mom? And my dad? You're serious? They left Mississippi and came *here*?'' Tears filled her eyes as she read the answer to her question in his smug expression. ''Oh, my stars! My folks?'' She hadn't seen them since before she'd married Dan. And now they were within walking distance? ''Oh, Heath. What on earth possessed you to—? You went clear down to Mississippi and—?''

A wealth of love shone in his eyes as he gazed down at her. ''You never would've been completely happy if you'd never been able to see them again. Every time you mentioned them, I could see how much you loved them, and that you missed them so much you ached. And I think all kids should have the chance to know their grandparents.''

"So, just like that, you went and got them?'' she asked incredulously.

"Not 'just like that.' It was damned difficult.'' He flashed her a teasing grin. "I got a crash course in down-home Mississippi folks, I can tell you that. Your dad never blinked about selling his place and all the equipment and all their furniture. He was so anxious to see his daughter, I think he would have parted company with his right arm to get out here. Just not with Spook.''

"Spook?''

"His pig. There was no way in hell he was leaving Spook. Do you have any idea how much trouble it is to transport a three-hundred-pound hog? And on an airplane, no less? There was no way that Spook could go in a truck all that way. Oh, hell, no.''

Meredith giggled even as she felt tears welling in her eyes. Heath had promised to do everything in his power for the rest of his life to make her and Sammy happy, but she'd never expected him to go to these lengths. Of all the beautiful gifts in the world she might have wished for, being able to see her parents again had to be the sweetest, most perfect gift of all.

"I love you so much,'' she whispered, unable to draw her gaze from his. "Have you any idea at all how much I love you?''

"As much as I love you, I hope.'' He sighed and loosened his hold on her, his mouth quirking at the corners as he began straightening her clothing and started to rebutton her dress. "Prove it by not staying over there too long this afternoon, all right? We're going to have supper with them, so you'll have all evening to catch up.''

Meredith caught his wrists. "I'm not going anywhere right now, Heath Masters.''

His smile deepened. "I'm not gonna hold you to that silly promise. I know you're dying to go see—''

She touched her fingers to his lips. "I'll go, yes. But later. And not without you."

The next instant, she was flat on her back across the bed with him straddling her hips. "Are you sure? I really don't mind if you go. I'll understand."

"Are you trying to get rid of me?" she asked.

Narrowing one eye, he started peeling away her clothing and throwing it in all directions. "Have I told you recently how much I love that dimple in your cheek?" He bent down to kiss the spot. "Dear God, Merry, I've missed you. Day and night, twilight and dawn. I couldn't get you out of my head." He jerked her shoes off. "I love your toes. Can I kiss your toes?" Next went her stockings. "You've got the cutest dimpled knees. Did I ever tell you that?"

Meredith giggled again. "You make me sound like a dumpling."

He canopied her naked body with his broad, darkly burnished one. "And every sweet inch of you is absolutely delicious, if I remember right." His eyes twinkled warmly into hers, and he gave her one of those slow, crooked grins that she loved so much. Then he bent his head to nibble at the corner of her mouth. "Oh, Merry. I love you so. You have no idea how very much I love you."

Meredith turned to kiss him fully on the mouth, murmuring that she loved him just as much, the words almost indistinguishable from her blissful sighs, which he drew into himself as if they gave him sustenance.

Heath. Being in his arms again was sheer ecstasy, and she knew deep in her heart that this was where she belonged. He had given her so much, this man. Gifts beyond measure. A sense of pride and a belief in herself. A happy, confident little girl. The strength to endure whatever came her way and to stand alone as she faced it. And last, but not least, he had restored her ability to believe . . . in magic, and miracles, and castles made of dreams. There really were heroes in this grim old world, after all. And right when you felt the most hopeless and least expected it, he could barge into your life, sweep you off your feet, and carry you off into the sunset to live happily ever after.

As their kiss deepened, Meredith remembered thinking as she left the ranch in Oregon that she would never see Heath Masters again. Now she realized how wrong she had been. Her fairy tale hadn't been over.

The most wonderful part of the story had only just begun. . . .